THE OT 'COCKLESHELL HEROES'.

With a Foreword by
Lieutenant Colonel P.R. Thomas.
Royal Marines. Rtd.

A Novel

by

Bill Hawkins.

© Copyright 2005 Bill Hawkins
All rights reserved. No part of this publication may be reproduced, stored in a retrieval system, or transmitted, in any form or by any means, electronic, mechanical, photocopying, recording, or otherwise, without the written prior permission of the author.

Note for Librarians: a cataloguing record for this book that includes Dewey Decimal Classification and US Library of Congress numbers is available from the Library and Archives of Canada. The complete cataloguing record can be obtained from their online database at:
www.collectionscanada.ca/amicus/index-e.html
ISBN 1-4120-5458-3

TRAFFORD

Offices in Canada, USA, Ireland and UK

This book was published *on-demand* in cooperation with Trafford Publishing. On-demand publishing is a unique process and service of making a book available for retail sale to the public taking advantage of on-demand manufacturing and Internet marketing. On-demand publishing includes promotions, retail sales, manufacturing, order fulfilment, accounting and collecting royalties on behalf of the author.

Book sales for North America and international:
Trafford Publishing, 6E–2333 Government St.,
Victoria, BC v8t 4p4 CANADA
phone 250 383 6864 (toll-free 1 888 232 4444)
fax 250 383 6804; email to orders@trafford.com

Book sales in Europe:
Trafford Publishing (UK) Ltd., Enterprise House, Wistaston Road Business Centre,
Wistaston Road, Crewe, Cheshire cw2 7rp UNITED KINGDOM
phone 01270 251 396 (local rate 0845 230 9701)
facsimile 01270 254 983; orders.uk@trafford.com

Order online at:
trafford.com/05-0356

10   9   8   7   6   5   4   3   2

Foreword.

Although Bill and I were in the Royal Marines at about the same time - and at one time I was Commanding Officer of the Amphibious Training Unit Royal Marines (ATURM) at Poole in Dorset that was "home-base" to the Special Boats Service - our paths never crossed until later on, in civilian life, when Bill was Chairman of the Portsmouth Branch of the Royal National Lifeboat Institution (RNLI) and I one of his Committee.

Although he hotly disputed the need, it is the RNLI policy that inshore lifeboat crew members should retire at the age of 45 and Bill was no exception. He had been coxswain of the Portsmouth lifeboat for 12 years during which he had achieved many notable rescues including a service in a Force 11 Storm for which he was awarded the coveted RNLI Bronze medal. It gave a sense of purpose having a fund raising chairman who knows what it is like at the sharp end.

Bill has the sea in his blood. He was born in Portsmouth and went to sea at 14; serving eight years in the merchant navy as a Second Officer. After National Service he had a spell in Portsmouth City Police before joining the Royal Marines Special Boat Service; the Royal Navy's equivalent to the S.A.S. After his arduous Commando training he would have completed the even more taxing swimmer-canoeist course where he would have learned the ship attack role, operating from submarines, escape and evasion, resistance to interrogation; all the operation skills which are the grist of this compelling novel that also faithfully records the normal repartee between sailors and marines. The obligatory sex scenes I cannot answer for.

Lest the reader believe the narrative to be far fetched think for a moment that in December 1942 Royal Marines Major "Blondie" Haslar led ten men of the "Boom Defence Patrol" in five canoes up the River Gironde to attack shipping in Bordeaux (Operation Frankton). Six men were captured and shot by the Germans but four ships were severely damaged. Only "Blondie" Haslar and Marine Sparks got back to England through the bravery of an English woman living in France.

I hope you will find this book as good a read as I did.

Peter Thomas.
Lieutenant Colonel. Royal Marines. Rtd.
Langstone, Hampshire. November. 2003.

Acknowledgments.

I am most grateful to Lieutenant Colonel Peter Thomas, Royal Marines. Rtd., for his kindness in agreeing to write a Foreword to this book.

Also, to Captain M.L.C. "Tubby" Crawford. D.S.C. and bar. Royal Navy, a former submarine commander, for his advice on 'The Trade' that an ordinary bootie paddler like me would have been unaware of.

In addition, my thanks go to Margaret "Maggie" Fleming who kindly read the earlier transcripts and corrected my many spelling and grammatical errors.

Bill Hawkins.
Portsmouth. 2005.

Author's Note.

In December 1942, No.1 Section of the Royal Marines Boom Patrol Detachment, who had trained off the beach at Eastney, Portsmouth, carried out a daring raid on enemy shipping in the French port of Bordeaux by paddling their flimsy canoes, called 'cockles', for eighty five miles up the River Gironde.

Of the five canoes launched at the mouth of the river from HM. Submarine TUNA, only two succeeded in reaching Bordeaux and sinking several German ships by placing magnetic limpet mines below the waterline.

Only two of the raiders returned to England. They scuttled their canoe and escaped, with the help of the French Resistance, after a four month overland route via Spain and Gibraltar.

Of the remaining eight canoeist, six were captured and later shot by the Germans despite still wearing R.M. insignia on their jackets, one was drowned and his body washed ashore, and the other went missing - fate unknown.

This raid, codenamed 'Operation Frankton', was immortalised by the 1955 film 'Cockleshell Heroes'.

The following story is a fictional account of what might have happened to No.2 Section - the ones not sent on 'Operation Frankton'.

Glossary.

For the benefit of readers not conversant with the ranks of German Forces and/or the terminology used in HM.Forces, especially "Navalese".

Bootnecks (or Leathernecks).	A name given to Royal Marines (usually by naval seamen) derived from the leather tongue which closed the opening of the collar in their old military pattern tunics.
Captain(S)	A four-ringed naval Captain in command of a submarine flotilla.
Cam-cream/ Cam-netting.	Coloured cream or netting used to camouflage the face and hands or an object
COHQ.	Combined Operations Head-quarters.
Compo rations.	Composite rations issued to troops. Highly nutritious but usually tasteless.
Deckhead.	The ceiling of a ship or cabin.
Freeboard.	That part of a floating vessel's hull above water.
Frogs.	Frenchmen. (Eaters of frog legs).
Galley.	A ship's kitchen or cookhouse.
H.O's.	Men enlisting in the armed forces for the duration of the war.
Horse's neck.	A cocktail drink of Brandy, Angostura and dry ginger ale.
Head or Heads.	Ship's toilet.
Jimmy.	"Jimmy-the-one". A ship's First Lieutenant.
Killock. (A type of anchor).	Name given to a Leading Seaman. He wears an anchor on his arm as a badge of rank.
Matelots. (Pronounced as Matlows).	A nick-name for naval seamen. Derived from French name for sailors.
NCO.	Non-commissioned officer. (Corporals, Sergeants etc).
O.D's.	Ordinary Seaman. (RN).
Oppo.	A close friend.
Pompey.	Nickname for the City of Portsmouth.
Pusser.	A term meaning "Service or Regulation issue".
P.O.	Petty Officer. Naval equivalent to an NCO.

PDQ.	Pretty damn quick.
Pilot.	Name given to the ship's navigating officer.
Ragheads.	Servicemen's nick-name for Arabs, Indians etc. Those who wear turbans.
Ruperts.	Name (usually derogatively) given to officers by ratings/other ranks.
Royal.	Another (usually friendly) name for a Royal Marine.
Rosbifs.	French name for Englishmen. (eaters of roast-beef).
Sitrep.	Situation Report.
Tommies or Tommis.	German name for British soldiers.
The Trade.	The name given to the submarine branch of the Royal Navy.
Whale Island.	The naval gunnery school in Portsmouth Harbour famed for being a centre of excellence and high standards of discipline.
Wood butchers.	Carpenters.
Yomping.	Term used by Royal Marines to describe a long march.

Ranks of the German Army (Wermacht) and S.S.

Oberschutze	Private (Army and S.S.).
Fallshirmjager	Parachutist.
Gefreiter	Lance Corporal. (Army).
Feldgendarmerie	Military Police.
Obergefreiter	Corporal (Army).
Geheime Feldpolizie	Secret Field Police.
Rottenfuhrer	Corporal (S.S.).
Oberleutnant	Lieutenant (Army).
Untersturmfuhrer	2nd. Lieutenant (S.S.).
Hauptsturmfuhrer	Captain. (S.S.).
Obersturmbannfuhrer	Lt. Colonel (S.S.).

THE OTHER 'COCKLESHELL HEROES'.

Dedication.

This book is dedicated to my late wife Valerie, to a very valued friend Larraine Hallman, and to all Royal Marines, past and present, especially the Swimmer-Canoeists of the Special Boat Squadron (S.B.S.).

Chapter One.

Eastney sea-front, Portsmouth.
August 2002.

The late afternoon sun felt pleasantly warm on the almost bald pate of the old man's drooping head as he fought off the waves of weariness that were dragging his heavy eyelids closed. Despite the whispers of a warm southerly summer breeze, his fleshless legs - that had supported him throughout eighty-odd years of trials and tribulations - felt cold, as if a draught were whistling up the legs of his shapeless grey trousers, but he had neither the energy nor inclination to do anything about it. His backside ached too. The wood-slatted seaside bench was not the most comfortable seat in the world, especially as he had no cushioning fat or muscle on his frail skeleton of a body.

An unseasonable shiver ran through his tired frame like a mild electric shock. He knew his body was dying on him even though mentally he was alive and well, but he had no regrets. He'd had a good innings and there was no one to mourn his passing; not since losing his long-suffering wife a few years back. Even so, he wasn't looking forward to the half-hour shuffle back along the sea-front to the loneliness of his terraced home, just as soon as the sun lost its heat.

Slowly, he raised a claw-like hand to his brow, shielding the sun, and lifted his rheumy eyes to squint out across the sparkling waters of the Solent that stretched, flat and featureless, into the distant haze; seeing the breezes ruffle the sea into a carpet of wrinkles. It was a view he hadn't taken much notice of sixty years ago, but now loved. Given the choice, it was where he would like to end his days.

On the intervening pebbles and grass patches of the sand-less beach, hundreds of almost naked sun-worshipers lay sizzling on sweat-soaked multi-coloured towels, turning themselves over now and then as though on a roasting spit, basting their bodies with lotions against exposure to the tanning rays which was what they had come out here for in the first place.

Away to his right, shivering in the heat, the low-lying undulations of the Isle of Wight spread darkly grey across the horizon with the two visible sea forts intruding like bad teeth. To his left, small wavelets splashed whitely onto the drying sands of the West Winner Bank, while fleets of seemingly unmoving sail splattered the sea like clouds of settling confetti, occasionally scattering before the charging cross-channel ferries that looked more like huge mobile blocks of maritime flats than sea-going ships. He felt at peace. His almost deaf ears unaware of the incessant roar of screaming children, the yelling of concerned parents and the boisterous shouts of sky-larking youths, as he watched a strutting seagull industriously forage for scraps on the pavement among the feet of passing promenaders, its beady eyes staring maliciously at the uncaring shoe that crushed a discarded chip.

Behind him, on the other side of the road had he been able to turn his stiff neck to see them, a small group of elderly ladies had been gallantly assisted from out of two taxi's by the drivers who now waited beside the meter-ticking vehicles that bore the City crest on their side-doors above a notice saying that they were *"Authorised bus lane users"*.

The ladies stood like fragile dolls, looking up at the massive bronze statue of a 'yomping' Royal Marine that stoically flew the Union Flag from the aerial of a radio-set on its back as it stood sentinel over the entrance gate of the famed Royal Marines Museum; a memorial to the fallen in the Falklands War.

A keen observer might have noticed a certain moistness in the eyes of the ladies as they cautiously re-boarded the taxis for the return trip to the Pier Hotel, to continue their reunion with other ex-Wrens who had proudly worn the Globe and Laurels cap badge of the Royal Marines and called themselves "Marens", more than half a century ago.

Had he looked, he would also have seen the dumpy, square clock-tower that once overlooked a magnificent parade ground being pounded daily by a thousand marching boots, and the long prison-like three-storey building that had been 'home' to countless marines over many decades. Now that same tower, with its silent clock and unmoving hands, looked down on the unaltered facade of those same buildings whose interior - no longer divided into separate 'barrack blocks' - now contained numerous highly expensive luxury flats that went by the incongruous name of 'Teapot Row' whose inhabitants now had the grass-covered parade ground as their 'front garden'. The once world-renown Royal Marines Eastney Barracks, was alas, no more.

Still squinting his veined eyes seaward, he placed both hands on the silver top-cap of the walking stick held lightly between his emaciated thighs, and briefly rested his chin on them; but the position was uncomfortable. Slowly he sat upright again and eased himself backwards, like a fakir onto a bed of sharp nails, until the unyielding slats of the bench supported his shoulders. He dropped his head back, feeling the cooling breeze fan the sweat-soaked creases of his flaccid turkey-neck, and closed his eyes looking into the past, trying to visualise this same area way back in 1942 when, as a young headstrong and adventurous marine, he had volunteered for hazardous service and been posted here - to this very spot. Memories came flooding back as he pictured the two buildings that had stood where the 'yomper' statue now dominated the skyline. They had been the Headquarters of his unit, where they stored their canoes and other equipment, and attended unending instruction and lectures. Where they rested fatigued muscles, and sulked with disappointment when No.1 Section were sent off on "extended exercises" that everyone knew would be a raid somewhere.

'Why couldn't it have been No.2 Section?' his team had asked themselves, 'what was wrong with us?'

Perhaps it had been just as well they hadn't known at the time what fate had in store for them.

He opened his eyes and stared, unseeing, up at the clear blue sky and the beginnings of a smile twitched the corners of his gaunt lips as he remembered the good times spent off-duty in the *Granada* pub with the other RMBPD lads, most of whose faces he could only vaguely recall. Then there was the homely atmosphere of their 'civvy' billet in St.Ronans Road with the wonderful Mrs. Montague who 'mothered' them all. It was good just to think of those carefree times, the happy days, but he still found it hard to accept he was the only one left of the chosen five.

Suddenly he felt very weary. Not sleepy – just tired. He closed his eyes, wondering what would have been his fate had circumstances been different, and these were his last thoughts as his chin fell forward onto his chest and he drifted off to sleep.

Chapter Two.

Royal Marines Barracks, Eastney. Portsmouth. November. 1942.

The Union flag – fluttering from its staff high up on the sturdy clock tower overlooking the swarms of marching Royal Marines on the parade ground below – gave off an agitated crackle, like a continuous volley of pistol shots, as the brisk winter breeze tried to rip it to shreds. Striding around the perimeter path of that same drill-square, oblivious to the stamping boots and shouts of frustrated NCO's, twenty-three year old Lieutenant Adrian Thomas, felt good. For some obscure reason, the crunching of his own boots on the gravel path made his return journey to the cold, damp atmosphere of the two hangar-like brick buildings of his unit's Spartan base (known, less than affectionately, as *The Shed*) that overlooked the beach, all the more satisfying. An hour ago he had not been so happy. Recent events had left him unreasonably depressed for the first time since taking over No.2 Section of the Royal Marine Boom Patrol Detachment; his first *real* command since joining the Corps three years ago, straight from University. He lengthened the stride of his long legs; stretching his nearly six feet tall body, luxuriating in the feel of the cold wind that ruffled the tufts of unruly fair hair poking out from under his beret, and made his eyes water.

In the early hours of that same morning, he had led his Section of six two-man canoes on a fast paddle across the cold dark waters of the Solent, to the Isle of Wight and back. It was not so much as an exercise than to take their minds off the bitter disappointment they all felt at having been left behind when their mates in No.1 Section had suddenly been despatched *"on extended exercises"*; a term that everyone knew to be a cover story for a pending operational mission. They were tough lads, his young marines of the RMBPD who had all volunteered for hazardous duty and found themselves sitting in fragile craft that were little more than a fabric- covered wooden frame. Yet despite their toughness, their heads were low, having had to wave their pals off the day before. They felt rejected, forgotten and, to be honest, second rate.

THE OTHER 'COCKLESHELL HEROES'.

The stiff westerly breeze had made conditions uncomfortable on the crossing, with each pair thrusting their Mark 2 "cockles" through the increasing swell as Thomas drove them to increasing effort. Beneath their camouflaged waterproof-suits, upper bodies ran with sweat, and muscles ached. Inactive legs and feet became numb and stiff inside the canoe's thin canvas hull, and as each paddle dug deep into the grey Solent waters, cascading drips torn from the upper blade by the raw wind splattering their faces like ice needles; stinging their squinting eyes with showers of salt spray. A keen eared seagull, swooping in a low fly-past over the canoes, may well have heard the time-honoured curse spluttering from the frozen lips of one or other of the discontented paddlers. 'Sod this for a game of soldiers. Roll on my bloody twelve!'

No sooner had they landed back on Eastney foreshore and stepped out, stiff legged, onto the pebbly beach from their canoes, when an immaculately dressed Royal Marine messenger approached stepping slowly and cautiously, like someone probing through an uncharted minefield. His face painfully aware of the damage being done to the highly polished toecaps of his boots by the stones and sharp-edged seashells.

'Lieutenant Thomas?' he asked of the group as a whole, his nose wrinkling in disgust, uncertain which of the bedraggled shambles was the officer. For several moments the rabble ignored him, as if he didn't exist, until one straightened up from bending across what appeared to him like a big long piece of soggy wreckage that he would never be seen dead in. He was a "Big ship, bullshit and blanco" man himself. Canoes were for madmen; no place for a proper marine.

'Yes.' answered the officer. 'That's me.'

The miffed messenger shuffled to a stony-beach style of attention. 'Major Blake's compliments, sir,' he saluted. 'He would like to see you in his office at your earliest convenience, sir.'

Thomas acknowledged the salute with a weary nod of his head. He knew that the politely worded request actually meant he was to report immediately. 'Say I will be along shortly, please.' He turned his attention back to his equally tired crewman. 'I'll give you a hand up to The Shed, Browning. I need to change my boots.'

Together, they hoisted the sodden, sagging length of the canoe onto their shoulders to portage it back up the beach and across the road, overtaking the boot-worshiping messenger still delicately picking his way across the stones, as though each pebble were a red-hot cinder.

'Ah!' greeted the grey-haired major sitting on the edge of a paper-strewn desk, swinging a polished shoe and scraping at the bowl of a time-worn pipe with a silver pen-knife. 'Thomas. Good man. Good of you to come so quickly.' His slate-grey eyes enviously scanned the weary face of the young man standing, self-consciously, in a growing puddle of seawater that drained from his alleged waterproofs onto the corticene floor covering of the office. How he wished he were twenty years younger and able to do something worthwhile, instead of being a "re-called from retirement" staff officer in Combined Operations. 'Sit you down, we need to talk.' He nodded his head to indicate a rickety wooden folding-chair that was the only other seat in the room. 'Drink?' he asked, knocking the loose dottle from his pipe into an ashtray on the desk and lifting a crystal glass decanter, waving it, like a grizzly bear grasping a struggling, newly caught salmon.

'No, thank you, sir,' Thomas answered, wishing desperately to say "Yes," to warm his chilled body. He could almost feel the burning sensation of a neat gin cascading down his gullet, creating an internal glow, calming the slight shiver, bringing life back into his frozen fingers and toes. But it was all imagination. He'd been in the service long enough to know that such an offer, from seniors to juniors, was just a formal courtesy, not to be taken seriously; acceptance being seen as a sign of weakness, frowned upon, and liable to lead to adverse comment in one's personal assessment report.

The Major, now sat behind his littered desk, was clearly made of sterner, more realistic stuff, as - without comment – he half filled a small tumbler and handed it across. 'Your Section feeling a bit pissed-off at the moment?' he asked, raising bushy eyebrows that seemed to reflect the dark circles beneath his eyes and leaning back against the back of his upright chair.

'A little, sir,' replied Thomas, sipping his gin. Longing to gulp it down and ask for another. 'But they'll get used to it. That's why I pushed them a bit this morning.'

'Yes, I noticed you were up and about early,' said the Major, leaning forward and sweeping a clear space on the cluttered desk with his hands and placing his forearms on the scratched varnished top. A vague smile creased his haggard face in anticipation of giving this young man the good news he undoubtedly wanted to hear. 'Well, there's no need for them to fret any longer,' he added, watching the spontaneous reaction to his words.

Thomas involuntarily straightened his back, squared his shoulders and gripped the edge of his seat to control his mounting curiosity. A questioning glint appeared in his eyes, waiting.

The Major walked his stubby fingers among the untidy jumble of files and papers littering the desk. Eventually, selecting one with a satisfied 'Ah, here it is,' he placed it between his resting elbows and, coughing into his fist, looked up at the Mickey Mouse clock with its revolving white-gloved hands – a present from his grand-daughter - that hung askew above a dog-eared map of Europe on the wall.

Thomas waited in apprehensive anticipation. Was this to be what he – and his men – yearned for? Was it to be operational orders, or another shattering disappointment?

Blake again looked at the clock with a slight frown, as if checking on a failing memory. 'It's 12.30 now' he began, 'so you haven't a great deal of time to waste.' He paused, absentmindedly turning the paper in front of him to see what was on the next page, then replacing it. 'There's a bit of a flap on,' he continued, 'so you will need to get back to your people P.D.Q. and choose a team of four to accompany you on a mission of no small importance. I suggest Corporal Pearman as one of them for reasons that will become obvious to you later. These four should return to their billet – and you to your quarters – and be packed ready to be collected by transport at 18.00 hours today. The remainder will prepare three of your "cockles" for loading onto a vehicle due at your Shed by 16.00 hours.'

'May I ask where we are going, sir?' queried Thomas, anxiety making him lean forward.

'Gosport,' was the laconic answer, followed by another shuffling of desk-top papers.

Thomas - his brain racing through its Gosport file and coming up with *Submarine base; Coastal Forces base and Naval Air Station* - knew that any further questions would be a waste of time.

The Major cleared his throat as if to read a prepared speech. 'You will report to a Major Tocher at HMS.Dolphin for a few days of intensive training. He will tell you what you need to know, when he thinks you should know it.' Another brief pause. 'Well, off you go then…' he said, standing with an extended hand and nodding his head towards the door, an unseen lump rising in his throat. '… and good luck'. He knew of the impossible mission this young officer and his marines were going to be asked to undertake, and it saddened him, such a waste. Bloody war!

Thomas rose and accepted the offered hand-shake. 'Thank you, sir,' he said, turning for the door.

'Oh! and by the way…' continued the Major, as though as an after thought, '…you can tell the rest of your chaps that they will be off to warmer climes in the next few weeks – probably before Christmas I shouldn't wonder.'

Thomas felt relieved. He'd had a fleeting concern about them having to face a second disappointment. But now, with adrenaline surging through his veins, he headed for The Shed; deliberately scuffing grooves in the gravel path, like a schoolboy kicking a tin can.

Corporal Eric Pearman - known to his mates as "Tonker" for some reason now lost in history - was not happy. In fact, like the rest of his Section, he felt bloody miserable. With his dark hair plastered over his scalp, he was sitting hunchback on a wooden crate in The Shed, beneath the dripping canoes now resting on their wall brackets after having been washed off with fresh water that now drained down onto the bare concrete floor. Mentally he contemplated his shrivelled navel, well hidden beneath several layers of clothing, most of it damp, if not sodden, and a shiver coursed through his six-foot rugged frame. He felt more like forty-four than twenty-four. What had he done to deserve this?

One of only two regular marines in the Section, he had defied the traditional service doctrine of never volunteering for anything, by putting his name down for hazardous duties. Anything, he had thought, to get away from the boredom of being Guard Commander at a P.O.W. camp in Scotland. He had, hopefully, imagined doing something more exciting, with maybe a dash of danger, and was among the first to be sent to Portsmouth to form the RMBPD. It was certainly different. The unit's name was a cover for their real job that - rumour said - had nothing whatsoever to do with patrolling the length of concrete blocks stretching from Eastney beach out across the Solent to Horse Sand Fort as a defensive boom, to prevent infiltration by enemy submarines into the naval anchorage of Spithead. Nevertheless, he was getting fed-up with the cold, wet monotony of paddling around the Solent, day after day, night after night. Trying to avoid the numerous patrol boats that (knowing they were there anyhow) took a perverse delight in trying to capsize them with near misses, and then adding insult to injury by shattering the arctic tranquillity of the Solent by calling out 'Sorry Mate. Thought you was the enemy. Ha!'

It was the knowledge that eventually, they *would* be tasked to do something worthwhile, that kept the Section going. They needed something operational to make them feel they were using their skills, and doing their bit. But then, when a job did turn up, what happened? The brass gave it to No.1 bloody Section… their boozing pals and hated opposition. Where are they are now? he wondered. What are they doing? He lifted his heavy head from numbed cupped hands and looked around at the others. They were all sat on makeshift seats and leaning back against the damp brick walls, waiting for the Boss to return from his summons to the office. They looked as miserable and depressed as he was. Much more of this, he thought, and I'm requesting a draft as a M.O.A. (Marine Officer's Attendant) and become a skivvy to some prat of an officer who didn't have the savvy to look after himself. Anything would be more exciting that this!

Apart from the continuous tapping of water dripping from the canoes and adding to the spreading puddles on the floor, all was quiet. No one spoke. Eleven men waited, depressed and shivering, as the coldness seeped up through their improvised seating into the stiffening muscles of their backsides. There was "Porky" Pine who, at twenty seven, was the oldest member of the Section. As tough as old boots and mild of nature, he was already half asleep. He could sleep on a clothesline. Then there was the baby of the Section, nineteen year old Dave "Bing" Crosby, the broad-shouldered ex-fisherman from Penzance, whose unruly red hair made him irresistible to the motherly type of female. According to his reckoning, he'd had more girlfriends than the rest of the Section put together, although those were not his actual words. No one doubted his claim.

Side by side, talking softly together on a rolled up sheet of tarpaulin, sat the two twenty-year old inseparables, Tom Nook and Alan Browning; their plimsolled feet stretched uncaringly across the floor. Alan - known as "Gravy"- came from London. He was a cheerful, thick-set Eastender who, as a schoolboy, had played rugby at National level, and acquired the obligatory crumpled nose and cauliflower ears in the process. He rarely lost his wicked sense of humour and had, amazingly, chummed up with Tom Nook, a rather serious character from Leicester whose nickname "Windy" had nothing to do with flatulence or cowardice. Both fresh faced, and an inch or two under six feet tall, they could easily be mistaken for brothers; until they opened their mouths.

Inside the classroom - a small partitioned area of The Shed with barely sufficient space to hold four low uncomfortable bench stools, and a table-mounted blackboard that still bore signs of a previous chalked lecture and a notice pinned to the top right hand corner that read *Dave to phone Maureen at six* - the other six lads were crashed-out, fatigued, and blissfully unaware of their discomfort. It had been a long, bloody awful morning.

They all jumped as the outside door was thrown open and a column of what passed for November daylight silhouetted the grey shape of their section commander as he entered, thudding the wooden door shut behind him. No one leapt to attention; it wasn't that sort of unit. Corporal Pearman swivelled his head towards the young officer, sensing - as all experienced N.C.O's can - an aura of excitement surrounding his boss.

'Right lads,' shouted the officer, hardly able to contain his enthusiasm as he walked through into the classroom. 'All in here. Chop - chop.' His cheerful ebullience aroused the weary bundles, who shuffled to their feet with questioning eyes beneath arched eyebrows, each searching the face of his mate as they stumbled to obey.

When they were all seated, Thomas looked around at their attentive faces. They looked like eager schoolboys at assembly, and he suddenly felt the weight of his responsibility for their welfare. He took a deep breath. He had already selected his team and didn't want to keep them in suspense any longer. 'Our turn has come at last lads…. at least for some of us,' he began, his heart still pounding with suppressed excitement. 'As soon as I dismiss you, I want Corporal Pearman and Marines Crosby, Nook and Browning……' he said, looking at each of them in turn and nodded his head, '…….to return to St. Ronans Road and pack your gear ready to be collected by transport at 1800 hours. The rest of you will clean and prepare our three best canoes for loading onto transport that will be here at 16.00 hours.'

Four happy faces looked back at him. The rest were unsmiling.

'Don't ask me what it's all about,' he pre-empted their questions, 'I can't tell you because I don't know myself. What I *can* tell you, is that those not named will also be moving in the next week or two; probably…..' he added in imitation of the Major '… before Christmas. And I am informed it will be to somewhere much warmer than here.'

A buzz of excitement swirled around the small room as glum faces broke into smiles and cheerful looks exchanged. Thomas was pleased to see relief on the faces of the ones not selected for his team. No one felt forsaken. They were all chuffed. 'Right, move it lads. We've no time to waste.'

The small eight-seater coach, and a three-ton truck carrying the canoes, came to a grinding halt at the barber-striped pole spanning the road at waist height. Two armed sailors, patiently waiting for the end of their watch and longing to get indoors away from the biting wind, stood crouching low into the collars of their greatcoats, unmoving and uncaring in the shadows beneath the highly polished brass name plate of HMS.Dolphin, the submarine base at Gosport. With little curiosity, and even less concern, they stared blankly at the pale faces of the marines sat inside the coach looking out through smeared holes sleeve-wiped in the fogged glass.

After a theatrical pause to enhance the power of his presence, the portly figure of a gaitered Chief Petty Officer emerged from the guardhouse like a waddling Toby jug and strolled unhurriedly over to the coach driver's window; the gold-wire badges of crossed guns on his lapels and rows of WW1 medal ribbons on his chest glinting in the shaded lights around the security barrier. 'Papers,' he barked, officiously.

The coach driver - a young marine who looked no more than eighteen years old - handed his orders out of the cab window. 'Evenin' Chiefy' he called cheekily, as he scratched industrially at the head of a pimple on the side of his nose.

The veteran's face seemed to swell and redden at this insubordinate disrespect. His neck began to bulge over the immaculate white collar of his shirt, and his eyes took on the appearance of a surprised frog. He was about to explode when Lieutenant Thomas leaned across from the passenger seat to quickly intervene.

'Good evening, Chief Petty Officer,' he said. 'Lieutenant Thomas and a party of Royal Marines…… for Major Tocher.'

Years of Whale Island training and ingrained tradition came to the Chief P.O's aid as he took a step back and gave a salute, like a Karate chop in reverse, that would have severed the peak of his cap had it travelled a fraction more. His malevolent eyes momentarily lanced into the uncaring driver's face, then dropped to minutely study every word of the orders.

'Thank you, Sar,' he shouted, at decibels just below eardrum shattering level as he strode slowly along the length of the coach, his angry eyes scanning the blurred faces on the other side of the steamed-up windows, treating the marines to a swift, professional survey to allow time for the colour of his offended cheeks to reduce to a mere brilliant scarlet. After a cursory check of the three-tonner's papers, the CPO returned to the coach, his anger now under control but wishing, with all his heart and soul, that the officer was elsewhere. He'd like to have given the insolent little bastard of a driver what for.

He pointed a finger into the unlit road ahead. 'Go to the end….' he snarled tight-lipped at the driver who was studying something interesting under his fingernail, '….. then turn left at the brown building.' He ducked his head, bending an unaccustomed spine forward like a rusty hinge, to look through the cab at the officer. 'Major Tocher's office is at the end of that road, on the left, Sar!'

'Thank you, Chief' said Thomas, his voice slightly irritated by the unnecessary delay. 'I was beginning to think we weren't expected.'

'Hif you 'ad't been expected Sar, you wouldn't 'ave got in,' shouted the CPO, his breath hissing in his throat as he straightened his back trying to add another half an inch to his height, and whispering 'Bloody orficers. Bloody bootnecks,' under his breath.

Thomas treated himself to a smile. He should have known better than to try to best a man with years of lower-deck experience under his belt. They knew all the answers, and all the responses. Been there – done that. They'd always get the last word in; never crossing the vague line into insubordination. It would take a very clever, and brave, man to get the better of a CPO Gunnery Instructor. 'I shall have to have a quiet word with this lippy driver too' he thought.

Almost defiantly, the young driver slammed the coach into gear and pulled away, deliberately staying overlong in the whining first gear, to annoy. 'How does that prat expect me to see a brown building in this darkness?' he muttered.

Chapter Three.

HMS. Dolphin. November 1942.

From the outside, in the dim reflected glow of the coach headlights, the indicated "office" appeared to be nothing more than a pair of green-painted metal doors looking more like the entrance to someone's garage.

'Wait here', Lieutenant Thomas instructed the driver. 'I'll see if this is the right place.' He stepped down onto the road, every move being watched from the coach by five pairs of listless, yet inquisitive eyes.

The road was barely wide enough for the vehicles, nothing more than a short, dark alleyway between unlit black buildings, through which the raw wintry evening breeze funnelled its way, like wind whistling through the gap in a door jam, from the submarine moorings in Haslar Creek to the wide expanses of the Solent's white-horse speckled waters. He slid the right-hand door open to reveal an apparently empty interior, as black as the infamous hole of Calcutta. He cursed, and was just about to slam it closed when he noticed a thin strip of light at floor level to his left. Was it from under a door? Was anyone at home after all? He shuffled his way towards it, groping with hands and feet, like a blind man in a strange house, his eyes slowly becoming accustomed to the darkness.

'Come in,' invited a voice like gravel, in answer to his tapping on the wood panelled door. 'It is open.'

His hands felt for, and found, the cold round door knob. He turned it and gently pushed, but the door didn't budge. He shouldered it harder and still there was no movement. Feeling slightly foolish, he pulled and the door opened outwards with a screech of protesting un-oiled hinges. The room wasn't a room at all, just a bare-walled closet barely ten feet square, and probably a store space originally.

A tall beanpole of a man sat hatless on an ordinary dining-room type chair, his battledress tunic - with the crowns of a Major on the shoulder epaulettes – unbuttoned, and his tie askew. Beside him stood a small coffee table - the only other piece of furniture in the room - laden with papers that had overflowed onto the wooden flooring around his feet. Light, shining from a single un-shaded bulb hanging on its flex from the rafter like a distressed spider, gleamed on the skin of his tanned head that, apart from a white tuft of hair above each ear, was as bald as a billiard ball.

'You must be Thomas,' said the ruddy faced Major of Marines, twitching his nose like a rabbit as if it were being irritated by the short bristles of a well trimmed moustache. 'Sorry about all this.' He waved an open-palmed hand around the claustrophobic walls. 'It's all they could find for me at such short notice…….. They're very busy.' He rose, uncoiling himself from the chair like a snake from a fakir's basket, and offered his hand. 'Tocher,' he said by way of introduction. 'Alistair… I'm here to help you over the next few days. Your chaps outside?'

'Yes, sir.'

'Right then,' he said, stretching his shoulders back, hands on hips like a posing ballet dancer. 'I'll get my M.O.A. over to show them to their accommodation.' He went down on one knee and fumbled among the papers on the floor, found the cable he was looking for, and traced it to the black bakelite telephone under his chair. 'Then I will show you to your quarters, brief you on your training schedule, and buy you a noggin in the Wardroom…. Adrian isn't it?'

Without waiting for confirmation, he spoke to whoever was on the other end of the phone and grunted, as if satisfied with a job well done, and replaced the receiver. 'In the meantime' he continued, 'get your men to off-load their kit and canoes. You have got them with you, haven't you?' His eyebrows arched as though to meet a long-gone hairline.

Thomas nodded, but before he could open his mouth to answer, the dynamic Major continued giving more orders as he straightened his recalcitrant tie and buttoned his blouse. 'Put them out there for now' he said, pointing a finger out of the door. 'Sorry there's no light. I'll leave my door open. You can dismiss your drivers then. I presume they'll go back to barracks?'

'Presumably, sir. I'll check.'

The marines, with very little enthusiasm after a long day, roused their aching muscles and clumsily unloaded the vehicles.

'I'll be glad when I've 'ad enough of this,' moaned Crosby, dragging the last of the kitbags into the gloom of the unlit garage. 'Bleedin' pack-horses, that's all we are.'

The others - vague shadows in the feeble glow from the impotent 60 watt bulb in the "office" - ignored him. All they wanted was the chance to get something to eat, thaw out, sink a pint and get their heads down – not necessarily in that order.

'Who's that?' whispered Browning, seeing the silhouette of a stranger enter the "garage" and walk unhesitatingly to the "office" to stand with his back framed in the doorway, almost eclipsing the half-light.

'Dunno.....' answered Corporal Pearman, squinting his eyes in an effort to pierce the darkness and identify the intruder. '.....but by the shape of his cap he looks like a Royal to me.'

'Ah! Henderson.' The Major's voice drifted out to them. 'Show Lieutenant Thomas' marines to their accommodation and see them settled in, there's a good chap,' he ordered. 'And tell them to be back in here by 0830 tomorrow morning.'

'Bleedin' hell', murmured Corporal Pearman, overhearing the instruction. 'We're getting a lay-in!'

Marine Officer's Attendant (MOA) Albert Henderson turned around, his night vision ruined by the "office" light, and peered into the blackness of the "garage" like an octogenarian at a strip-club. He was not happy. He had been a regular marine nearing the end of his service career when war broke out, and now, instead of being in Civvy Street and enjoying a good life as a Gentleman's Butler, he was 'retained' for the duration of the war. He longed for a return to the good old peacetime days when officers were gentlemen with perfect manners in immaculate uniforms. Now, they were nothing but young kids. And he did not much care for being a dogsbody to a bunch of H.O. marines who seemed to be enjoying their war, playing silly buggers. They were not marines at all. More like boys pretending to be soldiers.

'Bring your kit and follow me,' he called into the void that could have been empty for all he knew, then marched quickly out onto the road and waited. Four throats grunted as kitbags were hoisted onto protesting shoulders, and hobnailed boots scraped the concrete floor.

'He'd 'ave looked bloody silly if we hadn't been here,' said the irrepressible Browning, sotto voce, so as not to be heard by the officers. 'he'd have had a long wait.'

Heads bowed sideways under their burden, the four trailed after their striding guide who, incidentally, had forgotten to lend them a hand with their gear as he led them, muttering curses under their breath, through the maze of tall unlit buildings that seemed to overhang the road like an archway. At last, just as they were about to accuse him of leading them on a wild goose chase, the M.O.A. made a sharp left turn off the road and through a set of swing doors into a gloomy lobby lit by a blue police-light.

'Nearly there,' he called over his shoulder, in the better-than-thou voice he reserved for talking to other ranks, as he climbed a flight of concrete stairs. 'You're up on the first floor.'

Reaching the landing, he crossed to a door that bore a pinned notice reading "RMBPD". Beneath it, some wit with nothing else to do had added "Royal Marines Bed Poofs Daily". Holding it open, he switched on the lights saying 'Mess Hall is in the next block. Suppers should still be on, if you get your fingers out.'

The four weary marines mumbled their begrudged gratitude and edged crabwise past him into the room, each man endeavouring to inflict an accidental knock with a lumpy part of their kitbag. The last man - "Windy" Nook - ripped the notice from the door and presented it to the unsmiling door opener saying, 'Perhaps you'd like to give this to your officer?' Henderson sniffed his cold, runny nose disdainfully and departed, closing the door noisily behind him.

'Bloody Nora!' exclaimed Corporal Pearman, dropping his gear on the polished floor. Wide eyed, he looked around, removing his beret and scratching his head in astonishment. 'We've come to the bleedin' Ritz!'

A dozen beds - all piled with pillows and blankets - lined the brilliantly lit room with a wooden locker standing alongside each one, like an empty hospital ward. Several hot iron radiators gurgled against the walls radiating a welcoming warmth, and wooden frames covered in dark material blacked-out the windows.

'Wot! No bleedin' flowers?' joked Crosby, tossing his kit onto the nearest bed and easing his neck muscles. 'I bet the matelots get 'em.'

'Not on subs, they don't,' said Browning knowledgably, and then adding with a smirk, 'Not real one's anyhow.'

'What do you think, Corp?' called Nook, launching himself into the air and bouncing on his chosen bed like a trampoline. 'Bit of alright this. Better than Eastney bloody barracks anyhow.'

Pearman curled his upper lip, cynically. 'Condemned man's last wish more likely... Anyhow, I'm off to see if there's any scoff left. Coming Gravy?'

'Yea, why not. Providing we find the Naafi afterwards. I could kill a pint.'

'You have a lovely view out over the harbour entrance in daylight,' said Major Tocher from his seat on the edge of the bed in Thomas' allocated cabin in the officer's block, watching the younger man empty his suitcase and hold-all into the various drawers and wardrobe. 'In daylight, you can see the Round Tower and Portsmouth Point as though they were right beneath you.' His eyes glazed nostalgically, recalling happier days. 'The view over the city is quite breathtaking, and there's always something moving in or out of the harbour.' His rabbity nose twitched and he brushed his moustache with the back of a forefinger. 'Not that you'll have much time to enjoy it.'

'I don't suppose I………' began Thomas, but the Major butted in.

'Mind if we have our little talk in here, Adrian?'

'Of course not, sir. If you prefer'.

'Too many eyes and ears in the wardroom, don't you know…' mused Tocher as if contemplating a debate at Hyde Park Corner, '…and we don't want our business known all over the base, do we?'

If I know the Navy, though Thomas, it's probably all over the base already.

'Care to sit more comfortably, sir?' he asked, pointing to one of the two easy chairs. People sitting on other people's beds were one of his pet hates.

Almost absentmindedly, the Major stood and took a step forward to plonk himself down in the proffered chair like an obedient dog, as Thomas handbrushed the creases from the navy-issue counterpane. His blatant action being lost on Tocher who, with eyes half closed and chin resting on the tips of steepled fingers, started to outline the details of the forthcoming operation.

'First thing tomorrow morning….' he began, composing his fingers into a bridge and studying their tips, '….I want one of your canoes taken aboard *Tenacity* which is alongside the jetty here. During the next few days, your chaps and the sub's crew have to perfect the technique of getting it up from the forward torpedo compartment, through the loading hatch and onto the deck casing, in no time flat. It will be a tight fit. You will be meeting the sub's captain, probably tomorrow, and I can assure you that on your mission - which by the way, is named Operation Gladstone - he will not want to be on the surface any longer than is absolutely necessary.' He looked up and gave a cold smile. 'Also, you'll be exercising in the Solent with a picket-boat that has been fitted with a bow devise shaped like a letter "T" lying on its side. You will practice floating a line between the two canoes so that it can be snagged by the picket-boat coming between them. With the line around its bow it will then tow both canoes along behind.' He kissed his fingertips as though in prayer and massaged the end of his nose. 'You will perfect this method…' he continued after a brief thoughtful pause, '…and ascertain the highest speed manageable; we estimate this to be about eight knots. The purpose of all this will be disclosed to you in due course but…,' he said with heavy emphasis, '…even then it must not be divulged to your troops until you are aboard the sub on the way to your mission. You, yourself, will not be told of your destination until the very last moment I am sorry to say. This is for security reasons obviously, and in case the whole sheebang is cancelled.' He straightened his back, and took a silver cigarette case from the breast pocket of his battledress blouse with a theatrical flourish. Opening it, he selected one carefully, as if it were somehow different, then leaning over onto one buttock, fumbled in his trouser pocket for a box of matches with one hand as the other held out the case. 'Do you?' he enquired.

'No, thank you, sir' replied Thomas, trying not to wrinkle his nose. He hated the smell of nicotine and hoped his forceful refusal would strike home. It didn't!

At a second attempt, Tocher struck a match and applied it to the end of the cigarette. Inhaling deeply, he leaned back in the chair and tilted his head to blast an obnoxious stream of smoke up towards the ceiling through pursed lips, shaking the match violently to put it out.

'The plan….' he resumed, tossing the dead match into a tin ashtray on the bedside locker, '….is for *Tenacity* to take you as near to the French coast as its captain deems advisable. He will then surface and bring two of your canoes - each loaded with eight magnetic limpet mines - up onto the casing, leaving a third down below with a reserve canoeist in case of damage… or other emergency. With the crews already seated in them, the canoes will be hoisted in strops from a girder clamped onto the barrel of the deck gun that will then traverse outboard and lower them into the sea, like a derrick. This was an idea thought up by your own Major Haslar, actually,' he added as an afterthought. 'The sub will then submerge and continue on its patrol, while your two canoes paddle inshore towards the mouth of a river that has a heavily guarded seaport at its entrance. You will by-pass this port' he said, as if it were a tourist excursion, 'and continue upriver, in as few stages as possible, for approximately fifty miles, to another port where you will attach your limpet mines - with delay fuses - below the waterline of as many ships as possible, making your own choice of suitable targets'. He exhaled loudly, blasting another stream of smoke across the room, and leaned forward, elbows on knees. 'That's it in a nutshell….' he said casually, as though discussing arrangements for a forthcoming dinner party, '….although events may dictate changes and we must be ready to amend if necessary should the next few days of trials give good cause.' He gave Thomas the sort of look that only a chair-borne staff officer can give an operational commander – half pity, half envy – as a length of drooping ash fell from his cigarette and splattered on his lap. 'Well, what do you think?'

I think it is suicidal madness, thought Thomas. A scheme thought up by someone who didn't have to put his own life on the line. Lives were so easy to risk when they weren't your own. He felt stunned at the audacity of it, even though he was aware of the pressures that Prime Minister Churchill was placing on his Service chiefs to undertake such missions. "*To keep Hitler on his toes and boost the morale of the British people,*" as the great man had put it.

Out aloud he said, 'Do you think it can be done, sir?

'More's to the point….do *you?*' asked Tocher, sticking his lower lip out as though imitating the Prime Minister's pugnacious stance. 'Of course, we will go into more details later, but I would like to hear your initial reaction?' He leaned toward the locker and ground the stub of his cigarette into the ashtray as if trying to make a hole in it. 'And bye-the-bye' he continued, addressing the ashtray, 'you will be interested to know that your No.1 Section is training to undertake a similar raid to coincide with yours.'

Thomas tightened his lips, stretching the corners of his mouth into a grimace in an attempt to conceal the beginnings of a nervous twitch. Was the information about N0.1 Section meant ensure his compliance?

'Well….it sounds simple enough, sir, but I guess that is not how it's going to be' he said, wondering if Tocher could hear his pounding heart. 'In fact, it sounds decidedly dodgy. But I suppose that's what we volunteered for.' He paused, reflectively. 'I have two questions to ask at this time, sir, if I may?'

The Major's head nodded, expectantly.

'First, when do we go? Second, how do we get back?'

Tocher's face creased into a frown. These were the two questions he knew would be asked, and he dreaded answering. Annoyingly, he took his time replying, as though trying to put off the inevitable. 'I regret you have only a few days, Adrian.'

Thomas' face was a picture of undisguised dismay. How could he be expected to get such an act together in so a short time? Were they insane? Perhaps they think his chaps are supermen, capable of doing the impossible. They should have named it "Mission Impossible". A million questions buzzed around inside his head, each creating another. The lives of his men - and any chance of mission success - would rely on his ability, his decisions. He didn't know what to think, or what to say. His blood felt like solid ice in his veins. He knew he was afraid, scared stiff in fact, so he sat on his hands in case they were trembling. He knew that he wouldn't, or couldn't, ever refuse. 'And how do we get back?'

Seemingly indifferent - but with a heavy heart full of pity, admiration and compassion for the young man sat facing him who, he felt sure, had but a slim chance of returning safely - Tocher cleared his throat. 'After placing your limpets, you should paddle as fast and as far as you can away from the docks, and land on the northern or eastern bank of the river, while it is still dark. After removing your survival bags from the canoes you will scuttle them by ripping the hull fabric and weighing them down with whatever material is available. If the two crews have not already separated, it is essential that you do so at this stage and make your escape overland by heading southeast towards a small town where the French Resistance movement will be on the lookout for your arrival. Hopefully the enemy will expect you to head either north, or west towards the sea.' He paused to brush imaginary ash from his trousers and inspect his fingernails. 'The name of the town, and the means of contact, will be made known only to those of you actually taking part in the raid. Neither the reserve man remaining on the sub, nor the captain and crew, are to be made aware of this information. The French will return you to England via one of their escape channels. You should at all times - or until asked by the Resistance people to remove them - wear your Royal Marines shoulder flashes and Combined Operations patch so as to ensure you are treated as POW's, not as saboteurs, in the event of capture. He stopped briefly, and then added, 'I think that is enough for now Adrian. Let's go and have a noggin, then you can get some sleep.'

I will certainly have the noggin, thought the stunned, bemused Thomas, but I can't see me getting much shut-eye.

A fist, punching the pillow inches from his nose and rocking his head, brought Adrian Thomas back into the world. A brilliant flash of light exploded somewhere in the back of his head as one eyelid opened, fractionally, to reveal a blur of haloed faces hovering above him. Where the hell was he? He wanted to shout out for the violent apparitions to leave him alone, but his mouth seemed full of a vile tasting balloon.

The pillow pounding continued, and his brain felt like a bowl of water, sloshing about from side to side in his head, like the swimming pool of an ocean liner rolling from side to side in a heavy sea. He wanted to be left alone, to die. A disembodied voice impacted on his eardrums, screaming some sort of foreign gobbledegook that ricocheted around inside his skull. Who was torturing him like this? He forced his other sticky eyelid open. The faces, shimmering in a spectral mist like a mirage, gradually steadied to become one solid feature as his throbbing eyeballs began to focus.

'Come on, sir' said the distant voice, rapidly decreasing in decibels. 'Wake up.'

M.O.A. Henderson thought that the young officer on the bed looked like a proverbial village idiot. The swollen tongue pushing out from between parched lips, and uncomprehending eyes trying to uncross themselves to agree on some unified action, stared up at him from the pillow he had been pummelling. He felt sorry for the young officer. He had a good idea of what was to happen soon, so didn't blame the Lieutenant for going on a bender. Anyhow, he had seen plenty of drunken officers in his time. 'Major Tocher's compliments, sir. He'd like you to join him for breakfast in the Wardroom at 0800.'

Carefully, Thomas raised himself up on one elbow, nodding his tender head just once when he found his swollen tongue prevented him from speaking, and twisting slowly into an upright sitting position to put his feet on the cold floor. With bulging eyes, he watched Henderson dematerialize, the quiet slamming of the door sending shock waves around the room. For several minutes he sat perfectly still, his pounding head cradled in cupped hands, feeling sick, trying to get his bearings, and wondering which way was up. God, he felt awful. Forcing himself to his feet and straightening his back like an arthritic Chelsea pensioner, he took a faltering step towards the wall mirror. At first, he didn't recognise the shockingly distorted features of the reflected face. Black shadowy hammocks of skin supported drooping eyelids that half covered a pair of red veined eyes peeping like pinholes from a face of crumpled paper. It was grotesque. With difficulty, he pushed his bloated tongue out between cracked lips. It looked like a fat sea-slug giving birth. His queasy stomach retched. No way was he putting *that* back into his mouth.

He tried to recall the events of last night's bacchanalian orgy. Tocher's apparent insatiable capacity for gin was surely matched only by the size of his Mess bill. It must have cost him a fortune. The problem had been in trying to keep up with him. Not that he really wanted too, but it would have been inadvisable to refuse the senior officer's hospitality. Did the Major normally indulge in such excess? Or had it been a deliberate act to get him drunk, knowing that a sober Thomas would otherwise have spent a sleepless night with so much on his mind?

Showered, shaved and dressed, the walk to the Wardroom did little to benefit his general malaise, and the sight of the immaculate Major - who had probably been up and about for hours – sat at a table reading a newspaper, made Thomas even more aware of his own appearance.

'Morning, Adrian' welcomed Tocher brightly, waving his hand invitingly towards the vacant chair at his table. 'How do you feel? Have a good sleep?'

Not waiting for a response, as usual, the Major raised an arm above his head as a signal to the attentive steward waiting patiently against the wall who then turned with an acknowledging nod to disappear through a swing door.

Thomas lowered himself gingerly onto the upholstered chair, careful of his watery bowels, relieved to have the onus of immediate conversation taken away by the re-appearance of the white-coated steward wheeling a serving trolley containing two plates covered with stainless steel lids.

'Good morning, sirs' greeted the steward, placing a plate in front of each of the officers and removing its lid. 'Powdered egg, fried sausages and tomatoes this morning.' It was his well rehearsed speech, made every morning to enable his officers to identify what they were about to eat.

Thomas gave one glance at the revolting multi-coloured mess and felt his tender stomach heave. It looked more a mixture of frozen vomit, afterbirth, and a couple of lumps of what is usually seen at the bottom of a toilet pan. Delicately, as though touching something with a contagious decease, he pushed the plate away with the tips of his fingers. 'I'll just have a coffee, please.'

The steward removed the offending meal, wondering why all officers wanted to eat as though dining at the Savoy. Jolly Jack would enjoy such a feast. 'As you wish, sir.'

'Wot you got there then, Royal?' questioned the dungareed Leading Seaman standing near *Tenacity's* torpedo hatch, watching the two marines carry a canoe along the casing towards him.

'Bleedin' Venetian gondola init' answered Browning, sarcastically. 'What d'ya think it is?'

Unabashed, the Killock tilted his head to one side in mock examination, puckering his bulbous nose. 'Gonner put it in the 'oggin and give us a song then?' he asked.

'Bollocks,' smiled Browning, surrendering to the fencing of traditional naval humour as the two marines lowered the canoe onto the submarine's deck. 'It's all yours now, and mind you take good care of it. It's as frail as a Nun's fanny.'

The sailor bent over an open hatch and called down. 'Up top then, you shower. The bootnecks are 'ere wiv dair battleship.' He turned back to face the marines. 'Stoppin' for a wet, mates?'

'No thanks' said Nook, shaking his head to decline the offer of a cup of tea. 'We've got to be up the road by half past eight.'

The Killock stood to one side as four young capless sailors emerged from the hatch, blinking like early morning campers opening their tent flap to check on the weather. 'Next time then, eh?' he offered, then turned to the four seamen standing on the deck casing, their arms tightly folded against the cold wind driving through their off-white roll-top sweaters.

'Now, this 'ere is a canoe,' the two marines heard him instruct with the obvious knowability of a seasoned veteran, and grinned at each other as they made their way back onto the jetty by way of the connecting brow.

Chapter Four.

HMS. Dolphin. Gosport. November 1942.

'Looks more like a garage than our Headquarters doesn't it?' mused Major Tocher standing in the "office" doorway talking over his shoulder to Lieutenant Thomas who was slumped in the chair, suffering in shapeless misery. His eyes took in the four marines stood silently beside the two canoes on the concrete floor, as if they too were waiting for something to happen.

Thomas, endeavouring to lift his chin from his chest, was fighting a losing battle. His pounding brain came up with a response to the Major's comment but it took several seconds for it to be transmitted to his uncooperative mouth. 'That's what the men call it …. the garage,' he slurred, parting his parched lips hoping to release what felt like a bloated frog to slither out from his mouth and let him die in peace.

Tocher turned to gaze back down at the young officer and smiled, almost pitying. He knew from experience what was going on inside that bowed head. The turmoil, the longing to curl up and die. It would be some time yet before the wretched chap would be fit to function properly. Meanwhile, he would have to think - and act - for both of them. Perhaps, he thought, he may have overdone his good intentions last night.

Also looking, from outside the "office", Corporal Pearman was feeling a mixture of concern and disgust. He was annoyed at having to stand there, just waiting for someone to make up their mind what was wanted. He quite liked Thomas. He was a good officer, not afraid to muck-in with the lads and get his hands dirty. He'd do everything they did – and more – and was well respected by all the Section. Even so, it was the state he was in at the moment that was cause for concern. As commander of the unit, the Lieutenant had a responsibility to his men to always be on top of everything; not getting blind drunk and incapable. Bet that bastard Tocher had something to do with it, he thought. He hadn't liked *him* from the very start. Too bloody arrogant. Rarely did an officer get his approval, but like a good NCO, he kept a respectful silence; it was bad for discipline to slag off an officer in front of the men.

Nevertheless he felt angry and annoyed. If it had been him, or one of the lads, who had turned up for duty still half pissed, they'd have been put on a charge, hung, drawn and quartered, without hesitation. How come officers can get away with it?, he asked himself. They seemed to take every opportunity to knock it back. "Socialising" the prats called it. Wish they'd stay propping up a bar all the time and let NCO's run everything. Life would be so much better. Just because they've got money, and a degree in Greek pornography or something, they think they're better than us. In his book, higher education rarely meant intelligence and common-sense, but he had thought Thomas might prove the exception to the rule.

'Right, Corporal. Get your boats down to the jetty,' ordered the Major without looking up. 'The pinnace should be there by now.'

Pearman nodded to Marine Nook and together they hoisted their canoe up onto their shoulders. 'Ready Lads?' he asked the other pair, and marched out onto the roadway.

'Morning, Royals,' called a rosy cheeked matelot, pausing in his whistling and wearing his cap flat-a-back. 'Goin' on 'oliday, are we?'

'No,' answered Browning, witty as ever. 'Goin' fer our pay.'

'Flippin' eck!' grunted Pearman, halting in mid-stride and causing a collision behind. 'SPLITS!'

'What's Splits?' asked Nook naively, touching his cheek that scraped against the canoe in the sudden stoppage, and checking for blood.

The NCO pointed ahead with his free hand to where a pinnace lay tied-up to the jetty. At its bow, a short tubby Wren sat watching their approach with an excited twinkle in her eye. In the doorway of the craft's small wheelhouse another Wren stood, waiting. Even in her shapeless jacket with the badge of a Leading Wren on its sleeve, and sexless baggy trousers, she was still attractive. With wind-reddened cheeks, and blonde hair tucked into a round salt-stained hat with HMS embroidered on its tally band, she looked a picture to the admiring marines. The chinstrap of her cap framed a face that would be beautiful – if it smiled. Aft, a third Wren, thin and gangly, was bending over a hatchway like a fishing rod taking the weight of a heavy catch, apparently talking to someone below.

'Splits….' explained Pearman, turning his head 90 degrees to starboard and talking out of the side of his mouth. '….is women, you Wally. You know, Wrens, officer's bed-warmers, call 'em what you like. But don't get yer knickers in a twist, they won't look at the likes of us…..unless they're bloody hard-up, or just plain bloody ugly.'

They walked onto the jetty.

'Put your boats on the foredeck' ordered the Leading Wren, sternly. 'One either side.'

Marine Crosby, his face lit with a lusty smile, gazed at her, wide eyed in mock admiration. 'Thank you *so* much, Petty Officer,' he crooned.

'Leading Wren!' corrected the po-faced girl stepping back into her wheelhouse, a fleeting smile wrinkling the corner of her mouth. 'And don't be cheeky.'

The overweight Wren, still sat for'ard in the bow, puckered her lips enviously, swinging her booted foot to kick at the inoffensive anchor winch that looked remarkably like her Leading Wren's face. She knew why she never received the same sort of attention, but that didn't make things any easier. She couldn't help her size, it was her hormones; or the fact that she loved food.

Corporal Pearman stood uncertainly at the side of the wheelhouse, plucking up the courage to enter the Leading Wren's domain and offering an open packet of cigarettes as he introduced himself.

She glanced down at the packet, and then looked away. 'Maggie Day', she responded, treating him to a brief survey as though he were something obnoxious. 'And I don't allow smoking in here.'

Suitably chastised, he closed the packet and replaced it in his blouse pocket. 'Sorry.'

For a fraction of a second her face seemed to lighten, and her lips parted briefly, as though practising the strangeness of a smile. He looked at her profile as she stared out of the wheelhouse window, staring ahead at the submarines berthed two and three abreast in Haslar Creek. She *was* attractive, but with an aura of sorrow about her, and he wondered why. A girl with her looks could have any man she wanted, and probably there were plenty sniffing around. She had no competition from any of her crew, and that was a fact.

'The officers should be here shortly,' he said conversationally. 'What's the routine, do you know?'

She shook her head and, for the first time, looked into his face. Her eyes were a beautiful light blue and lanced into him like a Cupid's arrow. He could really fancy her, given the chance.

As if reading his thoughts she turned away again; remote, cold and untouchable. 'No idea,' she snapped, abruptly. 'All I know is that I've to take you out by the forts and do some sort of towing trials. They've put an awful contraption on my stem-head. Did you see it?' He said he hadn't so she offered to show him.

It was a typical dockyard bodge-up job. Ugly and unpainted. A three-inch wide iron girder stuck out like a bowsprit with another piece welded at the end like the top of a letter "T". One short end sticking up in the air and the longer length disappearing down below the surface, for about three feet, he guessed.

'Perhaps you're going to push us to wherever we're going' he laughed, but she wasn't amused.

'The sooner they take it off the better I shall be pleased.'

'Here comes the boss,' Pearman whispered, sighting the two officers approaching the jetty. 'He looks better already.'

Maggie raised a well trimmed eyebrow, but didn't question his enigmatic remark.

The NCO was to learn later that, at the Major's suggestion, the two officers had called at the Diving Store on their way to the pinnace, where a sympathetic P.O. Diver had allowed the lieutenant a few deep breaths of pure oxygen from one of his diving sets. It was a well-tried cure for a hang-over.

The Leading Wren saluted as they stepped aboard and Tocher touched the peak of his cap in reply.

'Permission to cast-off, sir?' she asked.

'Yes please, coxswain.'

Down below in the tiny after cabin, Wren Sarah Drew – the one that had been sat on the bow when the marines arrived – had her cuddly frame squashed delightfully between Crosby and Nook, enjoying the thrilling sensation of their hard muscular thighs jammed tightly against hers on the small bench seat. It was a long time since she'd been so intimately close to a man, and now she had two of them. She glanced down at Crosby's hand resting on his thigh, wishing it were on hers. She quivered as a spasm of arousal washed through her body, making her excitingly uncomfortable where it shouldn't. His hand moved an inch, sending her heart fluttering. He could have thrown her down on the deck and ravished her in front of the others for all she cared. Both of them could.

Crosby took a packet of duty free from his breast pocket and handed them round. Of all the splits in Portsmouth, he thought – relishing the sound of the new-found word – he had to be lumbered with this one who seemed determined to sit on his lap. She wasn't his type. He preferred long-legged blondes with figures like an hour glass. Visions of Rita, his last conquest in Pompey, swept into his mind. Jesus, she had been good; gorgeous to look at, exciting to touch, and as randy as a frustrated nymphomaniac in a chastity belt. In two wonderful weeks she had turned him into a physical wreck that had not been conducive to the hard demanding programme of his training, but what the hell! Then she started to get all serious, and he heard the warning clang of wedding bells. No way! Why do women always have to spoil a good thing? Why can't they just enjoy life?

On the seat opposite, the skinny Wren sat like a stick insect with her shoulders humped trying to make herself even narrower. Squashed between Pearman and Browning, her hands trapped tightly between her knees and looking scared stiff, she was unresponsive to their attempts at conversation. The atmosphere was like that of a dentist's waiting room. Little did the marines know she was one of that rare species - a virgin Wren, who also lived in mortal fear of men, and what they might do to her. *Had* they been aware, they would probably have cruelly assure her she had little to be frightened of – unless the man was very drunk.

'Oh! for the life of a sailor' sighed Browning, trying to inject life into the maritime mausoleum. The others glared back, silently.

In the wheelhouse, wedged just as tightly between the two officers, Leading Wren Maggie Day stood grasping the wheel, her feet as wide apart as possible to balance against the jerking pitch and roll of the pinnace as it plunged through the agitated waters of the harbour entrance. Despite her efforts, her body still thrust embarrassingly against first one man then the other; not that they were showing any undue interest, thank goodness! Steering by eye, and ignoring the swaying compass gyrating on the console in front of the wheel, she glanced sideways at the lieutenant who looked decidedly the worse for wear. With his handsome face haggard and drawn, pale lips clamped tightly together and eyes staring fixedly out onto the foredeck, he was probably wishing he were anywhere but here, she guessed, correctly. To her left the Major leaned forward, elbows resting on the console, his face loaded with thought and creased with worry wrinkles. Beneath the peak of his cap, crammed low on his frowning forehead against the brightening horizon, his eyes were sweeping the busy channel ahead.

Expertly moving the wheel a spoke at a time, she kept the pinnace in the main channel, keeping close to the red port-hand buoys and disturbing the unhappy seagulls standing on them with heads back, shouting angrily from their precarious perches. On No.3 Bar buoy a Cormorant stood spreading its wings to dry in the weak winter sunshine, like a fisherman exaggerating the size of his catch. Ahead, *Spit Sands Fort* became nearer and larger as a flash of memory pierced her brain. A tear moistened her eye and rolled down onto her cheek. Perhaps it was the closeness of the two officers that reminded her of happier days with her RAF Sergeant fiancé. Was his memory always going to cause such pain? She knew she would never forget him. Six months, with no news since he had been reported missing over Germany. He could still be alive, a prisoner or something – couldn't he? Her life was so empty without him. All their plans for marriage and having children, all gone.

'Take her around the other side of the Mother Bank, coxswain,' ordered the

Major, interrupting her thoughts and bringing her mind back to the present. 'There's calmer water beyond. Better to start our trial in.' He leaned back, looking behind Maggie's head across at the lieutenant's effort to pull himself together.

'Ready for a spot of boating, Adrian?'

Thomas looked at the Wren as though seeing her for the first time. The blinding fog seemed to be clearing from his brain. 'May we use your after cabin for changing into our gear Miss?' he asked, politely.

Maggie returned his look with a small, sympathetic smile. 'Of course, sir' she answered, handing him the wheel. 'I'll get my girls out.'

Off Gilkicker Point at the southwest corner of Gosport, and beyond the angry shallow waters of the Mother Bank, Maggie stopped the engine as directed and allowed the boat to drift quietly to a standstill, its bow dipping as it lost way and rolling sluggishly in the ground swell. A bitterly cold breeze blew from the west, not yet strong enough to blow the tops off the waves but certainly enough to make life uncomfortable.

Corporal Pearman blew hot breath into his cupped hands and his three marines cuddled theirs up under warming armpits, all waiting to get on with whatever they were going to do.

'Any chance of putting in for a draft to the Far East, Corp?' asked Marine Nook, hunching his shoulders with a shiver. 'Or better still, a trade swap with a stoker in a nice 'ot boiler room?'

Pearman turned a withering eye. 'You'd never pass for a Chinaman with that red nose and blue face,' he laughed. 'And your arse ain't hairy enough to be a bloody stoker.'

'This will do nicely,' remarked Tocher almost conversationally to the Leading Wren standing redundant at the wheel. He was looking with growing concern at the black humps of cloud beginning to gather over the distant island town of Cowes. 'Get your boats in the water Corporal. Better make a start before the weather turns nasty.'

'Easy lad,' muttered Pearman with quiet emphasis as he and Marine Nook bent to lift *Codling* up over the pinnace's side. 'Mind that cleat. Don't want to tear the bottom out of her.' They lowered the canoe carefully into the sea, struggling to keep their feet as the deck rolled, pitched and jerked, like a mustang with a burr under its tail.

Behind them, on the other side, Crosby and Browning had *Minnow* secured alongside and were sat on the deck fending the canoe off with their feet. Crosby started to inch forward, swaying from side to side on his buttocks, reaching out with one foot to get into the canoe.

'Belay that, Crosby!'
All heads turned towards the recognisable voice of Lieutenant Thomas.
'That's my job.'

A fleeting look of disappointed anger swept over Crosby's face and he cursed under his breath. He had already been told he was to be the reserve crewman on this little jaunt, but nevertheless he had harboured hopes that perhaps the boss would be too hung-over to take part, and then - without sufficient training - would count himself out of going on the mission. He knew in his heart that would not happen, but hope springs eternal he thought, holding on tightly to the bow line to keep the canoe close alongside. The lieutenant - trying hard to hide the agony of a splitting headache - stepped down into it with a coil of rope over his shoulder, carefully feeling with his foot for the centreline and thinking to himself that it would not do to capsize the flimsy craft at that very moment, with so many critical eyes watching.

Major Tocher watched in frowning silence as the two pairs settled in their seats and secured the waist aprons over the openings of the canoes to make the hull watertight; balancing their craft with skilful experience while joining the two halves of their paddles together.

The waves, so small from the deck of the cavorting pinnace, seemed even bigger from sea level, breaking over the canvas bows of *Minnow* and *Codling* as the four marines thrust forward with powerful strokes.

After a few minutes, Thomas stopped paddling and placed his hand, palm down, on top of his head, as a signal for the Corporal to come alongside into the "raft-up" position with all four paddles laid across both canoes to keep them stable and together.

'Sorry I didn't brief you before this,' apologised the officer, blowing cold seawater from his numb lips as it streamed down his face. 'Not much to tell, really. We will paddle off for roughly half a mile then stop about thirty feet apart with a rope floating between us. The pinnace will then snag the rope on her stem and tow us along trailing astern of her. The aim is to see if it is feasible, and to work out a safe system of speed and distance. That's about it.'

'Do I hold the loose end, with your end secured, sir?' spluttered Pearman, referring to the rope and quickly foreseeing possible problems.

The officer wiped a hand over his face, gratefully feeling better. 'Yes, Corporal. But watch for my signals at all times.'

Pushing against each other's boats they separated and began paddling with strong, steady strokes that drove them smoothly over and through the lumpy sea leaving the static pinnace corkscrewing in their wake, its mast clawing across the sky beneath a cloud of disappointed seagulls that had mistaken it for a fishing boat and provider of scraps. Spray pelted each marine's face as they pushed and pulled in a steady rhythm that could be maintained for hours, if necessary. Despite cold hands, and faces numbed with the driving shards of spindrift, they were all inwardly smiling. At last they were active and doing what they had been trained to do. They were in their chosen element.

Tocher stood silently beside the Leading Wren who still held on to the useless wheel to prevent being thrown bodily about the wheelhouse by the violent motion of the boat. Waves, coming aboard each time the side rails dipped to sea level, washed across the deck to the other side in a cascade of foam as the pinnace rolled, only to be defeated by gravity and rushed back by the reverse roll.

Maggie felt the first queasy murmurs of sickness in her stomach and wondered how her crew were coping. They didn't come outside the confines of the harbour very often. 'Shall I put a few revs on, sir?' she asked, hopefully. 'It would steady us up a bit.'

The officer either ignored her request or chose not to hear it, as he scanned the crowded waters of Spithead and the Solent. Warships of every size, type and description filled the famous naval anchorage. Some tugging at their anchor cables against the fast flowing tidal stream while others steamed slowly in or out of the harbour. Grey hulls against an even greyer background, with only the contrasting flutter of white ensigns and multi-coloured signal flags to break the dismal half-darkness. Dozens of small craft, some patrolling, others carrying everything from liberty-men to stores and ammunition, dotted the surface; buzzing around like bees. Occasional merchantmen - less immaculate than the "pusser" ships - waited with whispers of smoke being whipped downwind from their salt-stained funnels. Beyond them, sticking up from the dark landmass of the Isle of Wight, the tall steeple of Ryde church reached up like a pillar to support the low gathering clouds. On the near horizon, the three circular, weather-beaten sea-forts - *Spit-Sand, Horse-Sand* and *No-Man's-Land* - stood like guardian sentinels over the restless fleet.

Behind his bland, unemotional façade, Tocher felt a deep concern for the young marines who he - and probably their Lordships of the Admiralty too - knew were being sent to an almost certain death. Their task was suicidal and he had argued against it as much as he dared. But, like everyone else, he had to obey orders. His intention now was to do all in his power to give them every possible chance of survival.

'Put her half ahead, coxswain,' he said quietly. 'Keep her between the canoes, and *that*!' He pointed towards an armed trawler coming around Gilkicker Point towards them, with a bone in its teeth. 'When she is clear, you can head up to pass between the canoes and snag their connecting line with your bow contraption. Make it dead slow at first.'

Marine Browning looked across to where *Codling* lay drifting at the other end of the snag line floating in a curve between them. From the corner of his eye, he saw the head-on shape of the beamy pinnace steaming towards them and tapped the shoulder of Lieutenant Thomas sat in front of him. 'She's on her way, sir.'

The officer swivelled his upper body to see for himself, then signalled an indication to *Codling,* receiving an acknowledging wave in reply. A few strokes of their paddles placed both canoes stern-on to what they now called "Maggie's boat", and watched with professional interest as the Leading Wren steered expertly between them, a frown of concentration on her face.

'Steady,' said Tocher, totally unnecessarily, looking out of the wheelhouse window as the pinnace's stem ran into the centre of the snag line without the slightest sensation of arrest to its four knot forward motion. Tensely, his white-knuckled fingers gripping the window ledge, he watched the line tighten on either side between the bows of the pinnace and the canoes, seeing the two fragile craft drawn inwards under controlled rudder until they trailed astern, just a few yards apart, on the edges of the boat's wake.

'Stop engine,' he ordered, stepping out of the wheelhouse and walking aft to where *Minnow* and *Codling* were drifting slowly alongside their stopped mother-craft. 'Well! How did it feel?'

Thomas held on to the pinnace's side while Browning coiled in the snag line, now released by *Codling,* to prevent it from fouling the big craft's propeller. His hands were quite numb with cold, but the fresh air had cleared his brain and blown away the headache. He dangled his hands, one at a time, into the sea that felt almost warm compared with the air temperature, then took them out and rubbed them together vigorously to restore the circulation, in the mariner's age-old remedy for cold hands, as Tocher crouched down to hold on to *Minnow's* bow. 'No problem, sir' he mumbled through frigid lips, then stretched his neck to call across to *Codling.* 'How about you, Corporal?'

'Fine here, sir,' replied Pearman. He wasn't really. He was dying for a pee and it made him feel colder than he already was.

Tocher seemed pleased. 'Okay then. We will find a rougher patch of water and try again,' he told both crews. 'Once I have you in tow I will increase speed a few revs at a time, so make sure you give me a clear cut-throat signal as soon as it gets too much for you to cope with.'

Thomas and Pearman nodded their understanding as the Major released *Minnow* and returned to the wheelhouse, breathing hot breath into his hands. 'Slow ahead coxswain,' he ordered. 'Take her onto the Mother Bank.'

The second trial went equally as well. Maggie slowly increasing her speed in response to the circling finger of the Major who stood outside the wheelhouse with his head stretched forward looking aft, watching with concern the two canoes surfing in the wake among the tossing turbulence of the shallow water.

Thomas' arm felt a yard long as if being pulled out of its shoulder socket, and the snag line cut painfully into his forearm around which he had twisted a few turns. There was nowhere else to secure it. 'That's enough, Browning,' he gasped.

His No.2, sat behind, waved to the pinnace to attract their attention then drew his open hand edgewise across his throat. Immediately the strain came off the line as Maggie cut her engine, and Thomas rubbed his painful shoulder.

On *Codling*, Pearman gave a sigh of relief, his breath evaporating the air around his mouth. He too had wrapped the line round his forearm and was feeling the strain.

Back on board the pinnace, with the canoes safely hoisted and stowed, Tocher wanted a de-brief with Thomas and Pearman.

'Will you excuse me for a minute please, sir?' asked the NCO as he ran urgently and awkwardly to the stern to relieve his bursting bladder overboard; only just making it in time.

'You'll get frostbite, Corp,' laughed Marine Nook.

The skinny Wren looked away, shocked not only at such indecency but also at the blatant staring of her crewmate.

'Wonder you can find it in this weather,' added Crosby. He had spent a miserable morning in the cabin with the two Wrens who he had nicknamed Laurel and Hardy. Given the choice of either of them, he'd have preferred jumping into the sea…naked!

'Sir' cried the tall gangly Wren, peering outboard and pointing. 'I think that destroyer is trying to signal us.'

All eyes followed her extended arm to see the wildly blinking light on the anchored warship.

'Wants to know who we are and what we're doing' she continued, proud of her knowledge of Morse code remembered from an earlier signals course that she had failed.

'Ignore him' ordered Tocher, irritably turning his head away. 'Carry on, coxswain.'

By the time the comforted Corporal returned to the wheelhouse Maggie was already heading back towards the harbour entrance at full throttle, hugging Haslar wall for a good lee, grateful that her stomach had stopped lurching about. The wind had certainly increased to a strong breeze, causing the other small craft farther out to bob about alarmingly. No doubt there would be quite a few on board them with unseamanlike innards, staring into paper bags or feeding their breakfast to the fishes.

Pearman stood outside the open door of the wheelhouse, knowing he would not have been asked in – even had there been room. The bloody "Ruperts" might just as well have hung a sign outside saying *No Entry*. Not that he would have wanted to share his contagious impetigo and black plague with them, anyhow. At least they left the door open.

'I was just telling the Major,' said Thomas, trying to bring his NCO into the conversation. 'The only problem I had was when he increased the towing speed; it hurt my arm.'

The Corporal - twitching his defrosting nose and hoping the moustachioed Major wouldn't think he was taking the piss – thought *Blimey! Were they asking my opinion? That's one for the record book.* Out loud he said, 'Me too, sir. Reckon we need some sort of towing 'ook fitted if we're going to be pulled at that speed. Or, how about a small bollard through the foredeck?'

Tocher humped begrudgingly, thinking the suggestion should have come from him. 'Lieutenant Thomas and I will consider that and maybe get a chippy to work on it.' He turned his back on the NCO.

'I'll ask the Wrens to organise a cuppa then, if you're finished with me, sir,' said Pearman, thinking what a pompous, arrogant bastard that Tocher is.

Down in the cabin, the well-built Wren, who had by now given up on the chance of being seduced, or even chatted-up, huffily answered the request for tea. 'Get lost, Royal,' she snapped. 'We'll be alongside in ten minutes.'

Chapter Five.

HMS.Dolphin. Gosport. November. 1942.

'Oh! I say!' called the tubby, great-coated figure jovially, opening the door and pushing his bearded face into the Base Padre's office to survey the two marine officers whose cosy chat he had interrupted. 'Isn't this carrying the cloak and dagger stuff a bit too far?' He removed his cap and tossed it onto the table to reveal a bald head that gave him the appearance of having his head on upside down.

Major Tocher rose from a worn leather chair, a rare smile creasing his face at the sight of his close friend. 'Sorry, old chap,' he greeted apologetically. 'The base is so crammed full at the moment this is the only privacy they could offer us for our meeting; courtesy of the Padre himself, of course.' They shook hands warmly. 'Allow me to introduce Lieutenant Adrian Thomas….he's commanding the raiding party.'

Thomas stood to accept the offered hand as Tocher continued the introductions.

'Adrian. I would like you to meet my good friend Lieutenant Commander Richard Templeford, the Captain of *Tenacity*.

The Commander, rising on the balls of his feet to stretch his 5ft 9 inches of height, looked up at the youthful but obviously tough marine, noting what he assumed to be the heavy shadows of strain beneath the eyes. 'So, you're Britain's answer to Errol Flynn are you?'

'Sir?'

'Don't call me sir' said the sailor, not unfriendly. 'The name's Richard. Now, what's this all about? Let's get on with it.'

'Never mind him, Adrian,' interjected the Major, settling back into his chair. 'He's just an uncouth sailor. If he had a brain he'd be a marine.'

For several moments they sat waiting in uncomplicated silence as the Commander took a battered briar pipe from his top pocket and clamped it firmly between his teeth. With thick sausage-like fingers, he noisily scraped a match along the side of a Swan Vesta box and held it to the bowl, puffing like an excited goldfish and blowing clouds of pungent fumes from the corner of his mouth. Narrowing his eyes to keep out the smoke he tossed the spent match onto the table. It missed and fell onto the floor. Unconcerned, he ran a finger between his thick neck and the rolled collar of the white submarine sweater he wore beneath his navy-blue battle-dress blouse.

Adrian coughed discretely against the back of his hand as Tocher re-opened the conversation.

'No doubt you've read your orders Richard, so you'll know we don't have a lot of time at our disposal. I suggest we get our heads together to discuss the details, and any problems. However…..' he paused, dramatically, '….I have to mention that, at this juncture, Adrian is unaware of Operation Gladstone's location, and regrettably I'm under strict orders not to divulge it to him for some obscure security reason, until the very last moment. I don't agree with that decision of course, but there it is.'

Templeford, tugging at his beard, looked shocked. 'What a load of senseless rubbish' he muttered, centering his pipe between tight pursed lips and staring cross-eyed down at the glowing bowl. 'I suppose they have their reasons, but for the life of me I can't think what they could be. Hardly fair on you Adrian' he added, directing this last comment to Thomas, who shrugged in resigned acceptance.

'We've done *our* sea trials, Richard….' said Tocher, not wanting to pursue that line of discussion, '….and we are of the opinion that the top towing speed should not exceed eight knots. We may be getting the wood-butchers to fit some sort of small towing bollards through the foredecks of the canoes to facilitate this.'

Thomas raised an eyebrow in surprise. As the raid commander, he should have been consulted in any final decision on Corporal Pearman's suggestion, and if he lived to make a report after the raid, he would damn well say so.

The Major leaned forwards on his elbows towards Templeford. 'How are your trials going?'

Like a politician carefully choosing his words the Commander hesitated, thoughtfully puffing at his pipe, and then addressed Thomas. 'I would like you to come aboard my boat and witness an exercise Adrian. At the moment it's taking twenty minutes to get your two boats up out of the hatch and placed overboard by using the gun-lift.' … puff! puff!..... 'And I am not at all happy with the thought of being on the surface, in enemy waters with a deck hatch open, unable to dive for twenty bloody minutes. Not happy at all,' he added emphatically.

Thomas shot a quick glance at the Major, then decided to broach an idea he had been considering. He hadn't discussed it with Tocher as yet, but two can play at being silly buggers. 'I've had a thought, sir,' he said, talking to the Commander, 'which could possibly reduce your on-surface time to a few minutes….. if you thought it feasible.' He saw the sailor's eyes open with interest, the pipe poised motionless an inch from his mouth. 'How about the canoes being brought up on deck and placed across the casing –thwartships?, he continued. 'My chaps could then get sat in them while your men return below and shut the hatch. You then dive your sub slowly, allowing the canoes to float off and paddle away sharply to avoid being caught under your jumping wire. From my point of view, I can see no reason why this shouldn't work in say…mmm….two or three minutes,' he suggested optimistically. 'I realise we would need to try it out, and of course I'm not a submariner, but could it be done do you think?'

It did not take a trained psychologist to see the differing reactions.

Richard's face lit up. 'Damn good idea' he said after a few moments thought. 'I think it might work - and save me from a heart attack. We must try it out; I'll have a word with my boss.'

Tocher - his finger tips tapping an annoying tattoo on the tight leather arm of his chair - could hardly conceal a scowl of resentment. 'You haven't mentioned this before Adrian. It's the first I've heard of it.'

'I've only just had the thought, sir' lied Thomas, not at all concerned at having hurt the Major's pride and sensitivity. 'But if it works it will save time and, more importantly, reduce the sub's vulnerability.'

'You've trained your man well, Bull' placated the Commander, unintentionally adding to the Major's annoyance by using his nickname gained in earlier service, many years ago.

Thomas raised his fist to his mouth and coughed into his knuckles, trying to conceal a snigger with difficulty. He had not heard Tocher called by that name before and it suited the man, especially if one added a four letter suffix.

The Major, obviously miffed and unimpressed, was petulant. 'Sounds a bit hare-brained to me.'

'Nevertheless,' shrugged the sailor without rancour. 'If Captain (S) agrees we will slip out in the morning and give it a go.' Then, seeing the Major's face redden, added charmingly, 'I presume you will make your chaps available for a few hours, eh?'

Tocher, seething inwardly, clenched his fists behind the chair. He found it objectionable that his junior should be seen to take the initiative, especially when his so-called friend Richard enthused over the suggestion. He *could* say that he couldn't spare the men from their tight training schedule, but no doubt with Captain (S) likely to be getting involved he would probably be over-ruled by that higher authority, to his own detriment. And, he reluctantly admitted, there was some merit in the idea – if it worked. He looked out of the window. The view overlooked the lethal grey shapes of moored submarines in the creek, menacingly silent except for the low chugging from one that puffed out a stream of white smoke from its exhaust outlet. Outside, the grey, miserable day began to get dark as he nodded agreement.

Next day, on board *Tenacity* - already nick-named "Tin City" by the irreverent marines - Browning had sat himself on the uncomfortably hard racking in the oily atmosphere of the forward torpedo room with the other marines. They were enjoying the hospitality of the sub's crew as they lay alongside the jetty in Haslar Creek after their successful "floating-off" trials that morning. He held a mug of sweet tea in one hand and "smoked" a pencil stub with the other, studying a cross-word puzzle in the newspaper folded on his lap.

'What's a Caesarean Section, Corp?' he asked, trying to make sense of one of the clues and peering with deep interest at whatever was in the bottom of his cup.

'It's a unit in the Italian army, innit,' replied the knowledgeable Pearman facetiously, sipping from his own mug and not even bothering to look up from the woman's magazine he had found on top of a locker.

'Oh!......' said the baffled Browning, staring at the un-started puzzle with a deep frown splitting his forehead. His eyes ran down the list of other clues, following the tip of his finger. 'What's Nitrates then?'

The Corporal looked up at the submarine's pipe-strewn deckhead as if seeking divine guidance, inhaling a deep sigh of sufferance. 'Nitrates....' he said slowly, addressing the large wheel-valve just above his head and shaking his head in a gesture of hopelessness, '....is the bloody opposite of day rates, Prat!'

A nearby sailor, fiddling with a screw-driver trying to open the back of a watch, sniggered in amusement. He must try to remember that one.

In the Captain's cabin - nothing more than a curtained off broom cupboard - Tocher, Thomas and the Commander were also cradling the same sweet tea, this time served in slightly more delicate china cups that were taken out of their well-padded boxes only on high days and holidays by a protective steward; never when the boat was at sea. They had been discussing the morning's trial.

'So, we agree that we use the "float-off" method, gentlemen?' enquired the rotund Captain, delighted that his surface time had been so drastically cut to less than three minutes.

Tocher pouted his lips, and nodded. He had to admit the trial had gone exceedingly well and, to Thomas' credit, the young officer had made an obvious effort to praise the success as a team effort.

'It was a bit scary first time, sir' Thomas confessed, still not finding it easy to call the Commander by his Christian name. 'But both Corporal Pearman and I think it is by far the best method and….' he added, '…..providing you dive reasonably slowly and we paddle like hell, we don't see the necessity for you to un-rig your jumping wire.'

Templeford felt well pleased. The war was going bad enough as it was, without offering Jerry the present of a helpless sub on the surface. 'Let's drink to that then,' he suggested, raising his half empty cup and then lighting the foul-smelling pipe, much to Thomas' annoyance. 'You've done me a damn good turn, Gentlemen.' He nodded gratefully from behind a dense cloud of smoke, his eyes showing his pleasure. 'Now, perhaps I can return the compliment?' Using his elbows as a lever he lifted himself up an inch from the chair, shuffling his bottom into a more comfortable position. 'My orders are to drop you and your canoes off at a point six miles from the French coast.'

Tocher's heart missed a beat. Surely the fool wasn't going to disclose the location? There would be hell to play if he did. The orders were very explicit. Thomas was not to be told – yet!

'That's going to be a long paddle in hostile waters for you Adrian,' continued Templeford, 'so what would you say if, after you float-off, I submerge to periscope depth and snag a floating line between you to tow you in a bit further; as far as I safely dare? I have picked-up an agent in this manner before, and at low speed – say about five knots – I wouldn't harm my 'scope. Then, when I feel it necessary to leave you, all I have to do is down-periscope and you are free to continue on your merry way.'

The two marines faced each other in surprise. It was a very attractive proposal that was not - they appreciated - without danger to the submariner. Nevertheless, it would make the world of difference to the well-being of the canoeists. They would make their landfall in much better physical condition, and they *had* been training to do just that, albeit for another reason. A reason Thomas was unaware of at that time.

If only I knew what to expect when I get there, thought Thomas. How could they expect him, in his ignorance, to make contingency plans, or decisions? He was becoming quietly angry and frustrated.

'Sounds great to me, sir,' he answered appreciatively, and then turned to the Major. 'When *am* I going to be told the location of my target?'

'Tomorrow….. probably.'

Thomas lost his composure at this truculent reply. 'Well that's not good enough, *sir,*' he snapped with heavy emphasis on the last word. 'You expect me to put my life and those of my men at risk, without the courtesy and decency of being told *why?* What price loyalty? What do you think we are – spies? How am I supposed to plan my part in the operation all the time I'm being treated like a chattering housewife?' He stood, placing his white knuckled fists on the small table. 'Not good enough,' he said, tight-lipped. Angrily adding, 'Not acceptable.'

The major's face flushed. He wasn't used to being spoken to by a junior officer in such a manner, especially in the presence of a third person. 'Steady, Thomas!' he warned sharply. 'Watch what you are saying, and remember to whom you are speaking, or you may regret your words.'

Thomas stared down at the seated Tocher, eyes blazing with frustration. 'Oh! No, I won't,' he almost hissed. 'But *you* might think differently if I were to refuse to go. Treat me like a child and you can't blame me if I act like one,' he shouted as he threw the curtain aside, and walked out.

Tocher made to rise, but the Commander placed a restraining hand firmly on his forearm, holding him down in the chair.

'Leave him, Bull. Let him cool down before you both do something stupid. After all, who can blame him? I don't. I agree with him entirely. It's damnable to treat any unit commander in such a cavalier fashion, let alone sending him off blind on what is, seemingly, a suicide mission. Surely you aren't happy with that?'

'But my orders are.......' blurted Tocher.

'Your orders....' interrupted Templeford, '....as I understand them, are not to divulge the destination to anyone until the last moment, *at your discretion.* From what you have told me, the raid commander himself was not specifically mentioned. Good God, man, I am only the delivery boy and *I know!*'

Tocher's face crumbled, and he slumped like a melting snowman in his chair. Templeford was right. He had been over-exerting his authority by not taking the lieutenant into his confidence. He searched his mind for an acceptable excuse, and could not find one. Had he been afraid of losing face? Or failing in *his* duty, if Thomas refused to go when told the location of his objective? On the other hand, had he wanted to spare him the anguish of knowing he and his men had as much chance of returning safely as a chocolate oven glove? He wanted to believe it was the latter, but was honest enough to fear it was the former.

Templeford removed his hand from his friend's forearm and placed a sympathetic arm around his slumped shoulders. 'Go and find him, Bull,' he advised softly. 'Go and tell him, NOW.'

Back in the forward torpedo room of *Tenacity,* the Corporal and his three

THE OTHER 'COCKLESHELL HEROES'.

marines were feeling a mellow companionship towards the submariners who had all charitably spared them "sippers" from their daily tot. Crosby, Nook and Browning, had had little previous association with vagaries of Jolly Jack Tar, who's traditional feelings towards any "Bootneck" could change rapidly from open hostility to generous friendship - and, of course, the other way around. The present atmosphere in the cramped smelly compartment was, to say the least, amicable, and the three unanimously agreed that the "subbies" were a great bunch of lads; despite smelling like bilge rats and generally looking like unwashed tramps pulled through a hedge, backwards.

Pearman, in quiet conversation with a Leading Torpedoman, observed his three charges with disdain. He had enjoyed a few "sippers" himself, but wasn't acting like a prat, like them. One sniff of the barmaids apron and they were as pissed as newts. Call 'emselves Marines?

The Leading Hand, one eye closed against the smoke dribbling upwards from the fag end drooping from the corner of his twisted mouth, looked across to one of his fresh faced O.D's. who was listened avidly to Crosby's version of life in the hazardous service of Combined Operations. 'Hey, bollock chops,' he called, a Welsh tilt to his voice. 'Go to the galley and ask Cookie for some black coffee for the Royals'.

Browning, peering through the haze of smoke, focussed on Pearman's face. 'Hey, Corp....' he mumbled, waggling a finger in the vague direction of the sailors bunched around him, '....this bloke says a Caesarumem Section thing is summat to do wiv a woman 'avin' a baby!'

An expectant hush fell. Somewhere the dripping of water, or condensation, sounded like the beat of a drum. All eyes turned to look at the NCO, waiting for his gem of wisdom.

Pearman frowned reflectively, then raising his eyes and struggling to keep a straight face said, 'Don't take any notice of 'im lad. He's taking the piss. 'He's talking about an enema.'

'What's an enema, Corp?'

A group intake of breath, barely audible, went through the boat. In the heavy silence everyone waited, eager to hear the corporal's punch-line.

'Someone who's not yer bleedin' friend.' He answered casually. 'Now belt up.'

Chapter Six.

H.M.S. Dolphin. Gosport.
December 1st. 1942.

It was the faint shimmer of steam rising from the damp grey socks on his feet that distracted the attention of Corporal Pearman away from the Readers Digest he had propped up on his chest. He had been engrossed in an article about incest among the people of some obscure tribe in the remote regions of South America, and enjoying a few moments of rest and relaxation stretched out on his bed. I suppose, he thought, they never got to see anyone outside of their own village; probably never knew anyone else existed! His mind boggled at the thought of having sex with a female relative. His own twin sisters were only fifteen, and – Jesus! – no one ever thought of their own Mum in that way….did they? As for his one and only Aunt, well, she was built like a tank. He'd rather go without.

'What d'ya reckon is goin' to 'appen to us, Corp? asked the concerned voice of Marine Nook laid out on the next bed with his hands clasped together under his chin, like a corpse. He had been thinking all sorts of horrendous things about their forthcoming mission; his mind's eye seeing his mutilated body washed up on a deserted beach with eye sockets pecked empty by scavenging seagulls. He could not help being a worrier and knew he had too much imagination for his own good. There was a long silence. 'Well?' he persisted.

The NCO slowly lowered his book, and placing it face down on his chest, turned his head, his nose twisting in mild irritation. 'We're all going to die, ain't we' he grunted cruelly, running his fingers through the dark curls of his hair, then noticing the concerned frown on the young marine's face added with a smile, 'Eventually.' He too was worried about the immediate future, but dare not let it show for the sake of his lads. They only wanted re-assurance…. didn't we all? Of course he was scared. Who did they think he was, Desperate Dan? If he knew the score, he would be able to cope a lot better. At least he would have something to think about. Perhaps help with the planning and adding his own constructive thoughts and ideas; anything that would occupy his mind. It was the fear of the unknown that frightened him. He was not totally without imagination.

'You know what I mean, Corp….Now!'

Pearman lay back on his pillow gazing up at the raftered ceiling, noticing a bare patch where some idle decorator had left an unpainted "holiday". He cursed all officers and Major bloody Tocher in particular. What gave officers the right, he asked himself, to think they were better – more trustworthy – than anyone else? Easy for them to give orders, they didn't have to face the lads and live with their questions and fears day after day, night after night. It had always been the NCO's that ran the Royal Marines - and every other service for that matter - but when push comes to shove they were seldom consulted, or taken into confidence.

'Wish I could tell you, Lad,' he replied almost apologetically, hoisting himself up onto his elbows and letting his head sag between his shoulders like a weary tortoise, 'but I don't know anymore than you do. And, if I did, some gormless Rupert would order me to keep my mouth shut.' He looked across the room to where Browning and Crosby sat sideways on their beds with feet on the floor; interest aroused. They had learned long ago that when the NCO spoke it usually paid to listen. 'All I can say is…..' he continued, '….if *we* can't do whatever it is they want us to do, then no other bugger can.' He smiled encouragement. 'And remember, you all answered "Yes" when you were asked to volunteer for hazardous duties. It's too bleedin' late now to plead you didn't understand the question.'

'Don't worry about it, Windy,' called Crosby, stretching himself back on his bed, balancing a foot on the bent knee of the other leg to scratch its instep, like a puppy digging for a buried bone. 'You're in the Marines now and everyone gets treated the same… like shit!'

They all laughed. The grim mood was broken.

'Anyone for a game of crib?' invited Crosby, groping beneath his pillow for the peg-board and cards.

'Come in,' called Lieutenant Thomas unenthusiastically, in response to the timid tapping on his cabin door. The last thing he wanted was company, of any sort. He knew he had made a fool of himself on board *Tenacity* and would be well and truly in the rattle for insubordination. He shouldn't have lost his temper. It wasn't Tocher's fault, he was only obeying orders. Nevertheless he felt angry. With himself for blowing his top, with Tocher for being so bloody, bloody, rigid, and with Templeford for just being there and witnessing his outburst. He realised he would now have to make apologies for his behaviour in the hope of regaining his standing with the Major – but not yet; not at this very moment. More than anything he wanted to be left alone. Please, God, he thought, let this not be him.'

His prayer went unanswered as the door opened and the tall cadaverous frame of the florid faced Major filled the entrance, a claw-like hand combing his bristled moustache like a cat washing its whiskers. He stepped in and closed the door behind him quietly – apprehensively?

'Are you all right, Adrian?'

Thomas subdued the retort that sprang to his lips. No good making matters worse. They still had to work together; not forgetting the fact that Tocher was two rungs higher up the ladder!

'Yes, thank you, sir' he lied weakly, getting to his feet.

The Major flapped a hand to indicate his junior remain seated and nodded towards the vacant chair. 'May I?'

'I am sorry, sir,' said Adrian, as Tocher sat and crossed his legs. 'I was totally out of order.'

The Major swung his suspended foot annoyingly, as if playing ping-pong with another swinging shoe somewhere. One corner of his mouth lifting in what was a half grin, half grimace. 'Let's just forget it ever happened,' he said magnanimously. 'You had every provocation.' He leaned forward, detecting the smouldering anger and frustration behind the eyes, and felt a guilty embarrassment. 'If you are ready to listen I want to tell you about your mission.'

Adrian remained silent, absolutely motionless, giving no response. He wanted to cry out, *Too bloody late, the damage has been done*, but reason quickly returned. It was never too late.

Tocher sat back, eyes half closed, arranging his fingers into a steeple at the end of his nose, studying them almost cross-eyed. He took two deep breaths, like a hyperventilating sponge-diver. '*Operation Gladstone*' he began, 'is an attack on German shipping, using canoes and limpet mines, in the French port of.......'

'I have already guessed where it is, sir' interrupted Thomas, rubbing salt into the wound. 'Quite a few days ago, actually.'

Tocher raised a surprised eyebrow, comically twisting his moustache lop-sidedly. 'Oh!'

'Unless I am badly mistaken....' continued Thomas, '....and have completely misread your comments, sir, my target is the Port of Nantes.'

Tocher gave an audible gasp of astonishment. 'How the hell did you come to that conclusion?'

'I always excelled at geography, sir,' was the casual reply. 'And to my knowledge there are only three major ports in France that are situated up river. Rouen, Bordeaux and Nantes. I discounted Rouen because it is - what, eighty miles? - up the very narrow River Seine. It would have been impossible, if not suicidal to penetrate. Then I discounted Bordeaux because, even though the River Gironde is wide, it has - as far as I know - no heavily defended seaport at its entrance. That leaves Nantes on the River Loire, guarded by St. Nazaire where our people rammed the lock-gate a few months ago.

Tocher obviously had the wind taken out of his sails. 'Well I never' he said, flabbergasted, and looking at Thomas with new found respect. 'You are absolutely spot-on.'

'And probably dead,' ventured the young lieutenant thoughtfully.

'NO!' protested the Major, vehemently. 'That's not the case. We originally planned for Rouen, hence the snag-line towing drill. We had a tame barge-master on the Seine who was to have towed you for most of the way up river in the dark, ostensibly unaware of your presence, but he withdrew his offer at the last moment; he had too much to lose. The alternative of paddling all the way was deemed to be an unacceptable risk. So Nantes was chosen, after detailed assessments of the hazards, by a Combined Ops planning team that included your own Major Haslar. And, if it makes you feel better, I can tell you that your No.1 Section will be making a co-ordinated raid on Bordeaux, at the same time. Tomorrow morning you and I will go into full details using the chart I have in my cabin, but basically you will embark on *Tenacity* on December 4th and taken by a round-about route to a position approximately six miles off Pointe de St. Gildas. That is eight miles south of St. Nazaire where, during the evening of December 9th at low water, you will float-off. The sub will then submerge and, with weather and enemy activity permitting, tow you by snag-line as close to the coast as Commander Templeford thinks advisable. When released, you should steer to pass as close to the Pointe that the visibility - and your judgement – says is practicable, remembering Jerry has a coastal artillery battery sited there. You then continue across a shallow bay to Pointe de Minden opposite St. Nazaire where there are more coastal batteries and searchlights covering the mile wide entrance to the River Loire. As it will be just after low water, and a moonless night, you should be almost invisible among the mudflats. So you may decide to drift through this dangerous area with the flood tide using single paddles. The searchlights sweep the channel occasionally but never during an air attack, so the RAF will provide a diversionary raid to keep them occupied.'

He paused, uncrossed his legs and thankfully stopped his swinging foot by placing it on the floor. 'I will be as brief as I can, Adrian. I am dying for a

Horse's Neck, and I'm sure you are too.' He re-crossed his legs; the hanging foot remaining still. 'Once inside the Loire there are plenty of suitable places where you can lay-up during daylight hours. At the last one, which I shall tell you all about in detail tomorrow, you will meet with the Resistance people for a final briefing on the situation. That will be in the close vicinity of Nantes on the night of the 10th.. You will make your attack on the night of the 11th at approximately midnight, with your mines set on a ten-hour delay fuse to explode at approximately the same time as those being placed at Bordeaux. That should give Jerry something to think about. Tomorrow you will be given tide times, tidal streams and rates, positions of tide races and overfalls, gun and searchlight emplacements, weather forecast, moon phases and everything else you will need, including the latest intelligence update. *Tenacity's* navigator will be available to assist should you need him, and so will I. Your escape routine will be given you in sealed orders to be opened when you are on your way. These are for the eyes of the raid crew only.' He uncrossed his legs again and leaned forward, elbows on knees. 'Now shall we have that drink, before I die of thirst?'

'D'ya know what, Bing?' ventured Browning from his bed where he had been trying to yank a dangling hair out from a nostril.

'What?'

Browning took another tug at the hair, making his eyes water. 'I reckon it's Cherbourg.' All evening he had been considering the harbours on the French channel coast and decided this was the most likely. They wouldn't need a sub if they were only going across the Dover Straits, and he didn't fancy Dieppe or Le Havre.

Dave Crosby looked up from the letter he was trying to write on a pad propped on his knees, and gave his mate a pitying look. 'That's a load of bollocks.'

'Why?' queried the aggrieved Browning. 'It's as good a bet as any, ain't it? They're giving us a sub so it's got to be further than bloody Calais. Stands to reason.'

'I reckon he could be right, Bing' suggested Tom Nook lamely, swinging his bird-like face from one to the other in the manner of an owl watching a field-mouse. 'Must admit, I've been thinking the same.'

Crosby shook his head sharply, a movement that failed to disturb his unruly mop of wiry red hair one iota. 'Never'n a million yers,' he said in his broad Cornish accent. 'Oive bin there mate. A couple a times. And Oim tellin' you we wouldn't get past the bleedin' breakwater. You can bet yer boots they've put sodden great guns on 'em that'd blow us straight out the water without as much as by your leave.'

'If I had any money' said Browning, determined to get the last word in, 'I'd bet I'm right, and you're wrong.' He crashed his head down on the pillow to signal the end of discussion.

'You'd get better odds on Pompey winning the Cup, Gravy' predicted Corporal Pearman, solemnly pushing himself up on an elbow and giving up all hope of sleep while these prats were bickering like schoolboys. 'But if you promise to belt up and give me some peace I'll tell you where we're going.'

Tom Nook's head swivelled in a ninety degree turn, eyes bulging like a scared rabbit.

Browning sat up, the offending nasal hair held firmly between thumb and forefinger, like a trophy.

Crosby dropped his pencil onto the floor and twisted over on his side. Almost in unison they chorused, 'Where, Corp?'

Pearman swung his legs onto the floor, enjoying the warmth of the corticene under his stocking-ed feet and the attentive looks of his three marines who sat staring at him in awed curiosity. He stretched the silence for several minutes trying to suppress a grin. They really thought he knew! 'Well' he drawled, milking the situation for all its worth. 'In a day or two's time, we'll be going on that oily toothpaste tube they like to call a sub and be taken for a trip, probably out in the Western Ocean where you will all spew your ugly rings up. Maybe not you, Bing' he said looking at the ex-fisherman, 'but the others certainly will. Then, when the skipper thinks you've had enough, he'll pop up to the surface and put us and our pretty little paddly boats in the water, leaving us adrift so that he can get on with fighting the real war.'

'Then what, Corp?' asked the eager Nook.

'Then my lads, we'll paddle ashore and find us a nice big tree to sit under.'

'What for?' asked Nook again, a perplexed frown furrowing his narrow forehead.

'Cos, my lucky lads,' sniggered the amused NCO, 'that's the only known cure for sea-sickness.'

Still the penny didn't drop.

'Okay' said Browning who, like the others, hadn't seen the Corporal's little joke. 'But what's the target?'

Pearman pushed out his lower lip into a pout and shook his head. 'Dunno.'

'But you said you knew' insisted Nook, looking to his mates for support.

The Corporal raised an eyebrow; a picture of innocence. 'No, I didn't. I said I knew where we were going, not where we were going *too*!' He rolled over on his bed with his back to them, giggling to himself and listening as they cast quiet aspersions on his parent's matrimonial arrangements and threw imagined spears between his shoulder blades.

In the wardroom, Lieutenant Thomas finished his drink having firmly, but politely, declined Tocher's invitation to have "the other half". He had a lot on his mind and needed time to think. 'Goodnight, sir' he said, rising from the uncomfortable wicker chair that was normally reserved - so they said – for unwelcome visitors. Tonight, in the crowded smoke-filled room, it was the only one available; Tocher having made a un-officer like dash for the last arm chair when they arrived an hour earlier.

Outside, walking along the unlit jetty with its silent grey shapes and unseen sentries, the cold wintry wind quickly blew away the sickening tobacco fumes that seemed to cling to the very fibres of his greatcoat. Clean, almost unadulterated air, flushed his lungs and cleared his nostrils as he looked across the dark waters where the blacked-out city of Portsmouth lay as quiet as an abandoned broom in a cupboard. Would he live long enough to ever see it lit up again, he wondered? By the time he reached his cabin he felt quite chilled. Eagerly he undressed, carefully folding his uniform across a chair, and snuggled down under the blankets of his cosy warm bed, trying to picture *Juniper,* his two-and-a-half ton yacht he had last seen straining at her heavy chain mooring between two pilings in the upper reaches of Portsmouth Harbour, under the shadow of Portchester Castle's granite walls. He wondered if his father and Uncle were looking after her for him, as they had promised. The thought of never seeing her again made him feel sad, so he deliberately turned his mind to the last trip he made on her across to the Channel Islands. Surprisingly, he fell asleep.

An hour later Major Tocher, seemingly unaffected by the half dozen drinks he had consumed, strolled along the same darkened jetty, his hands sunk deep in the pockets of the greatcoat that had the collar turned up around his ears like a defensive rampart. With eyes closed to slits against the bitterly cold wind and a brain busy with a thousand and one problems, he was totally unaware of the many invisible eyes of casing sentries and others who enviously watched his passing, wishing they too had the early prospects of a warm bed and a belly full of glowing gin. Head bowed in the unconscious stance of many tall men he entered the officer's accommodation block, completely ignoring the omnipresent white-coated steward hovering unobtrusively in the entrance lobby, and made his way, mentally and physically exhausted, to his cabin. Stripping to his underpants he knelt on the carpeted floor and spread the chart of St.Nazaire and the River Loire region across the bed. It was an old chart given to him by COHQ, one that had been neatly updated in red ink, probably by a re-called pensioner clerk bored but happy to have landed a cushy number. For the umpteenth time his eyes – thought so cold and unemotional by many – took in every detail. His brain noted and catalogued every sounding, every buoy and marker. From the table drawer he took a hard-covered notebook that had seen better days and flipped through the pages until finding the one he wanted. What appeared to be a jumble of figures and arrows were, in fact, his very detailed workings and interpolations of tidal streams and depths of water that he had checked so many times he knew them all off by heart. On the next page - marked by a stiff-backed calendar card for the months of November and December 1942 - the moon phases and times of sunset and sunrise were listed, neatly and methodically. Again, his brain repeated its frequently asked questions, *Had he missed anything? Was there anything he hadn't foreseen?* His head ached, tormented by the knowledge that once Thomas and his marines sailed in the submarine he would have no control over their fate. It would be too late. Nevertheless, he was determined that whatever happened to them would not be due to any mistake or incompetence on his part. They would go armed with the best possible information he could supply.

After several minutes he reached out for the telephone on his bedside table. It was a secure line to COHQ in London and specially installed for this mission. He took a quick glance at the heavy diving watch on his wrist and flipped open the flap that protected its face and concealed the luminous hands and figures that glowed like a firefly. The thick hands, easily read even in pitch darkness, indicated it was eleven thirty.

'Ah, good!' he muttered aloud. '23.30. This will wake the idle sods up.' He dialled a number.

Almost immediately a disembodied voice answered. 'Duty Officer.'

Tocher gave his identifying code and waited the couple of minutes it took for a security check to be made.

'Good evening, Major Tocher,' said the satisfied voice. 'How can I help you?'

'*Operation Gladstone*' he snapped, not caring if the metallic voice belonged to a Lieutenant or Admiral. 'I want a full intelligence update.'

He listened to the shuffling of papers at the other end, and the unmistakable slamming of a steel filing-cabinet drawer in the background.

The voice came back on. The voice of a desk warrior. And for the next thirty minutes Tocher scribbled frantically.

Chapter Seven.

H.M. Submarine Tenacity.
4th. December. 1942.

Thirty-two year old, Lieutenant Commander Richard Templeford. DSO. DSC. RN., sat on his bed in the box-like captain's cabin of *Tenacity;* waiting. He was already dressed in his sea-going rig of a rather tatty and smelly uniform jacket that characteristically bore no sign of medal ribbons, and flannel trousers tucked into the tops of leather knee-boots. The gold wire badge, hanging askew on his battered peak cap, was almost green with verdigris. This was the start of his fifth war patrol.

'Boat is ready for sea, sir,' reported his First Lieutenant, Lt. Alan Willy. RNR., a former Cunard Line officer with a Master Mariner's ticket who, being built like a rugby scrum-half, inevitably acquired the nickname *Tiny* throughout 'the trade' – and for other reasons according to those less charitable.

Templeford shrugged himself into an equally shabby duffle-coat patterned with oil and salt stains, and climbed the vertical iron-rung ladder from the Control Room up through the Conning Tower, to his bridge. It was bitterly cold. Nestling his bearded chin deep into the thick woollen sweater that had seen better days, he leaned over the bridge breastwork and took a long look around, checking the way was clear for his stern-first exit from Haslar Creek. The boat seemed to breathe quietly, disturbed only by an occasional clang of metal against metal from somewhere deep inside the hull, the puttering of the engine exhaust, or a muffled curse.

There were no theatrical shouted commands of "Let go, for'rard" or "Let go, aft," on *Tenacity;* it wasn't that kind of boat. The enforced casualness of dress - and to some extent the discipline as well - and the close understanding built up over her five patrols between officers and men all reliant on each other, had welded the crew into an efficient unit without the need for authoritarian histrionics. He turned for'ard and raised both arms in the air, palms upper-most, then crossed them at the wrist in the agreed signal to 'let go the head ropes and hold fast to the bow spring'. A one-arm acknowledgement came from the fore-casing as he turned to face aft to repeat the two-arm signal without the crossing of wrists. Again the silent order was acknowledged as the after-casing crew hauled their icy wet stern-ropes clear of the boat's propellers.

'Slow ahead starboard. Port ten,' he ordered. Then seconds later called 'Stop starboard,' as the boat surged forward at the thrust of the propeller to put strain on the bar-taut bow spring and swing the stern away from the jetty. 'Slow astern together. Starboard ten.' He lifted both arms again and the fore-casing party pulled the dripping bow spring inboard as the men on the jetty threw its eye off the bollard.

A number of officers waved from the pier-head and Templeford returned their gesture with a relaxed salute, barely touching the peak of his old cap with the edge of his hand as *Tenacity* eased her long hull out of the creek.

'Stop starboard.'

The boat's head swung to port as the orders were repeated from below.

'Stop port. Slow ahead starboard. Port ten.'

The long grey-stone block of *Dolphin's* officer's accommodation building moved steadily across from port bow to starboard as *Tenacity's* head swung into the narrow entrance channel between the aptly named *Fort Blockhouse* and *Portsmouth Point*.

'Slow ahead port. Midships.'

More arms waved from both sides of the harbour as the men of the casing parties stood smartly to attention in the traditional "manning-ship" courtesy salute to senior officers; their white sweaters contrasting starkly with the rapidly fading late afternoon daylight.

'Half ahead together.' Templeford conned his command out through the well marked channel, following in the wake of a rusty minesweeping trawler that was herself starting out on yet another of her unglamorous tasks of keeping the approach channel clear. He hoped, uncharitably, that if there *were* any un-located mines floating around, the trawler would find them before he did.

At the back of the bridge, Tocher and Thomas stood - by special permission providing they kept out of everyone's way – listening to the sea hissing along the submarine's saddle-tanks and watching as the boat slipped almost silently past *Round Tower* and *Sallyport* from where Admiral Lord Nelson used to board his gig and be rowed out to Spithead to join his anchored flag-ship.

Southsea's pebbled beach, deserted at this time of the year, slid by and light rain began to fall as *Tenacity* followed the channel buoys on which even the resting sea-gulls looked miserable. Then, skirting the forlorn lump of *Spit- Sand Fort* to starboard and out as far as the Outer Spit buoy, she passed between the other two dismal looking shapes of the *Horse-Sand Fort* and *No-Man's-Land Fort* that stood out blackly against the darkening sky. Thomas, forgetting his own immediate future for a moment, wondered what life was like for the Royal Artillery soldiers stationed on the three offshore forts to man the anti-aircraft guns that helped to protect Portsmouth. They looked so cold, bleak and desolate. What a way to fight a war, he thought sympathetically.

The cold wind whistling around the confined bridge space, soon found a way through the greatcoats of the two marine officers who were quietly discussing the merits of life on a submarine compared with their own. With nothing to do they soon began to feel discomfort, so much so that the order for them to leave the bridge and climb down into the relative warmth of the oily fug below was very welcomed, and eagerly complied with.

Up on his bridge, Templeford shivered at the mere thought of paddling around in a canoe in such weather; in his opinion such flimsy craft were as seaworthy as a colander. The marines must be stark raving mad. Still, each to his own. His orders were to deliver his passengers and their canoes, then continue to a patrol area off of Lorient where he hoped to surprise any U-boat sailing from, or returning to, the massive submarine pens built there for protection against allied bombing. Hopefully he would find good pickings to add to his score of tonnage sunk, but he wasn't too happy about being two "fish" short having left them back at *Dolphin* to make space for the stowage of the three canoes in the re-load racks. Neither did he feel too happy at having Tocher aboard for the whole patrol. Despite their friendship, the man was an unwelcome addition to the already cramped officer's quarters. He blew sharply through his sodden moustache to scatter the rain droplets from the end of his nose and looked around at the Officer-of-the-Watch, two lookouts and a signalman who were still sharing the bridge with him. All were holding powerful binoculars and conscientiously searching the rapidly fading horizon, their heads crouched low inside the soggy hoods of duffle coats, like cowled monks. Each pair of eyes piercing the gathering gloom as the night began to draw its own blackout curtain across the sky. The rain turned to sleet.

'You can't trust bloody Jerry to leave you in peace, even in the Solent,' the Second Coxswain had been heard to say with the authority of eight years experience; three of them in wartime.

South of *Nab Tower* – the desolate pile of concrete that looked more like a ruined lighthouse covered in scaffolding than an important signal station and gun battery marking the eastern entrance to the Solent – the companionable minesweeper wished them "Farewell and Good Hunting" with her shaded signal lamp, then did a sharp turn away to begin another laborious, never-ending sweep.

Templeford, with rain dripping from the peak of his cap like an overflow from a gutter, turned to his signalman. 'Reply. Thank you. Will bring you back a pheasant.'

Accommodation on a submarine for both officers and crew is, to say the least, limited; certainly not five star by any stretch of the imagination. Even without their six Royal Marine guests the crew lived, ate, worked and slept in conditions considered poor; even by sardine standards. Hammocks were slung in any convenient space. Each of the very few narrow bunks, more like letter racks, had to be shared with another watch-keeper (although not at the same time; even the Navy drew the line somewhere). Known as 'hot-bunking', this was considered a luxury by those less fortunate who had to get their heads down in any space they could find, frequently among the spare torpedo racks. None gave a second thought to using several tons of high explosive for a pillow.

Tom Nook considered himself reasonably lucky to have acquired a narrow slot in the fore-ends between two of the canoes. Not that he cared. He had been seasick since leaving Pompey and would have willingly, and hopefully, died for King and Country, whichever came first and be quickest. The first night had been purgatory for him. The boat had completed a short dive – something to do with "getting a trim" according to one of the torpedo-men. The rest of the night, it (he couldn't bring himself to think of the oily cramped boat as a 'she') plunged and corkscrewed on the surface with jarring crashes that must surely cause it to sink. 'Please, God!' he prayed hopefully. He wasn't alone in his misery. Marine Browning felt just as bad, and so did some of the crew. They hadn't seen anything of the Corporal or the officers, but "Bing" Crosby – who sat unconcerned humming a tuneless song - seemed to be in his element, his cheerful chatter getting on everyone's nerves and earning himself several death threats from some of the sufferers; although most were beyond caring.

At daylight, when the boat dived, it seemed like heaven. Within an hour everyone was up and about, bragging they had been *only slightly* sick. The vomit-filled receptacles being emptied down the "head" gave lie to their claim. Even so, very few appeared to have appetites except, of course, Crosby who ate like a pig from a trough. Unfortunately for some, the daylight was short lived and at sunset *Tenacity* surfaced again. Thankfully the sea had moderated a little, although not enough to suit the many delicate stomachs, and Tom soon began staring, once again, at the blood splattered vomit in the bottom of his dish, wondering how the hell the sea-sick matelots managed to continue carrying out their duties.

The next few days, as the boat circled out into the Atlantic, were an eternity. The atmosphere in the sub deteriorated hourly with the stale air heavily laden with the smell of shale oil, diesel oil, sweaty bodies, cabbage and the acrid stench of vomit. To the amazement of the marines, most of the more experienced submariners took it all in their stride; not caring if they were submerged or surfaced with the hatch open. Tom thought they must all be mad to accept such discomfort and privations. Give him a canoe and fresh salt air any day.

Meanwhile, sat at the collapsible narrow mess table drinking a mug of thick sweet navy "ki" (cocoa), Crosby had found a kindred spirit; a brother-in-arms (or should it be in beds?). Able Seaman Alf Walters, a wireless operator, had been recapturing his many romantic escapades in Pompey during his last two leaves. At first Crosby was all attention, envious even, and then his mouth fell open, flabbergasted. One sounded very familiar.

'Bloody hell!' he stammered. 'So you knew Rita too?'

The seaman lifted tired eyes from the half-empty mug in his hands, a little worried that he had over-embellished the truth. 'Knew her, Royal….?' he said. '….I bin screwing the randy bitch for the last two months'. Then adding as an after thought, 'except for when we was away on patrol.'

Crosby wasn't the least perturbed. On the contrary, he wanted to hear more to make comparisons. 'Oiy only met 'er the week afore last,' he said.

'You're well out of it, mate' advised the seaman, feeling he was now on safer ground and could continue his boastful reminiscences. 'All she wants is someone to marry 'er. Preferably a matelot who'd be away most of the time and leave 'er to enjoy 'erself. I got a bit wary when she started on about 'avin' kids and things, but I dumped 'er completely when 'arry Nobes in the Naafi told me 'e'd seen 'er out wiv a marine… Hey!' he laughed, 'weren't you, were it?'

'Probably' said Crosby, beginning to feel a bit like a cuckolded husband. 'Oiy were wiv 'er most of the week afore we came to *Dolphin*.'

The sailor laughed again. 'Flippin' eck. We could've 'ad a punch up, mate.'

Crosby looked at the weedy looking bloke sat opposite and smiled. He could have flattened him with a fart, he thought crudely.

But there was no stopping Able Seaman Walters who was in full swing. 'Two things stick in my mind about Randy Rita' he continued, taking a slurping swig from his enamel jug and staring down at the almost solidified remains. 'We was at it on the kitchen table one night and just getting to the short strokes when she looks up at me and says "Did you know they're cutting the sweet ration next week, Alf?" I tried to ignore 'er, which was easy 'cos she just laid there quietly wiv out moving one little bit. When I 'ventually come, she glared at me and wanted to know why I'd finished. "*I was enjoying that*", she says….. Bloody cow!'

Crosby was remembering a similar position he had enjoyed with Rita and the memory awakened urges where it shouldn't. 'What was the other thing?'

Alf placed his mug down on the table and ran a dirty finger back and forth through his greasy hair, as if massaging his brain. A frown started to wrinkle his forehead, and then vanished just as quickly. 'Oh yea!' he smiled, remembering. 'That was just afore I jacked 'er in.' He sniffed and fingered his nose with a nicotine-stained finger, as though scratching an itch in his brain. 'We'd bin out to a dance in Southsea and went back to 'er 'ouse for a night-cap. We was at it in the same way as before wiv 'er laid back on the table, when the door burst open and 'er bloody Mum comes in! There was me wiv me trousers down round me ankles, me bare arse wobblin' and me knees tremblin',' he said in graphic description. "er Mum didn't turn an 'air. All she said was "You two want a cup-a-tea?" Don't reckon mine was the first 'airy arse she'd ever seen. Probably the table 'ad memories for 'er too.'

Their little tete-a-tete ended as a young blonde head poked itself through from the control room and shouted, 'Diving Stations in ten minutes.'

In the torpedo stowage space, Tom Nook lifted his white face and pushed the vomit-filled dish away from his mouth. He had heard the welcome shout and his dream of imminent death receded. 'Thank God!' he said, loud enough to be heard. 'Thank bloody God.'

An hour later, with all the pallid sea-sick faces beginning to look almost human again, Lieutenant Thomas mustered his marines in the fore-ends, with Major Tocher and the boat's First Lieutenant in attendance. One or two seamen hovered around, ears flapping, hoping to glean a few titbits of information that would enhance their reputation during mess-deck debates later on; until they caught the warning eye of "Jimmy" and made themselves scarce.

'Right, listen in, lads,' he began, opening a chart of the River Loire area and spreading it over the deck plating. 'At twenty-hundred hours tomorrow we will be floating-off the sub in this area here.' He knelt down on one knee and made a small circle with his forefinger on the chart. 'I will be in *Minnow* with Browning. Corporal Pearman will take *Codling* with Nook as his number two. Crosby will be in reserve in case of any injury during the debarkation and *Garfish* will remain below as replacement should either of the other two canoes get damaged.'

Crosby looked and felt thoroughly pissed-off. He didn't need reminding of the probability of being left behind. *Like a spare prick at a Portuguese wedding*, as he so elegantly described it.

'It goes without saying,' said Thomas straightening his back, 'that Corporal Pearman will take command if, for whatever reason, anything happens to me.

Crosby discreetly crossed his fingers behind his back.

'If, in spite of Crosby's wishes to the contrary….' smiled the lieutenant glancing towards the reserve marine, '….all goes well, the Captain may take us on a snag-line ride nearer to the coast. In any case, we will be given a course to steer for this headland here.' He tapped the chart. 'When we approach it, I will signal a turn to port with *Codling* keeping station astern within visual distance.' He glanced up at the Corporal, willing him not to ask questions in front of the Major. 'It will be low water and moonless, so make sure you don't get too far behind and lose sight of us. If you do lose us you must continue on your own, and if for any reason one of us has a problem, or makes contact with the enemy, the other is to continue without attempting to give assistance. The mission objective is paramount. There are gun batteries and searchlight positions here and here.' More chart tapping. 'We should be able to keep between the mudflats and be virtually invisible but when we reach this point here….' he pointed to the place named Le Pointeau on the chart, '….we will go to single paddles and drift in on the tide. With luck,' he said hopefully, 'we shouldn't be bothered by searchlights as the RAF will put on a diversionary raid, and if we keep in shallow water among the mudflats we shouldn't meet up with any patrol boats either. Once through the narrows….' he went on confidently, '….and in the Loire itself, there are several places where we can safely lay-up during the daylight hours, but like everything else, we will play things by ear. We should get to here….' he pointed at a marshy area opposite a place called Paimboeuf, '….well before daylight. During the second night a short paddle will get us to a ruined building on the left-hand riverbank that was once a recreational "rest hotel" for senior German officers, until the RAF bombed it. It is arranged for members of the French Resistance movement to meet us at these ruins to update our intelligence as to the shipping in the port. There's an abandoned boathouse right on the river edge at this point that the French will mark with white paint so that we shouldn't miss it. Also, they will do the same to a wooden stake at the river's edge about two hundred yards before the boathouse. That way, if we miss one, we will see the other.' He stopped, seeing Corporal Pearman raise a tentative hand shoulder high, like a nervous schoolboy. 'Yes, Corporal?'

The NCO had been following his officer's briefing, attentively. After all, his life could well depend on it, and the lives of the others; not to mention the success of the mission. So far, the plan seemed riddled with if's, but's and maybe's, and depended entirely on every German in the district being fast asleep. He could accept the concept of surprise tactics, especially as Jerry wouldn't be expecting an invasion by two canoes after the massive raid on St. Nazaire earlier in the year by half of the bloody navy and army, but this!......the chances of success were probably less than about 5%, and hopes of survival about bloody nil as far as he could see. Nevertheless, the powers-that-be said it should be done, so who was he to argue? But, as Section NCO, he had the right and duty to add his own pennyworth.

'Assuming we get that far, sir,' he said with a slight inflection of sarcasm in his voice. 'Won't Jerry be alerted if he sees new white paint being splashed all over the place?.... and how will we know which post is which?'

Thomas quietly sighed. He had been hoping for the Corporal's support in this hair-raising scheme. He could see the hazards and pitfalls more than most. Everything would depend on a huge overdose of luck and he wished he had all the answers.

Seeing the lieutenant's hesitation, Tocher interrupted. 'The first post will be painted with one stripe, and the second with two,' he said brusquely. The NCO's nitpicking questioning had irritated him. 'You will have to accept that we planners have *some* idea of what we are doing,' he said with undisguised sarcasm. 'As for timing, the painting will be done on the day before you are expected, and only on the river side of the posts.' He wiped a forefinger across his moustache, trying to quell his rising annoyance and wanting to tell this Corporal to "just get on and do as you are told". Why do NCO's always feel the need to question the ability of their officers?

Thomas, seeing the light of anger in the Major's eyes, responded quickly to forestall any further comment from either man. The last thing he wanted at this stage was discord. The Corporal's questions were perfectly reasonable, which was more than could be said for Tocher's sharp reaction. 'Good question, Pearman. We need all the input we can get on this job, from anyone,' he said pointedly, and flinched as he felt Tocher's eyes puncturing the skin between his shoulder blades. What price promotion now? he thought… if he lived! 'Subsequent actions will, of course, depend on what the Frenchmen have to tell us, but I propose to launch again at about twenty-two hundred hours the next night and drift the short distance to the docks on the flood tide. We will place our limpets on selected targets or, if there are problems, on targets of opportunity. Of course, events might dictate changes and we'll have to be ready for them.'

It all sounded so easy, so simple, but the look on each marine's face told a different story. Not one of them was under any false illusion. They knew this was not going to be the doddle that Major-bloody-Tocher tried to make it out to be.

Browning felt an unnatural sympathy for the lieutenant who was clearly in an unenviable position. He had to bite his tongue to stop himself from asking the question that everyone wanted to ask… *Will Jerry be asleep, sir?*

The anxious looks that passed between each face, the frowns and raised eyebrows, and the nervous fidgeting all told their own story. Three pairs of eyes strived to conceal the turmoil of worried minds as they forced false smiles in a desperate attempt not to reveal their fear. It was a gut-wrenching fear of an unknown future, the dread of capture, wounding, or even death; yet no one considered failure - it was not an option.

Crosby's eyes were anxious too, but not for the same reasons. These blokes were his mates, they had trained together. Now he almost wished for one of them to have an accident or injury, so that he could take their place. His dreaded the thought of being left behind. How would he feel if they didn't get back? How would he face the rest of the Section back home? How would they manage without him? He wanted to go!

Anxiety filled the lieutenant's eyes as well, but strangely enough he felt no concern for himself. This was his job, his responsibility, his *command*. He briefly studied the faces of the marines, all looking apparently unmoved, unworried and unafraid; waiting for his instructions and *his leadership*. Their stoicism was awesome. How could they *not* be afraid? He was! His fears were for their welfare and the possibility of his own failure. A fear of doing something - or not doing something - that would result in their injury or capture, or worse. They were relying on him, their officer, to do the right thing; to make the right decisions. It was a responsibility that weighed heavily on his young and relatively inexperienced shoulders, and he thanked God for the presence of Corporal Pearman.

The NCO shared many of his officer's concerns. He too had worries for his own capabilities. How would *he* react in the face of the enemy with the lads watching his every move? Would *he* show his fear, his doubts? They, and Lieutenant Thomas, were relying on him. He was the daddy of the outfit, the experienced NCO… *What experience?*…. He was as green as any of them. He felt, rather than saw, "Windy" Nook looking at him. He turned and stretched the corners of his mouth in what he hoped would be seen as a re-assuring smile.

"Windy", for once in his life, *was* living up to his name. His hands trembled, so he pushed them deep into his trouser pockets. He could face up to the possibility of capture and – surprisingly – even being killed, providing it was quick and relatively painless. What he did dread - and it was a morbid fear - was being seriously wounded. His pain threshold, he knew, was limited. The thought of being left sightless, disabled or disfigured for the rest of his life was too frightening to contemplate. He would rather die. At least that way he wouldn't have to go back to that bloody bank job when the war was over. He swivelled his head from side to side; no one else looked scared! Corporal Pearman even had a smile on his face and for some inexplicable reason it made him feel better. He didn't want to show them he was a coward. He smiled back.

Thomas coughed to clear his throat, and to attract their attention back to his briefing. 'When all the limpets are in place we will either drift with the tide or - depending on circumstances – paddle like hell to get as far from Nantes as possible while it is still dark. We should have several hours of flood in our favour. When the tide turns we land on the north bank of the river and, after removing the survival packs, scuttle the canoes by extensive ripping of the hull fabric. When they are well and truly sinking we give them a hard shove out as far as we can into deep water.' He paused as if to collect his thoughts, fiddling around with something in his trouser pocket. 'In your survival packs you will find a well-worn civilian overcoat, an over-size beret and a pair of boots that should - if the planners have done their job properly – fit reasonably well. We remove and hide our canoe smocks and waders, then put this overcoat on *over the top* of our battledress uniforms. This is to ensure our treatment as P.O.W's should we be unfortunate enough to get captured.' He stopped, and ran a dry tongue around his even drier lips, hoping the million questions he could see forming behind each pair of eyes would wait until they were away from the intimidating presence of the Major. 'You have all been trained in escape and evasion tactics so remember what you've been taught. If we haven't already separated we do so when we land. Travel by night; keep clear of roads and habitation, and lay-up during the day. Keep heading in a sou'-sou'-easterly direction for approximately forty miles, to a village that we will call Point X, for now. On arrival, enter the village and take a seat inside the café in the village square. When the waiter comes to you, ask for *"Un café, sil vous plez"*. Say nothing else. Your English accent will be recognised. If he brings a glass of red wine it means something is wrong. Remember red is for danger. Take a sip of it and then walk out. Do not return. If all is well however, the waiter will bring your requested coffee. Drink it and then, after about five minutes, leave the café and the village, by the same route you entered. Do not look back. Someone will follow you. At a suitable place, that person will approach you. Do exactly as he says, even if it means removing your protective uniform. Remember, these people are risking their lives, and that of their families for us. From then on we are in their hands.'

Corporal Pearman again raised a cautious hand.

Thomas gave an acknowledging nod. 'You are going to ask about contingency plans, Corporal?'

The NCO dropped his hand, grateful that Tocher hadn't joined in with six-guns blazing. 'Yes, sir. I…….'

'If all this fails ….'Thomas interrupted, '…it means things are up the creek and we are on our own. Head south towards the Med and use all the survival skills you have been taught. Only if you are absolutely desperate should you try to contact a sympathetic person who may put you in touch with the underground. There are many such people but they have a lot to lose if caught helping you. On the other hand there are those who will betray you to the authorities, for varying reasons. One last thing….' he said with an almost audible sigh, '….if captured, you have no plausible cover story – except on the first day in the estuary when you can claim you were washed overboard from a passing ship and drifted ashore with the tide. Whatever you do you must *not* reveal the nature of the operation until after the time for the limpets to explode has passed. After that there will be no harm in telling an interrogator a little of the truth – except for the contact with the Resistance bit – it may save you from an uncomfortable experience. Do *not* let your canoes be taken' he said with emphasis. 'Destroy them at all costs. Any questions?'

His offer was met with stony silence, from stony faces.

'Right. We'll go over this all again tomorrow, before we launch. In the meantime try to rest as much as you can. It may be sometime before you get any decent sleep again.'

Chapter Eight.

H.M.Submarine Tenacity. At sea.
8th.December.1942.

The air inside *Tenacity* was thick with the ever present smell of oil, the overpowering reek of boiled cabbage and the unwashed body odours of her crew. She had been dived for the last twelve hours. In the fore-ends, the marines – accustomed to an abundance of fresh air – were gasping.

'Loike livin' in a bleedin' sewer' moaned Crosby, sitting on the hard steel deck with his back resting against an upright part of the spare torpedo rack and holding his nose to keep out the sickening stench while gulping to fill his lungs with the oxygen-deficient air.

Browning, sprawled beside him and still weak from his marathon seasickness, lifted his pounding head. He wasn't feeling at all well. 'Think I'd prefer the sewer, Bing. 'ow do them blokes stand it?' he wheezed, pointing his nose at two submariners who were stepping over the marines like a pair of goose-stepping roosters. 'Ain't normal.'

'You should worry mate', growled Crosby feeling very sorry for himself. 'I got ter stay on this bleedin' thing fer weeks yet, while you blokes goes a swannin' off.'

One of the sailors - awkwardly carrying a large cardboard box through the maze of racks, valves and pipes - looked down on the prostrate marines. 'Hi ya, Royal?' he called cheerfully, obviously unaffected by the fetid atmosphere. 'Ready to go boatin' are we?' Their obscene reply was cut short by the appearance of Corporal Pearman, his face looking paler than usual. 'Start getting yourselves organised lads' he grunted. 'We'll be off soon.'

Nook levered himself up off the deck-plates, his ten-stone body feeling like a ton weight. Christ, he was tired, no energy at all. He tried to put his brain in gear in an effort to sort out his equipment and get dressed, but his mind was occupied with the thought of getting off this sardine can and out into fresh air more than with the forthcoming mission. Never, ever, he swore, would he set foot on a submarine again.

In the control room – dimly lit by red lighting to preserve the night vision of those who would soon go up on deck – Alan Willy stood looking over the shoulders of the two planesmen who were concentrating on keeping the boat at its correct depth. He had no thoughts for the deteriorating quality of the air. He wasn't even thinking of his new girl friend with who he planned to spend a passionate weekend in London when this patrol was over. He had other things on his mind. Like all good First Lieutenants he had three eyes; one pair continuously flicking from side to side, scanning the bank of gauges and dials in front of his planesmen, like a tennis umpire judging two top class players.

Every job in a submarine is important, but his was crucial. If the boat became too heavy it would sink like a stone, and no one would be happy. If too light, it would shoot to the surface, and death would be as nothing compared to the captain's wrath. His third eye – not between the cheeks of his backside as suggested by some of the less charitable members of the crew – he kept attentively on his captain. Ashore they were the best of friends; on board it was strictly a Captain/First Lieutenant relationship. As one of the very few RNR First Lieutenants in 'the trade', Alan knew he had to be the best. His captain demanded nothing less.

Richard Templeford was a good skipper. His were the only eyes to see outside of the boat when submerged, and he always made every effort to keep his team informed of what was happening "up top" by giving a running commentary, as if talking to himself, when peering through the periscope. It was a habit much appreciated by all of his crew, especially by Alan who was his second-in-command and understudy. Apart from having to be ready to assume command at a moment's notice should the need arise, it made Alan - and everyone else - feel part of whatever was going on; not just blindly obeying orders.

At that precise moment the Captain's eyes were staring down at the deck plating, his chin crushed against the roll-necked collar of his sweater causing his beard to stick out at ninety degrees, like a bowsprit. With hands clasped behind his back and feet planted slightly apart, he stood in the centre of the control-room looking the epitome of a bored husband waiting for his wife outside of a ladies dress shop. In fact, his outward appearance belied the mental activity whirring around inside his head. He raised one hand; palm uppermost to waist level, and an unseen watcher activated the periscope that then rose from the deep well of its housing. He bent to meet it halfway, grasping the handles and pushing his forehead into the moulded rubber eyepiece in the manner of a motor-cyclist racing down the straight at a hundred miles an hour. Twisting the handgrip to acquire the correct focus, he did a quick all-around search of the barely discernable horizon that was just a vague line separating the two grey/black shades of the sea and night sky. Then a slower search; every move followed by a seaman tailing behind - like an eager one-man queue waiting his turn to see into a 'What-the-butler-saw' machine - ready to read off bearings, or do whatever his Captain required.

'Black as a witches tit,' he said conversationally, using the description often quoted by his navigating officer in preference to the one heard from the second coxswain '*as black as a coal-miner's jock-strap*'. He smiled, wondering under what circumstances the two men had obtained such snippets of worldly knowledge, and stepped back giving an imperceptible nod that sent the 'scope humming back down.

'On station now, sir,' reported Lieutenant Blacklog RNVR, his thin, unathletic frame labelling him as a former academic with a brain that made him excel as *Tenacity's* navigating officer. He straightened his aching back from the plot, fingers crossed. Neither he nor the captain had seen sight of land or stars for the last hour and he confidently hoped his D.R. (Dead-reckoning) was spot-on.

Templeford closed his eyes to rub an eyelid with the heel of his thumb. 'Thank you, Pilot' he muttered, 'I'll take another look in two minutes.' He glanced sideways at his First Lieutenant. 'Are the Royals ready, Number One?'

Willy's eyes never left the gauges for a second. The marines had been reported as ready to go, apparently longing to get off the boat and eager to face Jerry or the Devil himself if it meant getting out into the fresh air. A smile flickered around the corner of his mouth, like a nervous tick, as he remembered his own reaction to life in a submarine in his early service days, before he became immune to the smells. Now, he loved the life. 'All ready, sir.'

'Up 'scope.' This time the commander's scrutiny was meticulous; checking every suspect shadow to ensure it wasn't a waiting patrol boat, seeing a tenuous silhouette of black land and an occasional white flash of a cresting wavelet. 'Bearing?'

'087, sir,' called his faithful attendant, skipping around behind his captain, following every step and reading the bearing from the indicator above the Commander's bowed head.

Templeford stared hard, comparing the land shape with the silhouettes supplied within the intelligence report he'd been studying for the past few days. 'Looks like Pointe de Saint-Gildas,' he said to no one in particular.

'Yes it is, sir,' confirmed the Pilot with a confidence he didn't truly feel. There was always some element of doubt under such circumstances.

'Sure?'

'Certain, sir.'

Templeford treated himself to a smile. He had already come to the same conclusion.

'Stand by to surface.' He signalled for the 'scope to be lowered. 'I shall want to know how close I can tow the canoes and still keep four fathoms under the keel at periscope depth, Pilot. He looked across the control-room. 'Anything on your box of tricks, Phones?'

The hydrophone operator, a very youthful Leading Seaman who had high hopes of becoming an officer one day, sat huddled over his set, his face towards the captain, pressing the electric ears close to his head. He didn't hear a word. 'Nothing, sir,' he replied. 'All clear.' He could lip read though.

'Surface.'

The atmosphere in the fore-ends was tense and faces looked drawn, almost spectral, in the dim red lighting. A Petty Officer sat crouched, like Quasimodo in the bell-tower, on the top rungs of the iron ladder leading up to the forward torpedo-loading hatch. Below him a seaman held *Minnow's* painter, ready to haul the canoe up on deck with the assistance of another waiting to push up from behind. Behind them, their faces blackened with cam-cream, Lieutenant Adrian Thomas and Marine Browning were anxiously poised. Next in the queue stood a seaman with *Codling's* pointed bow under his arm while at the stern end his "oppo", balancing the canoe on his shoulder, wiped his sweaty armpits with a lump of oily cotton waste, totally disregarding the distasteful looks from Corporal Pearman and Marine Nook standing close - too close - behind him. All eyes were on the communications rating – waiting.

A sudden, noticeable change in the heavy atmosphere caused one of the matelots to say, 'We're up!' Everyone fidgeted nervously; expectantly. Almost immediately the comms rating came to life clamping his hands over earphones that made him look like something from outer space. 'Open the hatch!' he yelled as though calling across the dockyard, relaying the order from the bridge.

Quasimodo spun the wheel on the underside of the hatch and shouldered it open until it clicked onto its retaining clip. A blast of cold sea air rushed passed them, and a shower of icy salt water cascaded down into the boat as the first men struggled out onto the casing, careful not to damage the frail fabric of the canoes on any protruding edges.

'Move it, you shower,' screamed someone, totally unnecessarily.

Within seconds the canoes were placed across the fore-deck, and the marines – inhaling deep breaths of reviving fresh air - were sat in them, all buttoned up and ready to go, as the seamen raced back below decks clanging the large hatch-cover closed behind them. From the bridge, the captain looked down on the canoeists, seeing them reach forward with their right hands ready for the first pull on their paddles to shoot them clear as soon as the deck was awash. He raised a hand to the peak of his cap in a silent salute, sadly wishing them good luck as the dark water surged whitely against the casing.

'Clear the bridge' he ordered, looking at his watch. Two-and-a-half minutes! He must remember to congratulate the crew on a job well done. He bent his knees and stooped to the voice pipe. 'Take her down gently, Number One!'

At periscope depth, Templeford searched the blackness of the moonless night for a sign of the two canoes. Several times he mistook a 'white-horse' for the splash of their paddles until, with an obvious sigh of relief, he spotted the two pinpricks of light from the shaded red torches carried specifically for this manoeuvre.

'Port five. Dead slow ahead.'

'Port five, sir,' answered the helmsman. 'Five of port wheel on.'

'Midships. Steady.'

Templeford conned the boat between the two specks of light and didn't even feel the snag line catch on the periscope.

In the fore-ends of the submarine, Marine Crosby irritably shrugged a friendly hand from his shoulder, ignoring the Leading Torpedoman's well intended condolence. 'Never mind, Royal. You can help us sink some Jerries instead.'

It was bitterly cold in the canoes, and the exposed faces of the four marines became numb as they waited in the slight chop of the sea, with the snag line floating between them.

'Here she comes, Corp,' whispered Tom Nook, seeing the feather of water made by the sub's periscope cutting through the water towards them from astern. He could feel the pulsing thud of her propellers, and imagined the concerned faces of her crew looking up, a few fathoms below.

The NCO half-turned in his seat. 'Right, you know the drill, Windy. Use yer paddles as outriggers, and enjoy the ride.'

The snag was perfect. Hardly a jerk and they were being towed at twice their paddling speed. Both No.1's kept pressure on their canoe's rudder bar with their outboard foot to keep in a sharp arrow-head formation. Only the increasing wind-chill felt unpleasant. It was an exhilaration that lasted for too short a time. *Tenacity* had towed them for the best part of two miles closer to the shoreline when its periscope dipped, and the snag line went slack.

'Bye, Bye, *Tin City*,' called Nook softly into the black night, as they paddled across to join *Minnow*. 'Thanks for the ride.'

'Everything okay, Pearman?' asked the officer, as they rafted-up for one short minute.

'Yes thank you, sir.'

'Good. Dump the snag line and torches and follow me.'

Chapter Nine.

The first night.

'One and two, and one and two,' chanted Marine Browning to himself, unaware that he was subconsciously timing his paddle strokes to keep in unison with the heaving smock-covered back of Lieutenant Thomas crouched in front of him. It was an essential rhythm, made second nature by months of training, and could be maintained for hours if necessary. Despite the slight chop of the sea and the chilling breeze that made life a little uncomfortable they seemed to be making good progress. His upper body had soon warmed with the effort, although his hands – already numb inside dark-blue woollen gloves and silk inner liners - were moulded around the paddle shaft.

It all reminded him of the thirteen-hour bash they had done a few weeks ago, up the Thames River on a training exercise when everything that could possibly go wrong did so. It had been pure hell, a total failure, and the Boss had really laid into them, with both barrels. In comparison this little jaunt was a doddle so far; but they still had a long way to go. He shot a quick glance over his shoulder. One of his jobs – apart from keeping a good lookout – was to occasionally check that *Codling* was still with them. There she was, powering along a few yards astern with a fine bone in her teeth, her wet paddle blades flashing in the darkness. Suddenly he felt sad. Her crew were two of the best, and over the last months he had built a bond of friendship, trust and respect with them, stronger and deeper than anything else he had experienced before; even among the so-called brotherhood of the East London gangs. He dreaded the thought, and possibility, of anything happening to them.

A quick flash of light fine on the starboard bow caught his attention, gone in an instant. He paused, and was about to tap his No.1 on the back to report it when the officer stopped paddling and swivelled his head around saying 'Dimmed headlights' from the corner of his mouth, his arm outstretched and pointing. 'On the coast road. Must be less than a mile away.'

Browning squinted into the black night, trying to see signs of the shoreline.

Nothing. The sea seemed to merge with the heavy sky without any apparent join.

They waited, drifting like flotsam; paddles placed across the hull for stability as *Codling* came swishing alongside like a sleek fleet destroyer. The lieutenant cupped his gloved hands to his mouth and called across, just loud enough to be heard. 'Single paddles from now on, Corporal. We'll turn parallel to the coast soon and let the flood tide take us in.' Pearman raised an acknowledging hand and the four marines broke their paddles at the central joint, placing the unwanted half into its fabric sleeve on the canoe's hull.

'Okay, Browning?' the officer asked his No.2.

'Fine thanks, sir.'

'Right. Let's go.' He raised an arm and waved it forward like a cavalry officer signalling a charge.

On *Codling*, the NCO concentrated all his attention on keeping *Minnow* in sight; not an easy job in the stygian blackness of a moonless night. He could see no wake to follow, just a faint splash of thrusting paddle blades and a shape fractionally darker than the ink-black sea. He dare not take his eyes from it even for a second, although he wouldn't be too concerned if they lost contact. Lieutenant Thomas had given him a thorough briefing on board the sub for such an eventuality, and he knew the location of the marshy area they were aiming for as their first daytime lay-up position. It would be better if they could keep together but if they became separated so what! They would still be in the same area and probably meet up at the start of the second night's paddle, or at the next lay-up in the ruined building. So focused was he on following *Minnow's* faint blur, that his mind didn't register the swing to port as they paddled with the tide along a shoreline vaguely seen as a varied shade of black. It was very close to starboard and being infrequently lit by the sweeping glimmer of dimmed headlights of coast-road traffic; and sometimes by a flash of brighter light, probably from an opening door with faulty black-out.

The early flood carried them silently along, with just an occasional thrust of paddle on one side or the other to keep them in the stream that swirled and gurgled its way through the concealing sand banks that were gradually disappearing beneath the rising tide. Once, they found themselves in a dead-end, and rather than wait indefinitely for the tide to rise sufficiently to allow them through, turned around to retraced their passage, cursing.

Marine Nook didn't share his corporal's problem. His eyes were free to scan the surrounding gloom as the tide swept *Codling* and *Minnow* through the deepening runnels between the low hills of sand. It reminded him of Langstone Harbour, the almost land-locked stretch of water to the east of Portsmouth that was a beautiful sanctuary for wild life and birds. It was also a pleasant place for artists and painters, if the tide was in, but at low water, it was a mass of smelly mud and a few deep-water channels. Not very pleasant, unless you were a hungry seabird searching for juicy lugworms. Much of the Portsmouth's sewage emptied into this maritime haven shortly after each high water, to allow the fast flowing ebb tide to carry the effluent out into the cleansing waters of the Solent. At low water the high banks of foul smelling, decaying sludge stank to high heaven, and this was the time when senior officers thought it best to exercise their marines in swimming, wading and canoeing. After all, they reasoned, who would expect marines to land, on a sewage-saturated beach?

Out here, off the coast of France, the only smell was of fresh, salt-laden, cold Atlantic air, and Nook felt content; albeit a little apprehensive at being in enemy controlled waters. Normally in a canoe, the lower part of one's body, the inactive part, soon became stiff and numb but he had remedied the problem by wrapping the camouflaged netting – used for covering their day-time 'hide' and usually stowed in the canoe's stern – around his legs. So, except for his hands and face, he felt reasonably warm and fairly dry. Now that they were using single paddles he didn't have to contend with the continual shower of dripping spray streaming from the upper blades of his No.1's paddle. He crossed his fingers and hoped it would stay that way as he dipped his paddle to sheer away from the bank.

Out in front, on *Minnow,* Lieutenant Adrian Thomas began to worry, squinting his eyes into slits trying to see the ditch-like channel ahead. The shallow creeks between the sandbanks were fine for concealment but gave him no room to manoeuvre until the tide rose much higher; and they were getting perilously near to the river's mouth. If they were to come across a pier or jetty with only a few inches of water running beneath it they would be in trouble; and if an armed sentry happened to be standing on it….. well! It didn't bear thinking about. Pragmatically, he pushed such thoughts from his mind as being unproductive. "What-if's" had broken many a man's nerve.

Suddenly, several searchlight beams lit the sky, their waving wands probing the darkness above the city of St.Nazaire ahead, and lighting the estuary in an eerie glow. Those same searchlights would have been scouring the sea surface looking for them, but for the diversion. A few minutes later brilliant explosive flashes flickered on the horizon as the RAF kept its promise, followed by distant rumblings and short sharp bangs.

Lieutenant Thomas - seeing a gap between two hummocks of sand that led out into deeper water - turned *Minnow* towards it, pulling hard on his paddle. Browning reacted immediately, using his paddle on the opposite side. *Minnow* shot forward. They had to get through the dangerous narrows at St. Nazaire before the raid ended.

Close behind, Corporal Pearman lost sight of them for a few seconds and momentarily panicked. Then, guessing what had happened, he too dug his paddle in and pulled hard, calling over his shoulder 'Paddle, man. Paddle!'

Marine Nook, thinking they had been spotted by the enemy, joined in with fear tightening his throat. His mind conjured up visions of patrol boats and lethal flying bullets. *Codling* flew over the surface like a surf boat and within seconds caught sight of *Minnow* again. Together they pushed on under single paddles like Eskimos stalking the future contents of their winter larder; the coastline to starboard seeming to fly by as the current doubled their paddling speed.

St. Nazaire, on the opposite side of the estuary, appeared to be ablaze, but Thomas knew only a few bombers were involved, so he assumed most of the explosions were from anti-aircraft guns and guessed, hopefully, that all enemy eyes would be searching skywards, not looking for two tiny canoes among the choppy seas.

The glowing seaport, with its fires and explosions, seemed to rush towards them with frightening speed as the four men pulled as hard as they could without creating too much splashing. On their side, Minden Point - the nearest place to St. Nazaire - loomed up ahead, and they stopped paddling to allow the flood tide to sweep them around the headland very close inshore, into the river itself. They crouched forward, holding their breath, noses touching the wet decks to minimise any silhouette. They were in the hands of whichever Saint looked after Royal Marines. Had a patrol boat, or shore-watcher, seen them there was nothing they could do except look like the floating, water-logged tree trunk that most matelots said they were anyhow!

Head down, perfectly still, Thomas prayed. Not to *the* God because he wasn't a religious man but to any god who would see them through, whether he be a sun god, moon god or any other kind of god; as long as he was a powerful one.

In the back seat, Marine Browning found, to his surprise, he had no feeling of fear. With his head bent to within inches of his officer's backside he had other worries that, in other circumstances, would have been laughable. He wasn't a church-going man either. He wasn't praying at all but certainly hoping with all his heart that someone, somewhere, was watching over them.

Drifting astern and keeping level, the crew of *Codling* were huddled forward in a similar position. Corporal Pearman, happier now that the two boats were together again, prayed silently. He had never been a believer in God but at this precise moment was open to suggestions.

Tom Nook, with his nose pressed harder to the deck than any of the others, openly admitted to himself that he *was* scared. Scared bloody stiff! What on earth had made him volunteer for things like this? He must have been mad! When he got back…No, *if* he got back… NO, *When* he got back!... he would put in to become an M.T. driver. Getting cold, wet and bloody scared like this was for the birds! All he wanted to do now was to start paddling, get to Nantes, blow up the bleedin' German navy and get the hell back home!

An eternity later, and following the lead of their officer, they all sat upright as the blazing fires of St.Nazaire dimmed into the increasing distance astern. They were through, and their combined exhaled breaths sounded like a train coming out from a long tunnel; loud enough to waken any hibernating hedgehogs on the southern bank of the River Loire a mere few dozen yards away. Now they had another problem. They had to cross the river's two-mile stretch of open water, and its deep-water navigable channel, to get to the northern side. At half flood there should be enough water covering the intervening shallows to allow the boats over. The planners said there would be; would they be right?

Still under single paddles they set off almost due north. The first half – in shallow water – would be relatively safe. It was the second part, the crossing of the navigable channel, where the danger from patrolling boats, and other eyes, lay. It was difficult to hold a paddle with fingers crossed.

Surprisingly they reached the southern edge of the main channel without touching bottom and having seen only one vessel, an unlit barge anchored in a narrow swatchway between two banks of sand. It was probably derelict but they took no chances and gave it a wide berth.

The tide was running strongly at this point, probably three or four knots Thomas estimated, and their attempt to hold on to a rusty, slime covered marker buoy - for a breather and last minute Council-of-War - failed miserably. Fortunately, they were no signs of river traffic of any kind, and the relieved officer chopped the air with an open hand to signal *Codling* to follow him straight across the channel. They bent their backs with a will and made the half mile crossing in a little over five minutes, all the time being swept upstream and nearer to the unseen town of Paimboef where, according to the planners, a number of patrol boats were stationed.

They made land-fall at the marshlands where they planned to make their first lay-up and, with several hours still to go until dawn, carefully reconnoitred the area looking for a good spot to land. They soon realised that almost anywhere would do. It was an almost perfect "Hide"; miles from anywhere with no apparent firm ground underfoot. They pushed their way into a narrow gap between two banks of tall reed until running out of water, then with stiff legs and aching backs, lifted the canoes up onto a relatively firm mound that hopefully would be above the high water mark, and placed them side by side.

'Everyone okay?' asked Thomas in a whispered voice, even though there was probably no one within several miles.

'Fine, sir,' answered the NCO untruthfully. He felt bloody frozen and dying to empty the night's contents of his bladder.

Browning nodded in the dark and Nook grunted; too cold to speak.

The officer looked at their dim shapes barely discernable against the black clouds, taking small comfort from the fact that they sounded as shattered as he felt. The stress and the strain of their night's work had taken its toll. They were mentally and physically drained.

'Right then,' he said in a reluctant effort to be seen to be in charge. 'Let's get the cam nets over the boats and get our heads down. We'll do two-hour watches. I will do the first, then Corporal Pearman, then Nook, then you, Browning.' He nodded to them each in turn. 'If any of you want a slash do it now so that you don't disturb the others. By all means get into your sleeping bags but we stay *in* the boats. Come daylight, if there's no one around, we'll have a brew and something to eat. But don't forget…..' he continued as the three stepped a few urgent paces downwind, 'If there's an emergency we wake each other by the silent method, and if I say "*Move*" we move, PDQ.'

Fifteen minutes later, all four men were snugged down, jammed tightly into the cockpits of the canoes, their sleeping bags in a right mess now they had wriggled into them still wearing their muddy waders. If discovered - although the probability of that was small – they would have had no time to dress. Under the cam netting, they were practically invisible from the air, or the ground. Nevertheless, thought Thomas as he prepared himself for his two-hour watch, no one knows for sure. His body ached with weariness, yet paradoxically, he was not sleepy.

The cold breeze had dropped to a mere whisper, and although the night remained as black as the ace of spades he could picture his surroundings by listening. He felt the silence closing in on him, like a blanket. Marsh birds and wild life - angrily disturbed by their late night visitors – had re-settled. The night air vibrated with the gurgling of the river water probing through the roots of the tall reeds, the chattering of the resting birds, the plopping and rustling of other unidentifiable marsh life and the occasional, less pleasant noise from one or other of the sleeping marines. He pushed all thoughts of the coming nights from his mind with an effort, to concentrate on the serenity of the present. It was all so peaceful. He uncovered his wrist-watch and lifted it close to his eye but the so-called luminous dial was nothing but a blur. He tried the old night-vision trick of looking from the corner of an eye and twisting the watch face, all to no avail. He tried again, looking from different angles and distances. Was it four o'clock, five or six? He wasn't sure. He wished he had been able to acquire one of the American diving watches he'd been shown by a Yank marine in the officer's mess at Eastney. That was *some* timepiece; with large hands and numbers glowing on a black dial that could easily be seen underwater, or in an unlit coal-hole.

A nearby bird cawed into the night as if in alarm, and a splash came from the same direction. From the far distance, a faint single bark of a restless dog echoed across the marsh and once – seemingly miles away – an almost inaudible rattle and rumbling noise that sounded like a tank on a roadway, lasted for several minutes.

Unnoticed at first, the eastern sky began to lighten with streaks of dull leaden grey as what would have been the dawn came grudgingly. It was the beginning of another day and nature was astir. The awakening of the marsh inhabitants brought Thomas out from his reverie. For one dreadful moment he thought he may have dropped off to sleep and he tried hard to convince himself that hadn't been the case. Christ! He would have put his marines on a charge if they done that! Gradually the darkness became less dense and from his low position the tall fronds of the reed beds grew in silhouette as the peep of day climbed the bleak December sky. At least it was dry, he thought, looking again at his watch and being surprised to see it was nearly seven o'clock. The last few hours had flown by. Guiltily, he knew he must have drifted into some sort of sleep, and roundly condemned himself for doing so. He might just as well let Pearman sleep on for another hour or so; to ease his conscience. Not too long though; he was dying for a cup of hot tea.

Keeping perfectly still, he felt like an alien voyeur. Birds began to chirp and flutter noisily and a pair of insect-seeking wader birds came close, unaware of his presence until one of the two sleeping figures in *Codling* gave out with a raucous fart that frightened them away. Something unseen slithered through the reeds, and a loud plop – like someone slapping an open hand on the mud – made him jump. He felt so close to nature that he almost forgot the reason why he was here. It was so pleasant listening and watching the world wake up.

After a while he eased himself up out of the canoe, slowly so as not to disturb the sleeping Browning, and straightened his stiff knees until he stood erect with his head lifting the cam net like the centre pole of a bell tent. The view, as he looked over the top of the shimmering reed beds, was of miles of desolation. Only in the very distance, probably a mile or more away, could he see the red tiled roof of a building. Childishly he felt the urge to yell out "is anybody there?" and then twisted around. The swollen river, less than thirty yards away, appeared empty until a faint thump-thump of what sounded like a diesel engine brought him up on tip-toe, and he stretched his neck. A disembodied mast drifted towards him over the rim of the reed tops like a submarine's periscope as the tonking engine got louder. A few agitated birds flapped irritably a few feet into the air as if to identify the intruder, then landed back at their starting point as though having completed a high hop. With nothing else in sight, Thomas decided to wait until the unseen vessel had passed, then he would put on a brew and wake the lads. That is *if* it passed. What if was a searching patrol boat! His heart began to thump with premonition. He watched, dry lipped, as the noise and mast came abreast of his hidden position to reveal itself as a long, heavily laden barge with barely an inch or two of freeboard, pushing a pile of white water ahead of its blunt bow, like a bull-dozer shoving sand. Right aft, a small one-man sized wheelhouse that presumably enclosed the helmsman, perched almost on the stern rail above the bubbling wake. She appeared deserted as she passed-by and hid herself once again behind the screening reeds.

'What was that, sir?' asked Pearman's sleepy voice as Thomas lowered his tent-pole body back into the sitting position.

'Only a barge going up river.'

'Oh!... What's the time?'

The officer flipped off the cover of his now clearly seen watch, glad of having someone to talk to. 'Nearly half-past eight.'

Pearman' crinkled his face into a frown, his sleep-sodden brain struggling with a simple mathematical problem of time. 'Shouldn't you have shook me earlier, sir?'

'Wasn't tired,' Thomas answered, climbing out of his sleeping bag and stepping onto the firm mud for a quick pee. 'And I was enjoying nature's dawn chorus.' Two minutes later, he wriggled back into the warmth of his sleeping bag and gave the yawning NCO a brief "sitrep", emphasising the need for a sharp lookout to be maintained, even though they were in an isolated situation. 'I'd murder my mother-in-law for a cup of tea, if you feel like making a brew. Then I'll get my head down.'

Pearman rubbed a hand over the bristle that decorated his chin and smiled at the unmarried officer who had just volunteered him as duty tea-boy. He eased himself out of the sleeping bag and canoe, luxuriously stretching his legs and straightening his back, grateful to feel the reasonably hard surface of the hummock beneath his feet. 'Fancy a soup before you turn in, sir?

Thomas thought for a moment. Actually he would have loved one but their

THE OTHER 'COCKLESHELL HEROES'.

'THE TENT-POLE LOOKOUT'

rations were meagre. Apart from the small personal packets of biscuits, sweets and chewing gum supplied for sustenance during the long hours of paddling, each canoe had just four cans of unidentified soup, two packs of inedible compo meals containing oatmeal blocks, cheese, tinned meat, ten cigarettes and – a delicate thought – two plastic bags and a wad of toilet paper. Also a gallon of water and ten packets of mixed tea, sugar and powdered milk in perforated linen bags. A hot soup would be more beneficial before they set off that evening. 'No thanks. Keep mine for later.'

The corporal opened a hexamine cooker pack wrapped in waxed paper and unfolded the four-inch-square tin stand that looked like a miniature collapsible picnic table. Inside, separately wrapped, were four blocks of solid, smokeless fuel made from compressed metholated spirits, one of which he placed under the stand and lit with a fuzee match. Filling one of their two cooking utensils – a two-pint sized can – from the water bottle he placed it on the dancing flames. 'How about crustless toast and marmalade, sir?' he joked.

About midday it began to rain. Only a drizzle but enough to make life even more unpleasant for Nook who was the only one awake; he too had been given an extra lie-in by the corporal. He had spent his time on watch in much the same manner as the lieutenant; keeping still and quiet. Enjoying the sights and sounds of nature. In his rural native Leicester he never had much time for such things. What with his work at the bank and his drinking and partying, he'd be hard put to tell the difference between a Marsh-tit and a seagull, even though he considered himself as somewhat of an expert in other forms of the former. A smile lifted the corners of his mouth as he recalled his last romantic escapade with a Wren named Hannah, in Southsea. Was that only three weeks ago? She'd been gorgeous, and very tactile; leading him on with blatant promises of better things to come. She'd cost him a few bob too, what with the entrance to the dance-hall and a few drinks, but she had given him high hopes of it being worthwhile later on. When they went under the pier for a kiss and cuddle later, he had thought his luck was in. Her response to his attention was passionate, and she giggled delightedly as he probed inside her blouse, but the wrath of God descended when he tried to move south of the border. She went berserk, and he began to worry in case passers-by thought he was attacking her. One of the nicer things she called him was 'a filthy lecherous bastard' as he had stepped back away from her in shock, watching with relief as she ran off leaving him standing under the dripping pier. Ah! Well. Win some, lose some.

He took a last look around the deserted field of rustling reed before deciding it was time to wake that lazy sod, Browning. He could do with another few hour's kip.

'Wakey, wakey, Gravy,' he called, pinching the ear lobe of his gently snoring mate. 'Your turn to watch the seagulls shit.'

Chapter Ten.

Second night.

For someone who said he wasn't tired, Lieutenant Thomas did very well. Despite the cold, cramped conditions of *Minnow's* less than five-star accommodation, he slept soundly until mid afternoon – much to the envy of his three marines who were enjoying a quiet afternoon's chat -and woke stiff, starving hungry and feeling like an unflushed toilet.

'Any chance of a brew and something to eat lads?' he asked, his unshaven chin rasping against the collar of his smock. 'My stomach's as empty as Browning's hospitality wallet.'

'We've been waiting for you, sir,' replied Pearman, smirking at the officer's feeble joke then turning to face Browning. 'Get the stove going, Gravy' he said, wiping two spread fingers across his own upper arm to indicate non-existing chevrons.

'Christ!' muttered the lieutenant, easing himself out of the cockle's cockpit and slowly forcing his stiff leg muscles to lift him into the standing "tent-pole" position. 'I feel like a pensioner.'

The disgruntled Browning placed a match to the solid fuel block under his small 4"x 4" "galley", not at all pleased with being lumbered as duty cook. 'Rather have a twenty-year-old Swedish nymphomaniac myself' he grumbled, earning himself a dirty look from the officer who was still considering an appropriate response when Pearman – never lost for a suitable reply - interrupted. 'Why's that Gravy? You giving up women?'

'Ha, bloody ha!' answered Browning. It was his turn to give a dirty look.

The grey, gloomy daylight was fading fast as Thomas scanned the vast expanse of marshland that stretched as far as the eye could see. The reeds rustled and swayed like waves in the raw breeze that swept over them. Birds fluttered and swooped, scavenging for their supper and making the last social calls of the day. The level of the river was beginning to drop, and although empty of human traffic, was busy with birds of all shapes and sizes whose antics momentarily made him forget the reason for his being there. Small darting birds skimmed the choppy surface of the river, chasing invisible insects. Larger more sedate ducks – like the ubiquitous Mallard – cruised like miniature warships in and out of the river's edge. An ornithologist's paradise, he thought. It was fascinating.

'All clear, sir?' Pearman's query brought him back to reality. Darkness was almost upon them, but it was not the pitch-blackness of the previous night. The land – or rather the tops of the reeds – looked like an undulating wave silhouetted against a deep-grey sky. Only the straight-edged outline of a distant building marred the feeling of absolute desolation.

'Yes, Corporal' he replied, reluctantly dragging himself back to the present. 'We can dispense with the cam-netting now and exercise our legs a bit. I think the world has gone to sleep.'

The faint glow from Browning's two stoves gave no cause for concern, anymore than the mouth-watering cooking aroma of the long awaited meal did. It was as if they were on another planet, a deserted one at that, as they stood working their lazy leg muscles until they ached, hoping Gravy's cordon-bleu effort would taste as good as it smelled.

But even Browning couldn't work miracles with compo rations.

Ordered to divide the food packs into three - one part for now and the others kept for tomorrow - he scratched the top of his head in frustration and packed tomorrow's share back into the canoes. What was he supposed to do with a few tins of soup, some blocks of oatmeal, a square of tasteless cheese, and canned meat that resembled Spam but smelled like rotten tripe? What could anyone do?

The hot sweet tea, quickly brewed, tasted wonderful to the men sat on the canoes, each cradling his steaming mug in numb fingers, eyes closed, luxuriating in the sensation of the scalding liquid pouring down a parched throat.

'Cor! That was great, Gravy' complimented Nook, keeping his eyes closed to make the glowing fantasy last. 'Beats Naafi char, any day.'

'Yea, great,' echoed Pearman, staring intently at whatever was in the bottom of his empty mug and offering it, hopefully, for a refill while massaging an eyebrow with a stubby forefinger. 'Really great.'

Thomas nodded absentmindedly in agreement. His thoughts, miles away, were on the forthcoming meeting with the French Resistance people. How would he know if they were genuine? What if they'd been caught and Jerry was waiting in ambush? He couldn't see an answer to the dilemma, they'd just have to go in with fingers crossed; there was no option as far as he could tell. He frowned, compressing his eyebrows as though trying to squeeze away the feelings of despair that he must not show, and shook his head in an unconscious gesture of hopelessness.

'What's for eats then, cookie? asked the corporal, seeing the look of worried concern wash over his officer's face and wanting to change the lieutenant's train of thought. 'Smells good!'

Browning continued stirring the warming soup, wishing he were back home doing his postman's "walk" and shoving people's mail through finger-trapping letter boxes. Now, that was *the* life. No worries, no responsibilities and an occasional glimpse of a young housewife in her nightie through an un-curtained window on a dark morning. The only hazard to life and limb being that bloody Jack Russell in the house next to the corner pub. It had an in-bred hatred of postmen's ankles, and the agility to avoid a size-nine hobnailed boot. Without lifting his eyes from the simmering pot or turning his head he answered the NCO. 'Well, you got oxtail soup or oxtail soup, 'cause that's all there is. Then, for afters, you can have a nice mug of hot porridge, a piece of cheese and some bloody awful meat that looks like plasticine. How's that for a mixture?'

'Better eat the lot, lads' advised Thomas, remembering his duty. 'It may not taste terrific but it's full of nutrition and you need it to keep you going.' But even he doubted the wisdom of his words as he looked down at the congealing oatmeal in his mug and bravely lifted a spoonful to his mouth. It was like wallpaper paste; lumps and all. The soup was delicious and very more-some, but the cheese was as chewy as a schoolboy's rubber. Worst of all, by unanimous vote, was the revolting meat. It looked as though it had been swept from the bottom of a parrot's cage and compressed, like a snowball, in a coalminer's unwashed hands. The snowball would have tasted infinitely more acceptable.

'Congratulations, Gravy' said Nook sarcastically, still chewing valiantly on his lump of "Best Cheddar cheese". 'That was bleedin' awful.'

Unabashed, Browning glared at his mate; his stare quickly changing to a grin of self-satisfaction. 'Never mind, eh! Windy,' he smiled maliciously. 'Your turn tomorrow.'

By seven o'clock it had already been dark for over two hours. Rested, fed and watered, they sat listening to Lieutenant Thomas give a briefing on the forthcoming night paddle. A chilling westerly breeze fluttered the rushes, ruffling the water into small wavelets. They considered that a bonus as it would make it difficult for anyone stupid enough to be out on such a wintry night, to see them.

'We've only about fifteen miles to go tonight, chaps….' said the officer, wriggling his numb buttocks on the unyielding wooden seat, '….and with the flood tide in our favour we should easily make it in four hours, at the most. It'll be a doddle. Low water's about 20.30 hours so we leave here at 21.00. The French Resistance people will be looking for us from midnight onwards but won't really expect to see us until between one and two o'clock. Don't forget you are looking for a wooden stake near the left-hand bank with one white stripe as a warning marker, then a dilapidated wooden boathouse a couple of hundred yards further on with two white stripes. It's a bloody black night so keep a sharp lookout. Any questions?'

Three heads shook, negatively. They'd been over all this before; several times. Their questions had all been asked, and answered.

'Okay then. Let's have another brew, shall we?'

Marine Browning offered up a silent prayer of gratitude to the designer of the cockle canoe for making it with a flat wooden bottom that slid easily over the soft glutinous mud. The first half of the twenty yards that separated the relatively firm bank of their first "hide" from the low waters of the river, had been a hard energy-sapping crawl through knee-high sucking ooze that gripped their wadered feet.

'Like walking in glue ain't it, sir' he said breathlessly, leaning across the canoe and pushing with one foot, sliding inch-by-inch across the mud like scooting a sledge. Startled wildfowl, screeching and cawing angrily, exploded from their nocturnal roosts with wings flailing as if being attacked by a swarm of hornets, cursing duck-like at the intruders who were disturbing their peace for the second night running.

'SHIT!' yelped Pearman in alarm, when a frenzy of beating wings from a frightened bird burst in his face as he and Nook thrust *Codling* through its own sea of squelching mud, following in *Minnow's* wake.

'No thanks, Corp,' panted his irrepressible crew-mate in a serious voice. 'I've already been. But I'll wait if you want to go.'

In the lead, Lieutenant Thomas – with wisdom beyond his youthful years – gave no rebuke to this noisy chattering. He recognised that their nervousness equalled his own, and anyhow there was no one within earshot. The last thing they would appreciate would be a bollocking from him. 'Nearly there,' he whispered over his shoulder, unable to see a thing but hearing the rippling and gurgling of the fast flowing river a few feet ahead. Almost immediately *Minnow's* bow splashed off the bank and into the rapidly deepening water. He swung his legs inboard – mud and all – to steady the canoe as Browning give a final shove off before climbing inboard himself. They drifted upstream for several yards getting themselves comfortable before the officer used his single paddle to turn *Minnow* around to face downstream.

'We'll wait for the others,' he called softly as the canoe rocked violently. 'What *are* you doing?'

'Just getting settled, sir' said Browning guiltily. He was following "Windy's" suggestion and wrapping the cam-netting around his legs for warmth while, at the same time, watching the shadow of *Codling* emerge from the reeds and slip safely afloat.

It was like heading into a black void. Only the small white splashes of foam - whipped from the tops of the wavelets by the blustery wind - and the dimmed blinking lights on the buoys marking the river's deep-water channel, gave any relief from the pitch blackness of the raw night. With a slow, effortless use of single paddles the four men allowed the flood tide to sweep them upstream, keeping position between the port-hand buoys and the river bank. Occasionally they passed pinpricks of lights on the land but saw no sign of life, not even when they drifted through a silent village keeping close under the overhanging bank, hearing nothing but a single plaintive bark of a curious dog.

Thomas' eyes ached from squinting into the night, hoping to see any danger in time to take avoiding action; his brain busily trying to foresee possible problems and planning how he would deal with them. Only briefly did he allow himself to think of his own destiny, then quickly put it out of his mind to concentrate on his heavy responsibilities.

Browning, his legs wrapped comparatively warm in the cam netting inside the canoe's hull, swivelled his head from side to side. He could see nothing but the blackness of the river bank and the dull gun-metal coloured surface of the water with its streaks of white foam that seemed to keep pace as he stroked gently along with his single paddle. The low moaning of the breeze and the dripping of water from paddle blades were the only sounds that broke the otherwise eerie silence.

After a while, the monotonous tedium of the rhythmic paddling and the strain of trying to penetrate the dark night, caused him to see every shadow as a challenging enemy. Illusory figments began to fuel his fertile imagination; just as they had during the long exercises paddling around the Solent and up the River Thames. He recalled his feeling of relief when, after one particular thirteen-hour exhausting "night bash", the others had said that they too had suffered the same mild hallucinatory effects; seeing life-like figures and shapes appearing before their eyes, straining nerves to breaking point. A military "trick-cyclist" later explained to them (in clear layman's terms, so he said) that it was 'a common auto-suggestive phenomena generating optical illusions resulting from stress and causing mild delusionary amentia'. They hadn't understood a word, and were grateful when their officer at the time - a Lieutenant Blacklog - offered an interpretation. It meant, he told them, they were all barking mad.

But of course, he added, he had known that all along. He wasn't a bad bloke - for an officer.

He struggled to fight off the hallucinations, trying to fill his mind with thoughts of home. Of his Mum and Dad back in their terraced house, and Dad's nightly visit to the *Three Crowns* where his fame as the local darts champion made him a celebrity. Remembering how he would watch, with bated breath, as his father poised to throw yet another accurate double top; *just like the men lifting their heads from the riverside reeds to his left…...* 'Bloody hell!' he cursed, shaking his head to clear away the images that were nothing more innocuous than a clump of bushes. He must concentrate on what he was doing.

But there was nothing wrong with his hearing.

He tilted his head, pointing an ear like an inquisitive owl adjusting its natural radar, as a faint rumbling noise came from astern. He turned to glance over his shoulder just as a white moustache of bubbling water, surmounted by red and green sidelights with a higher white light, came around the bend they themselves had passed a few moments ago. 'Boat coming up astern, sir' he said, urgently tapping the officer a little too hard on the shoulder.

Without comment, the lieutenant rammed his numb left leg onto the rudder bar and dug his right blade forcefully into the water, pulling hard with the obvious intention of gaining a dubious refuge among the rushes overhanging the bank. Automatically Browning followed suit, hunching low in his seat trying to make himself and the canoe invisible.

For the last hour or so the river's edge had been fringed with a variety of vegetation; marsh-reeds, bushes and undergrowth. Now Murphy's Law prevailed, and the spot they came alongside was bare of everything except grass. There was nothing they could do but lie doggo against the foot-high bank and watch as the launch – for that was what it was – rumbled by, pushing a large bow wave ahead of its bluff stem, and piling up a huge wash that coursed along the bank like a tidal wave, sending *Minnow* leaping and bumping, and breaking the tenuous grip the two marines had on tufts of grass. They could see two of the launch's crew standing in the dimly lit wheelhouse and another walk aft along the narrow side-deck into the cabin-well. All three were wearing uniforms of some description and only needed to turn their heads in the direction of the canoe to see it wallowing helplessly in their wake.

Thomas blew a long breath of relief. 'Eight lives still left eh! Browning?' he said, his heart thumping louder than the receding beat of the launch's propeller as it merged into the darkness trailing a thread of reflection from its white stern-light.

'Blind bastards' muttered Browning, quietly apologising to God for ever doubting his existence, and offering up gratitude to whichever Saint looked after scared marines.

'We'll hang on for a minute....' whispered the officer, trying unsuccessfully to grab a stubble of grass, '....to make sure *Codling* is alright.'

'They'll be okay, sir,' replied the marine re-assuringly, reaching out to dig his fingers into the earth bank. 'They're too wicked to die so...' he stopped suddenly, shocked, as *Codling* appeared out of the solid blackness and bumped alongside with two sets of white teeth grinning from blackened faces, like Halloween masks.

'Want a tow?' joked Pearman wheezily, grasping the lieutenant's paddle and trying not to show his relief at having found *Minnow* so fortuitously. A yard farther away and they'd have missed her altogether. They too had had a narrow escape, only seeing the launch at the very last minute and managing to get under the shadow of the bank; grateful for the lack of alertness on the launch and worrying if *Minnow* had been caught napping.

Unseen in the dark, the officer's eyebrows arched with pleasure at the sound of his NCO's voice. He felt more confident when the corporal was around, encouraged by his presence. Almost like having a father-figure, even though there was but a year's difference in their ages.

For a split second they all sat listening to the rustle of the restless reeds and the pounding of their own hearts. It had been a close call.

'Okay. Let's go,' he ordered quietly, his voice tight with solicitude.

A short while later, a glow appeared in the sky ahead, low down on the horizon like a rising sun, or moon. As they got nearer it rapidly became a string of lights on the right-hand bank that lit up the river like a peacetime football stadium; albeit an empty one. Thomas edged *Minnow* closer to the left bank, ensuring that *Codling* – who was trailing in his wake within inches of his stern - followed.

Despite the light reflected from the opposite bank, it came as a startling shock when a huge black shape loomed up over them, barely a few yards from their bow. Reacting instantly, Thomas thrust with his paddle over the left side to avoid what looked to be a solid pier jutting out from the bank, missing it by inches and drifting down the side of what was now seen to be a large barge moored to the river bank. Its length seemed endless as the officer watched it slide by from the corner of his eye. He had his face pressed hard down on *Minnow's* canvas-covered wood decking, praying that the other three had acted the same. But even he was not prepared for the surprise of seeing the blurred shape of a man sitting at the stern of the barge on the outboard side, silhouetted against the grey-black sky with what appeared to be a fishing rod between his knees. It was even more startling – as they drifted within a yard of his feet – to see him raise a languid hand as a sort of silent salute in recognition of their presence. A mixture of concern, worry and fear, raced through Thomas' brain. What was the man? Who was he? Was he a relaxing enemy sentry, a look-out for the Resistance people or just a harmless midnight angler? What would he do? Was he at that very moment racing to raise the alarm?

They let the tide sweep them a couple of hundred yards further upstream, away from the bright lights and the solitary fisherman, before raising their heads from the low-profile position. There were no flashing lights, no searching torches, no blaring sirens or shouted voices; nothing but the rippling of the flowing river, and the angry whistling of the wintry wind. Had they used up another of their eight lives?

It was a few more miles of easy paddling before *Minnow* found the first of the two markers by the simple method of colliding with it. Luckily it was only a glancing blow, but more than enough to shock the marines who had been searching for its one white stripe for the last half-an-hour with aching eyes.

'Start counting, Browning,' reminded Thomas as he pushed *Minnow* away from the post, worried in case their hull had sustained any damage that would have meant disaster at this stage, and thankful they'd hit with their port bow and not been swept inside the pile.

Browning began his prearranged task of silent counting. The officer had estimated the distance to the boathouse from the first marker would take about one hundred and fifty seconds and he was tasked to tap him on the shoulder when his numbering reached one hundred, for the final count-down. He concentrated hard, even closing both eyes tightly to avoid letting his mind wander with delusory images caused by the surrounding dark shadows. If they missed the boathouse they'd have a hard job paddling back against the fast current. Even so, he almost faltered in the trance-like count that was as sleep inducing as counting sheep; only just managing to drag his mind back as it wavered on the edge of reverie.

'Ninety-nine.....one-hundred.' He called aloud, tapping the lieutenant on the back, the simple act clearing his mind and throwing off the frighteningly spooky effects of the long paddle. He wondered if he had been counting aloud all the time.

Either the officer's Winchester College education had let him down or the river's flow was slower than estimated because more than a minute passed before Browning heard him grunt 'There it is.'

The marine stretched his stiff neck to look over the officer's shoulder, easily seeing the two white splashes in the murk, still some way ahead. The easy sighting was not surprising really, as each of the two stripes of paint on the side of the wooden building were very thick and long, in vast contrast to the narrow one on the first marker. They both dug their paddles in the water and held them firmly in a braking effect that allowed them to drift into the rushes at the side of the dilapidated shed.

'Keep an eye open for *Codling*' said Thomas, twisting his head and speaking from the corner of his mouth. 'Shout at them if necess…. SHIT!' he snapped, jumping with shock as a ghost-like figure rose up from out of the reeds and grasped *Minnow's* bow.

'Allo, Tommie,' it said, welcomingly.

Before Thomas could collect his wits and answer, *Codling* crashed in beside them, driving its stem into the squelching mud and causing the apparition to jump back in alarm.

'Mooring party?' queried the apparently imperturbable Pearman, fully aware that he had been as scared as any of them at the sudden appearance of the ghostly white, un-blackened face of their French one-man welcoming committee.

Sat behind him, his military mind working overtime, Nook spoke the words they were all thinking. 'Stupid Sod,' he snapped, referring to the Frenchman. 'If I'd had a gun he'd have had a bullet between his eyes.'

'Should 'ave smacked him wiv yer paddle, Windy' responded Browning.

The lieutenant step out of the canoe into the marshy slough to offer his hand to the gun-toting Frenchman who seemed reluctant to accept the gesture - probably not wanting to release his hold on what was obviously a British sten-gun - as he stepped back a pace and half-turned, motioning with his hand for them to follow him.

'Let's get the boats up onto the bank lads,' instructed Thomas as his three marines clambered stiffly ashore. 'You and Nook stay here, Browning, while the corporal and I go with this chappie to see what's what.'

'I could kill for a pint, Gravy' murmured Nook, echoing the thoughts of his mate as they watched the three shadowy figures trudge stiff-legged away into the night. 'Guess I'll have to settle for a pee…. Anybody looking?' he laughed.

Thomas and Pearman, with their French guide leading, crunched along a gravel path lined with unkempt waist-high bushes for about a hundred yards before coming to the ruins of what had obviously once been a very grand chateau. Tall brick chimney stacks, without supporting walls, poked gaunt fingers at the moonless sky as they stumbled over the rubble of the shattered building. The RAF had done a good job of demolition.

Following closely behind the Frenchman they passed through a topless doorway, stepping carefully across the floor of what had presumably been a large room, now roofless. Heeding a warning signal from the guide they began to descend a long flight of stone steps. Tip-toeing cautiously, with feet feeling for each step, they reached the bottom, and with hands probing ahead like blindmen in strange surroundings, groped their way along a passageway littered with rubble. Turning a sharp corner, they entered a musty cellar-like space lit by a couple of smoking oil lamps standing on a wooden crate. Around the crate - in a pool of light that threw eerie flickering shadows on the un-plastered bare-brick walls - three huddled figures sat in a circle on low wooden boxes, each with a cigarette dangling from bearded lips and holding a glass of red wine. In the sombre glimmer from the lamps, their faces looked like crumpled paper.

The guide, now revealed as a short young man in his mid-twenties who would never be mistaken as anything but a typical French farm worker, spoke rapidly in his native tongue. The three sitting men turned, almost disinterested, to look at their visitors from under bushy eyebrows. They looked like the Brothers Grimm; or the grim brothers. One of them, an elderly bewhiskered man of indeterminate age and wearing a beret that looked many sizes to big, picked up a machine-pistol and stood, straight-faced, regarding the marines with wary curiosity. His eyes sparkled with reflected lamp light. Thomas stepped forward, hand extended to introduce himself with the agreed codeword "Dover", and was surprised at the firm grip of the old man's gnarled hand.

'Calais,' grunted the old man, giving the correct response and baring his teeth in some semblance of a smile. 'Welcome Capitaine. Where boats?'

Accepting his rapid promotion with grace, the lieutenant explained that the two canoes and the other marines were still down at the boathouse. The old man appeared to be listening intently, then placing his weapon down on the box he had been sitting on, spread his hands in an expressive gesture and gave a Gaelic shrug of his shoulders. 'No spik Englis.'

'Oh! Dear,' said Thomas, not realising he had spoken aloud. It was apparent that the man - obviously the leader of the group - had already used up most of his English vocabulary, which was one hundred percent more than his own ability to speak French. This looked like being a difficult task. Surprisingly, and to everyone's amazement and delight, their lack of common tongue soon broke the ice as they communicated with a pantomime of childish sign language and drawing of sketches in the layer of brick-dust on the floor. Charles, for that was the leader's name, proved to be an intelligent man with a perceptive brain, despite looking like a caricature of a down-and-out tramp. He quickly understood what the British officer tried to explain and despatched three of his men to the river to assist in bringing the canoes up into the concealing shelter of the ruins.

The two leaders sat face-to-face across the smoking haze from the lamps, each studying the other, both wanting to ask questions and give answers, not knowing how to make a start. Charles waved a wine bottle wordlessly at the officer and, without waiting a response, emptied the dregs from one of the glasses on the crate onto the floor and filled it with the rich red liquid. Thomas, not a lover of wine, accepted it, deciding not to risk offending with a refusal. 'Cheers' he said softly, raising his glass in salute. He took a mouthful, and immediately changed his religion to "wine drinker". It was nectar.

The Frenchman went on to describe – with much waving of hands and arms, and to Thomas' great relief – that he had look-outs posted outside on the approach roads, and that they would be warned in good time in the unlikely events of any enemy approach or activity.

With the canoes safely hidden under broken wood and brick rubble, the marines carried their sleeping bags and other equipment down into the cellar with the willing aid of their new-found friends who the original guide, Alphonse, had introduced. Alaine, a tall gangling young man with tousled hair and ragged moustache, worked on the same farm as Alphonse, and shared his intense hatred of all Germans. Robert, on the other hand, was the complete opposite, being a benign middle-aged bean-pole of a man whose cauliflower ears would have earned him the inevitable nick-name of "Wing-nut" in any of the British armed forces. None of them had seen a razor for weeks, months even, yet despite the highly dangerous activities they engaged themselves in, they were outwardly jovial, sincerely friendly, and seemed eager to make the marines as comfortable as possible. Even so, they were not the type one would wish to meet in a dark alley, especially if one happened to be wearing a German uniform.

Carefully, so as not to disturb the brick-dust more than necessary, places for the sleeping bags were cleared of debris and more bottles of wine appeared from nowhere. The shortage of glasses did not deter the thirsty marines who upended the bottles and earned a quiet admonishment from Thomas who said, 'Take it easy, Lads. You don't want to wake up with a thick head.'

With two solid-fuel fires going, they were soon sharing a hot brew. The pot-mess of soup and compo rations "cooked" by Windy - which the Frenchmen politely declined with amused wrinkling of noses – was greatly enhanced by two big loaves of delicious fresh bread, donated by Charles. Only the stern warning eye of the officer prevented it all being washed down with copious draughts of seemingly unlimited red wine.

With the meal over, the bloated marines – tired, weary and slightly merry from the unaccustomed effects of the wine – sat around the oil lamps with their new companions, smiling occasionally at each other with mild embarrassment, talking with their hands and sharing their meagre ration of Woodbines with the very appreciative French, whose own cigarettes had the distinct aroma of (and probably tasted like) horse manure that had been soaked in the decaying sediment from the local sewerage.

Outside, the first faint streaks of a grey dawn smeared the eastern horizon as the four marines said their goodbyes to the departing resistance fighters who they would probably never see again; except for Charles who promised to return later in the day with the latest information on German shipping in Nantes and - more importantly - fresh bread. Pleasantly weary, and taking off their outer clothing for the first time since leaving *Tenacity,* the four marines shook the worst of the dried mud from their sleeping bags and wriggled into the welcoming warmth to settle down for an uninterrupted sleep, with the assurance from Charles that watchful eyes would be guarding over them through the coming hours of daylight.

Chapter Eleven.

Third night.

Corporal Pearman's eyelids snapped open and his eyeballs swivelled from side to side like an owl sensing a nocturnal rodent. A noise had startled him into wakefulness but he could see nothing in the total darkness. A tremor of fear filled his chest and gripped the nape of his neck – *something was covering his face* –. In a flood of instant panic he clawed it away, then suddenly felt stupid; it was only his sleeping bag. During the night he had slipped down into it for warmth, cocooned like a chrysalis, shutting out the world, disappearing without trace into a black void. He pulled the kapok material away from his face and fisted it under his chin, breathing in the relatively clean air of the cellar's atmosphere and allowing the foul smell – a mixture of dried mud and his own unwashed body odour – to escape from the confines of his sleeping bag past his wrinkling nose. How had he slept in that malodorous stench? He raised his head from the pillow of rolled waders and looked around the gloom of the cellar, seeing the hunched figures of his officer and the Frenchman, Charles, sat on boxes in a pool of soft light cast by the two oil-lamps. They were drawing lines and figures in the layer of floor dust with their fingers. He watched the officer nod repeatedly at the Frenchman's expressive hand gestures, and saw the shadows cast by the light accentuating the haggard lines of stress and tiredness on the young lieutenant's face, making him look as old as the aging Resistance fighter.

'Wassa time?' he croaked from a throat that felt like a tray of used cat's litter.

'Nearly four' answered the officer, not lifting his head or taking his eyes off the dust grooves that represented the outline of Nantes docks. 'Time you were up.'

'Zat a.m. or p.m?'

Not receiving the favour of a reply the NCO wormed his way out from the nauseous sleeping bag and slowly stretched upright, feeling the painful bruise on his left hip that had been in contact with the unyielding concrete floor for the last eight hours. Bladder pressure told him of another urgent need. Scrambling into his battledress, he crossed the cellar to the dim doorway of light, and climbed stiffly up the two dozen worn stone steps into a roofless square of battered walls that stood silhouetted against the heavy grey clouds of a late afternoon sky. It was rapidly darkening into another wintry night. Even though the air was bitterly cold it was the eeriness that made him shiver as he stumbled over the debris-littered floor to "pump ship" and irrigate the weeds growing among the brick rubble in the corner.

After the biting freshness of the open air, the fug that had been so sweet after leaving his sleeping bag smelled obnoxious as he descended back into the dungeon-like cavern where the two leaders were concluding their council-of-war. 'Cor! Stinks like a sewer down here…..' he muttered, '…..and freezin' bloody cold up there.'

Wordlessly, the Frenchman lifted an earthenware jug from the floor and, emptying the cold tea dregs from an enamel mug, filled it with red wine, handing it to the corporal.

'Ta, mate,' said the NCO, taking a hefty swig. He shivered and pulled a face as he swallowed. The wine that had tasted like nectar in the middle of last night now tasted more like vinegar. He took another mouthful; much better. A few more and he could get used to it, but a withering glare from the lieutenant persuaded him otherwise. 'Make a brew then, shall I?' he offered.

For reasons he could not or would not explain, Charles had to leave them, indicating he would return at nine o'clock. Struggling to his feet, arthritic knees creaking, he leaned heavily on a knobbly walking stick with one hand. The other clutched the German machine pistol slung over his shoulder; probably a souvenir from a long-dead soldier.

Pearman – hoping he would be happily retired with pipe and slippers by the time he reached the old Frenchman's age – couldn't help but feel admiration. What was it that drove an elderly man to such extreme measures? Was it patriotism, hate, vengeance? Or just plain bloody-mindedness at having his homeland occupied by the hated boche? Nevertheless, he still felt qualms at being in the hands of the old chap. He liked to be in control of his own destiny, not reliant on others, especially ancient foreigners who he didn't know from Adam, no matter how brave they were. For all he knew the Frenchman could be on his way to the Jerries now! He just hoped the powers-that-be knew what the bloody hell they were doing, and wondered how insecure his officer felt.

'Call the other two, Corporal,' ordered the lieutenant, deep in thought and not taking his eyes from the dust map on the floor. 'Then we'll eat and have a chat about tonight.'

Browning was already awake, sitting up and raking his fingers through the tangle of his thinning hair. Pearman offered him a mug of tea held at arms length, his head turned away to avoid the smell drifting from the sleeping bag like an evil fog. It was worse than *his* had been.

'Ta, Corp'. What's 'appening?'

'Not much, mate,' said Pearman, trying hard not to breathe. 'Kit and boot inspection in half an hour, then church parade.'

'And bollocks to you too, chum,' quipped Browning, his face turning pale as he caught whiff of his own B.O.

A muffled grunt and fart came from the heap in the corner where Nook still festered. No way did the NCO intend to get near that! Cautiously, arm outstretched, head leaning away, he placed a tea mug alongside the sleeping man's head and retreated to aim a kick at the region of the putrescent feet. 'Wake up, you idle bastard!' he called, stepping smartly back two paces. 'Go up top and air your rotten self.'

The face emerging from the sleeping bag looked ghastly, almost green in the low light, its eyes staring like a frightened frog.

'Jesus!' exclaimed Pearman, peering at the apparition and feeling sick. 'His face has gone gangrenous.'

'Wassa time?' slurred the revolting creature.

'We've done that bit, Windy,' answered the corporal from the far side of the cellar. 'Just get up, and go up top. You need ventilating.' He lifted his own mug and buried his nose into the steaming tea, using its vapours as a deodorising filter, then added as an afterthought, 'And take that stinking bag up with you. Perhaps Jerry will smell it and keep away.'

Nook uncoiled his thin frame and stood in some semblance of the vertical, his bird-like nose probing the gloom like an unlit torch. 'Funny bastard ain't we,' he rasped, obediently bundling the offensive material under his arm and shuffled towards the steps in socks and long-john underpants - still half asleep....until he stood on a sharp piece of brick. 'Ouch!' he yelped, hopping back to his bed space to put on plimsolls and battledress. 'That bleedin' 'urt.' Luckily for his blood pressure he couldn't see the amused grins on the faces of his unsympathetic mates.

'The last supper,' grumbled Browning, getting a look of disapproval from the lieutenant as he and Nook collected the cartons and papers that had contained the tasteless but filling meal of their compo packs. 'Only a joke, sir' he added almost insolently, shaking his head in disbelief at his officer's lack of humour.

Thomas bit his tongue, holding back a retort. This was neither the place nor time to enforce discipline for such a minor, but irritating, matter. 'Put all the rubbish over in the corner' he ordered, sharply. 'The Frenchies will sanitise the place after we've gone.'

Patiently waiting until they finished, he waggled his forefinger in a circle pointing downwards, 'Gather round lads.' He remained standing, looking at them with a grin on his face as they sat on the boxes, staring into the lamps. They looked like gnomes around a toadstool.

Using a long splinter of wood he pointed at the dust grooves on the floor. 'This....' he said, touching one of the grooves, '....is the northern bank of the river. This....' he moved the point of his stick an inch, '....is the southern bank. These....' He indicated three oval shapes, '....are three merchant vessels in the docks.' He moved the pointer across to the northern bank. 'Here are two more.' He sat down, jabbing at a lump of inoffensive plaster near his feet with the stick while massaging the bridge of his nose with the fingers of his other hand. There was a long silence, and the three marines looked at the officer's worry-wrinkled face, saying nothing; waiting. It was as though his mind had found somewhere better to go. Seconds passed like silent drips from a leaking tap. Suddenly - so sudden it startled his audience - he came to life as if rejuvenated with a second wind.

'Right' he snapped, looking directly at Pearman. '*Codling* will launch at about 22.00 hours and cross the river to the south bank. Then you make your way upstream, in low profile with single paddles. Drift with the tide as much as possible and time your arrival at the docks for around midnight. Charles has said the dockies work all night, so expect the ships to be well lit. You don't need me to tell you to stay in the shadows whenever you can. Circumstances permitting, you should endeavour to place three limpets on each of the first two ships; one aft to cripple the rudder and hopefully the propeller, one amidships in the area of the engine-room, and the third roughly between the two forward cargo holds. On the last ship, put one limpet aft and one amidships. If you meet with problems just select any target of opportunity. *Minnow* will launch ten minutes later and stay on the northern side of the river.' He didn't mention the warning from Charles that the northern bank would be the most dangerous for several reasons. 'We will also time our arrival for midnight and attack the two ships on our side, plus anything else that may present itself. When all limpets have been placed, we should let ourselves drift away from the lit area, then paddle like hell with the aim of getting as far away from Nantes as possible. We should have several hours of flood left, but it will be quite weak so far up river. When the tide turns we separate – if still together – and get ashore on the north bank where we scuttle the canoes and follow the escape route to the village where the Resistance will be on the lookout for us. God willing, and with a bit of luck and the help of the French, we should meet up in the *Grenada* in a few weeks time and you can all buy me a pint. Are there any questions?'

There were none. They'd been over every detail time and time again and tried to plan for every eventuality. No one was in any doubt that the job was fraught with danger. They would have to play things by ear and use their training and initiative. That's all they could do, except pray that Jerry would be fast asleep, and every Frenchman friendly.

Thomas looked at each man in turn, proud to be their leader and full of wonder at how they managed to appear so calm. His own stomach was churning like a water-wheel. Did they have no imagination at all? Surely they knew they were on a hiding to nothing! Little did he know that each one of the other three was struggling to hide his own feelings. Frightened above all of letting the others see his fear, and frightened in case he would let them, or himself, down. The glimmer of light from the lamps was a good camouflage for nervousness.

'We'll sort the boats out now, lads,' continued the officer, struggling to keep his own voice steady; throwing the pointing stick away and pushing against his knees with the heel of his hands to stand upright. 'I want everything taken out of them except the escape bags, placing rods, magnetic hold-fasts and limpets. Everything else, the sleeping bags, cooking gear, everything, will be left here. Anything the Frenchies want they can have, although I don't think that will include the sleeping bags unless they're very desperate,' he laughed. 'They'll dispose of the remainder for us. Then we'll get the boats down to the water.'

The limpet mines, paired on their keeper plates, were no light weight as they were taken from the canoes into the darkness of the dilapidated boathouse. Each would be fitted with an ampoule of liquid acetone as a fuse that would give an approximate ten-hour delay, once activated by a turn of a thumbscrew that would break the ampoule to release the penetrating agent. It was a job they could all do blindfold, had done many times. The thought that this time it was for real very much in the forefront of their minds, as they fitted the soluble plugs of the sympathetic fuses, and checked each other's work. They were not looking forward to sitting in the canoes with a lot of high explosive tucked between their thighs.

Nook whispered his concern to Browning. 'It could ruin your wedding tackle, mate.'

'Don't worry about it, Windy,' came the light-hearted reply. 'If one of them buggers goes off, your goolies will be spread all over Frogland, along with the rest of you.'

In the dark corner, cuddling a limpet on his lap, Pearman treated himself to a chuckle. His perverse sense of humour picturing the look on a Frenchman's face if he picked up a bloody testicle from a quiet leafy lane about twenty miles from the river. They eat frog-legs don't they? he thought. Perhaps they'll eat anything.

Codling slid almost effortlessly over the short stretch of hard mud as Pearman and Nook half-leaned on the flimsy hull to sledge it into the cold, fast flowing river. Goodbyes had been said with firm handshakes, good luck wishes, and promises of waiting pints back home. Charles raised his stick in salute and bade them "Bon Chance" with a sad look on his face, but they were uncertain if it was concern for their future or relief at seeing them depart after watching them start the limpet fuses. Somewhere in everyone's mind was the thought that, whatever happens now, the mines would explode - hopefully blowing a hole in one of Jerry's ships - in about ten hours time and preferable not before while still nestled between their legs.

As soon as *Codling* became afloat the corporal sat sideways on its deck, kicking his feet in the water to wash the worst of the clinging mud from his waders while Nook stood knee deep in the river – holding the frail craft steady. Once settled in his seat, he stretched his paddle outboard as a stabiliser to assist Nook in his feet-washing and boarding routine, then allowed himself a small grin of memory as he took a quick glance at the expensive, state-of-the-art diving watch on his left wrist.

He had acquired the watch from a gullible clerk in the stores of an army diving unit during a short visit a few months ago, by using the time-honoured "double B method"….bluff and bullshit. The Chief of Combined Operations at the time was Vice-Admiral Lord Louis Mountbatten whose name was held in awe by all service personnel. Also at that time, few people - other than high-ranking staff officers - were aware of planned special operations. It was a situation Corporal Pearman took full advantage of. The watch, he told the suitably impressed army store-man, was required for a secret mission under the personal direction of Lord Louis himself. He even hinted that he knew the Vice-Admiral personally and could be persuaded to "put in a good word".

'You'll have to sign for it, Corp','whispered the store-man, convinced he was now part and parcel of a covert Combined Operation.

'Naturally' answered the NCO, touching the side of his nose with a forefinger conspiratorially, and signing the chit *B.Nevis. Corporal Royal Engineers*. He had long ago learned the old adage, "If you don't ask, you don't get. And if you don't ask, you don't want". He also knew that the more outrageous the request, the more chance of success. All that anyone ever asked for was a signature on a piece of paper, to clear their yardarm of responsibility. He was also a great believer in another saying. "If you want a submarine, ask the RAF. If you want a tank, ask the Navy. If it's an aircraft or a diving watch, you ask the army"…..Well, not quite, but that was the principle.

He called the watch his *Woolworths Everright,* and told everyone he bought it for a few dollars in Singapore before the war, in case they thought it to be a real *Rolex Submariner* worth a lot of money….which in fact, it was! It was also his prized possession. The luminous hands showed 22.15 hours. They were a few minutes behind schedule owing to everyone playing it cool to hide their own nervous tension; don't hurry, don't panic, look calm.

Codling gave a slight shimmer as Nook made a meal of settling himself in. 'Okay, Windy?' hissed the corporal, pulling the hood of his camouflaged smock over his head and tightening the draw-string, almost covering his blackened face. He felt an affirmative tap on the shoulder and dipped a paddle blade in the water, sensing Nook's rhythmic response as they struck out across the empty, velvet-black river with only the icy breeze on their exposed right cheeks and an occasional wink of light from a channel marker to give them direction. The quick sprint warmed and eased their stiff muscles and it seemed no time at all before the blackness of the south bank loomed up a few yards ahead, causing them to brake with left-side blades and bring the canoe's bow round to face upriver; and to prevent them from charging into the muddy edge like a rampart bull into a cow-shed. Changing to single paddles they drifted, letting the flood stream carry them along towards their objective, only occasionally giving an easy paddle stroke to maintain position. Ahead, a low glow on the horizon rose higher and higher with each mile as they were swept along in a state of tense alertness, their eyes and ears searching for…anything.

A cold hour later, they were close enough to see the whole dock area of the city a blaze of arc lights; their glare reflecting up from ship's decks and river surface, lighting the undersides of the leaden night clouds streaking overhead. Obviously, Jerry wasn't too worried about a black-out, or RAF raids. Hopefully, thought Pearman, pressing his numb lips together and wriggling energy back into lifeless legs, they would be in for a shock.

Behind him, blissfully dreaming of nicer things, Nook was not suffering from the same problem of cold legs. Like Browning, his were wrapped tight and warm in the camouflage netting he was supposed to have left ashore. He wished he could say the same about his frozen nose that felt like an ice block stuck prominently on the front of his face, like the figure-head of a sailing ship crunching through pack ice. It was as times like this – and only such times – he wished he were back in the nice warm bank; counting money and bored out of his skull. He looked at the hunched shoulders of the NCO - vaguely silhouetted against the dock lights now only a few miles ahead – and wondered what he was thinking. He was a good bloke was Pearman, knew his stuff. He might look asleep but Nook knew different. His mind would be working overtime, thinking of potential problems and thinking ahead.

Nook had long ago convinced himself he would never make a decent NCO; didn't want the responsibility. He felt content as he was, doing this sort of job. Could he ever return to that mind-boggling existence at the bank after the war? He knew he couldn't – wouldn't. He fancied being a copper in a nice quiet village with a warm cosy pub to relax in; and grandchildren he could enthral with stories of how he won the war….that's if he ever found a wife in the first place.

Watching the two shadowy figures slide *Codling* over the mud into the river and paddle away, almost eagerly, into the darkness, Thomas stood on the broken floor of the derelict boat-house, and prayed. Being the only child of a small town vicar, religion had been rammed down his throat since the day his over-zealous father almost drowned him in the baptismal font. Church had been a chore to be endured every Sunday, and the frequent weddings and funerals at which he dutifully sang as a reluctant, unpaid choirboy, were an obligatory interruption to his young social life. He hated it. He wasn't a *real* atheist; neither was he a true believer. He couldn't accept the concept of there being a God, or a hereafter. The Bible he considered as a mythical collection of stories compiled by numerous story-tellers, embellished with the passing of time. For seventeen years he had lived - almost unloved - with his timid mother, and an oppressive father who would hypocritically preach love, goodness, tolerance and forgiveness to his "flock" and then return home to rule his family like a despot. Even later in life, during his infrequent visits home from college, he was always treated like a child. Told what to do, and when to do it. The Royal Marines had been his saviour, his escape to freedom and adventure, from an existence that never included *sincere* prayer.…until now. Now a heavy foreboding filled his mind. He had the awful premonition he would never again see the two hooded figures disappearing like wraiths into the dense night; leaving nothing but a ripple of muddied water in their wake, and a few whorls on the surface from their thrusting paddles. He turned away and crunched leaden-hearted, back along the gravelled track to the ruined chateau, stumbling into unseen bushes and tripping over the broken edging blocks that once kept an immaculate path free from encroaching weeds and undergrowth; forgetting for a moment he was in the middle of enemy occupied Europe.

At the bottom of the stone steps, framed spookily by backlighting from the oil lamps, Browning greeted the return of his officer with a grin that put a white splash of teeth in the middle of his cam-creamed face. 'Left us 'ave they, sir? he asked with a jollity he didn't feel, trying to put a smile on the lieutenant's grim features. He hadn't enjoyed the last ten minutes left behind in the company of the unspeaking Charles.

Grateful that the gloom hid the look of annoyance that clouded his face, the young officer bit back a sarcastic response. Browning's irrepressible Cockney humour grated on the nerves at times but he was a good man to have around. Better to be that way than to be one of those miserable depressing types. 'Yes,' he said, guiltily suppressing his irritability. 'Time we were away too.'

For mile after mile *Minnow* drifted with the flooding current, being blown along like a straw by the raw breeze; the two cowled occupants slumped low in the hull with the rigid edge of the cockpit pressing uncomfortably hard under their armpits. The dull orange glow over the distant city loomed on the horizon but Thomas and Browning were very much aware that – just when they needed the concealing cloak of a pitch-black night – it would get brighter and more revealing the nearer they got. Trust Jerry to light-up the world at the wrong bloody time, thought Browning, wriggling his toes and buttocks to keep the blood circulating in his idle legs, and praying for the RAF to make a surprise raid to black-out the city. He turned his head to look back, in case anything should come creeping up behind…*like a bloody high-speed launch for instance!* They were keeping close to the bank, in the shadows of increasing numbers of tall buildings, most of which appeared to come right down to the river's edge. They figured the chances of being spotted by anyone out so late on such a diabolically bone-chilling night, were less remote than being caught mid-stream by a passing patrol boat that might not suffer from the same untypical German indifference to vigilance as the first one.

As Browning took yet another quick glance astern he heard a sharp squeal, like a startled animal, come from the lieutenant. He snatched his eyes back to see the officer frantically digging his paddle deep on the left side, his shoulders heaving. Spontaneously he raised his own blade, uncertain whether to assist with a sharp brake on the right side or to add to a forge ahead on the left. It was a decision he never had to make. Outlined blackly against the backdrop of city lights that lit the low-lying clouds, a dark shape reared over them. It was barely a yard or two ahead and swinging rapidly to their left as the canoe turned; too late! In the second or two before they hit, he saw another shape rise from the first and become erect, like a cobra getting ready to strike.

'Shit!' he heard the officer uncharacteristically swear; then felt the rush of cold water pour into the canoe.

Chapter Twelve.

Nineteen-year old Oberschutze Albert Mulhousen of the 243rd Artillery Regiment was thoroughly fed-up. Nothing seemed to be going his way since he had joined the Wehrmacht…and on top of everything else he was frozen! Why they needed a guard on a wooden-decked jetty made from heavy scaffolding bars was beyond him. The blasted thing was miles from anywhere and only used by the weekly river barge that serviced the needs of his anti-aircraft battery across the road; and it wasn't as if it were anywhere near the front-line. He sat himself down on a cold iron bollard, sinking his head low into the collar of his greatcoat until only his eyes were visible between the two upturned lapels and the rim of his helmet. He was feeling seriously sorry for himself. First he had been denied entry into the Waffen S.S. because of his tall but extremely thin stature. He wasn't a Nazi, but had always admired the smart uniform and dreamed of being in such an elite and respected unit. Then his application to join the Panzer Corps had been refused on the grounds that his two-metre height was too tall to fit into a tank. In desperation he applied for training as a fallshirmjager – he wanted to be someone special, do something special – but instead, found himself posted to this battery in the backwoods of France where everyone hated the sight of his uniform…well, almost everyone. One or two pretty girls had given him a smile on his rare days off in Nantes, but his officer had warned against fraternisation. The girls could be working for the so-called Resistance, they said, and be likely to lure unsuspecting soldiers down dark alleyways for "political discussion" with knuckle-dustered partisans. Not that he had ever heard of any incidents like that himself. It was probably scare mongering by the officers, who wanted the girls for themselves. And now he was being threatened by his battery commander with being given a dreaded posting to the Russian Front. All because he had requested compassionate leave, to visit his widowed mother in Dresden who was dying from some sort of cancer. Of course - his officer told him - he could take his request to higher authority, but he did not dare. That would make the posting inevitable. He had heard the Russians were animals who never took prisoners, and ate the bodies of any German soldiers they could find, dead or alive, because they were so hungry. He shivered, as much in fear of such a prospect as from being so cold. Better to keep a low profile and stay anonymous, even if it meant no medals or heroics.

The chance of being caught sitting down on duty by his guard commander did not worry him at all. It was too dark to be seen from the road and he would hear the approach of the Obergefreiter's heavy, clumsy boots in plenty of time to put on a sentry-like pose; assuming of course the lazy *schweine* deigned to lift his fat backside off the fireside chair in the guardroom in the first place. But to be stupid enough to light and smoke a cigarette on guard duty was something else. Someone would be bound to see, and his next duty *would* be in Stalingrad.

Misery flooded his thoughts as he looked down at the black river gurgling past the supporting stanchions of the jetty, a metre under his feet. What would become of him? Where would he spend the war? *Would he survive it?* He had little to be cheerful about, and Gott! it was cold! He tucked his gloved hands tightly up under the armpits of his greatcoat and wriggled numb toes uselessly inside his boots. Elbows on knees, he let his head slump forward, staring unseeing at the piece of decking between his boots. What was there here for him to guard against?

From the corner of his heavy eyelids, a movement on the river attracted his attention and he saw a black floating mass, darker even than the black water, approaching the end of the jetty. For a few seconds his idle mind wondered if it was a clump of reeds torn from the riverbank, and then a movement and splash made him jump. A shouted word blasted from the clump and he leapt to his feet in alarm, forgetting in his panic the rifle slung across his shoulder.

'Halt! Wer da?' he screamed, his throat constricted with fear. Then, remembering his rifle, swung it to point at whatever and whoever was now impaled on the scaffolding bars projecting from the ends of the jetty. His whole body trembled, and every muscle contracted as his jaws clamped together like a vice. A hand, then an arm followed by a black face, reached up from the dark mass that he now saw as a small boat of some sort. From below a pair of staring eyes, a white-rimmed hole appeared in the black face, calling out words he didn't understand, but instantly recognised as English.

'Mein Gott! *Tommis!*' he yelled aloud, and wet himself.

Another pair of hands shot up to grasp the decking. He jumped back, fumbling for the whistle dangling from the buttonhole of his greatcoat with trembling hands, finding it difficult to locate his mouth and force the cold metal between bloodless lips. He blew, and blew, and blew repeatedly, the strident screeches blasting the air as his bulging eyes saw two figures emerge from the water and crawl up onto the decking, almost touching his boots. He wanted to run but could not; his legs frozen into immobility. Everything appeared to be happening in slow motion and it seemed an age before he felt and heard the thudding of several racing boots approaching.

'Was ist…?' panted the aging Obergefreiter, seeing his sentry pointing a rifle at two men sprawled half on, half off the decking, and quickly taking in the situation. It took a lot to shake the composure of an NCO who had been through the invasion of Poland, Belgium and France. He had seen too many frightening and shocking sights in his time, and been wounded for his efforts.

Oberschutze Mulhousen, nervously recovering his self-control and feeling the flood of relief surge through his veins at the sight of his NCO, felt the tightness in his throat ease. '*Tommis*. Obergefreiter' he croaked, thrusting the barrel of his rifle towards the two figures now struggling to their feet.

'Hands hoch' shouted the NCO, tilting the point of his drawn pistol at the marines and rapping out a string of orders to the four accompanying young soldiers scampering up behind him who apprehensively began searching the two Englishmen. None of them had seen the enemy face-to-face before, let alone touch one. His own chest, beneath several layers of jerseys and a heavy greatcoat, was swelling with controlled excitement. The two men, he had no doubt, were members of the infamous Commando's – a force he, as a soldier, secretly had a great respect for – their capture would reflect great credit on himself, and his section.

'Well done, Mulhausen,' he said to the young guard who had added another five centimetres to his already towering height, despite the fact that his uniform trousers were now wet and cold against his leg. 'This will probably get you the compassionate leave you've been asking for.' He made a mental note to remind the young soldier to "put one up the spout" and release the safety catch of his rifle should he ever confront the enemy again. Now was not the time.

Slightly deflated, Mulhausen replied 'Danke Obergefreiter.' Wishful thoughts of an Iron Cross 2nd Class decorating his chest drifting away.

'Come' said the NCO in a friendly manner, nodding at the two marines and stepping to one side waving his revolver to indicate they should move.

Leaving one soldier behind to salvage the damaged canoe impaled on the projecting scaffold bars, and sending another on ahead to waken the battery commander, the NCO marched his prisoners and their escort - including the proud but wet Mulhausen who was glowing under the open admiration of his mates - along the jetty. Across the riverside road, at the guardroom of the gun-battery site, an open-mouthed sentry stood so awestruck at the sight of the two enemy soldiers that he failed to follow his strict orders to challenge everyone, every time.

Oberleutnant Gustaf Glieb leaned heavily on the walking stick that supported his crippled leg. A leg supposedly smashed by an enemy bullet, but actually mangled when he fell off the back of a tank on which he had been hitching a lift when it made a violent acceleration, near the beaches of Dunkerque.

In the few minutes since being woken by one of his excited soldiers with the news of the captured British soldiers, he had quickly dressed with fumbling fingers and limped across the grass to his Headquarters office. This would go down well on his service record and hopefully win him a transfer away from this dead-end command. He wasn't a gunner; never had been. He'd been a signals officer up until his – er – wounding. It would also give him the opportunity to practice his rusty English, rarely used since his five years in the German Embassy in London, way before the war.

'Come' he commanded, in response to the respectful tap on the door, and watched with growing excitement as the two bedraggled Englishmen were herded in by his NCO and three escorting soldiers, to stand in ever increasing puddles of river water before his desk, stiff backed and truculent. Typical English, trying to show their superiority, he thought, running his sleep-filled eyes over the wet smocks, noting the Royal Marines shoulder flash and Combined Operations badge on the sleeves. He glanced down at the expensive, wafer-thin watch on his wrist, acquired from a badly wounded French officer before it could attract the attention of a pillaging infantryman who wouldn't appreciate it value.

'Good evening, gentlemen,' he greeted amicably, seeing the pips on the shoulder tabs of one of his prisoners and the lack of any rank insignia on the other, who he then proceeded to ignore. 'I am Oberleutnant Glieb, the officer commanding this unit. And you are Lieutenant...?' he raised a querying eyebrow that made his haggard face look lopsided.

Thomas looked the German squarely in the eyes, observing the lined, middle-aged face beneath a high-fronted peak cap that looked like a ski-jump, and the supporting stick that gave meaning to the pain-filled eyes. He also recognised the equality of their respective rank. 'Lieutenant Adrian Thomas. Royal Marines' he answered, endeavouring to match the friendly tone of the other man.

The German smiled. He could almost read the mind of this arrogant young Englander. 'Ach, so. And your man?' he asked with typical Teutonic disregard for other-ranks.

'My man, as you call him' snapped Thomas, glaring angrily at his captor. 'Is a British Royal Marine who understands the English language and is perfectly capable of answering your questions for himself.'

Glieb smiled again, totally unabashed at this pompous response from the quick-tempered Englander. 'I hope' he said quietly, 'you will conduct yourself with more respect if and when you are confronted with S.S. or Gestapo interrogators.'

If either marine felt qualms at the mention of these organisations, whose reputations for cruelty and sadism were rapidly spreading throughout the world, they showed no sign.

'Marine Alan Browning' snapped the East Londoner, trying to stop his officer from dropping himself in the SH One T, and staring at a calendar on the wall an inch above the German's left ear as he rattled off his service number so fast that it was incomprehensible, even to an Englishman.

Thomas suppressed a grin. Trust Browning to be as politely insubordinate as possible.

The German continued to ignore Browning. 'And what is your unit, Lieutenant?'

Thomas swivelled his right arm across his chest to point at his left shoulder. 'Royal Marines, as I've said, and as you can see by my shoulder flashes.'

'And your mission?'

The silence that greeted the question was solid.

'Well?' he said again, knowing he was wasting his breath.

The two marines stood absolutely motionless. No physical response whatsoever. Glieb groped discreetly at the seat of his trousers, pulling at the underpants that he had hoisted too high in his hurry to get dressed, trying to ease the discomfort. 'And you…' he asked, turning reluctantly to point his hawk-like nose at Browning. 'What were you doing?'

Thomas shut his eyes and pursed his lips in a silent whistle. He knew the sort of answer that would be forthcoming.

'Night exercise, sir. We got lost.'

Thomas snorted, unable to control the reaction.

On the other side of the desk Glieb clenched a fist behind his back, inwardly fuming. He would court martial one of his own men for such blatant insubordination.

'You may think it funny, lieutenant' he snarled. 'But I doubt your man will be quite so clever when the Feldgendarmerie get their hands on him.' He put his stick across the desk-top and raised a hand to his forehead. Hesitating a moment, he then removed his cap and carefully placed it alongside the stick where it looked more like a ski-slope than ever. Slowly bending his good knee, and supporting his weight by grasping the arms of the leather buttoned chair, he eased his stiff leg under the desk and lowered himself gently onto the seat, as though he had a painful boil on his backside. Neither marine felt sympathy.

Fixing his gaze on Thomas, he leaned back away from the desk and hooked a thumb in one of the breast pockets of his tunic; his other white-knuckled hand tightening on the end of the chair's arm. A frown creased worried folds in his forehead and he twisted his mouth as if biting the inner side of his cheek.

'I have a dilemma, Lieutenant' he said, noting the Englishman's unconcerned raised eyebrow. 'I can either phone through to my District Commander's office and report your capture – in which case he will be extremely annoyed at being disturbed at this God-forsaken hour – and have you dragged away before you can say ... er... Jack Robson. Is that your saying?' he inclined his balding head, waiting a moment for the answer he didn't receive. 'Or - if you give me your parole as an honourable officer - I will accommodate you in here, under guard of course because I have no cell to place you in. I will then inform higher authority first thing in the morning. Well!... Do you give your parole?'

Thomas looked around the room at the Obergefreiter and his armed guards, who had overcome their initials apprehensions and were trying to look fierce behind their rifles and machine-pistols. There was no chance of escape, so his options were limited. Besides which, what the German was offering was exactly what he wanted. He put his mouth near Browning's ear. 'Trust me' he whispered, and then straightened to address the German. 'Providing we remain together, we give our parole to you, until dawn.'

Glieb dropped his eyes to hide his relief, failing to see the questioning frown on Browning's surprised face, or the slight headshake given in reply. Bad leg or not, he would be off to the Russian Front if he allowed these two to escape. He rattled off a string of instructions to the NCO who, in turn, despatched two of his men on errands. Lifting himself from the chair with both hands he stood up with difficulty, and picking up his stick and cap from the desk, stomped out of the office, bidding Thomas a terse 'Goodnight,' and leaving his concerned Obergefreiter in charge. Browning he ignored completely.

As the door closed behind Glieb the German NCO visibly relaxed, smilingly trying to give friendly signals. He liked the British. If only they could be on the same side, he thought wistfully. They were good soldiers and he preferred their public-school type officers to his own arrogant Prussian bastards who were mostly medal-seeking, promotion-hunting types who treated other ranks as sub-human and snivelled around the backsides of their own superiors. He caught Thomas' attention and pointing a finger, went over to the desk to walk his fingers across the top while shaking his head from side-to-side in a mime to confirm their promise not to escape. Thomas nodded with a smile, and gave a thumbs-up sign that prompted the NCO to take a packet from his tunic pocket and offer cigarettes to the marines. His disappointment at their refusal was obvious, until they indicated they were non-smokers.

Several minutes later the two guards returned carrying camp beds and bedding. One foolishly propped his rifle against the wall while helping to assemble the two beds. The Obergefrieter's angry rebuke left no one in any doubt as to his feelings, least of all the embarrassed soldier who snatched his weapon back as though from a flaming fire. The marines had seen the rifle standing unattended, like a forgotten broom, and both – for a split second – regretted the parole decision.

Knowing their conversation could not be understood, Browning almost snapped at his officer. 'Why?'

The Germans turned to look at this sudden outburst, amazed that a soldier could address an officer in such an abrupt manner.

Thomas, knowing what was being referred to, answered. 'Don't you see? By staying here we won't be questioned by anyone before the others get the job done, and it will give them chance to get away. If, in the morning, we get questioned and say something we shouldn't, it will be too late for them to do anything about it, and as a bonus we get a good night's sleep'. He looked at the guards furtively. 'They seem decent enough blokes here, and if we were to be whipped away *now* and let something slip, accidentally, they could still get *Codling*.'

Browning nodded. He understood the lieutenant's reasoning but the thought of willingly surrendering his freedom to a bunch of squaddies was irksome to say the least. 'Well,' he agreed reluctantly, looking down at his wet plimsolled feet. 'We couldn't do anything helpful even if we did escape, could we.'

'Good man. Now let's get our heads down.'

What with their fear of the coming morning, the uncertainties of their immediate future, and the disconcerting presence of armed guards sitting in the same room watching over them, neither man found it easy to sleep. Both would deny having slept at all. The night had seemed endless, yet when they were woken by the shrill ringing of the desk telephone, the first thing they noticed – apart from strands of daylight peeping grudgingly around the edges of the curtained windows – were the new faces of the guards who had obviously been changed during the night, unheard by the sleeping marines.

After half a dozen unanswered rings, one of the startled guards – having received encouraging nods from his colleague – reached out a timorous hand and lifted the phone from its cradle as if it were a delicate piece of china and lowered his head to the earpiece.

'Ja?' He said uncertainly, jumping upright as though on the receiving end of a red-hot poker, as a shouting voice from the phone filled the hushed office. The wretched man blanched as he stared, wide-eyed up at the wall clock's jerking minute-hand ticking quietly across the Roman numerals X11. 'Ja, Herr

OberLeutnant' he croaked, clicking his heels together and replacing the receiver carefully, as though it were fragile. He shouted something to his comrade, then went into a miming act for the benefit of the two marines; pointing at the clock and extending the five fingers of one hand, twice, while waving the other in a beckoning motion and stabbing a forefinger at the floor.

'I think he's trying to tell us someone big is going to be here in ten minutes, or maybe ten o'clock,' said Thomas, rasping a fist over his stubbled chin, feeling like something the cat dragged home.

Browning nodded. 'By the look of panic on his face he's scared shitless, sir. So I'd bet on ten minutes.'

Thomas agreed and, looking at the guard, made a drinking gesture with his hand. 'Coffee?'

The panicking soldier almost had an epileptic seizure. 'Nein. Nein' he choked, looking at the clock and shaking his head violently. Couldn't these stupid Tommies understand simple sign language? He extended his arm and lifted his hand, palm up. He needed them on their feet, like NOW!

'I do believe he wants us to get up, sir' said Browning, running a furred tongue over his coated teeth. 'Christ! I feel mankey. And I need a crap.'

Thomas, not wishing to get the worried guard into trouble, put his feet on the floor and stretched upright. 'Toilet?' he asked, cupping a hand between his legs as if in a urinal. The German grunted something that sounded like 'Snail. Snail', and pointed to a panelled door in the corner of the office, pushing him gently to indicate urgency.

'You first, sir,' invited Browning, smiling in mock respect and crossing his own legs. 'Don't be long though… please.'

Several minutes later, feeling extremely smelly and scruffy, the two marines jumped with shock as the office door crashed open to admit the battery commander and two, six-feet tall, broad shouldered, unsmiling gorillas wearing brass gorgets bearing the words *Feldgendarmerie* hanging from chains around their necks. Without a word the two Military Policemen's hob-nailed boots crashed across the floor and turned the astonished marines around to handcuff their hands behind their back; none too gently.

Clearly embarrassed, Oberleutnant Glieb looked on with a hangdog expression. 'I am so sorry Lieutenant' he apologised. 'The matter is now out of my hands. I am in trouble for not reporting your capture immediately, so I am afraid my next command will be on a desert island, somewhere,' he joked humourlessly, knowing how true his prophecy might well be. Roughly, the two marines were bundled past him, out onto the broken concrete pathway where a dun-coloured van waited with a stiff-backed driver behind the wheel. It all happened so quickly, and they were hustled in the back to sit on hard seats with hands painfully secured behind their backs, next to the two M.P's.

As the vehicle drove out of the camp, along the road paralleling the river, a huge explosion rocked it on its springs making the occupants jump in alarm.

'Was is das?' yelled the M.P sat next to Browning. The marines smiled at each other. They knew.

'Where d'you reckon they're taking us, sir?' asked Browning, endeavouring to sound nonchalant and trying to rearrange his manacled hands more comfortably. But before he could be answered one of the gorillas nudged him.

'No talking, Tommy' he said, baring his teeth into something resembling an unaccustomed smile. 'If you do, I am ordered to stop you.' His English was as good as the strongly nasal, Brooklyn-American accent would allow. He bared his teeth even more and added, as if in explanation. 'Hamburg-Amerika Line.'

The drive seemed endless, but in actual fact lasted less than an hour. Their cuffed wrists bruised and painful, both marines were hungry, thirsty and fearfully apprehensive of what awaited them at their destination. They could see nothing from the enclosed back of the van and had no idea in which direction they were heading. The enforced silence made it worse. Eventually they turned off the smooth tarmac road and drove over crunching gravel until coming to a sliding halt.

'Out,' ordered the M.P's, throwing open the back and stepping down on to an immaculate driveway leading to the front of a magnificent chateau that, in other circumstance, would have been astoundingly beautiful. Huge swastika banners, hanging like drying laundry from the upper floors, almost hid the ivy covered walls and the small leaded windows that peeped timidly through the luxuriant growth. The people inside had their national emblem as permanently drawn curtains blocking out the light from the outside. A reward for their patriotism.

Marble steps led up to a large ornamental front door flanked by tall carved pillars and two statue-like soldiers, whose highly polished knee boots and ominously black uniforms with Nazi arm-bands, gave a sinister tone to the splendid French building.

'S.S.' hissed Browning knowledgably, as they were hustled up the steps past the immobile guards and into the breathtaking splendour of a cathedral-like hallway. Massive – and probably priceless – chandeliers sparkled above a wide, carved-oak central stairway that wound its way right and left to the upper floors.

For one fleeting moment, Thomas imagined the figures climbing and descending the staircase, to be elegant, finely dressed aristocrats, instead of the sedately strutting officers – many of them of high rank – who were being carefully avoided by the army of messengers and other minions in black, field-grey and other various hues of uniforms, scurrying to and fro like headless chickens.

Very few took any notice of the handcuffed marines being hurried around the hall close to the walls, and being pushed through a heavy wooden door concealed by thick curtaining under the grand central stairway. It led into a narrow tunnel with white-washed concrete walls not more than seven feet wide, or tall, and the polished-steel helmets of the two Feldgendarmerie almost scraped the undersides of the widely spaced overhead lights, as they pushed their prisoners along at a fast pace.

Both marines were trembling with the fear of the unknown. Where were they going? What was to happen to them? Thomas, being more imaginative, suffered most. He had heard of the S.S. and Gestapo cruelty, and couldn't help but be scared at the prospect of being tortured. How would he cope? Ever since boyhood he had known his pain threshold to be low. Would he cringe, pleading for mercy like a coward? He felt sick.

The atmosphere was damp, cold and frighteningly macabre as they reached another solid door that was opened for them by a figure in the ubiquitous black uniform of the S.S. Browning, for all his hatred of the Nazis, couldn't help feeling compassion for the wretched man. What had he done to warrant this miserable, solitary duty in such dreadful surroundings?

The other side of the door revealed a huge cavernous cellar that reminded Thomas of pictures he had seen in magazines of wine cellars belonging to the rich and famous – which it probably had been. The low brick archways of the roof hovered menacingly dark, like the wings of a gigantic bat, echoing the tread of the M.P's studded boots on bare stone flooring, and it was only when these faded to a single pair that Thomas turned his head to see, to his horror, that Browning and his escort had disappeared! Dread filled his heart. Suddenly he felt desperately alone. The marine's presence had given him courage. Now he was gone, and blood coursed through his veins like cold water. His own guard – the former Hamburg-Amerika Line seaman – stopped at an iron door that featured a small grilled aperture fitted at eye level, and ushered him in.

It was an empty, windowless space not more than ten feet square. A single, low wattage light bulb, hanging motionless on a few inches of flex, lit the brown-painted bare walls. The total absence of furniture added bleakly to the awesome ambience. The rough concrete floor sloped slightly down and inwards to meet a small central hole that attracted the officer's eyes like a magnet. Surely it must be for cleaning purposes? It couldn't be a toilet. They wouldn't expect him to stay in here with no bed, chair or anything…...would they?

'Besta luck, Tommy,' said the guard, almost apologetically, as he slammed the heavy door closed with a resounding thud that echoed around the cell like a single toll from a deep-toned church bell, leaving the scared and desolate marine in solitary isolation.

Chapter Thirteen.

Codling, being carried like a piece of flotsam on the tide, drifted closer to the brightly lit docks, its crew crouched low into the hull and peering up under the enveloping hoods of their camouflaged smocks.

In the glow from the arc lights flooding the decks of the working ships, the two marines felt exposed and vulnerable even though they knew from experience that those same glaring lights would blind any watchers, and create deep concealing shadows alongside the ships. Also in their favour, the icy breeze had formed small breaking wavelets on the river, splattering the surface with dirty white streaks of foam that would make it difficult for them to be seen by any other than a very alert and keen-eyed sentry. Nevertheless, they still felt as conspicuous as Jews in a mosque as they glided into the deep shadow under the towering stern of the first rust-streaked freighter.

A deep echoing clunk, frighteningly loud, sounded as Nook attached the magnetic holdfast to the ship's side near the rudder post and held on, feeling the tug of the tide, to keep alongside.

In the front seat, Corporal Pearman wriggled to extract the folded placing-rod from alongside his thigh, and after opening it to its full six feet length, delved between his legs to pull one of the limpet mines free from its keeper plate. Hooking it on to the end of the rod he lowered it over the side into the water, as deep as he could reach, before edging it close to the ship's hull. With a dull, water-muffled thud, the mine magnetically seated itself among its natural, parasitic name-sakes. When the rod was unhooked and withdrawn, Nook released the holdfast to allow *Codling* to drift along the big vessel's waterline.

Cascading water, pouring from the ship's condenser discharge, indicated to them the position of the engine-room where they placed a second mine. With pounding hearts they drifted forward under the discharge, getting soaked in the process, until reaching a position they considered to be opposite one of the two huge forward holds that they hoped would rapidly flood once holed, and placed the third mine.

They continued on, passing under the ship's flared bow, to glide across the short stretch of open water to the stern of the next freighter. Shouting voices, coming from the deck high above their heads, scared the living daylights out of them as they kissed *Codling's* wooden decking in their endeavour to become as invisible as possible while drifting into the heavy shadow of the second ship's overhanging counter-stern. Both held their breath and reached out to grasp the barnacle-covered rudder. Nothing happened. There was no more shouting. They hung on for several minutes, ears straining for the sound of more voices above the low whistle of the wind. Still nothing. Easing forward a few feet, they placed their fourth mine and were letting themselves drift towards the region of the engine-room when they were startled by another shout from the ship. A probing beam of torchlight shone down on the water ahead of them, searching the surface along the ship's waterline. Instinctively both marines grabbed for their single paddles and pushed *Codling* away from the ship's shadowed side before the light reached them. Careful not to cause too much disturbance in the water with the blades, they thrust quickly across the patch of overspill from the arc lights into the welcoming darkness beyond. The torch beam still swung along the vessel's side, searching in vain. They hadn't been spotted.

Out in the middle of the river they coasted to a stop and looked over towards the northern bank, wondering if *Minnow* was marauding in the shadows among the ships there.

'Reckon we'll stay out here a while, Windy' said Pearman over his shoulder. 'When the ruckus dies down we can have another go; but we'll give that bugger a miss.' He nodded in the direction of their last target.

'Wonder what all that was about, Corp" asked Nook, referring to the shouting and flashing torch.

The back of the NCO's hooded head shook. ''spect some silly bastard thought he'd seen something, and reported it. He won't be very popular now,'

Another five, long, cold minutes past before the corporal spoke again.

'Better not let her drift too far......' he began, and then stopped suddenly as both men heard a continuous throbbing noise, faint at first then getting louder. Through *Codling's* flimsy hull they could feel the water around them begin to pulsate. Visions of an alerted patrol boat flashed into their mind's eye as their heads swivelled, trying to locate cause and direction while they joined the two halves of their paddles together into double blades, in readiness for an escaping sprint. They were drifting sideways across the river.

'There!' shouted Nook, his voice hoarse with alarm as he pointed an outstretched arm.

Pearman turned to look, and his heart leapt. Thundering down towards them from around the corner of a pier-head and pushing against the weak but still flooding tide, a huge ocean-going tug lit by the dock lights and her own dimmed navigation lights, was shouldering a high, foaming heap of white water before its blunt, rope-fendered bow. This was no sleek patrol boat to be easily avoided. It seemed to fill the whole width of the river!

'Paddle' he yelled, digging his own paddle hard and deep with a strength increased by fear as the mountain of water rapidly bore down on them. It was too late. No way could they get out of the monster's way. He heard a shrill scream, unsure if it was Nook or himself, as the tumbling bow wave crashed down onto their port side. *Codling's* bow leapt into the air and he heard a loud crack of splintering wood. The air filled with a frenzy of boiling water and Pearman gasped a mouthful of vile, oily river water as the canoe capsized, throwing him clear, away from the pounding goliath and down its side into the turbulent wake. He could feel his waders filling with water, pulling him down, and reached out in desperation for the broken upturned hull of *Codling*, providentially floating a few feet away. Gripping the canoe's stem with a panic that would surely kill him as easily as the water itself, he struggled, one arm at a time, out of the sodden smock that was dragging him under. Barely able to keep his mouth above the surface, he snatched at the shoulder braces of his water-filled waders and kicked them off with a deep sigh of relief. Still holding on to the wreckage he felt around, one-handed, for the inflating tube of his lifejacket and blew into it until the comforting bulge crept around his neck.

'That was nearly my lot,' he said to himself, shaking with fright at the narrowness of his escape and looking around for signs of Nook. 'Windy,' he called softly, though there was no chance of being heard. 'Windy' he called again, louder. With the security of the buoyant lifejacket around him, his heartbeat stopped racing and began slowing to a gallop.

Nook was nowhere to be seen, and it didn't take a genius to know that if he hadn't managed to hold on to the canoe he would have sunk like a stone – as he himself nearly had.

For a while he hung on to the drifting water-logged hull, regaining his breath and composure, and mourning the certain loss of his mate. The tide had carried him upstream from the docks, now half a mile away, and he could feel it slackening. It would soon be high water and the last thing he wanted was to be swept back by the ebbing tide. Now was the time to leave. Affectionately, he patted the canoe's upturned bottom. She had carried him many miles in training, and on this little jaunt, and served him well. 'Cheerio, old girl' he whispered, as if the wood and canvas were a dear departed relative.

With a last fleeting look around, he let go of the faithful *Codling* and turned to face the northern bank of the river, striking out for the few lights flickering over the ruffled surface, unaware that he was leaving the drowned body of his

THE OTHER 'COCKLESHELL HEROES'.

COLLISION

friend and crewmate hanging upside down underneath the canoe, trapped by the camouflage netting tangled around his legs.

Encumbered as he was in lifejacket, battledress and plimsolled feet, Pearman soon became breathless as the icy cold water soaked through to his skin. Trying to swim in sodden clothing felt like trying to move through treacle. It seemed forever before he reached the bank, not realising at first that the extra drag at his legs was, in fact, the soft mud. Exhausted after his long swim and the sucking climb up onto dry land, he sprawled lifeless and uncaring on the first piece of firm ground he could find. Every muscle screamed for rest, and his heaving chest gasped in the bitter night air. He wanted to stay there for ever, but knew he couldn't. He had to find shelter out of the coldness that had crept deep into his bones. Somewhere warm where he could hide until he recovered; and he must find it in the next few hours – before dawn. He climbed unsteadily to his feet shivering uncontrollably, his teeth chattering like frenzied castanets as the wind pierced his wet clothing with a million needles. His numbed mind told him to start running, to get circulation going for warmth, but his reluctant body was in an argumentative mood. Training and pure necessity won the day and he stumbled forward, slowly at first in the manner of a drunk in a hurry. Gradually the energising blood began to pump through his body, reaching the extremities and slowly warming the stiff aching muscles until he was jog-trotting in a staggering fashion, across field after field. He crossed a paved road, luckily deserted, and passed a row of unlit houses in which a barking dog made him jump and alter course. Bloody dogs need shooting, he thought with the conviction of a dedicated dog-lover.

He had no idea where he was, or in which direction he was heading, but he felt warmer; that was something. He came across a wood and stumbled through the trees for an hour or more, not knowing if he was going around in circles, or not. Branches lashed at his cheeks even though he held his hands across his face like a frightened blind man, and he frequently tripped over hidden roots, stubbing his toes and crashing to the ground among the undergrowth. He was reaching the end of his tether, his strength draining away, and he began to seriously consider burying himself in the tangled undergrowth. It wouldn't be dry or warm but he would be hidden come the dawn; and he could sleep. His survival training told him it would also be fatal, but he felt so overwhelmingly tired. He would carry on for just five minutes more. His mind started to wander, and he imagined seeing Windy sitting propped up against a tree wrapped in a blanket. He called a greeting, out loud, before realising it was a dream. It worried him. Had he been hallucinating or just asleep on his feet?

Suddenly it occurred to his befuddled brain that something was different.

There were no lashing branches whipping his face and body, no roots to fall over or tangled undergrowth. He was on a path! It wasn't much of one, little more than an animal track, but a path nevertheless. He knelt down, feeling the compressed earth with cold fingers. Someone must use it, a farm-worker perhaps? It must lead somewhere out of this bloody wood, he thought, and his weary body felt sorely tempted to follow it along, hopeful of finding shelter of any kind. But common-sense, and the first signs of a lightening sky showing through the canopy of leafless branches above his head, prevailed. The path offered an easier alternative but with far more danger of being discovered. Reluctantly he stepped back into the forest of trees, shaking his head trying to shrug-off the consuming need of warmth and sleep, and creating enough noise to waken the dead.

In his state of mental and physical exhaustion, the rapid change in his visual surroundings failed to register at first. The dark, impenetrable blackness was slowly becoming slate-grey and only when he tripped and fell headlong did he realise it was near daylight. Was this France? Kneeling on hands and knees in the muddied mulch of rotted leaves it looked more like a Malayan jungle.

The simple act of getting to his feet drained his last reserves of energy. He felt giddy and nauseous, just about all-in, as he staggered on, elbowing a way blindly into the thick undergrowth, knowing that if he gave-up now it would be the end. The damn wood had to finish sometime but could he last out? Was this god-forsaken corner of Europe to be his grave? Even in his state of near collapse he still wanted so much to live. He wanted to end his days peacefully in the *Grenada*, keeling over and spilling his beer among friends – not here!

As if in answer to his unspoken prayer he stumbled into a small clearing that seemed, even in the dismal December daylight, to be like a heavenly sun-lit glade. Drooping, hands on knees with exhaustion, his weary eyes searched for signs of shelter, but there was nothing; until they came to rest on a bundle of something in the far corner. He lurched over, realising as he got nearer, that it was a body. He'd seen plenty of bodies before but even his shattered system felt shock at what he saw. The body lay on its back in a black leather jacket type of uniform. It had no left arm and the expose face and hands had been ravaged by animals until only the skeletal bone remained. His stomach heaved, and momentarily he averted his eyes, until survival instinct kicked in.

Despite the missing arm the thick jacket looked enticing; as did the knee high boots. Would they fit him? Certainly the dead man had no further use of them. Gritting is teeth, and feeling like a grave-robber, he knelt beside the body to unzip the jacket. Opening the front he was relieved to see the uniform underneath was that of a German airman. At least it wasn't a British lad, he told himself in consolation – but did that really make a difference? He tried convincing himself it did, but knew in his heart that he would still do this, no matter what the nationality as he rolled the body to remove the jacket and boots.

The gut-wrenching stench that hit his nostrils was that of flesh not yet fully decomposed. Obviously the corpse hadn't been there for all that long and only his desperate need drove him to continue. He could see no sign of an identification disc around the airman's fleshless neck and didn't feel inclined to rummage through the pockets.

The warmth of the jacket around his shivering shoulders was a god-send and renewed his will to live. Would the boots fit too? He sat on the wet ground to remove the tattered remnants of his plimsolls and took a quick look at his bruised and bleeding feet. The boots were too large but that was better than being too small. Perhaps he could find something warming to pad them out. They would be drier, warmer and more protective to his battered toes. Even so, he decided, he would keep the plimsolls, just in case.

'Don't suppose you know where I can find some old newspapers do you, Fritz?' he asked the unresponsive corpse. He looked down at the woollen socks on the German's feet, resisting the urge to take them as well. At least the jacket and boots had not actually been in touch with the dead flesh.

How had the poor bloke ended up here? Had he been shot down? – There was no sign of a parachute. Had he been murdered, perhaps by partisans? Or maybe just lost? Why the missing arm, what had happened? Someone, someday would find the remains and ask themselves the same questions, and if he didn't get his finger out and find a place to hide and sleep they'd be finding his rotting bones too. He wished he could bury the German but had neither the strength nor means to do so.

He felt reluctant to leave the openness of the clearing, and even more unwilling to renew his battle with the trees. They were like ramparts, enclosing him within their prison-like walls; him and the Jerry. He had to move on, if only to get away from his unsavoury companion whose grinning skull looked happy at having donated the life-saving clothes. The leather jacket felt so warm and the slopping boots were like Cinderella's slippers on his battered feet, but nothing could relieve his bone-aching tiredness. Giving a silent salute to his saviour he struggled to his feet and staggered trance-like back into the woods, not caring in which direction he headed. Did it matter?

After a few minutes – or was it hours – the denseness appeared to be thinning. He could see daylight between the trees ahead, or what passed for daylight in mid-winter. Almost asleep on his feet his knees gave way and he fell forward, landing beside the trunk of a huge fallen tree that gave shelter from the biting cold wind. He had no strength left to continue, it was all over. Like a child cuddling into its mother he nestled against the comforting bulk, trying to bury himself as far under as possible, not concerned with discovery, only yearning for sleep and escape from Mother Nature's cruelty.

His last waking thoughts, as a black void of oblivion enveloped him, were… This is where I die.

'Gravy' Browning hardly had time to feel really afraid. No sooner had he been thrown into the corner of his cell (that was, had he known it, identical to the one his officer now occupied) than the door opened again to admit two grim-faced gorillas in brown shirtsleeves and Jodhpur style trousers. With hands the size of a Grizzly bear's paws, they lifted him off his feet without any sign of exertion. Unceremoniously hustled out of his cell, he was frog-marched – almost on tiptoe – along a short corridor into a room where they rammed him down onto a plain wooden chair.

In front of him, behind a plain, empty desk, a civilian in white shirt and black tie, his face grotesquely shadowed by an unshaded ceiling light bulb, sat cradling his fingers beneath his chin as though in deep meditation. Browning, now convinced he was about to be interrogated, kept repeating in his head the instructions he had been taught during training, mentally ticking them off on his fingers; it helped him to stop thinking less pleasant thoughts. In his mind's eye, he could still see the unsmiling face of his instructor who, it was said, had endured months of interrogation and torture at the hands of his captors during the Spanish civil war. If anyone should know, he should.

"Be polite and respectful to your captors" he had told the marines. "Do not react, retaliate or show anger to anything they may do or say, no matter what the provocation. Answer their questions in the pretence of co-operation without giving away information that may harm your colleagues, or be of value to the enemy. Act naively and unintelligent. Admit only to having vague knowledge of your mission. If your captors are Field Police, S.S. or Gestapo, do not expect to satisfy them with only your name, rank and number. They do not respect the Geneva Convention and you will only leave yourself open to abuse and violence." There were other items of advice given about resistance to interrogation, but his worried mind couldn't recall them as he waited fearfully, his nerves stretched bar taut.

After a few minutes of deathly silence – probably designed to intimidate – the civilian dropped his hands and leaned forward, letting out a long drawn-out sigh that whistled across the desk in a blast of garlic.

'Name?' he demanded, pen poised over a notebook.

'Alan Browning, sir.'

'Rank and number?'

'Marine. Number....' he recited, watching the pen scribbling away.

'Unit?'

'Royal Marines, sir.'

'I asked, what unit?' snapped the interrogator, irritably.

Browning raised an innocent eyebrow. 'No unit, sir. Just Royal Marines.'

The German paused to consider this answer. 'What is your trade or specialisation?'

'Driver, sir,' responded the marine who had never driven anything more mechanical than a push-bike.

The civilian (if that was what he was) sat back in his chair holding claw-like hands together beneath his chin as though in prayer. In the changed angle of the overhead light he could now be seen as a thin, almost bald man, with sagging cheeks and wide staring eyes, who looked as happy as an undertaker seeking a misplaced client. For some inexplicable reason this gave Browning courage. His questioner was no superman. He tried to sit up straight but his cuffed hands were hurting, so he wriggled his buttocks forward onto the edge of the chair to answer the endless but seemingly innocuous questions. What did it matter to this Wally where he was born, or where he lived, or if he was married? ....Or what he did in civilian life?.... So far, it was all harmless stuff.

Suddenly the German leaned forward menacingly, a tight-lipped smile like a zip across his face, as he slammed a hand down sharply on the desk top, causing the marine to jump and the empty coffee cup to rattle in its saucer. 'What was your mission?'

Browning thought for a split second, knowing that any hesitation in answering would be misconstrued as thinking up a lie. *Codling's* crew would be well away by now so he saw no harm in revealing half-truths. 'We was to blow up your ships with mines, sir.'

'Where?' demanded the interrogator, leaning further forward, expectantly.

'Dunno, sir. I was never told the name of the place, but I guess it must be somewhere here, in Germany.'

The German smirked at the Englander's stupidity. He didn't even know he was in France! 'How many of you were there?'

'Only two, sir. Me and Lieutenant Thomas.'

'LIAR' yelled the German, jumping to his feet and spitting in the marine's face. 'We know there were more!'

Browning hardly had time to say 'No, sir' before what felt like a camel's hoof hit him in the face, nearly knocking him out of the chair. He tasted blood and rose instinctively to retaliate, forgetting his cuffed hands. He never made it to his feet before his world exploded.

Two floors above the crypt-like cellars, Obersturmbannfuhrer Ernst Rhomdahl sat leaning with his elbows resting on the highly polished desk, his broad nose held between the tips of long, well-manicured fingers. The heavy brocade curtains pulled across the bricked-up window, and the numerous Nazi flags draped around the office, did little to muffle the monotonous hum of the recently installed air-conditioning apparatus that fought an endless struggle with the ancient, uncontrollable heating system to maintain his office temperature at an acceptable level. He was fuming. Not enjoying the best of days.

First, he had to castigate the idiot Battery commander at Nantes for delaying his report of the capture of the two British saboteurs for nearly eight vital hours. Then, a few minutes ago, came reports that two of his investigating officers had been killed by an explosion, presumably caused by fused mines left undiscovered in the Britishers sunken canoe. Then more reports from Nantes, and Bordeaux, of ships being sunk or damaged alongside the wharves, by so-called "mysterious explosions" that he now knew to be the actions of the enemy canoeist, one of whom had been found drowned in an overturned canoe in Nantes docks. Thankfully, he had two others in captivity. That made three, with one unaccounted for from the Nantes canoe. How many more were there? That was the big question. He was not concerned with the Bordeaux raid which was outside his jurisdiction, but he had to consider the possibility of the raiders from there using his area as an escape route. How did they plan to get away? He had no naval knowledge himself but he could not envisage them canoeing back down the river. Not when they must know that half the German army would be looking for them! They had to have an overland evacuation plan, he was convinced of that, and his staff officers were already organising search parties to comb the banks of the Loire River and surrounding towns and villages, as well as checking everyone on roads, lanes and railway stations. Whether the escapees numbered one or a dozen he swore they would not get away. It wasn't too late. He would make his prisoners talk, and then......He looked down at the papers on the desk between his elbows. The top sheet was a copy of the Fuhrer's top-secret *Commando Order* that decreed "All enemy commando saboteurs be denied all quarter and mercy, and to be killed out of hand or pursued to the death".

No more than they deserve, he muttered to himself, for their murderous action. He would, of course, obtain confirmation of the *Order* from his superior, then take great pleasure in complying – but only after his staff had "persuaded" the marines to talk. Then he would deal with his own people, in no uncertain manner. He was well aware he had enemies in higher echelons, and had no doubt they would derive great pleasure in placing the blame for all this on his doorstep. He, in turn, intended to limit that pleasure by ensuring that the idiots serving in *his* command, who *were* responsible, would suffer the consequences of their own incompetence.

He reached out and placed a hand on the cold bakelite phone, pausing to collect his thoughts; then lifted the receiver wearily to his ear.

Chapter Fourteen.

They came for Lieutenant Thomas eventually, and he almost felt pleased to see them; almost, but not quite. For what seemed like hours he had been squatting in the angle of the two walls of his cell getting colder and thirstier. His hands, secured tightly behind his back, were numb and the wrists felt red raw. Apart from his bottom being sore, painful and seriously uncomfortable against the rough concrete, he was scared stiff. He desperately wanted a toilet and looked calculatingly at the mysterious hole in the centre of the floor - any port in a storm - but he wondered how he could manage with his hands cuffed behind his back. It was then, before he could put his bladder-relieving plan into operation, that he heard the approaching heavy-booted tread. The door clicked open and two men, muscles bulging under brown shirts, entered and lifted him bodily by the upper arms as though he were weightless. Feeling as powerless as a snared rabbit – and just as frightened – he was carried with his feet reaching unsuccessfully for the floor, through the grim vaulted cellar and along a corridor to a door that the two thugs shouldered open.

The room they entered was in darkness, except for a dim pool of light cast onto an uncluttered desk by a single low-wattage bulb suspended from the ceiling in a tube-like shade, and he was thrust down hard onto a wooden seat that did his aching backside the world of good. The silence was deafening. A classic setting for interrogation, he thought, quivering with suppressed fear. He leaned forward, as much to ease his aching wrists as to try to pierce the sinister gloom. He could sense the presence of his two escorts standing behind, one either side, and as his eyes became accustomed to the dark he made out the vague shape of someone sitting on the other side of the desk. A disembodied arm appeared, waving its hand, and to his astonishment the two guards lifted him to his feet. He tensed, waiting for the blow that didn't come. Instead, and to his great relief, they uncuffed his hands. He began to massage them back to life, but before he could enjoy the pleasure they were grabbed again and secured at the front, and he was dumped back in the chair. Be thankful for small mercies, he thought, hoping his treatment wasn't to be as bad as he expected. Perhaps they were going to respect his officer status? After all, the Germans aren't that bad; very much like us really. The few he had met seemed decent enough fellows, in fact quite likeable. His hopes quickly plummeted as a thin face loomed out of the penumbral shadows and entered the pool of light like a spectre, its features made more cadaverous by the heavy shading from the overhead light. It also revealed his civilian attire. Jesus! Was this the infamous Gestapo? The cold, penetrating look from the sunken eyes sent a shiver of terror down his spine but instead of the expected tirade of grilling questions, a low voice speaking excellent English began reciting his own personal details.

'Lieutenant Adrian Thomas. Royal Marines' he began, as a statement not a question. 'Aged Twenty-three. Single. Until recently commander of a commando unit detailed to attack shipping in the port of Nantes with mines placed from canoes. Am I correct?'

The marine's mouth fell open in surprise. How the hell did they know all that? Even if Browning had talked he wouldn't have known his age, or that he was single. Did they have a dossier on everyone?.....'Yes. That is correct,' he answered.

The staring eyes probed deep into his head as if trying to read his mind. 'And is it also correct that, after these acts of sabotage, you intended to meet up with members of the so-called French Resistance with the intention of escaping overland, or assisting them in their murderous activities against soldiers of The Reich?'

'No. That is not correct.'

'Explain yourself,' said the soft voice. 'What is not correct?'

Thomas swallowed the cricket-ball sized lump of fear in his throat. He mustn't antagonise this man who seemed to know a hell of a lot, but he had to be very careful what he said. He didn't want to jeopardise *Codling's* crew, or the French. He decided to act subservient, to gain time. 'All of it, sir.'

'Please, lieutenant,' admonished the German, regarding the Englander with a deep contempt. 'We know differently. What we wish to know is, how many of you were involved?' He hesitated, dramatically, to add emphasis to what he was about to reveal. 'You should be aware that two of your fellow saboteurs are dead. They were killed before being able to place their mines, and the body of your Marine Nook was unfortunately badly disfigured by a patrol boat's propeller. So you see it is useless for you to remain silent. It will not go well for you if you continue to be – er – unco-operative.'

The shock of this news stunned Thomas. He felt like a balloon deflating; all the spirit and defiance draining from of his body. Poor Pearman and Nook, they were good lads and he wondered how they had met their deaths. He was horrified. The whole mission had been a tactical and strategic failure. Two men dead and two captured. For what? He cursed the staff planners for devising such a suicidal operation, and the top brass for authorising it. May they rot in hell, he thought angrily, wishing he were dead too. If his interrogator had the idea that this news would make him talk he was badly mistaken. If anything, his resolve was strengthened. He would not dishonour the memory of his brave marines. They could do their worse. He would rather die.

The German noted the Englishman's reaction with professional interest. First the visible physical and mental collapse, followed by an almost immediate straightening of the back. Then the tightening of the mouth, and a hard look of defiance appearing in the eyes. Had he made a mistake in mentioning the second canoe and telling the lie about the death of both its crew? He searched the marine's face for signs of the earlier fear that had been so obvious and expected, but there was none. All he could see was an obstinate, almost challenging stare. Blast, he said to himself, now he would have to take off the velvet glove. He felt no pity, no remorse. His job was to get information, and although he never hesitated to use force – in fact sometimes found it pleasurable – he much preferred to obtain it voluntarily and leave the physical side to others, like the two psychopaths assigned to him today. He would try once again and judge the response. 'How many of you were there taking part in this raid, lieutenant?'

Thomas heard the question as though it were an echo from far away, and understood the menacing threat it contained. He knew the consequences his reaction would bring, but he no longer cared. His marines were dead. He had no right to live. He had failed them. 'Lieutenant Adrian Thomas. Royal Marines,' he answered calmly, his voice full of disdain. That was all they were going to get out of him from now on.

The German, admitting defeat for his non-physical tactics, flapped his hands as an indicating to the two escorts that Thomas should be stood up.

Thomas felt himself lifted and saw the nod of his interrogator's head. He held his breath – waiting. He didn't wait long. A force like a steam-hammer hit him in the kidneys, throwing him forward with an arched back until held by hands not unlike steel traps. The indescribable pain surged up and down his spine, sending muscles into spasm. His whole body felt as though it had exploded and he heard himself scream like a wounded animal. His knees gave way and he sank to the floor in agony. They lifted him again, straightening his back against the unbearable pain as the bile rose up in his throat, and he vomited. Had he seen the questioner jump up from his chair, cursing loudly, and leap back as the puke spewed over the desk, it would have given him a great deal of pleasure, but he saw nothing through the red mist of excruciating agony. Another pile-driving blow slammed into the small of his back, this time on the opposite side. His back arched convulsively as the impact threw him across the room, legs flailing like a discarded rag-doll, and he felt himself fall into a black pit as his bowel and bladder emptied.

'Mein Gott!' bawled the interrogator, clapping a scented handkerchief over his crinkled nose and mouth. 'Get that filth out of here and get the place cleaned up,' he ordered over his shoulder, hurriedly leaving the room.

The two guards looked at each other and shrugged their broad shoulders in annoyed acceptance; their fun spoiled. They had volunteered for this work to escape from front-line duties – and come to like it. It was an outlet for their ingrained violent nature and the sadism that had gotten them noticed in the first place. This cleaning up was part of their duties, but they didn't like it anymore than they liked being bossed about by that little runt who hid behind his S.S. rank.

Grabbing hold of the unconscious marine by the shoulders they dragged him from the room out into the corridor, leaving a trail of filth to be cleared up later. Back at his cell they threw him in, head first, enjoying the thud of his head colliding with the floor. Taking one leg each, they snatched off his plimsolls and dragged the soiled trousers and underpants down, unconcerned by the vile stench. It was not the first time they had done this, and probably wouldn't be the last.

Leaving the cell door open for a few minutes, one of them went to fetch a bag for the marine's soiled clothing that would help feed the furnaces in the boiler-room, while the other opened a cupboard in the cellar wall and uncoiled a fire-hose. Standing with the hose nozzle pointing at the half-naked body sprawled on the cell floor, he waiting for his mate to return and open the valve. He looked down at the Tommy's pathetic body. So this puny specimen was one of the famed – and feared by some – Commando's? Doesn't look too tough to me, he thought, I've seen better among the starving in Warsaw. If this is the best they have to offer there's no doubt who is going to win this war. It didn't look as though he was much good in the sexual field either, his penis was so small. Or perhaps he was a poof? He wouldn't put that past the Tommies. No guts either; fainted in the first few minutes. Even the effeminate French had stood up to more than that. He recalled one man, in Paris, who hadn't lost consciousness during seven hours of torture. They'd beaten him black and blue, ripped out his finger nails, crushed his thumbs and burned him all over with cigarette butts, and still he just stared back at them; until he "accidentally" lost his eyes. That had been good, one of the better ones, but he still preferred to work on Jews, he hated those hook nosed bastards. The more he could make them suffer the better. They had fleeced the Fatherland for decades, until the Fuhrer had taken the necessary steps that the rest of the world was afraid to.

Now, there *was* a man - Adolph Hitler – he had the right ideas. The only thing he couldn't understand about The Leader was that he confessed to actually liking the Tommies!... Strange that.

He waited as his mate scooped the shitty clothes and shoes into the bag with a stick and then, with the valve opened, directed the stream of water at the lifeless figure. He stood well back as blood, faeces and water bounced off the inert body and splashed over the walls, and he wished the Englander would regain consciousness to feel the pain of the strong jet striking his testicles. It would serve him right. He watched as the corpse-like body moved about like a drowned man being washed back and forth by waves at the water's edge, wishing it would come back to life so that he could see the suffering. He smiled to himself. At least the bastard would be hurting and cold when he did wake up. Pity I wouldn't be around to see it, he thought.

Chapter Fifteen.

It was a sharp, flint-like pressure against his forehead that switched on the light inside Pearman's head. Or maybe it was the bitter cold, the numb ache in his bones or the uncontrollable waves of shivering surging through his very soul. Pictures of memory flashed on the screen of his closed eyelids as he began to recall the events of the last few days. Of poor old Windy, the freezing swim in the river and the agonising cross-country trek. Slowly, like opening Venetian blinds, he forced his unwilling eyes open, feeling the sting of a thousand needles in the pupils. All he could see was a brown shapeless mass. Was he blind? *Was he even alive?* He certainly wasn't in Hell, the temperature was all wrong.

Concentrating hard, he tried to focus on the brown mass until he became cross-eyed and recognised the rough bark pressing on his face. Of course – the tree!

Forcing his stiff reluctant body into a sitting position, he looked around his strange surroundings, seeing nothing but trees in every direction and the dull-grey streaks of daylight piercing down through their wintry nakedness. What was the time? How long had he been asleep? He lifted his trembling wrist, but it shook too much for him to make out the blurred hands on his *Everrite*. He knew he was showing early signs of hypothermia - he'd seen it before, in others - and that he must do something about it, quickly. He was also aware that, in any other circumstances, he would be already dead. He owed his life to the jacket and boots. 'Thank you, Fritz' he mumbled in his throat, unable to move frozen lips.

Struggling against quivering muscles and resisting joints, he rose to his feet like an arthritic pensioner, pulling the jacket tighter around his chilled body and stumbling forward, step after unsteady step, towards where the trees seemed less dense. Numbed by cold and thirst, and his body on automatic, he plodded for mile after mile through woods and across fields as the short daylight faded, and night drew its cloak over the countryside.

At one time he heard the lip-trembling whinnying of a horse and stopped to listen as a cow bawled a sympathetic answer. He must be quite close to a farm, and that meant food and water. The very thought reminded him of his raging thirst, and the parched throat and lips that tormented him. Recklessly he turned and took a step towards the farm, just as a yapping dog started to bark.

He froze for a second, and then cautiously retraced his steps backward until the dog – satisfied a dozen clawing cats were not about to attack– became quiet and returned to dreams of juicy bones. It had been a close call, and Pearman shook himself back to awareness. He didn't want to be caught yet, but thirst, hunger, cold and tiredness were taking their toll and making him carelessly light-headed. If only there was a light at the end of the tunnel, he thought. That would give him a goal to aim for. As it was, he had no incentive. He could wander around for ever, probably in circles, and would either drop down dead or be captured. He might just as well give himself up now!

Memories of Nook, Browning and the lieutenant came into his mind. Would old Windy have given up so easily? Were the other two still free and suffering as he was? Would they give up? Would they, Hell!! He squared his shoulders; if they could do it so could he. He'd get back home, for their sakes.

For several more hours – he didn't know how many as he purposely refused to check the time, thinking it might help – he trudged on until he blundered into an unseen brick wall. Well, it felt like a brick wall. In actual fact it was the wooden side of a dilapidated, semi-collapsed barn. Hand over hand, he felt his way around the outside until coming to a broken door hanging half open on one rusty hinge and supported by knee-high brambles. He peered into the dark interior, hearing a scuffling. Rats, he thought, or some other wild life. Half of the corrugated iron roof had gone and the other half rattled on loose fixing bolts in the raw wind that whistled through the many gaps in the rotten lapped-wood sides.

Fumbling around inside, he discovered a pile of decaying hay in a corner smelling rotten and *warm*, and was about to collapse, dead-beat, into its mouldy heat when his groping fingers touched something solid that made him jump. It was the spoke of a rimless wheel on a large upturned wooden cart. Poking his head underneath, he found a wide coffin-like space not more than eighteen inches high that stank to high heaven; but it was dry and warm, and looked like paradise.

With the last dregs of energy he stuffed it with armfuls of the musty hay, and crawled in. He was asleep before his cold and exhausted body sank into its blanketing heat.

A sharp pricking sensation behind his ear shocked him awake and his hand flew up protectively, fearing the worst, but it was only a hard stick of straw. He puffed his cheeks and exhaled in relief, turning over onto his back to stare up at the bottom of the cart – now his roof – just a few inches above his nose. His blanket of straw felt comfortably warm and dry but a raging thirst told him he must move. He licked his dry lips with a tongue that felt like a bloated slug, and wriggled his way out. A glance at his trusty Woolworth's *Everrite* told him it was nearly four o'clock, and the low grey clouds that hovered over the hole in the barn roof showed it was afternoon. Looking around, he took stock of his situation; he must sort himself out. What were his priorities? Well, he wasn't in a hurry to go anywhere! For a start he didn't know where he was and had no idea which way he should go. Even if he had he couldn't remember, for the life of him, the name of the town where the Resistance people could be contacted. Anyhow, he consoled himself, the longer he remained free the more chance there was of search parties getting fed-up and going home. So, his first desperate need was a drink. Then, if possible, something to eat. If he was successful, he might also be able to return to his straw bed. It would mean staying all night and probably another day before setting out again. That was a wonderful thought; it would give him the chance of getting fully recuperated.

Slowly poking his nose around the rotting edge of the barn doorway, his first impression was of still being in the middle of the wood he had fought through last night. His heart sank. He didn't fancy the prospect of having to do that again, even in daylight. Stepping out, inch by inch, into the small clearing in front of the door, he could see to his left that, apart from a tangle of bushes and undergrowth, he was on the very edge of the wood. Three more steps and he came to an almost overgrown path that led through the bushes. He pushed his way through. It was only a couple of yards long and the view through the web of leafless branches was of open land. At the end of the path he carefully parted the bare twigs with both hands and peered out. He was in the corner of a large uncultivated field. To his front, two parallel hedgerows - one either side - separated his field from others and stretched several hundred feet towards the far end where low buildings made the fourth side of an oblong. The centre building was a two-storey farm house with lights from candles or lamps flickering gloomily from the ground floor windows. Even from this distance, and in the half light, it had the appearance of being spookily neglected. To either side of it, extending out to the corners, other buildings that could be barns, chicken coops, stables or covered animal sheds, looked equally tumbledown. Fences sagged wearily in disrepair and if it wasn't for the blurred window lighting and the wisps of smoke being dragged downwind from the tall, leaning chimney pot, the whole scene could have been of uninhabited desolation. Apart from the noise of the wind groaning through the trees and rustling of bare undergrowth it was deathly quiet. There were no human noises, no mooing of cows, no bleating of sheep or cackling of geese. No whinnying of horses or clucking of chickens and, thank God, no barking dogs. Even the occasional startled bird fluttering among the starkly nude branches of the trees did so as if apologetic. An artist would probably have viewed it as being tranquil and secluded. To Pearman's fearful mind, it seemed threatening and foreboding; too quiet, like a trap waiting to be sprung. He knew the dangers of the situation, it was his freedom at stake, but his thirst was driving him mad and this was only the second day; if he didn't find a drink now he wasn't sure how much longer he could last. Dire need over-rode his caution and training; he had to take chances.

High-stepping out from the tangle of concealing undergrowth and crouching almost doubled over he inched his way through the long grass, staying close to the bushes until he reached the corner of the field, then turned towards the buildings, keeping low against the camouflaging back-drop of the hedgerow.

The winter wind began to creep through the serge of his battledress trousers and up under the leather jacket, draining away the warmth accumulated from his rest in the hay. Mentally he added another item to his list of priorities – clothing; anything that would keep the cold out from his bones. Perhaps, he thought, if he could acquire some sort of disguise he could travel by day!

With the dim light from the waning sun trying to filter through thick angry clouds, he crawled slowly towards the farm, alert to any movement or noise, heading for a pile of sawn tree trunks heaped against the hedge within spitting distance of the nearest out-house. Dodging quickly around the moss-covered pile he crawled the last few yards on hands and knees through the damp coarse grass to the nearest neglected wood-clad building and peered around the corner. Still no barking dog!

Peeping through a wide gap between two distorted wall slats into the dim interior of the building, all he could see was a dust-covered heap of dilapidated farm implements and what looked like a rusty tractor. In the last of the fading daylight his eyes quickly scanned the other buildings, searching for anything that may be a source of drink – or food. A tantalising smell of cooking, wafted past his nostrils by a capricious breeze, sent his taste-buds into overdrive. His nose lifted, searchingly the air like a Bisto kid in the advert, then it was gone leaving him hungrier than ever.

At the corner of a barn-like shed that stood halfway between where he was hidden and the farmhouse, he saw a wooden water-butt with a down-pipe hanging into it from the roof guttering. Rain water! With commendable restraint and a great deal of caution, he groped his way nervously towards it, anticipation adding to the thumping of his racing heart. It was no more than thirty feet away yet it seemed to take forever, but it was worth it. Beneath the broken lid of the cask a film of dirt and dead insects covered the surface of the nearly full barrel, but that was no deterrent to him. He put his hands together as if in prayer, gently parting the scum and scooping a handful of the stagnant water to his lips. Ordinarily he would have vomited at the thought of drinking such vile tasting stuff but at that moment, it was like champagne.

Just as he lifted a third cupped handful to his mouth he heard a noise from the farmhouse, and froze. It was the click of a heavy door latch. The front door opened and a man, momentarily back-lit by the gloomy house lighting, shuffled out leaning heavily on a crutch and carrying a small jug in his free hand. In the waning light he could have been anything between thirty and sixty as he hobbled across a narrow cobbled area to place his jug on the surrounding wall of … A WELL! Pearman hadn't seen it in his preoccupation with the buildings.

With a great deal of squeaking from the hand-winch the man lowered the well-bucket and then hauled it back up onto the wall to fill his own jug before awkwardly returning back into the house. The marine hadn't failed to notice the well-bucket left standing on the surrounding wall and his mind filled with wondrous thoughts of *fresh* water. It had a magnetic attraction, but it was not yet dark enough for him to dare venture out over the open space. He looked up at the black boulders of clouds scudding across the slate-coloured sky like huge wads of dirty cotton wool. It was getting darker by the minute, and over the farmhouse roof with its numerous slipped and broken tiles, the last strands of daylight were fading. He closed his eyes in dreamlike expectation, imagining the cold, clean well water swirling around his tongue, trickling down his throat and washing away the foul tasting, gritty rainwater from the butt that had so recently tasted wonderful. All he needed to find now was food; anything that would satisfy his ravenous hunger and the gnawing at his innards aggravated by the rich, savoury cooking smells that defied the dispersing efforts of the cold breeze. He must look in the other out-buildings while some vestige of natural light remained. Even a raw potato or an egg would be welcome.

A shed standing next to the house, looked promising. It wasn't as ramshackle as the others and had the appearance of frequent usage. He stepped out from behind the cover of the water butt and took a furtive step towards it when he heard the shout. He stopped dead, paralysed into immobility. The crippled man was standing in the opened farmhouse doorway framed by the dim golden internal light. Panic stricken, with blood pounding through his body like storm waves, Pearman felt impotent and vulnerable. Surely the man *must* see him; he stood out as conspicuous as a mitred Bishop in a brothel. Perhaps he was blind as well as crippled?

'Adele!' called the man again, looking straight at him.

Another shock stunned the marine when the door of the shed he had been heading for, opened. A woman came out, and without looking in his direction, closed the door behind her and walked towards the house. In a long ankle-length dress and scarf-like hood over her head she could have been any age, but from the back she appeared tired and weary. She greeted the man silently with a hand on his upper arm and led him back into the house. Perhaps, thought Pearman, the chap *was* blind after all; or poorly sighted. He stayed stock-still, as motionless as a cold marble statue, waiting for his racing heart to slow. Christ! he thought, that was a close call. I shall have a heart attack at this rate.

For several minutes, he remained that way, not even thinking to step back behind the water butt, watching the door and seeing an occasional shadow of someone passing behind the downstairs window, between it and the flickering lamp light. He still waited, getting colder by the minute, fearful of being seen or heard, until the movements inside the house stopped. All seemed quiet, and he hoped the woman had been called in for a meal and was now sat eating at the table. Concerned about the rapidly fading light he began edging over to the door of the shed from where the woman had emerged, every nerve tensed for the least sound or movement. Holding his breath he inched the door open, ready to stop at the first sound of a squeak, and slipped inside. His first impressions were of a workroom-cum-storage place lit only by two wall windows covered on the outside by bird dropping and cornered on the inside by cobwebs filled with dead insects. Even in broad daylight it would be dismal but now, in the weak greyness coming through the dirty windows, it was almost dark. How had the woman managed to do whatever she had been doing? he wondered, groping around blindly, touching and feeling cautiously, careful not to knock or kick anything that would make a noise and alert the farmers.

On a rough wooden table, his fingers touched a large metal container full of what felt and smelled like compost, or maybe animal fodder; whatever it was he felt sure it wasn't edible. Shuffling around, feeling with hands and feet, he came across a shelf of various sized flower pots. Must be a gardening shed, he presumed. All he found of interest was a ball of string that he put in his pocket. Continuing around the table he found a shallow wooden crate that, to his delight, held what his fingers and nose identified as tomatoes. Greedily he sank his teeth into one, feeling the succulent juice and pulp slide down his throat and chin. It was hard and probably an unripe green, but nevertheless tasted heavenly.

Alongside the crate lay a pile of empty paper sacks, the large multi-thickness type used for peat, or cement powder. Holding the top one open he dropped some of the tomatoes into it, fighting the temptation to eat more of them, there and then. He wouldn't take too many, not wanting to make their loss obvious and possibly creating an alarm that might make life difficult for him. Further along the table more crates contained other vegetables. Some were potatoes and others either carrots or turnips, he didn't care. A few of each joined the tomatoes in the sack. Having checked the rest of the shed as well as he could, and hoping he hadn't missed anything, he was about to leave when he recalled something else from his earlier survival training. He took three more of the sacks and folded them in with his haul.

Once again he went through the worrying routine of slowly opening the shed door, and after making sure the coast was clear, made his way back to the water butt to hide his sack of goodies. Now for the water, he said to himself, licking his crusted lips in anticipation and wishing he had found a suitable container in the shed to carry some away in. The house remained quiet as he edged his way warily across the small yard with as much stealth as his nerves would permit, cursing his stupidity for wearing the heavy boots instead of his plimsolls.

The bucket still stood on the wall of the well, like a tantalising magnet. Reaching out, he lifted it down and carried it around the far side, relieved that its weight gave the promise of sufficiency that would save him having to risk using the squealing winch. Bending his knees and tilting the bucket to his lips he unavoidably spilt the precious liquid down the front of his tunic as he gulped copious mouthfuls, gasping at its cold freshness until he had quenched his immediate thirst before resting it back on the wall. God! That was good. A life saver!

What he needed now was a container or bottle to take some away in. He looked towards the house through the gap between the winch-drum and the tiled roof of the well. He dare not knock and ask for help, or contemplate breaking-in later in the night. That would set the cat among pigeons and be asking for trouble, the sort of trouble he dare not risk. He wasn't that desperate – yet. Anxiously, his eyes swept across the yard trying to pierce the almost total darkness, looking for…anything, and nearly missed the garden watering can standing on the lid of a box near the front door. It wasn't ideal for his purposes but better than nothing.

At that moment, the houselights went out.

Hoping it meant the occupants were going to bed, he lifted his wrist-watch to within inches of his eye, moving it to and fro to focus and catch any scrap of natural light. The blurred image of the hands looked like it was half past six. Bloody hell! He cursed silently, where had the last two hours gone? He waited, as still as his cold bones would allow, hidden behind the well. He knew that English farmers often retired early so as to be up and about again by four-ish in the morning to tend their animals. Did the 'Froggies' do the same? He hoped so.

After what he estimated to be about ten minutes without any further sound or movement from the house, he began shivering with the cold, his whole body trembling; he couldn't stand still any longer. He came out from behind the well and with as much stealth as the floppy boots would allow, crept across the yard to the doorway and the watering can; his nerves stretched bar taut waiting for a shout of alarm, the bark of a dog, or a shotgun blast into the rigid hairs on the back of his neck.

Like a thief in the night – which he was – he took the can and tiptoed furtively back to the well, all the time feeling as if he had a bull's-eye target pinned on his back.

Slopping a mere cupful of water from the bucket into the can he swirled it around and emptied it quietly onto the cobbles; he wasn't hungry enough to start eating spiders yet. Draining the bucket almost filled the watering can. Carrying its awkward weight and keeping his eyes glued to the farmhouse windows, he returned to the water butt to retrieve his cache of vegetables. With his thirst quenched, and the prospect of getting back into the welcoming blanket of straw to investigate his ill-gotten gains, he lurched back along the shadows of the hedgerows. The can of water knocking awkwardly against his leg and the sack of goodies slung over his shoulder, like a robber's swag bag.

Chapter Sixteen.

'Bonne nuit, mon Cheri. Dors bien' whispered Adele Montange, tucking her crippled husband into his downstairs bed and bending to touch her lips lightly on his damp forehead.

His pale, wan face gave no sign of acknowledgement. With eyes closed he looked more like a cadaver than the wonderful man she had once known. She blew out the oil lamp and turned away, to climb wearily up the creaking wooden stairs to the bedroom she hadn't shared with her husband since the first dreadful days of the war when he had left her and the farm. He went, like all patriotic Frenchmen, to serve his country; only to return a few months later, almost deaf, blind and crippled from horrific head and leg wounds. Now just a shell of a man, he needed her constant care and nursing. He did his best to help where and when he could, and was an excellent cook considering the dearth of available food, but with a healthy active mind within his shattered body she knew his life must be purgatory, although he seldom complained.

Their farm, once thriving, was rapidly falling into disrepair but she felt fiercely determined to keep it going somehow, until she could find a buyer for it. Not that she held much hope of that until the damn war ended, one way or the other. All she had left were her treasured memories.

Mounting the dark narrow staircase, she deliberately forced her mind away from a growing depression, back to 1938 and her wonderful marriage to Jules, the tall, handsome, up-and-coming young farmer whose drive and ambition would have made him a rich man. Much sought after by the local m'selles, Jules showed no interest in women. Twenty-five years old and the most eligible bachelor for many miles he lived only for his farm. It was his heart and soul, his whole life – until he set eyes on Adele.

They first met during his visit to her hometown buying equipment for his farm. It was a two-hour ride on his rattly old motorcycle and a journey he was destined to make many times during their months of courtship. She had been the twenty-three year old, brown-haired, green-eyed daughter of Bertrand and Brigitte Falconel who ran the small *tabac* he had called in at to purchase something or other. Her sensual beauty, as she served him from behind the counter, had hit Jules right between the eyes, like a bolt from the blue. From the very first moment he had wanted her desperately; and she, him. They shared a tempestuous love, seldom apart for more than a few days at a time, and married within six months. Their parents were delighted, and the local girls – who had all enjoyed imaginary affairs with the handsome young farmer – were green with envy. Life was idyllic, much of it spent in the bedroom to the detriment of the farm. Jules worshiped his beautiful wife and she adored him. They both wanted children but try as they might - and they certainly tried - they were not blessed with a pregnancy. Then the dreaded war came, and the hated Boche.

Fortunately, she and the farm remained unmolested while Jules was away fighting his short war and during his long stay in hospital. The Germans made occasional visits to the nearby village but left the people in peace. When eventually discharged from the military hospital, Jules came home a shattered man, and all hopes for even a partial recovery faded as the weeks and months past; he would always need crutches. His patterns of behaviour varied from brave cheerfulness to self-pitying misery, as changeable as the weather. They received no government pension or income of any kind, other than from the sale of their meagre products. She had no expertise in farming or growing crops, and despite working every day from 5am until 6pm, caring for Jules and doing whatever she could on the farm, the buildings and fences were falling into ruin. All the animals, except for one cow and a goat, had been sold. Even their beloved bulldog had to be got rid of to a neighbour; they couldn't afford to feed it. All they had left, apart from the cow, the goat, a few chickens and acres of uncultivated land, were a few vegetable patches. How was she going to continue to manage and feed the two of them? she thought, despairingly. How long would the war last?

Reaching the top of the stairs and opening the door of her room, she crossed its darkness with the confidence of a blind person in familiar surroundings, skirting the lonely bed to the grey square of window. She never bothered lighting the oil lamp in the room; she knew every inch of its bare coldness and saved a few centimes into the bargain. Neither did she close the blanket-like curtains she was so ashamed of; not that anyone ever saw them - or saw her for that matter.

Heavy cloud scudded angrily across the night sky, driven by the biting wind that whistled eerily through the gaps of the window frame as she stood looking down onto the empty gloom of the cobbled yard. Tears glistened in her tired eyes, and at first she thought they were causing her to see things…..like a fleeting shadow crossing the yard! She blinked, screwing her face to squeeze the weeping drops from her eyes. Staring hard, she saw another movement over by the well. Too big to be a prowling fox, and too upright. Her heart began pounding and she involuntarily stepped back half a pace from the window, her hand flying protectively to her throat. Another movement close to the well convinced her it was a human, but who would be out there at this time of night, and in this weather? It couldn't be a thief, there was nothing to steal. It must be someone desperately thirsty. Could it be a prisoner on the run, or even an escaping allied soldier? Her heart fluttered, but not from fear. It was the thought of a man being so near. A long-forgotten sensation tingled in her groin as she undressed, throwing the thick unglamorous clothes onto the bed without taking her eyes from the bleak yard and feeling the icy evening coldness on her bare skin. Quickly she draped a warm flannelette night-gown over her head, feeling an arousal as the material brushed over excited nerve endings as it fell down around her ankles. Trance-like, she stood motionless for several minutes, staring out into the darkness, her imagination running wild; but there were no more heart-fluttering shadows to be seen.

Forcing herself away from the magnetic window she slipped into bed between the rough enveloping blankets and lay staring up at the black ceiling. Without a doubt, it had been a man, and apart from the old men and very young boys in the village, she hadn't been near a man since Jules went off to war. It had been a long time. Why had fate left her to share the rest of her life with a cripple? Why her? She was still a young healthy woman with feelings, and needs. Her eyes turned to the dim shape of the door, willing it to be opened by a tall dark stranger, or even a short blonde one, provided he wanted her as much as she needed him. Her breasts heaved with excitement, her mind a whirl of fantasies, wanting a man's touch to rekindling the desires she had been unconsciously suppressing for so long. Never before in all her young life had she needed a man's love as much as she did at that very moment.

Her fingers walked the night-gown up, inch by tantalising inch until it bunched around her waist, allowing her hands to brush sensually over her quivering stomach. Squeezing her eyes tightly shut to blot out the disappointing reality of being alone she arched her back, feeling the tingle that started in her toes to flood through her body like an electric shock that curled her toes. Gasping as an orgasm surged up inside her like an unstoppable train she collapsed exhausted onto the sodden pillow… but the door remained closed.

Chapter Seventeen.

Gravy Browning woke with a start as an agonising pain shot through his body to remind him where he was. The side of his face - pressed hard against cold concrete - felt numb, but the rest of his head pounded as though being hit with a steam-hammer. With an effort of will, he opened his swollen eyelids, forcing his brain clear of the mist of hysteria blanketing his mind, and gazed along what appeared to be a wall of rough stone. Slowly he began to realise he was curled up in the foetal position on the floor of his cell, his arms pinioned agonisingly behind his back. He swallowed as waves of nausea threatened to overwhelm him and, despite the ice coldness of his dark prison, he began to sweat – the sweat of fear.

The handcuffs securing his wrists bit cruelly into his flesh, each movement sending excruciating pain coursing savagely through every fibre of his body. A moan escaped his puffy lips as the returning circulation began revitalising numbed nerves, increasing his already intolerable suffering. He lay unmoving, feeling sick and helpless, getting colder and more frightened than he had ever been in his life, his mind and body becoming numb until he lapsed into a sort of dream-like trance that seemed to lift him outside of himself to look down on his own wretched body. Had he died? Was he dead? He had heard stories of similar experiences from people who had survived near-death. Was it his own soul hovering briefly overhead before dashing off 'with all despatch' as the Admiralty would say? Was it now soaring up to join the angels – or more probably the stokers in hell in his case? He seemed to be falling, drifting off into a void of oblivion, when suddenly a blood-curdling scream blasted his eardrums. A searing pain shot up his arms as he attempted to lift his cuffed hands from behind his back to cover his ears, then he tried to bury his bruised head into the stone flooring; anything to blot out the piercing screeches that echoed around the dank walls.

Heart pounding, eyes staring wide with fear, nerves jangling like a tambourine, he wondered if it had been himself until his tormented brain located the sound as coming from somewhere outside. He shuddered at the image of some poor soul suffering the unendurable agony of torture as another terror-filled cry rent the air followed by the thumping of heavy blows, and he fought to retain his own precious sanity. 'God in heaven' he prayed. 'I hope that's not Lieutenant Thomas.'

Just a few yards away, within calling distance had either man known it, those same agonised ululating screams vibrated around Adrian Thomas' cell, jerking him back to consciousness and the anguish of his battered body. The throbbing ache of his bruised back reminded him of his present situation as he fleetingly relived the hell of his interrogation. He cringed as another shrieking howl pounded his ears, and his first thoughts were for Marine Browning. What were those merciless fiends doing to him?

A violent, uncontrollable shivering brought his thoughts back to his own predicament, and the shock of finding he was laying on a cold floor naked from the waist down scared the living daylights out of him. His shirt and battledress blouse were wringing wet and his befuddled mind registered the fact he was freezing cold. He tried to sit up and drag his shirt down over his trembling knees but his cuffed hands and throbbing back made it difficult. He felt as if he had been kicked by a particularly vicious horse – with both hooves! The pain made him fight for breath in short gasps, and the imminence of further torture – or even death – clutched at his heart.

He didn't consider himself to be a brave man, and felt very aware of being near the end of his physical and mental tether; could he take much more? Everyone has a breaking point, even the bravest, but he didn't want to be seen to be a coward and let his men and family down. Death was preferable to that and he set his mind to considering ways of killing himself before he broke under torture.

Sitting up, he wriggled his bare bottom over the rough floor, hardly feeling the abrasions it caused, until he was able to lean his painful back against the damp wall. The effort briefly subdued the convulsive shivering but, by God, he was so unbearably cold. The numbness of his bare flesh was doing little to alleviate the agony, or lessen the sickening fear that gripped his stomach, as he envisaged what the immediate future undoubtedly held in store for him. Why was he cursed with such a vivid imagination?

Again a shrill, deafening scream sent waves of sheer funk and cold sweat swirling through his veins as he tried in vain to shut them out with cuffed hands that would barely open wide enough to cover his ears.

Then came an abrupt silence. A silence so total that even his shattered eardrums could hear the scuttling of cockroaches over his cell floor, and the droning buzz of pestilent flies.

In utter misery, he tensed his muscles until they ached, trying to ease the violent shivering that raged unstoppable through his body from head to toe. His whole being felt like a block of solid ice, and in the darkness he imagined his fingers and toes already taking on the grey-white hue of frostbite. 'Gangrene next' he thought, 'and if they don't torture me to death I'll be a cripple for the rest of my life.'

For some inexplicable reason the fact that he had never married gave him a morsel of comfort, and he rested his head against the rough concrete wall wondering how hard he would have to smash his skull against it to bring a quick, relatively painless death.

'Switch that damn contraption off' snapped Obersturmbannfuhrer Rhomdahl, stomping a jack-booted foot irritably on the floor and pointing his forehead at the gramophone player standing on a green-baize covered table under the draped swastika flag that curtained one of the high-ceiling walls of his office.

Rottenfuhrer Herman Lamden bent his grey-haired head and lifted the undulating arm from the spinning record, and switched off the loud-speaker system as ordered. No way was he going to risk the wrath of his arrogant superior who would not hesitate to send him back to the front line away from this comfortable job without giving it a second thought. Not at his age and with two lumps of shrapnel still embedded in his leg. Being wounded while serving in the Waffen S.S. had got him this job, and he wasn't going to do anything that would jeopardise the possibility of making it last until the end of the war, even it did mean listening to the recorded screams and howls every time this monster wanted to scare the life out of anyone. For the hundredth time he asked himself how the record had been made. It sounded very authentic. Was it a real tortured victim they had recorded, or just a clever actor? He would never know.

Presuming on his long service, his age and being a loyal dogs-body to the powerful Rhomdahl, and in the hope of currying favour with this very senior officer who had thought up the idea of the psychological effect such a record would have on prisoners, he ventured a complimentary remark. 'I hope your record frightens the prisoners into talking Herr Obersturmbannfuhrer' he said. "cause it scares the hell out of me.'

The S.S. officer stiffened. He had been secretly admiring his reflection in the full length mirror on the back of the oak-wood door. For all his forty-two years he still had the athletic body of a younger man, and looked good in his perfectly tailored black uniform with the glittering decoration – presented to him personally by the Fuhrer himself – adorning his throat. The soldier's impertinence had riled him and he turned to scowl at the wounded veteran.

'When I want your assessment or opinion, Landemann, I shall ask for it' he snarled. 'Until then just do as you are ordered and keep your mouth shut.'

Lamden, his face as immobile as his rigid body, fumed inwardly. This bastard, who hadn't even fought on the front line and probably never fired a weapon at anyone other than a helpless victim, couldn't even get his name right!

'Komm,' snapped the officer in response to a rapid double-tap on the heavy door.

The door opened to reveal the thin death-like face of the unit's senior interrogator whose civilian suit hung from frail shoulders like wet clothing from a hanger. 'You sent for me, Herr Obersturmbannfuhrer?' said the man, stepping aside to allow Lamden to unobtrusively slip out into the corridor.

'Ah! Kruger,' acknowledged Rhomdahl, looking down his broad nose distastefully at the weed of a man who he knew to be highly intelligent and utterly ruthless, even though he cut a comical figure when wearing his uniform of an S.S. Hauptsturmfuhrer. 'How are you getting on with the two Englanders. Any information for me yet?'

Kruger felt a slight trembling in his knees as he faced the only man he had ever been scared of. This man, who held the power of life or death in his hands, could - and would - ruin a man's career at his slightest whim. It was said he had the ear of Himmler himself, and was infamous for his treatment of incompetent inferiors.

'I regret I have nothing to report from my initial interviews Herr Obersturmbannfuhrer. I am of the opinion that the NCO has nothing of value to tell us and I intend to concentrate my efforts on the officer in the next ……..'

'I want answers, NOW!' interrupted Rhomdahl, slamming his fist down onto the highly polished drinks cabinet, rattling the glasses. 'If the marine is of no use to us get rid of him – and make sure his officer is a witness. Perhaps then you will get results.'

'Of course, Herr Obersturmbannfuhrer' replied Kruger, automatically clicking the heels of his civilian shoes together as he turned to the door, somewhat shocked. He had unmercifully tortured many during his three years of service but had never taken the responsibility of an execution. He closed the door quietly, and walked thoughtfully along the carpeted hall, a plan of action quickly formulating in his mind. He would pull rank and delegate that cocky young Berliner, Weiss, do the dirty work. He would probably enjoy it. His hatred of the tall, blond-headed Untersturmfuhrer knew no bounds. Weiss was a near perfect Arian and a fanatical Nazi, already gaining the admiration of his superiors for his unrelenting and pitiless pursuit of the so-called Resistance.

The ringing of iron-shod boots on the stone flagging outside his cell and the clanging of the door latch warned Thomas' benumbed brain that he had visitors. Two burly pairs of hands grasped his upper arms, lifting him to his feet and holding him there as his knees crumbled. He had lost all sensitivity in his arms and legs and felt cold beyond human endurance, like a carcass of frozen meat; too numb to feel pain. Only his brain felt alive, albeit sluggish like a drunk as he tried to focus on the tall, black-uniformed figure standing in the doorway without a trace of human compassion on his face. It was the type of face that rarely displays any expression, or emotion; like an automaton.

Thomas sensed his time had come as his two bearers followed their officer into the cavernous cellar scraping his bare, unfeeling feet over the rough concrete flooring. He let his head droop, he hadn't the strength or will to look up as the officer opened a double-door and ushered his two gorillas with their deadweight burden inside.

The room was several sizes larger than his own cell, with whitewashed walls and a barred window at shoulder height in one wall. Apart from the dull daylight filtering in from the window, the only illumination came from an unshaded light bulb hanging from the centre of the high ceiling; it looked like an empty storeroom with not one stick of furniture. They dragged him across to the window, forcing his chest against the wall and pressing his face against the window bars. He heard the door slam shut behind him and guessed the officer had left him alone with his two supporting thugs. He tried to reason what was happening. Was this some kind of torture? What were they going to do? What was he supposed to do? The uncertainty only added to his mounting fear. He looked out of the window; there was nothing to see except high windowless walls surrounding an empty courtyard and low black clouds racing across the small square of leaden sky above.

Browning had managed to painfully get himself in a sitting position in the corner of two walls. His bladder was at bursting point but none of his commando training had taught him how to get his fly-buttons undone with hands cuffed behind his back. It was nearly as painful as his bruised body and if somebody didn't arrive bloody soon and get him to a toilet he would wet himself.

As if in answer to his prayer he heard the sounds of heavy footsteps outside and tried to shuffle to his feet, but his knees wouldn't work. The American-speaking guard entered with another thug and lifted him as though he were a weightless child.

'A toilet please, quickly,' pleaded Browning.

'Later,' answered the pseudo Yank, averting his eyes as if shamefully.

'No, NOW. Please!' Browning begged urgently, but his words fell on deaf ears as they frog marched him from the cell and across to a small door that was so narrow they were forced to crab through, sideways.

A blast of freezing air hit them as they came out onto an empty courtyard and the marine shivered as the wind cut straight through his battledress – or was it his premonition that something wasn't quite right. Across the courtyard, on the far wall, they shackled his handcuffs to a ringbolt and left him without a word.

'Christ!' he thought. What sort of torture is this? Were they going to leave him to freeze in the open until he talked? His thoughts were interrupted when the small door opened again and four rifle-toting soldiers and an S.S. officer emerged. He smiled to himself. The bastards were going to put him through a mock execution in the hope he would crack at the last moment. He had heard such stories from the lads who were evacuated from Dunkirk. Well, it wasn't going to work with him. Two can play at games of bluff and silly buggers.

The four soldiers lined up in front of him and on the order from the officer, raised their rifles to their shoulders, eyes sighting along the barrels. Browning looked back at them and at the four black dots of the rifle muzzles, and saw the officer raise his arm. Determined not to crack before they did, he concentrated his thoughts on watching the wind spin dead leaves in angry spirals around the yard. The officer dropped his hand but the marine heard nothing of the order to fire before his body was slammed back against the wall, to hang lifeless in a pool of his own blood and urine.

Chapter Eighteen.

The uncertainty of what was going on filled Lieutenant Thomas with a dread that made his head reel. Why were two yeti-type paws crushing his chest against the wall and his cheekbone hard onto the rusty bars of the window? Were they giving him his last view of the outside world? If it was an attempt to make him crack, they were failing dismally; he wasn't impressed. All he could see were the dark and forbidding clouds rushing past at roof-top level and the three blank walls enclosing the cobbled courtyard.

Unexpectedly, a movement in the periphery of his left eye caught his attention. He tried to turn his head but one of the iron bars was jammed hard between his eyebrows and down one side of his nose. Swivelling his eyeballs until they hurt he saw two guards march onto the courtyard dragging something effortlessly between them. Even before his straining eyes could focus, his brain told him their burden was human, and shock stunned his already tensed body as he recognised the uniform and mop of black hair on the sagging head. His blood ran colder than the iciness of the dank room and dread gripped his heart like a steel clamp. He looked on, mesmerised and powerless, as they hauled Browning across the yard, and it was only when they reached the far side and turned him around that he saw the marine was still alive; not only alive but smiling to boot, as though goading his captors as they chained him to the wall. Thomas saw Browning lift his chin up defiantly as four armed German soldiers and an officer marched across the yard to line up facing the shackled marine. Thomas' mind whirled in a turmoil of stupefied horror and fury, paralysed and impotent, as the four soldiers raised their rifles to the firing position, pointing at the wretched marine whose face still stretched in a smile as though enjoying a secret joke. The German officer raised his hand and Thomas' heart stopped. The hand dropped, but the command 'Fire' unheard as the four rifles volleyed as one, shattering the eerie silence. He watched as Browning's body crashed back against the wall and then rebounded as if in slow motion, to hang, head bowed on a bloodied chest, almost in a kneeling position, suspended only by his shackled arms.

'Bastards' Thomas shrieked, blood from a bitten lip spraying through clenched teeth. 'Bastards, bastards, bastards.' It was only the firm pressure of the guard's hands forcing him into the wall that prevented him from smashing his head against the iron bars in pure seething anger as tears of frustration and sorrow poured from his pain-filled eyes that stared, unbelievingly, as big as saucers. He was in no doubt they had made him witness the callous murder intentionally, presumably in an attempt to weaken his resolve. Well, he thought, they'd made a gross miscalculation. They would get nothing from him now, and the quicker they put him out of his misery the better. With all his men gone he wanted nothing more than to join them.

The pressure on his shoulder blades eased as the two brutes pulled him away from the window and turned him around, inane grins of sadistic gratification splitting their gorilla-like features. His anger erupted, he wanted to smash the evil grins through to the back of their bull necks, but his manacled wrists never lifted above waist level before a huge paw back-handed him across the face in an unsuccessful attempt at decapitation. His neck seemed to stretch, then recoil like a weak spring and it felt as though his skull imploded. He wanted to scream vile abuse at his tormentors but his mouth flooded with the sweet viscid taste of the blood that oozed from the corners of his mouth. He was like putty in their hands as he fought to cling to consciousness. Somewhere in the back of his spinning brain he heard one of them shout something so guttural that it sounded as if he were hawking spit from his throat. Whatever it was, it was rewarded by an incongruously girlish giggle from his mountainous colleague. At least *they* were enjoying themselves, he thought, as his bare toes were once again dragged over the stone flooring.

There was a touch of déjà vu about the room they bundled him into. Despite the semi-darkness his blurred vision made out the steel table, its bareness spotlighted by the narrow beam of light from the ceiling bulb. Two hands on his shoulders pushed him down onto the uncushioned wooden chair that his bare bottom recognised. Yes, he had been here before. He felt suddenly very tired, but strangely not afraid. He'd gone beyond caring. They could do their worst now; the sooner the better.

For several minutes he sat there, his dazed mind drifting off into a sort of dream-like mist, his body held back in the chair by the unyielding grip of his silent guards, then a door opened beyond the table and quickly shut again before he could raise his head. The hands on his shoulders tensed and the shaded light swung slightly in a zephyr of draft. He felt sure someone had come in but still it remained silent, like sitting in an empty church. Several moments passed, the only sounds being the quiet rasp of controlled breathing from the guards standing behind him, one on either side, and the heavy beat of his own heart still pumping a trickle of blood from the gash inside his mouth. His eyes tried to pierce the sombre shadows beyond the light but there was no movement.

If someone was there he was being very clever in creating an atmosphere of menacing intimidation.

A sudden screech of chair legs scraping the floor made him jump and he sensed, rather than saw, someone sit quietly down on the other side of the table, beyond the light; yet still he felt no fear. Apart from the dull thumping ache of his battered head it was as though all his nerves and feelings were numb. It was several more moments before a disembodied voice broke the heavy silence.

'Lieutenant Thomas?' it said, making a question out of a known fact.

The marine stared through the beam of light into the blackness beyond. 'Bollocks' he spluttered, dribbling blood down his chin onto his battledress blouse and bare thighs. He had forgotten he was naked from the waist down and wondered why he wasn't feeling the cold. The expected retaliatory blow from behind never materialised; only more silence, which was unnerving to say the least.

'You really are being stupid you know, Thomas' said the voice. 'We know who you are and the names of your men. We know your unit and your objective, and *you* know that all of your men are dead. There is nothing more you can tell us of any value, except your escape plans.'

There was a long pause, and then like the bow of a ship emerging from a dense fog, the gaunt face of the speaker appeared over the table from the shadow, its glaring eyes and sagging cheeks heavily shaded by the imperceptibly swinging ceiling light.

Thomas stared back fearlessly; he had accepted his fate and only wanted to be reunited with his men again. Besides which, he wasn't going to show fear to this grotesque German.

'Jesus' he replied. 'You're bloody ugly.'

He heard a sharp intake of breath as the skeletal head disappeared back into the black fog, and relaxed his tensed muscles, feeling better now that he had let the scrawny runt know he wasn't to be intimidated.

'Do you want to die, Thomas?' asked the German from the darkness. 'Do you really hope to save a few Frenchmen who we will get eventually, with or without your help? All you need to tell is who, and where, you were to meet and we will send you to an officer's POW camp to spend the rest of the war in relative comfort. Not too much to ask, is it?' he sneered.

Thomas wasn't listening; his shocked mind still picturing Browning's slumped body in the courtyard, the mangled corpse of Nook and the bloodless face of Pearman both drowned in the river - for what? - To get more medals and honours for some brass-bound, red-tabbed desk wallah in Whitehall who had murdered his lads just as surely as the Germans.

I wonder where the chaps are right now, he asked himself. Probably having a good laugh at his expense and supping their beers wherever dead marines go for a drink. He smiled. Would that be upstairs or down?

The smile on his prisoner's face infuriated Hauptsturmfuhrer Kluger sat scowling in the dark, cracking his knuckles in frustration. Was the Englander being deliberately obtuse, or had he lost his reason? The two stupid guards had no right, or authority, to beat their captive without his knowledge; he'd sort them out as soon as he finished here. Perhaps a few winters in the trenches would be in order. He turned his attention back to the British officer. He had to get results, and soon.

'Well, Thomas. Are you going to talk to me or must I force it out of you?'

His only answer was a dull, almost amused stare.

'Put your hands on the table, Lieutenant, and spread your fingers,' ordered Kluger. 'Let us see how steady your nerves really are.'

Obediently, Thomas allowed his guards to lift his manacled hands onto the table and spread his fingers, palm down. He knew his nerves were rock steady. He would show this Kraut.

There was a movement at his side and the flash of a bare arm, and he felt the crunch of fragmented bone. He looked down and saw the hammer's head resting on what remained of his shattered forefinger. Shock delayed the immediate pain but when it came it shot up his arm like a surge of high voltage electricity. He sensed he was screaming but it sounded as though it came from somewhere else, in the far distance. He tried to withdraw his cuffed hands, to cradle his mangled finger to his chest, wanting to stop the agonising throb of returning circulation that felt like a knife repeatedly stabbing the back of his hand, but his arms wouldn't work. His whole body seemed paralysed as if in a nightmarish stupor, unaware the guards were still holding his hands on the table.

'Well?' asked Kluger, ominously.

Thomas spat the blood from his mouth to answer, unintentionally showering it over the table and splattering his interrogator who saw it as a deliberate act of defiance. Kruger gave another nod of his head and again the arm flashed as the hammer descended on the marine's left forefinger to detonate excruciatingly, like an explosive.

The marine stared trancelike at the mashed fingers, wanting to ask God for the strength to withstand the torturous agony. He pleaded for His mercy, then realised he didn't believe there was a god; never had. Was now the time to start? He mumbled his apology for ever doubting the Lord's existence, and asked for forgiveness.

'What did you say?' demanded the German, thinking the Englishman's ramblings were addressed to him.

Thomas dropped his chin onto his chest and shook his head. He didn't want to talk; his brain wasn't functioning and the pain from his hands obliterated every other thought.

'Answer me,' screamed Kluger in desperation. His career and reputation were in the balance if this pathetic man didn't talk. How could he report his failure to the Obersturmbahnfuhrer? He shouted an order to the two guards who released the Englishman's hands and hauled him to his feet where one supported him as the other gleefully began to pummel his body with fists like a railway engine's buffers.

Thomas only felt the first few blows that pounded his stomach and chest. Then he vomited and emptied his bladder as everything went numb. His attacker began to sweat with effort and Thomas watched the fists sink into his body without any feeling, as if with another's eyes. He knew most people have a breaking point, even the bravest of the brave, but he stayed unconcerned. He no longer felt human. He would die soon and he wanted to do so without betraying anyone; it was the least he could do as he waited the approach of the dark grave of death. He felt he was falling, falling into a black pit. Somewhere in the back of his mind the voices of past instructors were telling him he had to remain silent for twenty-four hours, for his own survival and to give others the chance to escape – *But there are no others* – he screamed silently within his brain – *and I don't want to survive. Not now.* He heard shouting and felt himself drop – or thrown – to the floor. A booted foot kicked him hard in the ribs and he felt bones snap. A stabbing pain lanced his side causing him to curl up on the floor like a tortured animal and he prayed for an end to the suffering. But it was not to be; not yet. Renewed agony pierced his side as he felt himself hauled upright, stretching his broken ribs.

'Please,' he gasped through the red mist of pain threatening to envelope him, and turned to face his tormentors.

The harsh voice of Kluger seemed to rise in volume, starting from a faraway whisper until it exploded violently against his ear. 'Tell me about the French' he yelled, his hawkish nose within inches of Thomas' bloody face. 'Or you will suffer more pain that you could ever imagine possible. You will die a thousand deaths and plead for mercy before I've finished with you, unless you talk.'

The marine sensed the closeness of his torturer and saw the blurred outline hovering over him, like a vulture. A frenzy of anger surged up inside his brutalised body and he tried to hawk phlegm up from his throat to spit at the demented face, but he had neither the strength nor the ability.

Another excruciating pain shot up his leg as a studded boot stamped hard on his bare foot breaking more bones. His knees gave way and he slumped, barely conscious, in the supporting hands of his two warders. As his head dropped forward, a fist – it could only have been Kruger's – came up from the floor and slammed into his already battered face. Surprisingly, it felt more of a stunning shock than painful. He tried to inhale through the broken nose and failed, then through his blood-filled mouth. He wanted to spit his defiance at Kluger, but couldn't even manage a puff as the free-flowing gore poured from his nostrils and split upper lip. Fighting waves of fear and pain he struggled to breath, moving his head from side to side, but each move earned yet another punch from his persecutors. He tried remaining still, forcing breath into tortured lungs that were clamouring for air. During a short pause he tensed every nerve for the onslaught he knew was still to come; they weren't finished with him yet. Then the blows began again. He felt the dull thudding impact of each blow a fraction of a second before the searing pain that followed, until it merged into one overwhelming agony that eventually ebbed away as the blackness engulfed him.

How long he had been unconscious he didn't know, but he became aware of being dragged by the feet, face down, along the stone floor as renewed waves of agony swept through his broken body. There wasn't a nerve, muscle or bone that didn't hurt. He had passed his pain threshold and knew nothing more could hurt him as he silently commended his soul to his newly-found God.

At the door of his cell, the two guards dropped him, callously banging a further wound on his forehead against the side of the door as they opened it with a jangling of keys. He was flung inside in the manner of being thrown into the sea, cannoning off the wall to end up like a rag doll strewn across the floor. Every bruise, every cut, every battered muscle flared in maddening agony. His whole body seemed to be on fire burning the flesh from his bones until, mercifully, his brain succumbed and he dropped into the welcoming arms of oblivion.

Chapter Nineteen.

A burning pain tearing at the muscles of his stomach woke Corporal Pearman with a start. Instinctively he tried to raise his knees to ease the anguish, only for them to hit against the floor of the upturned cart that was now his roof, before they were hardly bent. The shock made him realise where he was but he gave no more thought to it as another gut-rending spasm turned his bowels to water. He gasped as the urgency of his situation became very apparent, and wriggled his way – on shoulders, elbows, backside and heels – out of the tomb-like hide, hoping he would make it outside before he had an accident.

A third agonising cramp, like a bolt of lightning in slow motion, hit him as he emerged and he charged heedlessly from the tumbledown barn, out into the undergrowth. He only just made it. The relief when the almost liquid excreta voided from his body felt as pleasurable as a sexual orgasm as he squatted among the brambles, eyes closed and head bowed in the manner of a silent worshiper. It was only after some blissful moments that he opened his eyes to look up through the canopy of leafless branches above his head. Lumps of dirty cloud, windblown across a dull grey background of sky, seemed to scrape the tree-tops. It was daylight; or at least what passed for daylight in the middle of winter.

A glance at his watch showed it to be two o'clock and his bare arse was beginning to feel the icy coldness. He stood up, hauling his trousers over goose-pimpled legs when, almost immediately, before he could fasten his stubborn fly-buttons, another searing pain contracted his stomach forcing him to drop his trousers and crouch again. Jesus! He cursed, what was wrong with him? He recalled his return from the farmhouse last night and eating the tomato, then scraping the dirt from a potato and removing the worst of the peel before munching it like an apple. Surely that wouldn't have caused his problem? Then he remembered drinking the life-saving rain water from the water butt, and the surface scum he had to push aside to get at it. Of course, that was it! That was what had upset his stomach and gave him the trots. Had his guts been more sensitive and delicate it could have killed him, he supposed. Thank God for the well water.

Twice more he tried to stand, hoping the pain had disappeared, and each time he only managed to half-mast his trousers to knee level before dropping back into the leg-breaking crouch, hissing through clenched teeth as renewed agony ripped his tortured stomach muscles. Irrationally, he wondered if women giving birth suffered like this; if they did he was glad to be a man. Eventually – his bum frozen like a cold jelly – he was able to stand and dress himself; all the time on edge waiting for signs of the gripes returning. How the hell could the Japs commit Hari Kari voluntarily? The thought made him shiver.

Mentally keeping fingers and everything else crossed he shuffled back into the relative warmth of the barn, away from the bitterly cold wind. He felt weak and utterly exhausted as he lowered himself carefully onto the cushioning straw.

Deciding he had no strength or inclination to do anything else, he took a mouthful of water from the watering can and crept gratefully back into the sanctuary of his bed beneath the cart. As he lay there, silently staring up at the dark underside of the rotting cart barely a handbreadth above his nose, sleep evaded him. No wonder, he reasoned, he'd just slept for more than twelve hours.

Resting his hands gently on his tender stomach he began to think about his situation in some detail, and the options available to him. He hadn't the foggiest idea of his whereabouts in France, other than being somewhere north of the River Loire and to the east of Nantes. Which way should he head? Always assuming he could find a method of ascertaining direction. To go westward towards the Atlantic coast would be to invite capture. The Jerries would guess he would go that way and swamp the area with troops. To head north to the English Channel was equally as risky, despite the tantalising appeal of getting nearer home with every step. No, he decided. There would most likely be dozens of escaping soldiers, sailors and airmen in that area with the Gestapo thick on the ground searching for them. East was out of the question, he didn't want to get nearer Germany. So, south it would be, towards neutral Spain, if he could find his way. Maybe there would be fewer German down that way, and perhaps it would be easier to contact the Resistance people; there must be hundreds of them down there. On second thoughts, he'd go east for a bit, to get away from Nantes, and then turn south.

Awkwardly, because of the lack of space, he went through the contents of his pockets one at a time to muster his possessions, such as they were. They consisted of the small ball of string from the farmhouse, a box of sodden matches ruined by his swim in the river, an escape compass that pointed in a different direction each time he looked at it and therefore useless, his commando dagger in its leg sheath and one hundred French francs wrapped in a durex. Plus, his trusty *Everrite* watch that could be used as a makeshift compass - *if* the sun ever came out - a dirty handkerchief and – surprise, surprise – a small tube of Ovaltine tablets he had forgotten about. His other assets, apart from the boots on his feet, the plimsolls and his uniform clothing, were meagre. Two raw potatoes, three tomatoes, some vegetables that looked like carrots but tasted more like turnips, three paper sacks that he intended to use as protective clothing and, most valuable of all – his can of water. He popped three of the Ovaltine tablets into his mouth and chewed them hoping they would settle his churning stomach, then realised his stupidity. There were only seven left and they might have to last him for a very long time. Against his better judgement he decided he would have to make another visit to the farmhouse after dark; providing his upset stomach allowed. There must be more food and things he could acquire from there before he moved on.

Thoughts of food brought back memories of the tantalising cooking smells from the farmhouse last night and his mind wandered to the delicious Sunday roasts the wonderful Mrs. Montague served up for "her lads" in her crowded dining room at Southsea. There were times, he recalled, that they had even left some of the meals because of earlier over indulgence at the *Granada* pub where the landlord boasted of the finest liquid breakfast west of Suez; and of course he was right. Such were the dreams rolling about in his mind as he drifted into an exhausted sleep.

It was pitch-dark when he awoke and his first thoughts were for his stomach. Was it still upset? Was he going to suffer a repeat of the debilitating diarrhoea? He rested his hands on his belly, fingers probing gently for the slightest sign. So far, so good. It still felt bloody sore and tender inside but as yet, none of the crippling pain seemed apparent.

Lifting his left hand close to his nose he tried to make out the time but no amount of wrist-twisting could persuade the luminous hands of his Everrite to reveal their secret. He was full of a great longing to curl up in the warm hay again and go back to sleep – like forever – and it was only by an effort of will that he wriggled his way out.

The night was as black as a witch's heart. Overhead, heaving lumps of cloud – fractionally lighter than the darkness of the wood – tumbled so low they appeared to be passing through the barren tree branches that quivered in the raw wind and howled eerily through the many cracks and gaps in the barn wall. Pearman shuddered. Only nature's own noises disturbed the inhospitable desolation.

Picking up one of the paper sacks taken from the farmhouse he slashed the bottom open with his knife and stepped into it like a skirt, securing it around his waist with a length of string. With the second sack he cut a smaller slit in the bottom for his head and two holes in the corners for his arms and slipped it on, his head emerging like an inquisitive turtle. With this also tied around his waist he began to feel the warming benefit; the oil impregnated paper being impervious to the piercing wind. He cut the third sack down the full length of one side. This would act as a hooded cape to keep his head warm and dry when it rained. He was beginning to feel almost human again. If only he could find something better than the dead German's oversize boots for his feet and get over the weakness of his Gyppy tummy.

Several hours later, estimating the time to be well past the bedtime of the people in the farmhouse, he changed the boots for his plimsolls and retraced his steps of last evening. Still keeping cautiously in the shadows of the hedgerow he felt more confident, knowing where he was going; grateful there were no dogs to raise the alarm and give him heart failure. With a little care and stealth, he thought, it should be possible to give the place a thorough search without rousing the occupants. Would he dare enter the house? Probably not. He was desperately hungry, but not enough to risk capture so soon, even though he could do serious damage to a plate of fish and chips.

Skirting the woodpile, he crept towards the hut containing the rusty tractor, wondering what else he might find in there. With cold fingers he reached out and lifted the wooden latch, tentatively pulling at the door. Nothing moved. Anxiously he pulled harder creating a short squeal of protest from the rusted hinges. He stopped and held his breath, hoping the squeak hadn't been heard above the wailing wind, then pushed the door closed again and dropped the latch. That was a definite no-no. Too bloody noisy.

Working his way warily over to the next barn he paused at the water-butt, silently cursing it for the pain and discomfort it had given him. A few feet along, on the side hidden from the farmhouse, he found a door with a latch that thankfully lifted noiselessly. Gingerly he pulled and the door opened with a low groan that wouldn't carry far, and in any case could have been mistaken for a million other things like a swaying bough. Crab-wise, he slid in through the narrow gap and started to feel his way unhurriedly around the walls and shelves that held a variety of tins and pots filled with unknown contents, best left alone. In the centre stood a solid wood table that his sweeping hands discovered was completely bare except for an enamel jug about eighteen inches tall that would easily hold a gallon or two of water. His probing fingers brushed over its chipped lip and warily dipped inside as he prayed it would not contain some sort of corrosive acid – it was empty. Much relieved he took possession; it was better than a watering-can, and easier to carry.

Disappointed at not finding anything of real value – like food – he left the jug at the side of the water-butt and edged his way over to what he now thought of as 'the woman's barn'. As he reached for the latch, a brief break in the low clouds allowed a dim glimmer from the blanketed moon to light the courtyard and give just enough time for him to glance at his watch. It was eleven forty-five.

Certain that the farmer's family would be snoring their heads off by now, he opened the barn door and entered with the deliberate slowness of someone feeling their way through a minefield, his hands and feet sweeping for any sign of obstruction as he worked his way along the wall shelving, touching and smelling the dozens of pots, tins and packets, searching for anything he may have missed on his previous visit. He found nothing except a string bag and an old beret that he stuffed in his pocket. Turning his attention to the central table, his fingers explored every inch. Nothing had changed since yesterday, so he filled the string bag with several more tomatoes, potatoes and the other turnipy carroty things.

Beneath the table, his foot touched an object. He knelt down awkwardly, encumbered by his new fashion paper outfit, and found a pair of Wellington boots, heavy with dried mud. Sadly his joy was shattered as he tried one on; it was far too small. He stood up to consider if there were any ways to possibly alter them; like cutting the toes off, but immediately dismissed the idea as being a quick way to loose his toes through frostbite. It was then that a short, sharp pain shot through his stomach, doubling him up and taking his breath away. It died away for a second then returned with a vengeance as he threw himself outside in a panic, barely avoiding an accident as he ripped his string belts, paper skirt and trousers down around his ankles. With relief came depression and as he squatted, elbows on knees, head in hands, he wondered how the hell he would be able to move across country in such a state. No way could he remain hidden in his barn for ever. He would have to give himself up to Jerry if it didn't improve, or make an open approach to the French in the hope they would be friendly. He even considered trying *this* farmhouse, it was as good as any, but as the griping pains ebbed so his senses returned. No, damn it! he thought. He'd crawl all the way to Spain trailing his shit behind him if necessary rather than surrender himself voluntarily.

Adjusting his dress he collected the enamel jug from the water-butt and anxiously tip-toed across the open courtyard to the well. The bucket still stood on the wall but to his dismay it was almost empty. Not wishing to trust his luck with the noisy winch he lowered the bucket by hand on its rope. It was a hell of a long way down, and even longer coming up. Inexperienced in such matters, he filled the bucket to its brim and had no way of spilling any out as he hauled its heavy weight up, hand over hand, his tender stomach pressing painfully against the edge of the wall. Even his hardened hands were sore by the time his aching back and arms heaved the slopping bucket out and down onto the cobbles so that he could drink a couple of cupped handfuls before rinsing out the jug and filling it.

He looked longingly at the two barn-like buildings on the far side of the farmhouse, wondering what goodies they may contain, fantasising about the possibility of eggs, or even bread and cheese. With a great deal of regret, his common-sense advised against any investigation. Firstly, he would be pushing his luck; he might disturb noisy chickens - or even worse - cackling bloody geese. Secondly, and more important, his watery guts and aching stomach might not hold out. The sooner he returned to the privacy of his own barn the better.

Carrying his ill-gotten gains he made his way back to his hide, leaving behind – had he but known it – what could have been a safe house, and the care and comfort of a lonely woman. He hadn't seen her white face in the corner of the bedroom window watching his every move, her mind torn between wanting to call him inside, and fear.

Luckily he made it back without any emergency stops on the way, although there were two false alarms – more painful than false - and gratefully he crawled back into the warmth of the straw bed where he lay, savouring the juicy pulp of a tomato; his mind a kaleidoscope of worries. One thing was a certainty in his mind, there would be no more staggering blindly along paths and through woods at night. Now that he had covering for his uniform he was determined to start moving by day. After all, he reasoned, who in their right mind would be suspicious of a tramp dressed in paper sacks and carrying a jug of water? And if he were stopped and questioned by the Jerries he could always pretend to be a dumb itinerant, couldn't he? Was he that good an actor? Okay, so when would he start on his way? He'd have to leave that decision until the morning to see if his guts improved. He closed his eyes, tired and very weakened by his disabling condition, but still he couldn't sleep.

He would have sworn to not having slept a wink when another racking pain stabbed him. Scrabbling from under the cart like an inverted beetle he almost made it to the scrub – almost but not quite – and he had to spend a cold, bum-freezing few minutes trying to clean himself and his clothes as best he could with a few handfuls of straw. It was only then that he realised it was dawn and instinctively noted the direction where the lead-grey sky looked brightest. Now he knew which way was east, not that it mattered at that precise moment, he wasn't going anywhere yet; not in his state. He felt dizzy and nauseous squatting among the undergrowth with watery faeces draining from him. His exposed bottom half was freezing in the cold wind, but his head and top half burned hot and feverish. Please God, he prayed, it was nothing more serious than a touch of gastric infection, or food poisoning that would soon pass. He felt so weak and his knees trembled with effort as he rose and struggled back inside the barn to collapse half in and half out of his bed, his head swimming almost deliriously. His last conscious thought was that Jerry would have no trouble finding him now. And he didn't care.

Chapter Twenty.

Hauptsturmfuhrer Horst Kluger stood rigidly at attention nursing his bruised knuckles, very aware of his pounding heart and trembling knees as he stared at a spot on the wall above the head of the officer sat behind the large, ornate desk kissing the tips of his steepled fingers. His pulses had started to race when he first received the summons to Rhomdahl's office. He had been waiting with trepidation for the response to his report of failure to extract any information from the British officer, and was in no doubt as to what he should expect. Rhomdahl would rant and rave, and hurl verbal abuse at him for incompetence and threaten to send him to some remote mud-filled trench in the front line. His boss was a vicious, vindictive brute, and Kluger was well acquainted with his senior's feelings towards him, as had been made perfectly clear on more than one occasion in the past. He knew people considered him as not physically suitable to wear the coveted black uniform of the S.S. – especially Obersturmbannfuhrer Rhomdal - yet, in his own mind he knew, that what he lacked in appearance he made up for in superior intellect - far superior to that of the oaf sat at the desk judging his ability. He drew a small crumb of comfort in the fact that someone, somewhere, had recognised his intelligence and mental usefulness, otherwise he would not even *be* in the S.S. Naturally, he envied his contemporaries, most of whom were fine physical specimens of blonde-headed Arians and former Hitler Youth, who looked so magnificently menacing in all black, trying to conceal their lack of brainpower behind a façade of intimidation and – in most cases – awesome power. It was a power they enjoyed exerting, even over officers of superior rank in the Wehrmacht, Luftwaffe and Kriegsmarine. As far as he was concerned he felt like a professor among imbeciles, yet nevertheless for the first time in his living memory the cold fingers of fear touch his spine.

Much to his surprise and astonishment things hadn't turned out as expected. Rhomdahl had sat perfectly still, listening to his account without as much as an interruption as he described his interrogation of the British officer, and detailing the physical methods used to force him to talk.

'All my efforts were in vain, Herr Obersturmbannfuhrer' he whined, totally confounded by the uncharacteristic attitude of this infamous despot. 'The Englander *wanted* to die. *Wanted* us to kill him. There was no mistaking his determination to remain silent, no matter what we did to him.'

Rhomdahl raised his head until the fingers supported his chin, his squinting, cold-grey eyes boring into his subordinate's face like rays of solid steel. He had nothing but loathing for the skinny runt who was a disgrace to his S.S. uniform, and regarded him with open contempt. 'Do you think – perhaps in hindsight – that your tactics could have been er-different?' he asked in an ominous whisper, inclining his head questioningly.

'No, Herr Obersturmbannfuhrer. I do not,' answered Kluger with false confidence. 'The man has resigned himself to his death.' He nearly went on to say more but sensibly decided the least said the better. Nothing he could say would alter what Rhomdahl had in mind for him. He knew he had been pre-judged, found guilty, and sentenced to whatever this evil man considered suitable. His fate had already been decided, even before entering the office.

Rhomdahl dropped his hands onto the arms of the buttoned-leather swivel chair and stood up, stretching to gain every terrorising millimetre of height. 'And that is your professional opinion?' he mocked, turning to face the portrait of Adolph Hitler hanging ever so slightly askew on the wall and raising a finger to adjust it.

'Yes, Obersturmbannfuhrer. It is.'

There was a long pause of consideration before Rhomdahl turned around to face his wretched inferior, his face wrinkled with controlled anger. He sniffed. 'As you have failed so utterly in your present duty Kluger' he snarled, 'perhaps you will be more successful in doing something different.' He sat back in the chair, a sneer of sadistic self-satisfaction tightening his upper lip against unseen teeth. 'I have two tasks that you will fulfil for me…and the Fuhrer.'

Kluger clenched his hands until the nails dug into his palms, sending shooting pains up his arm from a throbbing fist - he had convinced himself that he had a broken bone in there somewhere - and every muscle tensed. He was not a stupid man, something awful was forthcoming and his heart sank like a lead weight. What did this callous animal have in mind?

Rhomdahl gripped the lapels of his immaculate tunic, very lightly so as not to crease the material, thumbs twitching. 'You will take the prisoner to Point Eight this afternoon' he said, 'and execute him yourself, by order of the Fuhrer. You will then submit a written report to me that you have done so.' There was a short hesitation as though he were conjuring up additional malevolence. 'Oh yes!' he added. 'You may as well get rid of the French woman at the same time.'

Kluger felt stunned. This was something he wasn't expecting. He had never personally killed a man, let alone a woman - albeit that she was a terrorist who had murdered three German soldiers - and his skin crawled. He ground his teeth, and a surge of anger that he dared not show, boiled in his gut. This bastard intended to keep his own record clean by ordering him to do the dirty work and report, in writing, an action that would convict him as a war criminal in a Court of Law, should the unthinkable happen and the Fatherland lose the war. But he had no option. He must obey a direct order….or get shot himself.

'Your second task' said Rhomdahl, warming to his vindictive revenge and obviously relishing Kluger's humiliation. 'Will be to clear your office and pack your bags… tomorrow will do. Your inefficiency has earned you a position of more-er-interest.' He made a dismissive gesture with a wave of his hand, adding 'My report on your service record will not make good reading Kluger, but you have brought it upon yourself.' He allowed himself a smug smile as the door closed behind the contemptible little man. The insignificant, almost effeminate weakling had been a thorn in his side for some time. Anyone can brutalise people, he thought, nothing clever in that; but to physically extract information from an unwilling captive was an art form. Perhaps a spell of duty in a concentration camp for Jews would teach him a few lessons – although perhaps not…. He will probably enjoy it.

When the guards came for Thomas he was barely conscious. For what seemed like hours he had been laying on the cold slab of his cell floor wearing nothing but a sodden shirt and battledress blouse, but with no sensation of pain or coldness. His shocked nervous system had shut down, his body numb, yet in the back of his brain a small awareness still flickered as they bent down to take hold of his wrists. He couldn't stand by his own effort, he had no strength. They didn't necessarily want him on his feet anyhow.

Pulling him out by the hands they dragged him from the building, uncaringly scraping his bare thighs on a rough concrete path, to a waiting lorry. Despite being a dead-weight in their hands they lifted him as easily as they would a broken doll and threw him into the back of the vehicle like a bag of rubbish. He landed awkwardly, banging the back of his head, and tried to shift his reluctant body into a better position. It was then that he felt a soft hand touch his face like a soothing brush of silk and looked up at the battered face of a woman floating over him like a wounded angel. She lifted his shoulders and shuffled her knees under him so that his head rested on her lap. He tried to speak, to say hello and thank her, but couldn't. Tenderly she caressed his swollen face with bloodied, nail-less fingers and began to rock him in the manner of mother and child, humming softly and leaning over him as a lock of her tangled hair fell onto his cheek.

A warm feeling of compassion began to flow from deep within him at the presence of this comforting human being and he struggled to raise his own mangled fingers to touch hers. Her tears fell on his cracked lips and he forced his tongue to peep out to taste their sweetness. Who was this woman? he wondered, as four armed soldiers climbed into the truck stepping carefully to avoid the two shattered bodies on the floor.

With an inexpert grinding of gears the vehicle lurched forward on its journey to…. where? How long the trip lasted he neither knew nor cared. Intuitively he knew this was his last journey, his last few moments on earth, and he had no doubt that this brave, brutalised women knew the same. The drive seemed relatively smooth until they came off the road onto a rutted track that bounced them violently around the unyielding steel floor. They sensed the soldiers trying to help as best they could by using their legs as braces, but none of them spoke; probably under orders not to. Thomas heard his lady angel give a sharp cry of pain and felt so impotently useless, incapable of giving her any comfort; instinctively wanting to protect her in a natural masculine way, but it was she who provided the succour.

When the truck eventually came to a juddering stop the four young soldiers solicitously edged around them and – after lowering the tailboard – jumped down to the ground. Between the four of them they gently eased Thomas out and laid him on the damp grass, and were helping the woman with equal care when an officer appeared from an escorting car, screaming at them to hurry and get her off. Under the supervision of the demented officer, Thomas and the woman were taken across the field, supported – almost carried – by the soldiers who bound them securely to a pair of trees. Thomas looked up through the waving branches at the racing clouds thinking that in a few short minutes from now his soul, and that of the woman, would be winging its way up through those same clouds. What would happen to their bodies? Would they be buried here, forgotten and undiscovered, in this remote corner of France? He wished it could be an English field that would soak up his blood; preferably in Dorset overlooking the Channel, or maybe in Kent near a hop-smelling oasthouse. This wintry countryside was not his first choice for a final resting place.

He turned his head to look at the woman, trying to give her as much of a comforting smile as his broken jaw and split lips would permit. Her eyes met his - were they blue? - and tears rolled down her bruised cheek as a brave smile lit her face. I bet she had been a beauty before Jerry had added his own brand of make-up, thought Thomas.

They were still looking at each other, these two strangers, when the rifles fired.

Not far away, a sixty-year old shepherd – alerted by the sound of the approaching vehicles – was crouched hidden in the undergrowth wrapped in an old army greatcoat, its huge collar up around his ears like the walls of a castle. Stunned, he watched as the soldiers carried two bodies – one a half naked man in a military type blouse, and the other a woman – from a lorry parked on the far side of the field, across to two trees a few dozen paces to his left. Under the orders of a yelling officer the soldiers roped the two people to the trees, then stepped back with their rifles to form a line facing them. The reality of what was taking place before his eyes hit him like a thunderbolt and he nearly jumped to his feet in angry protest. The Germans were going to shoot the poor souls!

On a shouted command the soldiers raised their rifles to their shoulders, tilting their helmeted heads to sight along the barrels. The officer lifted his hand and held it there as though to deliberately prolong the wait. His shout and the sharp bark of the rifles were simultaneous, and tears cascaded down the shepherd's whiskered face as the two bodies slumped down into the binding ropes. Two of the soldiers handed their weapons to the others and went to release the bodies one at a time, lowering them almost reverently to the ground. The officer stepped forward, strutting like a peacock, obviously not appreciating the mud ruining his highly polished jackboots and, unholstering his pistol, shot the dead man in the head. The troops turned to face away as the officer moved over to the woman and bent over to lift her skirt. For several seconds he leered at her naked thighs then flicked the skirt back down.

In the hedgerow the enraged shepherd etched the officer's face deep on his memory and vowed that, for that one act alone, he – Daniel Mordan, formerly of the elite 120th Regiment of Bombardiers and now an active member of the newly formed Maquis - would ensure this particular Nazi would die a most painful death.

He closed his eyes. He could not witness the next callous act of putting a bullet into the woman's head. She was already dead, thank God.

Chapter Twenty One.

Hunched in an old cane armchair drawn up to her bedroom window, and wrapped in the blankets from the bed, Adele sat with her forearms spread across the sill staring reflectively out onto the dark emptiness of the courtyard below, unable to sleep even though feeling tired and drained of all energy.

With each passing day, she tried hard not to let the drudgery of her life get her down. The wearying routine of rising at five every morning, seven days a week, was taking its toll. Caring for the animals, cleaning the grate, lighting the fire, tidy the house and prepare the meals for the day before waking Jules and helping him wash and dress, was just the start. Only then could she allow herself a short rest for breakfast prior to starting the unending work on the farm. That, apart from another short break for a snack lunch, comprised her normal day until the evening when Jules would call her in for dinner. Cooking the main meal of the day was one of the few things he could manage, for which she felt grateful.

By six, or soon after, having bedded Jules down for the night, she would be huddled in her own bed enjoying an exhausted, dreamless sleep…..normally. But life over the last twenty-four hours had not been normal, far from it! The excitement of last night's furtive shadow around the well – that she was now convinced was that of an escaping Allied soldier or airman – still remained vividly in her memory and had been all day long; sending her mind into a whirl of wild fantasies instead of concentrating on her chores. Even in the barn, in the dull mid-morning light, she felt herself blush embarrassingly with wanton thoughts.

'Mon Dieu' she said, half aloud, scolding herself for such shamelessness and thinking she was already an adulteress, in thought if not in deed. Now, late into the night, sat by the window in her bedroom, she thought back to the last lunch-time at the scrubbed-wood table with Jules.

In the usual homely atmosphere of companionable chitchat, they sat at the table sharing their few precious moments of quality time together holding hands, talking of the past with a mixture of love and sadness, of the present with worry and concern, and of the future with hope. During the meal she had looked deep into Jules' sad eyes and felt ashamed and guilty over her impure thoughts. His life was far worse than hers. At least she enjoyed good health and had endless chores to keep her mind occupied. He, on the other hand, had nothing but her and the pencil drawings he was so good at. What was he thinking? she wondered. Were his loving and sometimes pain-filled eyes reading her mind? Could he sense her mental infidelity and the needs pulsing through her veins? She tried to console herself that her cravings were only for sex; she loved Jules, and yet she yearned for…..?

It was then than a sharp rap on the kitchen door made her jump up from the table with a start and look at Jules with the wide eyes of a frightened rabbit; they rarely had visitors. Her first thoughts, and fears, being that the caller would be her shadowy, phantom lover. Jules raised questioning eyebrows and nodded towards the door. Blood pounded in her breast. What would she say if it were him? With trembling hands she lifted the latch and pulled.

'Bonjour, Madame Montange. Sorry to disturb you.'

With a flood of relief, Adele saw the uniformed figure of the aging Albert Dongalue standing there touching the peak of his kepi that looked as though it were sitting on top of a ledge of thick bushy eyebrows, with a forefinger in polite salute. At sixty-four years of age he was well passed retirement age but happy to have retained his position – albeit temporarily – as the local gendarme.

'Bonjour, M'sieur,' replied Adele breathlessly, stepping back as an unspoken gesture for the policemen to enter and inviting him to join them at the table. Gratefully he accepted. His legs and back were aching from the two-mile cycle ride from the village. He wasn't getting any younger and this was only his second call of the day! Removing his cape, he draped it over the back of a chair and then took off the cap to reveal a contrasting, almost bald head with just a few wispy strands of thin hair above the long tangle of eyebrows. He stooped sideways and placed his cap on the floor beside his chair.

After the usual round of pleasantries and enquiries as to their well-being, he laid his notebook on the table and flipped open the pages with a pencil, feeling unusually uncomfortable at visiting this couple who he had not seen for a long time. He had been stationed in the area for many years so of course he knew of their tragic circumstances and frugal lifestyle, that's why he refused their offer of refreshments with the excuse he was on duty.

Apprehensively, the Montagnes watched as the policeman came to the last entry in his notebook and scribbled something in it. They had no idea of the reason for his visit – it could not be anything good!

Dongalue looked up, crimping his gaunt cheeks and stubbled chin in a tired grin. 'Have you heard about the British raid at Nantes the other night?' he asked loudly for Jules' sake, hunching his shoulders and leaning forward conspiratorially.

The Montagnes shook their heads dumbly. How could they have heard anything about anything? Visitors were as rare as snow in the desert and Adele could not remember the last time she had seen a newspaper. They waited patiently for the policeman – who was a great believer in the saying "people are ignorant if they didn't know something you had just learned" - to continue.

'They were soldiers' he said with a touch of amazement in his voice. 'Not aeroplanes.'

Again the Montagnes waited with growing impatience as the gendarme fidgeted on his chair, leaning over first one way and then the other to remove the cycle clips from the bottoms of his trousers. The thought of how British soldiers came to be in France never entered Adele's unmilitary mind but the frown lines on Jules' forehead indicated his questioning brain was already asking...... *How?*

'They sank two ships and damaged a few more' exaggerated Dongalue, getting into his stride as a story-teller. 'Some of the soldiers were captured, some got away, and I've been ordered to tell everybody in this neighbourhood to be on the lookout and report anything unusual.'

Adele gave a short gasp and raised her hand to her mouth to quickly disguise it as a cough; a loud voice in the back of her head shouting *'That's who he is!'*

'Such as?' queried Jules, still frowning.

'Anything at all. Anything suspicious, or out of the ordinary. Unusual noises or things missing. You know what I mean!'

Adele cleared the lump in her throat. 'And what' she asked, 'do you expect us to do *if* we see or hear anything?'

The gendarme dropped his eyes and spent a few seconds scraping dirt from under his finger nails with the nail of his thumb. He had no reason to doubt the patriotism of the Montanges. He knew they were as loyal to France as he himself was, yet one could not be too careful. In the early days of the occupation, many sought to line their pockets or curry favour with the Boche by denouncing fellow Frenchmen for the least indiscretion or remotely subversive word or action. Caution must be his watchword. In his position, he could fulfil a minor - possibly important - role for France; but he had to obey German orders, or at least be seen to do so. He would not wish to lose the job, and certainly had no desire to face a firing squad like some poor souls he had heard about. The ordinary Germans were not too bad and tried to act with correct decency, but the S.S. and Geheime Feldpolizie were inhuman bastards. He knew, he had to work with them! He coughed politely into his fist. 'If you do, and wish to report it to me officially, then I will act officially and do my duty,' he said, choosing his words carefully with as much innuendo as he could. "The choice will be yours, but I must warn you that the Germans intend to severely punish anyone found harbouring or assisting these men in any way.'

Jules, equally as cautious, lifted his chin and inhaled a deep breath. He was a Frenchman and proud of it, and no way would he collaborate with the hated Boche who had crippled him for life and then occupied his country. In his condition there were very few things he could do but, he vowed, collaboration wasn't one of them. He had known Albert Dongalue since well before the war. In fact he felt indebted to the old man for not reporting a minor illegality he had committed once on his motor-cycle.

'What do you mean by *officially*, M'sieur Dongalue?'

The policeman chewed his lip, pausing to consider a suitably ambiguous reply. This was getting into dangerous waters. Yet, he told himself, if he could not trust these good people whom could he trust? Unfortunately there were others involved, others to be considered, other lives at risk. Could he take the chance? He decided he could.

'Well, M'sieur Montagne' he said quietly, causing Jules to lean his head forward and to one side. 'If there were things you didn't consider worth reporting officially, but still wished to mention as casual interest, you could do one of two things.' He scratched an imagined itch on the back of his hand. 'You can either talk to Father Lorrette the village priest, or invite me for an off-duty glass of wine.' There, he had said it now! Committed himself and placed his future in the hands of these two – hopefully – good people.

For several moments, the policeman sat nervously twiddling his thumbs, with niggling doubts as to his own wisdom in getting involved. Jules, who had followed the conversation mainly by lip reading, was delighted at having found what he believed to be a kindred spirit. He also felt concerned by the look he had seen on his wife's face. She looked – disturbed? Surely she wasn't afraid?

Adele, feeling her face redden and fighting to control the flush of emotion brought on by the news, could sense her husband's concerned eyes staring at her. She knew she looked flustered – she felt it! She had to do something, say something, to allay his suspicion. 'Do you think they would be dangerous?' she asked in a little girl's voice.

Jules stretched out his hand, seeking hers comfortingly and gently squeezing it. 'Of course not' he said with a tight smile.

'No, Madame,' said the officer in an attempt to re-assure what he saw as her understandable fear. 'Your husband is quite right. In the unlikely event they are anywhere in this area, they will be scared for their own lives. Apparently, so I am informed, there are thousands of troops out looking for them, so their first priority will be to get away as far as they possibly can. The last thing they will want is to be seen, and they are probably expert at hiding themselves. No, Madame,' he emphasized. 'They will be more scared than dangerous, believe me.'

'Poor devils must be frozen in this weather,' said Jules in the sort of loud voice normally used by the partially deaf. 'Unless they have planned to meet up with - ah - friendly people.' He arched his eyebrows almost questioningly and looked directly into the gendarmes eyes. 'I believe such people exist, don't they?'

The officer shook his head slowly, trying desperately to think up a non-committal reply, feeling his way through a veritable minefield of potential hazards. There was something almost overtly challenging in the crippled farmer's query.

'They probably do,' he answered, closing his notebook and pushing himself to his feet. 'But I must get on. I have to visit so many people. Still, better me than the Boche –eh?' He laughed, and took a step forward to place a restraining hand on the shoulder of Jules who had reached for his crutch and began struggling to get up. 'Stay where you are, M'sieur. I can see myself out.'

Adele opened the door for him, letting in a blast of bitter wind as the officer threw his cape around his thin shoulders and replaced the cap on his bushy eyebrows. 'Thank you, M'sieur,' she said.

He pause for just a second, not wanting her to keep the door open any longer than necessary. Her eyes had a strange, almost pleading look that he found disquieting. Was she trying to say something to him? He touched the peak of his cap, courteously. 'Remember that I am not always on duty Madame,' he said, stepping out into the bleak courtyard, hoping his comment would not be lost on this obviously troubled lady who, it appeared, desperately wanted a shoulder to cry on.

The rest of Adele's day had been a blur of confused thoughts. The soldier was probably miles away by now – long gone. But what if he wasn't? What if he returned to the well tonight? How would she know if he did? She couldn't stay awake, on watch, all night. And if she did, what would she do? What could she do? So many questions, so few answers. The stress brought on the beginnings of a headache that became progressively worse, so it was with grateful relief that she eventually climbed the stairs that evening after clearing away the detritus of the meal and getting Jules settled with almost indecent haste, using her pounding head as an excuse. She had looked out of her window, briefly and hopefully, at the black shape of the well but the thumping ache at the back of her eyes sent her to the healing comfort of her bed and unexpectedly fell asleep as soon as her head felt the soothing balm of her pillow.

She woke with a start, relieved to find her headache gone. Was it five o'clock already? Had her body clock woken her to start another depressing day? She turned her head to look out of the uncurtained window, sensing something was not quite right. It didn't *look* like five o'clock! Wrapping a blanket around her shoulders she crossed to the window wishing she had a clock to verify the time. Had it been something else that had woken her? Had it been a strange noise? A sixth sense, or a woman's intuition? Whatever it was she knew she would never get back to sleep again. It was then she took the other blanket from the bed and dragging her one and only armchair up to the window curled herself into it, like the picture of a Mexican Indian having a siesta she had seen in a magazine many years ago.

Nothing moved in the sombre courtyard below her window. Nothing but the fleeting shadows of the night as the black clouds flew overhead like an angry ocean. Listening to the wind whistling through the gaps in the window frame where the paper she had jammed in had come out, her mind drifted between thoughts of the British soldiers out there in the bitter night, to Jules and the gendarme who had clearly been trying to give her a message. Even to the Boche themselves who – in her limited experience – seemed no better or worse than anyone else. Nevertheless, she hated them for what they had done to her, to her marriage and to her country, but what could she do except survive and hope for better times to come.

She jumped, like a frog, almost out of her chair as a shadow – more dense than the others - moved slowly across the cobbled yard. With a beating heart and racing pulse she leaned forward until her forehead touched the cold surface of the glass. With each passing second the figure grew into a solid shape but to her dismay it wasn't the uniformed silhouette of her previous night's visitor. It looked more like a traditional tramp wrapped in cardboard, or paper. Or was it? Could it be her soldier? Had he found some sort of material to cover his uniform and keep out the cold? She watched with heaving breasts as he disappeared behind the roof of the well and it seemed ages before he reappeared to tip-toe back across the yard to the water butt where he bent down and lifted something. Straining her eyes in the darkness, frightened she would lose sight of what was rapidly becoming an indistinct blur, she followed his movement around the woodpile into the camouflaging background of the hedgerow. Staring unblinkingly hard, she felt sure of seeing a head bob above the outline of the bushes several times. So, she thought with a mixture of satisfaction and excitement, he was hiding in the woods at the bottom of the field. Her heart sank like a lead weight. She would never find him in there, especially if he was an expert at concealment. Nevertheless, she decided, in the morning daylight she would go down to the wood and just walk around making friendly noises.

Perhaps, only perhaps, he may be tempted to reveal himself. Apart from her other feelings she genuinely wanted to help, to keep him out of the clutches of the Boche and, maybe, into hers. Then, in a flash of memory, she remembered the barn just inside the edge of the wood. Of course, that's where he'd be. She had not been down there for well over a year and it was probably a ruin now, but it would provide shelter and warmth for the soldier who she now thought of as *her man*. Tomorrow first thing – or was it today – straight after breakfast, as soon as it was light enough, she'd go down there and see. Getting back into bed with dreams filling her head and every nerve tingling, she slowly fell into a restless sleep.

Despite her disturbed night, the automatic alarm of her mental clock still jangled its customary routine call, and instinctively – this time - she knew it was five o'clock as she sat up and twisted around to put her feet on the bare floor, shivering in the cold air after the warmth of her bed. Quickly throwing off her nightgown she dressed, her heart palpitating as she recalled the night's events, and the prospects of the day to come with the possibility of meeting her soldier.

In the bone-chilling early morning freshness, she went about seeing to the needs of her animals – always a priority in her mind – by the dim inadequate light of her hand-held oil lamp. Then, back in the comparative warmth of the house away from the numbing wind, she knelt before the ash-filled fireplace to scoop out the cold grey clinker into a bucket. It was a chore she hated more than most, but with a skill born of daily practice she soon had the kindling burning and began placing the split logs onto the spitting fire, waiting to ensure they caught alight and, as always, seeing so many images in the dancing flames that cast their flickering glow around the gloomy room.

In the kitchen, standing over the stone sink preparing the vegetables that Jules would cook for the evening meal, her thoughts drifted off again, imagining a romantic meeting with her soldier in a sunlit wooded vale, he in a smart military uniform and she in a beautiful new dress that flared out coquettishly as she danced for him, happy to see the longing in his eyes and the need in his outstretched arms.

Inattentively she splashed dirty water from the sink down the front of her skirt. She stepped back to brush it away and suddenly felt ashamed of her tatty but clean clothes. Her wardrobe of clothing was small, virtually non-existent, and what she did have was old, outdated and very much the worse for wear. God only knew when she would be able to afford more – if ever. She dreaded the thought of anyone, least of all her soldier, seeing her like it. A hot flush coloured her throat and neck as she thought of the underwear she had on. Practical and warm they were; feminine they were not. Jules was the only man ever to see her in underwear and that was a long time ago. They were sexy in those days, deliberately so, and made her feel good. There was no doubting that they pleased Jules too. She would die if anyone were to see them now; not that there was a chance of that happening – was there?

Sat at the table eating his frugal breakfast Jules appeared to be in good spirits, almost animated, chatting away to Adele mainly about yesterday's visit from the gendarme and the improbability of anything happening in their neck of the woods.

'They'll be long gone by now,' he said knowingly, referring to the British soldiers involved in the raid. 'It will have been planned down to the last detail, probably with our people being involved in their escape in some way. The "Rosbifs" don't go in for suicide missions. Well, not in my experience anyhow.'

Guiltily, Adele rose from the table with the two empty plates, feeling slightly annoyed. Of all the mornings to be talkative he had to choose this one, when she wanted to get away. She was determined to visit the old barn as soon as full daylight made it possible, and there were jobs to do first. Excitement put butterflies in her stomach and impatience made her irritable.

'You're probably right,' she called from the kitchen, putting her threadbare coat and muddied over-shoes back on. 'Anyway, must get on. See you later,' she added stepping out into the grey yard wrapping a thick woollen scarf around her head and ears and closing the door behind her, gently.

In the dark potting shed, working on the real priority jobs by the light of the flickering lamp, she watched through the dirty window as what would have been the dawn came slowly and grudgingly; each passing minute adding to her growing anticipation. She knew, without doubt, he had been in this very shed, things were missing, and the thought of his being so close caused her to tremble with pleasurable fantasies.

After an hour her excitement became irrepressible. Outside it was as light as it would ever be and no longer could she contain her impatience. Her shaking hands lifted the latch. Would she be brave enough to go through with it?

Without so much as a look back over her shoulder at the house she walked the length of the field, her shoes leaving a trail of scuffed tracks in the crisp, virgin hoarfrost on the grass, her heart beating like a drum as though to give warning of her approach. Nearing the wood she saw, through the bare leafless branches of the trees and bushes, the dark outline of the old barn and a shiver of apprehension fluttered her nerves. She could hear no sound, nor see any sign of movement other than the rustling of the wavering treetops. A gap in the bushes that looked freshly made, attracted her attention and cautiously she high-stepped through it trying to avoid catching her shabby coat on the groping branches. Tip-toeing to the broken door she paused, eyes and ears alert. Her nose crinkled. The clean fresh air now carried a tainted, unpleasant smell coming from inside the ramshackle shed and she wondered how – if – anyone could live in there. As she edged her way inside, the revolting smell grew stronger and she cupped her hand over her mouth. It smelled like a sewer pit.

Slowly her eyes became accustomed to the gloom but all she could see was what appeared to be the wreck of the upturned cart she vaguely remembered being dumped here when its wheel broke, and piles of mouldy, stinking hay; certainly no sign of life. With a mixture of relief and disappointment, she was about to turn away when a movement – almost at her feet – made her jump back, frightening the life out of her and making her already pounding heart race like a frenzied drum-tattoo. She gasped a mouthful of the fetid stench, retching as it hit the back of her throat, and looked down at the dark shape on the floor. Realising it was a human being she quickly recovered her equilibrium, controlling shattered nerves, allowing her natural caring instincts of mothering and nursing – although she was neither – to come to the fore.

The man, for it was a man, lay curled tightly in the foetal position, his face buried in hay against his knees. Fighting off waves of sickness generated from the revolting smell, Adele took hold of the man's shoulder to turn him so that she could see his face. As she did so, he began to shiver violently, twitching, his closed eyes screwed up in pain. His forehead felt boiling hot to her touch and there was no doubting he had messed himself. It didn't need a doctor to tell her the man had a raging fever and was very, very ill. She panicked, momentarily; what should she do? Obviously he needed help and medical care urgently, and logic told her that what help she couldn't give, she must get.

Overcoming her revulsion, and trying to recover her self-control without breathing, she took off her coat and tucked it around the sick man, thinking ruefully that this was not the way her fantasies had envisaged their meeting. Taking one last look at him she hurried out of the barn, carelessly brushing through the short path and out onto the field. To get help for the poor man was her only thought, but she had no idea from where, or how, as she ran back to the farmhouse, heedless of the biting wind needling through her jumper and skirt.

Chapter Twenty Two.

Life had not been kind, decided Jules. He was suffering from one of the increasingly frequent bouts of self-pity that he considered himself entitled. The stinging pain in his hip and the never ceasing throb that pulsed through his brain were gradually driving him crazy. At times, it felt as if his eyes were bulging from his head. There was no getting away from it. It was with him for ever and he wondered how long he could bear it. He was useless, of no use to anyone, least of all to Adele. His life was nothing except pain and misery, and if it were not for her love he would end it tomorrow, somehow.

He shrunk his head deeper into the rough collar of his well-worn army greatcoat like an indolent tortoise retiring inside its carapace. Even the crackling log fire did little to warm him as he sat staring with blank concentration into the smouldering embers, his cold fingers moulded around the stub of pencil, periodically adding another line or scribbling more shading to the drawing of farm animals grazing in a summer field, balanced on his wasted lap.

He always tried desperately hard to put on a brave face in front of Adele. She had to live her own life of misery and hardship, looking after him and the farm, trying to make ends meet, working like a slave from dawn to dusk. But at times, when alone, virtually helpless with nothing to do and no future to speak of, he easily succumbed to deep depressions. Tears filled his weary eyes, he loved her so much yet felt worthless and effete; just another mouth to feed. If only he could do something to help make her life easier, but there was no way. He was physically useless, sexually impotent and mentally...... boring? He could barely struggle on his crutches as far as the well, or to the toilet. Even standing for more than a few minutes was agony.

He looked down at the covering of his thin trousers, his watery eyes seeing the emaciated legs, just skin and bone, all muscle wasted away. They'd never be any different, ever. Probably get worse. Not for the first time he contemplated suicide – but how? He could not consider anything bloody or violent. She would be the one to find him and that would make it even worse for her, and he could not think of an alternative method. Of course she would suffer and grieve, and hopefully miss him, but eventually time would heal and she'd get over it. In the long term, it would be better for her without the millstone of his crippled body around her neck. He ran stiff fingers through his tangled hair, feeling the deadness of the scar where the Boche bullet had torn away half his scalp just before another had ripped into his back, shattering his pelvis. How had he survived? *Why* had he survived? He closed his eyes, listening to the wind. Those brave stretcher bearers who had dragged him to the field hospital had done him no favours.

The loud clack of the door latch made him jump half out of his chair, and he grabbed at the drawing that almost fell from his lap into the fireplace. Wide-eyed, he turned to see Adele stumble in, cold, coatless and obviously distressed, her hands reaching out as she staggered towards him.

'Mon Dieu, Adele,' he shouted fearfully, holding out his hand to her. 'What on earth's the matter?'

She fell to her knees, burying her head in his lap as she sobbed out the full story of the British soldier, sparing him the details of her own turbulent emotions. 'He is so sick, Jules. We must do something for him quickly.'

He placed a comforting hand on her head, wishing he could take her in his arms and kiss her cares and worries away. He knew she had been troubled over something these last twenty-four hours, the trouble he had related to fear. Why hadn't she told him earlier? Wisely he decided not to ask; now was not the time. He must think of how they could help the soldier….if only for her sake.

'Take the velo, my love. Ride to the village and tell Father Lorrette. We can trust him; he will know what to do.' He struggled out of his greatcoat. 'Here, put this on or you'll freeze to death.' Nodding numbly, she did his bidding and left wordlessly, hugging the coat tightly and gratefully about her chilled body. Even though old, it was still better than the one that now covered the sick Englishman.

Crossing the yard to what had once been the cowshed, she hauled the ancient and rarely used bicycle from beneath a tarpaulin and checked the tyres, finding them almost flat. Cursing, she snatched the air pump from the frame and hastily inflated them with just enough air to take her weight. Still breathless from the run across the field and her energetic pumping, she wheeled the creaking bicycle out onto the hedge-lined country lane. It had been a long time since she last rode it, and felt grateful that it was all downhill to the village as she pressed hard on the pedals causing the chain to slip on the worn cog with a jerking crack. Fighting against the icy wind, standing on the pedals and wobbling violently from side to side across the narrow lane, she gradually gained enough speed to enable her to attain proper control and sit down onto the hard, uncomfortable saddle to ease the strain on her leg muscles. If it was not for the damn headwind, she thought, she would be freewheeling along the gently sloping lane at a fair rate instead of puffing and panting with her skirt pressed hard against her thighs, like a tent on a windy ridge.

Less than half a mile from the village, rounding the last bend in the narrow lane, she nearly ran into a small stationary military truck and a group of four armed German soldiers. Braking hard to a slow juddering halt, the brake-blocks grinding noisily against the rusty wheel-rims, she almost collided with a baby-faced soldier who stood his ground before her erratic approach and giving an officious signal that looked almost like a Nazi salute.

'Bonjour, M'mselle,' he said in an atrocious guttural accent that probably used up all his French vocabulary, not taking his eyes off the outline of her legs beneath the plastered skirt. 'Papieren bitte.'

'*Madame!*' corrected Adele, haughtily, pulling at the overcoat to cover over her skirt. 'My papers are at home. I came out in a hurry.'

The young soldier looked confused. He hadn't understood a word she said. 'Papieren, bitte,' he repeated, politely, in the slow style of speech that people use when talking to foreigners.

She leaned the bike against her hip and raised her arms sideways, palms facing the young German. 'I haven't got them with me.'

Seeing the young man's puzzled embarrassment, a middle-aged soldier with chevrons on his sleeve stepped out from behind the vehicle and walked towards her. 'May I see your identity papers please, Madame,' he requested courteously in passable French.

Adele repeated that she had left them at home, having left in a hurry. Her husband was unwell, she told him, and in her panic, she had not given them a thought. She was on her way to the village to see Father Lorrette who acted as an unofficial, and untrained, chemist-cum-doctor in the absence of both in such a small village.

'Please open your coat, Madame.'

She undid the only two remaining buttons and held the front open for his inspection. 'No machine guns,' she smiled, disarmingly.

'Army?' he queried, arching his eyebrows under the rim of his helmet and feeling the coat's lapel between finger and thumb, trying not to return her smile in response to her brave joke.

'Yes, M'sieur,' she answered with a nod. 'It's my husband's. He was badly wounded at Dunkerque.'

'Merci, Madame,' he said, stepping to one side and gesturing her to pass with a gallant military salute. 'My apologies.'

Gathering speed after another cranking start she puffed out her numb cheeks and blew a huge sigh of relief. She had heard that travelling without papers was considered a serious offence by the Germans. Perhaps they weren't *all* bad!

The streets of the village were empty with no sign of life as she screeched to a halt, scuffing her heels on the ground, outside of Father Lorrette's house. Propping the velo against one of the two moss-covered stone pillars that guarded the gate-less entrance to the small, yet imposing building, she crunched her way up the short, pebbled driveway to the front door.

'Yes, Madame?' demanded the imperious voice of the wizened lady who answered the door.

Adele suppressed a smile, amused that such an authoritative sound could come from someone who looked like a stick-insect in an over-sized dress. 'I'd like to see Father Lorrette, please.'

'He's out.'

Adele paused for a moment, hopefully waiting for further information that wasn't to be forthcoming. 'When will he be back?'

The face, like wrinkled paper, stayed without expression. 'No idea, Madame. Try again tomorrow' she said, slowly closing the door, dismissively.

Muttering an unchristian like ingratitude to the exasperating woman, Adele returned to her bike. What could she do now? The nearest doctor lived miles away in a town half-way to Nantes. Her soldier would be dead by the time she rode there and back. And who's to say the doctor would come anyhow? He might even report her to the Germans, or the Gendarmerie. The thought of the latter reminded her of Albert Dongalue's remarks yesterday. Would he help if she asked him – unofficially? Mentally crossing every finger she made her decision. There was only one way to find out.

Two minutes later she scuffed to a stop outside of his grey-stone cottage, very relieved to see smoke streaming downwind from a single chimney and his bicycle leaning against the ivy covered wall beside the door. The thought of what she would do had he not been at home had been worrying her during the short journey through the village.

He answered the door in shirtsleeves, with braces dangling down from the waist of his trousers and a crooked briar pipe hanging precariously from the corner of his mouth.

'Madame Montange,' he uttered, removing the pipe and blowing smoke sideways from pursed lips, surprised to see the distraught woman standing on his doorstep and immediately sensing a problem. 'Please, come in.'

A blazing log fire warmed the cosy living room, and electric lighting made everything bright and cheerful as the gendarme ushered Adele to an upholstered armchair that he drew close to the fire. Exhausted, and chilled to the marrow, she sank into its comfortable depth extending numbed fingers to the leaping flames.

'Can I get you a drink, Madame? Perhaps you'd like something hot?'

Adele shook her head, dragging her eyes from the soporific glow of the fire. 'No, M'sieur, thank you. I call on a matter of great urgency. Please help me?'

He sat down in his own armchair facing her, reaching out to hold her hand protectively - fatherly. It saddened him to see this lovely young woman so obviously distressed. 'Tell me how?' he asked, although he had a feeling he already knew.

Rapidly she related the story, falling over her words in haste. 'There's no time to waste,' she urged with pleading eyes, clutching his hand between hers. 'The man is dying.'

He placed his pipe on the small side table and their four hands linked together. 'Stay here and thaw out for a few minutes' he invited, squeezing her hands gently. 'Go home when you are ready and stop worrying. Everything will be all right. I know where to find Father Lorrette. We will do whatever is necessary.' He stood, and hooked the braces up over his shoulders. 'Would you be able to have this sick man in your house until he is well enough to be moved?'

Without a second thought, Adele nodded. 'Of course.'

'You do appreciate the risk?'

Again she nodded, knowing Jules would eagerly agree. He would feel he was doing something useful and worthwhile, and to hell with the Boche.

'Good,' acknowledged the officer with a tight grin, 'and we will see what can be done to help out.' He leaned forward and put a hand on her shoulder. 'Don't worry Madam, you are among friends now.' With that he turned and left the room, his footsteps clumping up the stairs, and she heard the floor boards creak above her head.

Feeling the wonderful warmth from the fire seeping through into every fibre of her body, and knowing things were going to be done by people who knew what they were doing, she began to relax, letting the cosiness envelope her like a fleece blanket. Woman-like, she surveyed the room. Clean and orderly, it was the home of a tidy man, yet something was missing. Suddenly it became obvious; it lacked a feminine touch. Only a silver framed photograph of a handsome middle-aged lady that stood on the mantle over the fireplace gave relief from total masculinity, and even that had a piece of black ribbon across one corner. She heard his tread coming back down the stairs.

'Don't forget what I said,' he called, poking his head around the door. 'Stop worrying and go home when you're ready.'

He shut the door and then the front door slammed. He was gone and she must go too, soon. Just a few minutes more. Jules would be anxiously waiting, and the soldier getting nearer to death. Involuntarily she shivered as though someone had walked over her grave, and she prayed it was not an ill omen.

The German roadblock had gone by the time she reached the bend. One less obstacle to overcome, she thought, standing on the pedals that kept clanking as the straining chain slipped over the worn teeth of the rear-wheel cog. Rarely able to sit on the uncomfortable saddle, the uphill struggle soon had her breathless as her aching legs pumped the wobbling bike along the lane aided only by the ever increasing wind at her back.

As expected, Jules whole-heartedly supported her decision, and they agreed the soldier would have her room so as not to be disturbed during the daytime. She would make-up a bed for herself under the living room table, near Jules, but they both knew most of her time would be spent nursing the soldier. She threw another log on the fire and curled up on the floor at Jules' feet. With more than a touch of envy she gazed around her sparse impoverished home comparing it with the homely comfort of the policeman's.

The waiting for help to arrive seemed an eternity. She could not dispel the image of the sick man curled up alone in the barn, from her mind. He was probably dying while she sat in front of a blazing fire. How was she to clean him up before putting him in her bed? There was no way could she do it in the house. She asked Jules if he had any ideas.

'Why not use the table in the potting shed,' he suggested, 'I am sure the people who are coming will wait long enough to move the man into the house and upstairs, afterwards.'

Adele thought this the best solution - actually she could think of no other – and began putting on the army coat to go out to the shed when a tap-tapping came on the front door. She opened it, grateful and relieved to see it was her expected visitors, and gestured for them to enter.

'Bonjour M'sieur, Madame,' chorused Father Lorrette, Albert Dongalue and two elderly gentlemen carrying a stretcher, almost in unison. They all looked exhausted after their ride up to the farm.

The Father, a portly man with a thick fringe of hair hung over a low forehead, looked every inch a man of the cloth. 'Bless you my child,' he panted taking her hand, 'Will you show us the way?'

Buttoning her coat and slipping into her overshoes, Adele led the way across the field, explaining the mess the soldier was in and her dilemma for getting him clean.

'Worry not, Madame,' said Father Lorrette in the manner of an undertaker contemplating an embalming. 'We will see to that. May I suggest you return and clear the shed table? We will need water – warm if possible – and cloths, and a blanket or two.' He had obviously assumed command of the situation and the others clearly accepted his leadership.

An hour later, with Pearman's washed body wrapped in clean sheets and blankets peacefully sleeping upstairs, the six of them sat around the kitchen table drinking a bottle of red wine that the Father had mysteriously produced from beneath the folds of his flowing gown.
Outside the window it began to get dark.
'Well!' said the gendarme softly, as though not to disturb the sleeping man upstairs, and raising his glass in salute. 'Here's to us, and to hell with the Boche.'
'Amen to that,' responded Father Lorrette surprisingly, looking around at the etched lines of exhaustion on the tired faces that cracked into smiles at his unexpected blessing. He paused, staring into the bottom of his empty glass as if seeking divine guidance. 'We should be going now.'
Adele stood with her four angels of mercy. 'Thank you all, so very much,' she said, her voice thick with emotion.'
'We will look after him.' called Jules, although he was beginning to worry about the question of *how?* as the four trooped outside to their bicycles leaning against the side wall.
'Stop fretting, my child,' said the Father solemnly, placing his hand reassuringly on Adele's upper arm. 'A doctor will call tomorrow and I will organise a helping hand for you, and some food. Later on we will think about clothing for the English marine, and as soon as he can be moved we will get him on his way back home.'
'Marine, Father?' she queried, failing to sound unconcerned.
He smiled at her transparent interest. 'Yes, my child. He is a naval soldier and worth saving perhaps? Take good care of him, he won't be with you for too long.' He turned to go, then stopped again. 'There were some other things left in the barn that the Germans would be interested in, including a pair of their soldier's boots. They have been disposed of safely,' he added, 'along with his British uniform.'

Chapter Twenty-Three.

All that night, in the glow of a turned-down oil lamp, Adele sat sleepless in the armchair alongside her soldier's bed, huddled like an orphan, cold and cramped, fearful of disturbing the sick man who's condition alternated between periods of death-like sleep - that caused her to frequently check if he was still breathing – and frighteningly violent shivering, twitching and incoherent mutterings during which she sat on the side of the bed bathing his forehead and crooning soft, soothing words as if he were a fretful child. Once – and only once – as he began to settle after a particularly bad spell, she lay beside him on top of the bedding to give added warmth and comfort, and as he became quiet and drifted off into a silent sleep, so did she.

She woke with a start, her heart beating with premonition, and a crawling shame began welling up inside her when she found herself huddled up to her soldier with an arm and a leg thrown across his still body. Fearfully inching her fingers over his chest she touched his exposed neck to feel the slow pulse that brought a surge of relief. She had no idea how long she had been asleep but assured herself it could not have been very long as she eased her chilled body off the bed back onto the unwelcoming chair, wantonly wishing she could undress and slip beneath the blankets to cuddle into her soldier's naked body. The very thought sent every nerve tingling and filled her mind with lustful fantasies. She longed to be touched and loved, to feel his body on hers, moving, wanting her.

Sat sideways with knees tucked up under her chin she dragged the hem of her dress down around her ankles to cut out the icy draught that found its way into the smallest gap, wishing there were more blankets in the empty cupboard, or a roaring fire in the equally empty grate. Stretching her neck she peered over the collar of the greatcoat that was doing little to keep her warm. He lay motionless, no physical response whatsoever, and guilt replaced her shameless thoughts. The poor man was seriously ill and all she could think of was adulterous sex. It was disgraceful, disgusting, and yet………

When her body-clock told her it was five o'clock she stood and wrapped the greatcoat tightly around her shivering body. She'd never been so cold. What had been a long endless night, now – in retrospect – seemed to have passed quickly, so she must have slept some of the time although it didn't feel that way. She was still dead tired and every aching muscle felt stiff, but the animals needed her attention. The sounds of a howling wind screeching through the ill-fitting window, and the thrashing of wind-lashed tree tops outside, gave her no incentive to move as she looked longingly at the shapeless heap of bedclothes and the white face buried deep in the vee of a pillow. At least he had made it through the night, she thought, creeping down the creaking wooden stairs as quietly as possible to where Jules lay snoring in front of the cold, grey ashes in the fireplace. Her feelings of guilt returned. What had poor Jules done to deserve such a selfish, unfaithful wife? Hadn't he suffered enough? She must control her emotion or it would all end in tears.

Wrapping a heavy woollen scarf around her neck and head, and toeing her feet into a pair of damp rubber boots, she gently lifted the door latch to slip out into the freezing early-morning wind.

A heavy rat-a-tat on the front door woke Jules and it took some moments for him to collect his senses. It was daylight – or a grey pretence of daylight – and he was still in bed! Easing himself up into a sitting position and twisting to place his bare feet on the floor, he felt the returning pain of his hip wound and winced as it ripped around his pelvis. With tight lips he tried to take his body-weight on his hands, closing his eyes as the nail-biting spasms made him light-headed. It was always the same first thing in the morning, and didn't get any better as the day went on unless he stayed laid down, which he was determined not to do. He had long ago reconciled himself to the fact it would never improve, and would probably get worse; he'd live with it as best he could.

He opened his eyes. The logs in the grate burned merrily as he stood resting his hand on the stone fireplace, thoughtfully gazing into the crackling flames that gave an illusion of warmth to the cold room. Where was Adele? He hadn't heard her light the fire. Why hadn't she woken him?

Rat - a - tat.

Pulling a blanket around his stooped shoulders and leaning heavily against the wall, he edged painfully towards the door.

'Bonjour, M'sieur Montagne' greeted the old man stood on the doorstep alongside a woman of equal vintage clutching a wicker basket in her gloved hands. 'Father Lorrette sent us to help you while you are – er – busy.' His wizened, bewiskered face – just visible beneath a huge beret pulled down over his ears and eyebrows – looked pinched and drawn; not surprising as they had just walked up from the village. An elongated dew-drop dangled momentarily from the end of his beak-like nose before being wiped away with the cuff of the over-sized greatcoat that still wore the faded badges of some obscure French army unit as he nodded his hidden forehead towards his companion. 'Voici ma femme, Marie,' he said raising his rheumy eyes imploringly. 'May we come in?'

'Oh! please, yes, sorry,' flustered Jules, stepping back and holding on to the door for support. 'Sorry, I didn't mean to be rude.'

The pair shuffled past him and made straight for the fireplace, extending their mittened hands into the flames.

Jules shut the door and reached for his crutch. His head was beginning to throb. 'I'm sorry' he said to the two hunched backs obliterating the fire, 'I don't know where Madame Montagne is at the moment.'

The old lady unwound the thick scarf from around her neck and pushed back the hood of her threadbare coat to reveal an unsmiling face of wrinkled parchment beneath a head of thin grey hair. Her veined eyes surveyed the room with professional interest, taking in the unmade bed and the blanket-shrouded Jules. 'Have you had breakfast yet?' she croaked.

Jules shook his head at her small, yet commanding figure.

'You get yourself dressed while I find my way around' she ordered, already opening cupboards and drawers to check their contents. 'And Henri will need to know what needs to be done outside.'

'Bonjour M'sieur, Madame. Bonjour Jules.'

They all turned to see the bleary-eyed Adele coming down the stairs in her stockinged feet. She had gone upstairs to check on her patient after lighting the living room fire, sat down for a second, and fallen asleep.

'Ah! There you are darling,' answered Jules, his face lighting up with pleasure. 'This is M'sieur……..' he turned to the old man questioningly.

'Erignan, Madame. Henri Erignan,' said the old man, bowing slightly. 'And this is my wife Marie.'

Jules turned his eyes back to Adele who now stood at the foot of the stairs holding out her hand to the old couple. 'They've been sent by Father……..'

'You get yourself back upstairs my dear' interrupted Marie Erignan waving a knobbly forefinger at Adele. 'You look worn out. I'll call you when breakfast is ready.' She had obviously been well briefed.

'But…..' began Adele, guiltily.

'No buts, Madame' snapped the old woman who they were to get to know as a sweet, caring person. 'Do as you are told. I've all I need here.' She waved the same bent finger at the wicker basket standing on the table as she busied herself around the kitchen. 'And you, M'sieur, can make a list for Henri of jobs that need doing' she said bossily, then adding, 'after he's had his breakfast.'

Thirty minutes later, the four were sat around the kitchen table pushing away their empty plates and breathing in the air still wonderfully heavy with the smells of fried eggs and bacon given, Madame Erignan assured them, by Father Lorrette.

Henri scraped his chair back over the stone floor and clasped his scrawny hands across the lap of his work-worn overalls. 'That was *some* meal,' he said appreciatively, looking at his wife with a small smile that creased the corners of his thin mouth.

'Certainly was,' agreed Jules, licking his lips with relish and gleaning every scrap from between his teeth with his tongue.

Adele smiled. 'It was lovely, Marie. Real Rosbif stuff. Thank you.'

Marie glowed, trying to hide her happiness as she placed a couple of new logs on the fire. 'Thank Father Lorrette, not me,' she said, wiping her hands and mouth on a spotless apron. 'Now, you get back upstairs and look after your invalid. We'll be here until after dark and be back tomorrow at nine.'

Adele rose to do as she was bidden just as a heavy knocking rattled the front door. She answered it and raised an eyebrow at the tall, cadaverous man standing there completely enveloped in a thick, expensive coat that reached down to his ankles who raised a leather bag with one hand as the other held on to the brim of a top-hat perched precariously in the wind on a skull-like head.

'Madame Montagne?' he enquired, then continued without waiting for her confirmation. 'Doctor Pelleau. I believe you have a patient for me?' He stepped forward, almost forcing an entry. 'Damn cold out there,' he sniffed. 'Lead on.'

Still in a state of surprised shock Adele obediently led the way upstairs, offering to take the doctor's coat as they entered the bedroom. He declined with a shrug of his narrow shoulders and placed his bag on the bed, opening it as if it were a toolbox.

To the best of her ability, Adele answered his string of questions regarding the sick man's recent history and symptoms as he pulled back the blankets to prod the pale body, listening intently with his stethoscope. Not once was the patient's nationality or profession mentioned, and she wondered with amazement at the extent of Father Lorrette's power and influence.

A surge of embarrassment washed through her, and she felt her face redden as the doctor pulled the blankets down to probe his patient's stomach, groin and testicles. So far all he had said was 'Mmm' a dozen times, which did nothing to allay her fears and concerns. Anxiously she waited for him to say something, anything, and to cover her soldier's nakedness before her blushing became obvious.

Eventually the doctor straightened like a fishing rod that had just lost its 'catch-of-the-day' and stretched thin lips tightly across his gaunt features as if in preparation for making a gloomy announcement. Adele's heart missed a beat.

'Nothing much to worry about Madame' he grunted, rubbing his unshaven jaw between thumb and forefinger, and twitching his aquiline nose from side to side. 'His temperature is very high, but that's to be expected if – as you say – he's been feverish. Physically he's fine and it is likely he has been poisoned through having eaten something he shouldn't have done. Of course, I can't be sure of that until he wakes and can tell me how he feels, but I'm confident that he's suffered a particularly nasty strain of food poisoning, or some-such.

Adele felt almost deflated with relief at the diagnosis. 'Will he be alright, Doctor?' she asked with obvious concern.

The doctor's eyes twinkled, knowingly. 'I think you'll find he'll be fine in a day or two, probably very weak though. Keep him warm and rested. I'm assured by Father Lorrette that he will be well fed and cared for here, but don't leave him alone for the next twenty-four hours or so, just in case he's sick – or something.

Adele forced a smile, a little concerned about the – *'or something'*, knowing she would cope, whatever it was, if she had to.

The doctor handed her a small bottle of tablets. 'When he wakes up, get him to take one of these every four hours. It'll help get rid of the nasties inside him. I'll come back again in two days but in the unlikely event of him needing me before then just contact Father Lorrette.

She followed him downstairs and saw him give a perfunctory nod to the others over his shoulder as he went out of the door and walk around the side of the house. Through the window they saw him climb into an ancient Citroen and drive away with a nonchalant farewell wave, narrowly missing a corner stone and a frightened chicken.

A feeling of unease began to wriggle deep down in Jules' stomach as he listened to his wife relate the doctor's diagnosis to them over a cup of excellent coffee and sandwiches from Marie's basket. He could see she was trying hard to suppress an excitement that he hadn't seen in her for a long time. Her eyes were twinkling and there was joy in her voice. Did she have feelings for the Englishman? Surprisingly he felt no jealousy. He loved her so much and it hurt to see such a lovely, vibrant young woman turning into a drudge with no social life, no passion. He had seen, at times, the efforts she made to hide her feelings, her desires, and the depressions. Luckily for him, there had been no other men to add to her problems, but now the soldier was around. Did *he* excite her? Strangely he almost hoped that was the case. She deserved more than the mental love that was all he could offer. He would do anything to keep her, and to see her happy. Time would tell. He would see how things turned out, and play the cards that were dealt him. If the situation troubled her too much he would talk with her, and try to understand.

Chapter Twenty-Four.

A bright light switching on in the back of his head heralded Eric Pearman's return to the world of the living, and for some seconds he lay staring into a shining mist that slowly dimmed and cleared as his eyeballs began to co-operate and synchronise through lids that blinked like a car's windscreen wipers in a thunderstorm. Gradually, and reluctantly, they focused on what appeared to be a beamed ceiling above his head and it dawned on his recently awakened brain that he was in a bed. Whose? Raising himself up onto his elbows he surveyed the alien surroundings. Apart from the bed, only an ancient wooden wardrobe leaning tiredly against the wall and a cushioned armchair furnished the room. Even the window that framed the wintry outdoor scene was uncurtained and rattled excitedly in a gusty wind. Where the hell was he? He closed his aching eyes to concentrate. The last thing he remembered was staggering back to the barn at the bottom of a field near a farmhouse, feeling like death. What had happened to him after that? He must have been found by someone and brought here….. *but where was here?*

Hearing a noise from the direction of the door he tried to sit up, and some kindly soul started to bash a bloody great brass gong inside his head sending exploding fireworks racing around his skull. He fell back onto the pillow pressing the balls of his hands against his eye sockets, his forehead feeling as though it were bulging like an inflating balloon. He gasped involuntarily, waiting while the pain slowly receded, leaving him exhausted. He thought he felt hands grasping his, pulling them away from his face, and a soothing wet cloth being placed on his brow. So cool, so comforting. He relaxed, letting the brain-storm drain away. Fingers were stroking his stubbled chin with a soft touch of an angel. If this were heaven, he would willingly prolong his visit. But he was not dreaming. The hands were real, and so was the wet cloth. With an effort he opened his eyes, dreading what he would see. Would it be someone in a black uniform with swastikas all over his face and a little square of moustache on his upper lip? Or a red-faced apparition with horns sticking out of his skull like a Viking helmet, breathing fire and brimstone and holding a pronged trident? Please God let it be neither, he prayed, as the spectral mist cleared and the shimmering face hovering over him steadied and settled.

His prayers had been answered, it was neither a Nazi nor Satan, but a beautiful woman sat on the edge of the bed holding his hand, her smiling lips moving soundlessly. Was she real? He crushed his eyebrows together into a deep crevice and closed his eyes to squeeze away what he was convinced was a visual fallacy of a guardian angel; not real at all, just a fantasy in his tormented mind….. wishful thinking?

Anxiously he opened his eyes again expecting the worst, but she was still there, still smiling and talking to him in a soft caressing voice with words he couldn't understand but recognised as French. He wanted to tell her how beautiful she was and ask a million questions, but his mouth would not respond. It tasted like sandpaper from the bottom of a budgie's cage as he tried to lick his parched lips with a tongue like a carpenter's rasp.

As if reading his mind, the angel dabbed water around his mouth and spooned drops of the cold liquid between his lips. He relished the trickle of it down his throat, richer than the finest champagne. Adam's ale, the elixir of life. He wanted more, lots more, and opened his mouth like a hungry chick wanting to be fed. Smilingly she shook her head and wisely continued with the dribbles from the spoon, deliciously tormenting him until he felt better. His head stopped spinning and aching but he was worn-out, dead tired.

Resting his head back onto the pillow he tried to muster up a smile of gratitude but all he could manage was a vague, twitching, re-arrangement of his lips.

He was woken by voices. Voices near him, voices around him, all chattering unintelligibly until his brain kicked into gear – Frogs. He'd recognise the language anywhere. Opening his eyes he raised his head, gratefully realising it no longer hurt, and looked enquiringly around the room at the two hazy figures at the side of the bed. He blinked and re-focused. One was his lovely guardian angel nurse, the other a scrawny man whose head scraped the low ceiling.

'Ha!' grunted the man, leaning over him and wrinkling his nose as though he were examining a particularly obnoxious specimen. 'You waken, goot. I am a doctor. 'ow you feel?' He looked like a skeleton in a long coat and his English was atrocious, heavily accented, but to Pearman the sound of his own language was like music in his ears.

'Where am I, doctor?' he asked, turning to give the woman a quizzical smile and seeing she was not the beautiful angel his addled brain had first imagined, but an ordinary flesh-and-blood woman who was nevertheless very attractive; even though wearing a working dress that had clearly seen better days.

The doctor fiddled about in his valise at the bottom of the bed with long fingers that looked like the claws of a spider crab. 'Firss things firss' he answered, looking up with the protruding eyes of the aforementioned crab. 'Tell me 'ow you feel?'

Pearman suppressed a giggled and nearly replied 'With my hands'. I must be feeling better if I can make a joke, he thought; and the doctor's English was a thousand times better than his own French, so who was he to scoff? He could have been landed with someone with no English at all!

The doctor stood silently listening as Pearman told of his symptoms from the very beginning, relating his visit to the farmhouse and of the things he had eaten, and the water he'd drunk. Suddenly the thought struck him…...*Perhaps this was the farm that he'd stolen from. Perhaps this lady was the owner!* His embarrassment was saved as the doctor began his examination by fumbling with his stethoscope, pressing it heavy-handed on his chest, asking questions all the time; and it was only when the bedclothes were pulled down – thoughtlessly or carelessly – to check his lower half that Pearman realised he was naked. He grabbed at the blanket to preserve his modesty… too late. With a faint smile stretching her lips, the woman turned away and left the room thinking she had already seen all that the Englishman had to offer. The thought renewed her excitement.

'No sink wrong wit you, M'sieur' declared the doctor pulling the covers back over his patient's freezing body. 'No sink that a few days rest and goot French cooking will not cure. Goot job you are a strong, 'ealthy man. Yoost take it easy and let Madame Montagne look after you. She is a goot woman.'

'Thanks doc' said Pearman. 'I'll do as you say.' He sat up cuddling the blankets around his bent knees. 'Now will you tell me where I am, and what's going on?'

The Frenchman stared almost absentmindedly into his valise as though seeing something unusual in it that he had not seen before, then sat on the bottom of the bed to tell the marine all he knew of the recent events and how he came to be here. 'You muss be told….' he added, '….that in the 'ighly unlikely event of you being found by ze Germans it could be bad for Madame Montagne and 'er invalid 'usband.'

'Then I can't stay here' snapped Pearman, starting to pull the bedclothes off. 'I must leave now.'

'You muss do as you are told' said the doctor, restraining the attempt with a shake of his head and glaring eyes. 'You must stay. Many peoples know you are 'ere so you muss remain 'idden for their sake as well as your own.' He stood up, straightening the things in his bag and clicking it shut. 'Now you muss eat. Plis do as you are asked and do not make things difficult. You are among friends 'oo will get you back 'ome as soon as possible.' He turned to the door. 'I will send Madame Montagne up.'

After a few minutes Pearman heard the front-door slam shut and then the sound of footsteps climbing the stairs followed by a soft tap on the door. 'Come in' he called.

The relief that Adele felt on hearing the doctor's favourable report was equalled only by the excitement that set her emotions alight. Her soldier would be fine in a short while, and in the meantime she had nothing to do but care for him and her animals. Henri and Marie Enignan would do everything else, and bring all the food required. It was like being a little girl again, in a dream world with few cares or worries. She wanted to dance and sing. Even Jules was different towards her, encouraging her in her nursing duties, saying the Englishman's welfare was paramount. Not many husbands would allow their wives to sleep in the same bedroom as another man, even under these circumstances. She wondered if Jules was aware of how she felt; wondered if he could sense her excitement. Somehow, deep down, she intuitively knew he did, and understood. He was that sort of man. He would want what was best for her….. wouldn't he?

What would the next few days bring? Would she allow her emotions to override commonsense? And if she did, would her soldier be interested? Maybe he would throw her out of the room in disgust, but somehow……… And what about Jules?

Her heart leapt at the sound of Pearman's voice as he called for her to enter in response to her knock. He was sat up in the bed, the blankets discreetly over his lap, pillows propped up against the bed-head, smiling a broad smile that somehow camouflaged the dark shadows under each eye and the pain lines that etched his face. Her hands, carrying a heavily laden tray, shook, causing the cups to rattle in their saucers and the knives to tinkle against plates as she lowered it onto his lap. The closeness of his bare muscular chest and the musk of his body smell sent her heart into palpitations and her libido into overdrive. Unashamedly, she wanted him there and then. If only he would grab her and pull her into bed with him. Inwardly she was in a state of wanton turmoil; outwardly – she hoped – she gave no sign of her needs, her desires or arousal.

She had brought breakfast for two. A real English breakfast of eggs, bacon, fried bread and beans, that came from God knows where by hand of the wonderful Elignans. It wasn't the kind of food she cared to eat first thing in the morning but it would be what her soldier was used to, so she would share his pleasure….. But not yet; not until her hands stopped shaking.

At first – not having a common language to share – they were both embarrassed in their efforts to communicate using childish mimes and hand signals, pointing at themselves saying 'Me Eric' and 'Je m'appelle Adele,' like Red Indians in a Hollywood western film, but soon the troublesome mimicry became enjoyable and they ended up laughing, and began learning the odd word or two of each other's language; even making up suitable words of their own for things that were unpronounceable. It was fun, the ice broken.

After the meal - that Eric enjoyed and Adele only picked at - Adele stood and reached for the tray with the intention of taking it down to the kitchen where Marie noisily crashed around with her cooking and cleaning chores, but before she touched it Eric's hand shot out, grabbed hers and pulled her firmly to him.

'Thank you, Adele,' he said huskily, releasing her hand and cupping her face between his hands. 'Thank you for saving my life.'

Gently, he drew her toward him and she went willingly, eagerly. Their lips touched in a long, full-blooded, intimate kiss that conveyed their mutual passion and she could feel his arousal under the blankets, against her breast. She was in a whirl of ecstasy, longing to feel his body on hers… but this was not the time. Reluctantly she pulled away from him, her face flushed red, miming the message for him to get well and strong first.

Pearman acknowledged the mime gratefully, understanding the meaning. She was right. Even though aroused, he had no strength. At that very moment he was good for nothing. Certainly his mind was willing but his bodily strength felt like a wet weekend in Ramsgate…a hopeless, useless flop….and she *was* a married woman with a crippled husband. He shouldn't try to take advantage of her vulnerability, he told himself, as he watched her pick up the tray and leave the bedroom.

Gratefully, he dropped his aching head back onto the pillow and closed his eyes. His last thought as he fell into a deep sleep was….*but she seemed willing.*

The look on Adele's face, as she came down the stairs balancing the tray of dirty crockery on the palm of one hand and holding the rail to steady herself with the other, told Jules that his fears – no, not fears, assumptions – had been correct. Her face was glowing; glowing as only a woman who is sexually excited can. Something had happened, but what? Surely the Englishman would be too weak, too drained by his sickness, for it to be anything physical….unless he had unbelievable powers of recuperation, but weren't British marines reputed to be tough?

He watched his wife closely as she sidled into the kitchen, almost as if trying to hide her face and its give-away expression from him. A pang of jealousy gripped his stomach yet he was surprised at its weakness and the lack of any angry reaction, and he thanked God his mind was as sexually dead as his body.

It would be a frustrating hell for both of them if he felt desires that he couldn't physically comply with. He knew his shattered body was impotent. He was no longer a man in that sense of the word, and Adele needed a man. His heart bled for her. She had always been a good, hard working woman, and a loyal, caring wife. She would not *want* to do anything behind his back, no matter what the provocation, but like any normal red-blooded female she had desires that needed fulfilling. He wanted her to be happy and contented, to see her glow. It would make him feel less guilty of his own incapability; providing of course she didn't leave him. He couldn't manage, couldn't cope without her. He would die if she left. She was his life. All he had. All he would ever have.

He took a deep breath, listening to the clatter from the kitchen where Adele and Marie were doing the things women do in kitchens without pausing for a break in their conversation. Both were talking, neither listening. He turned his worrying eyes back to the fireplace, staring unseeing at the spitting logs and the flickering shapes and shadows of the dancing flames, and came to a momentous decision, feeling better for it. This evening, after the Elignans had gone home, he and Adele would talk. He would give her his blessing to do whatever she wanted without cause for guilt. If the Englishman could make her happy – even for a short while – it would be alright with him, providing it was what *she* wanted. He'd also ask to meet the man as soon as he was able to come down the stairs. He wouldn't want him to feel guilt either.

The room was full of darkness when Pearman woke. Rain lashed against the windowpane like pellets from a gun, and somewhere above the howling of the wind, an irregular banging told of a loose door or shutter tormented by the gusts. But it was neither the wind nor the rain that had disturbed his sleep. It was something more urgent, more painful. His bladder was about to burst! Pressing his legs tightly together in an attempt to hold back the tide, he put his feet on the floor and stood, hunched almost doubled over, to wrap a blanket around his shoulders and stagger knock-kneed to the door. 'Jesus' he cursed aloud, panicking at the thought of reaching bursting point before getting to a toilet.

'Hello,' he called urgently down into the black void of the stairway, the effort increasing the unbearable pressure. He had seconds before exploding.

Her anxious face appeared, looking up from the foot of the stairs.

'Toilet, please!' he shrieked, biting his lip and writhing cross-legged in considerable discomfort.

Understanding the almost international word, and seeing her soldier's urgent need, Adele waved for him to come down, and opening the backdoor, pointed to another just outside while trying to keep a straight face. Eric's pain and obvious distress filled her with compassion, she had felt that way on more than one occasion when out in the field, yet the sight of his pigeon-toed, hunched-back, blanket-wrapped, Quasi Modo like figure shuffling across the floor and rushing passed the startled, departing Erignans, would have made a hangman laugh.

The outdoor privy, although attached to the house, was a real old fashioned thunder-box. Just a round hole in a wooden bench seat, dark and primitive. To Eric it was heaven and his relief indescribable – at least until the pervading draughts froze his exposed backside and thighs.

'Christ!' he blasphemed. 'This is worse than Eastney barracks in the rush hour.' Not a fair comparison really seeing as he was alone, whereas at Eastney he'd have been but one of a queue of dozens, all equally as desperate.

Back in the house, a much relieved Pearman gratefully accepted Adele's invitation to join her and her husband at the fireplace. Feeling embarrassed, and not a little self-conscious wrapped only in a blanket shroud, he reached for the flames; his numb hands unable to register any warmth at first.

'Voici mon mari' said Adele, pointing an open palm at the figure sat in a worn armchair in front of the crackling log fire wearing an enveloping overcoat. 'Jules.'

Pearman, guessing she was giving him an introduction to her husband, offered his hand to the thin, pale-faced man who looked sixty but was probably only half that age, as Adele rattled off another sentence presumably announcing him because he recognised his own name that she pronounced as 'Air-reek.'

The marine bobbed his head in acknowledgement as he looked down on the gaunt face and accepted the limp, almost lifeless handshake. Jules' skin, like thin parchment stretched tightly over protruding cheekbones, accentuated the dark sunken eyes that conveyed a mix of pain and intelligence as the Frenchman flattened his thin lips against strong teeth in semblance of a smile.

'Please to meet you, Jules,' said Pearman awkwardly, feeling guilt for his earlier advances towards the poor man's wife. 'Thank you for having me in your home.'

Jules hadn't understood a word of the soldier's strange tongue but got the gist of what was said as Adele added her interpretation. The Englishman seemed a nice sort, albeit scruffy in his unwashed state and whiskered chin, obviously very fit even after his spell of sickness. How he envied his healthy body.

Pearman felt a light touch on his arm and turned to where Adele stood cupping her hands to her mouth and moving her jaw to convey the meaning "would he like a drink and something to eat?"

'Yes, please,' he said, suddenly feeling very hungry.

She shook her head and again the marine felt twinges of attraction as her brown hair cascaded around her cheeks.

'Non! Eric' she scolded, waggling a reproving forefinger from side to side like a bad actress reprimanding a naughty puppy, determined to teach him to speak French. 'Oui, S'il vous plait.'

'Wee, civil play,' he answered with a laugh, hugging the blanket tighter around him trying to eliminate the draughty gaps.

She gave a Gaelic shrug of hopelessness but her annoyance could not conceal the pleasure that lit her face as she turned to listen when Jules spoke to her, then she left the room.

Several minutes of embarrassing silence between the two men passed before Adele returned, cradling a pile of men's clothing that she offered to Pearman with a raised eyebrow as though to say "hope these will fit", then mimed for him to go upstairs while she prepared them something to eat.

Only those who have attempted to climb steep, narrow stairways in the dark, in front of an audience, while carrying a pile of clothing and trying to retain one's modesty by clutching a recalcitrant blanket that seemed determined to surround one's ankles, can begin to imagine the difficulties that Pearman had to overcome with sheer guts, determination, and a huge portion of luck.

The clothes, that he rightly guessed came from the good Father Lorrette, fitted where they touched and – although spotlessly clean – were far from new. Nevertheless, it felt wonderful to be properly dressed again, even though he probably looked like a typical French country peasant which, he presumed, was the intention.

With a huge show of self-consciousness, and dressed in a suit and collarless shirt, he returned downstairs in his bare feet. Someone had forgotten to include socks, and the boots were several sizes too small. Still, he thought, you can't win 'em all. At least he felt warmer now.

Adele called 'Bravo,' and clapped like an excited child, and Jules nodded his approval as they watched Pearman do a dramatic pirouette that earned him extra grins and exaggerated approbation that lasted until he pointed down at his feet. With a look of horror Adele clapped her hands around her face and rushed out of the room to return almost immediately carrying a huge pair of heavy leather thigh-boots that she held out to her soldier. Graciously – to keep up the foolish charade – he put them on and stood posing, arms akimbo, like Napoleon on parade. They all burst out laughing, giggling hysterically, like children, until their sides ached.

Pearman, always the joker and feeling as ridiculous as he looked, clumped across the floor like a land-bound deep-sea diver and collapsed breathlessly into a chair. Tears streamed down Adele's cheeks and a wide grin covered Jules' face as they watched the marine mime a parody of shaving himself; then the penny dropped. Jules took a cut-throat razor from a drawer in the fireside cupboard and offered it. Pearman took it and turned his head from side to side, asking 'Where do I go?'

Adele led him out to the kitchen and poured half a cup of hot water, left over from making the coffee, into a small bowl and handed him Jules' shaving brush and soap, indicating the hand-mirror propped on the window sill.

'Mercy' said Pearman, showing off the first word of his newfound vocabulary, and jumping as she stamped her foot in simulated anger.

'Non, Eric. Mairsee,' she corrected phonetically, and shaking her head in despair left him to his ablutions.

He eyed the open razor with trepidation. It was an evil looking weapon; lethal. He'd never used one before, always had a safety razor. Come to think of it he'd never seen anyone else with one either. Perhaps they weren't allowed in the services?

The clean-shaven face, albeit with several bloody nicks, that presented itself a few minutes later, brought another round of applause from his admiring hosts. It was the first time he felt really clean since the night of the raid, and for a few fleeting seconds he was overcome with sadness, remembering that time among the reeds, sitting beside the canoes in the mud, cleaning themselves and their equipment, joking light-heartedly to cover their inner fears, not knowing if they'd ever see each other again.

Adele literally felt her heart leap as Eric came into the room. He looked so boyish without a beard, and so handsome. A smile covered his face and yet it seemed his eyes were sad. She wanted to rush to him and cuddle him in her arms; wanting to feel his arms around her, to have his body pressed against hers. Could he hear her pounding heart?

At least he had taken those stupid boots off, thank God.

They ate their meal in silence, finding it difficult to hold a miming conversation while holding a knife and fork. Pearman appreciated the quiet time that gave him time to think. He was very mindful of the fact they were risking everything for him, possibly even their lives. He liked Jules, and felt guilt-ridden because of his lustful thoughts about Adele. Yes, she was very attractive, beautiful in a way, and desirable, but the poor bloke was helpless, unable to defend his wife's honour. Only a total bastard would think of taking advantage of the situation, and he didn't consider himself to be *that* bad. No, he decided, he would explain that he wanted to sleep downstairs from now on, in the makeshift bed under the table that Adele had mentioned. That would enable her to get a good night's sleep and ease his conscience. Now that he was well again, it would be hard to control himself if they were to continue sharing the room, especially if she were to come on to him! So, he occupied the last few minutes of the meal planning how he could convey his wishes to her without giving offence, or showing ingratitude for her nursing and unstinting care. It would be difficult, but he'd manage it, somehow.

Chapter Twenty-Five.

In the dark bedroom, Adele lay with the blankets fisted tightly up under her chin with her eyes wide open staring into the blackness of the beamed ceiling, her thoughts washing over the days that had passed since Eric first came downstairs. She smiled at the memory; the sheer panic on his face as he tried to control his bursting bladder, the pleasure of seeing his unshaven face for the first time, and those stupid looking thigh boots!

So much had happened during that time; or rather so much *hadn't* happened. The Elignans no longer made a daily visit - not after Eric became up-and-doing and insisting that he share the outside chores – although they continued to trudge up from the village every third or fourth day to deliver a box of goodies from Father Lorrette, including a larger pair of shoes for Eric.

Apart from tending the animals, that Adele insisted on doing herself, Eric took over all the external jobs, leaving her to manage the cooking and domestic work. In those few days he had worked wonders. Fences and gates were mended, walls and roofs repaired, vegetable plots tilled and hundreds of other, long neglected tasks, attended to. He revelled in the physical activity and, he said, it kept his mind off other concerns such as the possibility of being captured by the Germans, and of his mates who were either dead, prisoners, or back home by now; and of his own uncertain future.

She jumped at the sound of a creaking. Was it a floorboard, or a stair-tread? Was he creeping up to see her – to share her bed? Or was it her imagination playing tricks? Holding her breath she waited, her heart palpitating madly. Had he at last noticed her unspoken invitations? He had already proved himself as a normal, red-blooded male. Surely she wasn't that unattractive. Or was he keeping his distance because of Jules?

She recalled the evening when Jules had told her she was free to do whatever she wanted. She had hung her head in embarrassment and shame as he talked. Had she been *that* obvious? Sat beside him, holding his hand, in front of a dying fire, she assured him she would always be faithful, and meant every word. He was her husband and she loved him dearly.

'Cheri,' he had said, squeezing her hand and lifting her chin to look into her moist eyes. 'I love you with all my heart and hate to see you so miserable, so - er -,' he stumbled to find a suitable word, '- unfulfilled. You must do whatever it is you want. Get it out of your system. Be happy and enjoy yourself. You don't have to love him to want him. Use him as he will be using you. Ships that pass in the night, so to speak. Anyhow, it will be with my knowledge and permission so it wouldn't be an act of infidelity; you wouldn't be being unfaithful. To be honest,' he lied, 'it would make me feel better; less guilty at not being a proper husband to you.'

Burying her head in his lap, she cried tears of remorse, thinking what a wonderful man he was, who must love her dearly to make such an offer, such a sacrifice. Nothing more had been said, then or since. Whatever happened now would up to Eric; *if* he wanted her. She would make no more advances. Perhaps Jules would have a similar talk with him, when they were able to com municate better.

She had been amazed at Eric's ability to pick-up her language, and he was a good pupil. To help him, she insisted they speak French all the time despite having a strong wish to learn English, for his sake. As each day passed, so their reliance on sign language became less, and they shared many a laugh at his efforts.

Only last evening, returning from a final check on the animals, she had found the two men deep in a stilted conversation that seemed to end abruptly as she entered the room. Has they been talking about her?

The thought was foremost in her mind as she eagerly strained to hear another creaking sound, or the squeak of the opening door, but the only sound came from the howling wind in the eaves. Disappointed, aroused and excited, she closed her tear-filled eyes and let her head drop back onto the pillow, allowing her hands to do what he should be doing until, exhausted, she eventually fell asleep.

Twenty miles away, in the cramped living-room of a terraced cottage that lined the main road through a small market town, two men sat facing each other across a bare wood table in front of a fire-place with its end-of-day glow of red embers almost engulfed by cooling white-grey ashes. They could not be more different in size, shape or character. At one side a heavily bearded, stocky, almost six feet tall, middle-aged figure, speaking immaculate school-boy French and fingering the end of his bulbous nose, faced an elderly man probably in his late sixties, who's thin, wizened, five-foot six-inch frame, and gaunt, whiskered face, seemed fragile in comparison. Both were twiddling half-full glasses of red wine, thoughtfully staring with deep interest into the contents as though expecting it to burst into flames.

'So, what you are saying….' summarised the taller of the two – who was in fact an unlikely looking British Intelligence officer codenamed *Le Major* working with one of the many clandestine organisations operating on the continent. '....is that you have four people waiting to be moved on. Two with Father Lorrette and two with the Funeral Director chappie; and they can't be shifted because your escape route has been compromised by one of your own people who, you suspect, is a Gestapo agent, or at least a Nazi sympathiser.'

Pierre Huet, the old man, placed his hands palm down on the table, piercing his unblinking eyes into those of the Englishman. He had a great respect and admiration for the man who spent much of his time limping around the countryside wearing a specially designed boot, in the guise of a cripple. 'Not suspect, M'sieur....*Know!*' he said with quiet emphasis.

'If you say so,' concurred the officer, finger an old scar on his chin acquired as a school-boy in a back alley religious debate. 'So, what do you intend to do about it?' His bushy eyebrows arched, reaching for a receding hairline. 'What do you want *me* to do about it?'

The Frenchman raised his glass slowly and deliberately to his mouth, and emptied it through his unkempt, filtering moustache without taking his eyes off the officer. 'The bastard is going to die,' he said, simply.

Several moments of heavy silence followed as both men gave free rein to their thoughts; a silence made more intense by the regular, sonorous ticking of the huge clock hanging over the fireplace. It was eventually broken by the throaty cackle of the Frenchman voice.

'I need your suggestions, M'sieur,' he said, wiping a forefinger across his nicotine-stained moustache. 'I want him disposed of in a manner that will not cause the Boche to think local people were involved. They would only take reprisals and innocent Frenchmen – and women – would suffer, probably die, as a result.'

A frown creased the already stress-lined face of the Englishman who could hardly keep awake. He had been sleepless for over twenty-four hours, and the drink wasn't helping to keep his eyes open. 'Any British chaps among the escapees?'

'Yes, M'sieur. Father Lorrette has a British marine. The others are fliers.'

The officer's face lit up. He himself had been a Royal Marine officer before changing to his present job. He knew a marine's capability. 'Grand' he murmured. 'Just what we need. Give me some time to think up a plan and I'll be in touch.' He stretched out the palm of his hand to cover his glass, too late to stop it being re-filled.

'Sante,' called the old man, raising his glass in courteous salute.

Oh! My God, thought the officer, gazing in horror at his brimming tumbler. He had a five mile cycle ride ahead.

At the door of the potting shed, standing stork-like on one leg and scraping the accumulation of mud off his boots from his day-long efforts in the marshy field, Pearman struggled with his conscience; fighting the conflict between his need for Adele – who he would hate having to reject – and the guilt complex he felt over Jules. He fancied her like crazy yet regarded Jules as a good friend to whom he owed a great deal. No way could he deceive him and make his life even more unbearable. That would be no way to repay his debt; and Adele would surely regret it after he'd gone, and yet……. ?
His mind had been in turmoil since Jules had spoken to him in a mixture of sign-language, gestures and slowly spoken French. He still couldn't believe what the Frenchman had said! Jules had begun by emphasising how much he loved his wife and wanted more than anything to see her happy. He went on to curse the Boche for causing the injuries that had turned him into an impotent cripple, unable to be a real husband to a wife who was still young and in need of physical loving. 'I understand those needs Eric,' he'd said. 'Without them she will never be really happy and will end up being a dried-up old woman, all because of me.' Sniffing back a tear, he clasped his fleshless hands. 'I've seen the way you look at her, and the way her eyes twinkle when you are near. It's only natural for you both to want what the other has to offer.' His sunken eyes were pleading. 'Please, Eric. Do me a big favour and make my wife happy, for my sake as well as hers.'
Eric had understood almost all of what Jules had been trying to say, and for once in his life, was speechless. How does one respond to such an obviously sincere invitation? The poor guy must love her to distraction to make such a selfless, sacrificial proposal. What could he say? It was like being offered an expensive present by a pauper. Dumbly he had taken the Frenchman's hand, gently squeezing it to convey the compassion he felt, and with a sad smile, pointed to his own head and watch. Jules had understood his need for time to think, and given a return smile just as Adele re-entered the room, queryingly raising her eyebrows at the two sombre-faced men.

New Year's Eve at the Montagne farm was special. At Adele's insistence, only necessary chores were undertaken. It would be a restful day, to make up for the Christmas that had passed, uncelebrated. Thanks to Father Lorrette, their roast chicken dinner - washed down with endless glasses of the rough red wine - left them bloated and just a little tipsy, giggling like children as they played simple games in front of the roaring fire that blazed away adding a real festive cheer to the otherwise undecorated room. Outside, under a heavy layer of dark-grey clouds that hung motionless like an oppressive blanket, the weather had improved. There was no sign of snow as yet but it was still bitterly cold and the ground lay under a coating of white frost; the naked trees unmoving in the mere whisper of wind.

Towards the end of the evening, with each sat quietly thinking their separate thoughts and gazing into the cooling embers of the dying fire, Adele noticed the faraway look clouding Eric's eyes. He looked so sad, she wanted to hug him. Instead, tapping him on the arm to get his attention, she pointed to his head saying the one word 'England?' He grinned a tight smile and nodded, not knowing how to explain his true thoughts to her. Yes, he had been thinking of home, but not in the way she imagined. Of course he would have liked to be at home among his mates, probably getting drunk in a local pub and nodding off by a roaring coal fire. He had many such memories, but now he did not want to be anywhere but here, with her. His family had never been a close one and ever since leaving school he'd been a loner – except for his service friends who, as far as he knew, could all be dead by now – or pissed. He could picture them in his mind; Lieutenant Thomas, Windy and Gravy, Bing and Porky, and all the other lads back at Eastney who were most likely far too busy doing something else to be thinking about him. No, he wanted to be here, to stay here. He had nothing to go back home to, neither did he feel unpatriotic. He'd done his bit for the war effort, for King and Country. He could be happy here. He loved Adele and God only knew how much he wanted her, but he also felt very strongly about the bond of friendship between him and Jules. They spent hours together, often in companionable silence, and the Frenchman had become almost brotherly. He would never wish to deliberately hurt him. Yes, of course he pitied him, his war had been devastating. The poor man had no future and nothing to live for – except Adele. The situation was impossible. How could he, a foreigner, a passing acquaintance, even consider stealing the chap's wife? It wasn't as if he wanted her just for sex, although that was very much in the forefront of his mind. No, he wanted her permanently! How could that ever happen and still keep Jules' friendship and respect?

When Jules started yawning, Adele and Eric took the hint and agreed it was time for bed, Eric helping Jules out to the toilet while she prepared the two beds and stirred up the remnants of the burning logs that barely gave any warmth to the room. Her room, she thought with a shiver, would be like an ice-berg, and just as lonely.

As soon as the two men returned, already chilled from the arctic outdoors, she helped Jules into bed and bent to kiss him lovingly on the forehead as he held her hand tightly. She kissed him a second time and straightened to wish the men "goodnight", but he would not release her hand. Instead, holding out his other hand, he beckoned Eric over to his bedside.

'Goodnight, old chap,' said Eric in English, grasping the Frenchman's proffered hand, thinking that was what was wanted.

Jules, lifting his head from the pillow with a tired effort, joined their two hands, sandwiching them between his and squeezed them together.

A thrill like a mild electric shock coursed through Eric's veins at the touch of her hand and he couldn't stop himself from looking at her longingly, seeing the wistful ache in her eyes, each feeling the other's need.

Jules also saw the exchange and spoke softly to Adele. 'Take him with you, my love,' he said, pushing them both away. 'Be happy, for my sake.'

Wordlessly, she knelt down beside him and kissed him full on the lips, her tears falling on his face and wetting his pillow. Gently he pushed her away. 'Go, please?'

Eric had only a remote idea of what had been said. It had been too quick and too quiet for him to follow, so he was surprised and startled when she stood up, weeping tears that ran down her cheeks from red-rimmed eyes, and faced him. For a few precious seconds they looked deep into each others souls. He, wanting to hold her tight in his arms and dreading the moment she would say "Goodnight", and leave him. She, dazed at the jumble of sadness and excitement whirling around inside her head; sure of what she wanted, unsure of what to do. It was seeing the desire burning in his eyes, the open lust that matched her own, that made up her mind. She needed him, yearned for their bodies to be together, craving his touch, wanting his love. And Jules *had* encouraged her – *for his sake*, he had said.

Jules watched as she led the bewildered Englishman by the hand across the room and up the stairs. Suddenly, he felt dreadfully alone, empty and lost, his leaden heart full of self-pity as he let his head fall back to stare up into the black void, and silently cried himself to eventual sleep.

The third day of the New Year brought an unannounced visit from Father Lorrette that enabled the Montagnes and Eric to thank him for his generosity and goodness. He had walked the two miles from the village in a light drizzle of rain that had soaked through his ecclesiastical cloak and bowed the wide brim of his hat soggily down around his red-cheeked, tubby face, like a drooping petal of a dying flower.

'Please, do not thank me, my children' he said, warming his hands by the fire and watching the steam rise from his cloak hung over the back of a chair to dry. 'They are God's gifts, supplied by my small organisation in time of need.' He cupped his hands gratefully around a glass of wine. 'It is good to see you all looking so happy.' He turned, his eyes looking up at Eric through the curtain-like fringe covering his forehead that gave him the appearance of a mad monk. 'And you, M'sieur. You are well?'

Pearman smiled down at the Buddha-like figure huddled in a chair to who he owed so much. 'Very well, thank you Father.'

The cleric nodded acceptance. 'We are doing our best to get you started on your journey home, my son,' he said. 'Sorry for the delay. Please be patient.'

This was something the marine had given a lot of thought to during the last few days. He knew what he wanted, *if* the Montagnes agreed. 'I don't want to go home, Father,' he said in English, then added in his best French, 'I want to stay here, with Jules and Adele, if they'll have me.'

For several long moments the room filled with a deep, impenetrable silence. A flea, had there been one around, could have been heard breathing. Shock was written all over the three wide-eyed, open-mouthed faces.

Apart from her pounding heart, Adele's first reaction to this startling and totally unexpected news was a breathtaking thrill. Her lover *wanted* to stay with her. God, let it be so, she prayed inwardly, looking at the Father and Jules to judge their response.

Jules was not surprised. He had been expecting something, but what he didn't know. It never crossed his mind that his friend would wish to stay permanently; a delayed departure perhaps, after the novelty had worn off. Nevertheless the idea didn't displease him. He and Eric had become firm friends, his presence a great boon around the farm, and without a doubt, his wife was a changed woman; happy, loving and extremely attentive now that she had more time to spend with him. Her being in the house with him most of the day was an absolute joy. He was no longer lonely and he felt no jealousy towards Eric. The longer the situation stayed that way the happier he would feel; and to hell with the Boche.

Father Lorrette, on the other hand, felt momentarily stunned. 'No, my son,' he snapped, almost angrily. 'That cannot be. You are needed back in England to help beat the Boche and free this country. That is what my organisation exists for. Besides, it would be extremely dangerous for the Montagnes if you were to stay. Sooner or later you would be discovered. Without papers you cannot leave the farm, or be seen. Certain people might object to your remaining here, and a word may be placed in the wrong ear.' He paused to let his words sink in, pinching his fleshy nose between thumb and forefinger, nervously. 'Apart from the danger to you and others,' he continued, 'these good people…' he nodded at Jules and Adele, '…can barely feed themselves, let alone an extra mouth, and my limited resources are so low that I offer a prayer every day for you to be on your way before they run out.'

Eric's dream collapsed. The very thought of being with Adele and Jules had kept him going, stopped him from thinking of any other future.

There must be a way. 'Could you not get me papers that would enable me to stay Father?' he asked in desperation. 'I would work hard to feed the three of us and no one in the village need know I am here.' He sought vainly for other plausible reasons. 'I'm learning to speak French quite well, enough to fool a German any day,' he added, lamely, knowing in his heart that the Father was right; it would be too dangerous for everyone.

The cleric was adamant. 'No. It is out of the question, even if the Montagnes did agree – which they haven't. For everyone's sake you must go.' He looked at each of them in turn with knowing eyes. He had had years of experience dealing with human frailties and emotions. He was no fool. Their situation was like an open book to him, but he was a man of God, not a Judge. It was the war! 'I am sorry, my son,' he said almost in a whisper. 'You will – must – go, as soon as arrangements can be made. I have no idea how long that will be, it could be days or weeks, but you must be ready to move at very short notice, and remember, others are risking their lives for you, so please do not be ungrateful.' Then, cleverly, he changed the subject. It was useless to discuss it further; there was no alternative.

'This marine of yours, Pierre,' said *Le Major*, revisiting the old Frenchman as promised. 'I'd like to meet him.'

'Not *mine,* m'sieur. He is with Father Lorrette and it will be a long ride for you if you want to see him. Over thirty kilometres.'

The officer shook his head, dismissing the warning.

'And' continued the Frenchman, leaning forward on the table, his elbows either side of the ever present glass of wine, 'I've heard it said he doesn't want to return home. Wants to stay where he is.'

'Does he now!' was the brusque reply. 'We'll see about that.' *Le Major* bunched a fist with controlled annoyance and lowered it slowly onto the table, lips tight with anger, eyes fixed on the huge clock above the fire. 'He is still a member of His Majesties armed forces and will do as he is told.'

The Frenchman remained silent for several minutes, allowing the officer's vexation to subside, and then asked, 'Have you considered a plan for getting rid of my traitor?'

Le Major had been annoyed, bloody annoyed. It was inconceivable to think that any serviceman - let alone a marine - would even consider putting his own selfish interests before the needs of his country. It was complete anathema to him. Who the hell did the man think he was? There were French people putting their lives at risk to get him home and all he could think of was his own comfort and safety. He'd bloody soon sort him out. He forced himself to calm down and returned his attention to the Frenchman.

'What do you think of the idea of putting this marine into the escape chain and getting him to do the necessary in such a manner as not to involve the locals, Pierre?' he asked.

'How, m'sieur?'

'Well. I could get London to send out a commando dagger, or an officer's revolver, or anything that the marine could conceal on his person and use. Then it could be left at the scene to convince Jerry it was a British assassination job. I can work out the details later.'

Sagely, Pierre Huet nodded, picking his nose while pretending to brush his wayward moustache. 'Sounds good to me,' he said. 'If you can get the marine to do it.'

The agent straightened his back, bristling again. 'He'll do it alright. I'll make him.'

His prophecy turned out to be correct. The long cycle ride through wet, wintry country roads and lanes was tiring and when he eventually arrived at the farmhouse he stayed outside, out of sight, while recovering his breath and composure, quelling his resentment of this marine's attitude. He must remain calm and in control. Much better to get the man's willing co-operation than to be heavy handed and incur his enmity.

At first, the marine welcomed him, happy to meet one of his own countrymen, and for half-an-hour they talked amicably in English and French, about anything and everything. The Montagnes were delighted to be included but both frowned at the rudeness when the conversation changed, purposely, into rapid English. They were excluded and assumed it was for some specific reason; their assumption proven correct when they saw Eric's face harden.

As diplomatically as he possible could, bearing in mind his own suppressed irascibility, *Le Major* outlined his proposed plan. He assured the marine – who would not even divulge his surname or how he came to be at the farm in case the officer was not who he claimed to be – that it would expedite his return home and do England, and the French, a good turn. But the marine obstinately refused to listen; he wanted to stay.

Temporarily defeated, and not wishing to invoke his commissioned authority unless, or until, it became necessary, he took a mental step backwards. Offering his apologies to the Montagnes for his rudeness, he explained to them the bones of his conversation with the marine.

Adele, ever the hopeful peacemaker, poured wine for everyone and frowned at Eric to remove the look of anger on his face. The pause gave the officer time to re-think his strategy.

'How about you entering the escape chain and removing this enemy agent for us, Eric?' he asked in English, quickly continuing so as not to give the opportunity for interruption. 'In return, I will get documents for you – forged of course but as good as any original – that will enable you to return here for as long as you wish.' His eyebrows arched, interrogatively.

This unexpected turn of events surprised Pearman. Was this the way out of his problem? He could do his duty and then stay with the blessing of an authority. 'But I've never killed a man in cold bl……..'

'That's as may be,' interrupted the officer testily. 'Nevertheless you are a marine, as I was, so you know how. That is what you've been paid to do. Or are you a coward?' he added. Instantly regretting having said it.

Pearman's face flushed, and he balled his fists at his side desperately wanting to smash them into the smug face. 'I'm no bloody coward, mate,' he snarled, placing his face a few inches away from the officer's nose. 'And if and when you can prove you are who you say you are I'll tell you why!' He took a deep breath and exhaled loudly through his nose. 'I'll do your bloody killing job for you, but I'll see the papers first…..right?'

The expression on the agent's face remained bland but inwardly he felt a rush of relief. He'd done it. He'd get the blasted fellow his damn papers but he wouldn't hand them over until after the job was done. He still questioned the man's guts and whether he'd have the courage to go through with it. He may be a marine, who on his own admission had never killed, but would he do so now? Probably yes, he thought, to get back to the girl and her cuckolded husband; the situation was blatantly obvious. His smile never reached his impassive face. Of course he would honour his word and get the papers, but would the marine make it back afterwards to collect them? There were more ways than one to skin a cat, he thought, malevolently.

Chapter Twenty-six.

For the next few days time hung heavily for Pearman. Fortunately the hard manual labour working on the farm during the short daylight hours kept his mind occupied, but the early nights to bed – after the lovemaking that was now more tender and caring once their initial frantic lust was satisfied – seemed endless. They would lay together, cuddling like spoons in a kitchen drawer for warmth, his hand and forearm stretched along a smooth thigh no longer covered by her discarded nightgown, feeling the slow rise and fall of her breathing close to his chest and the wonderful feel of her body nestling into his lap. He should have been in a heavenly world of happiness, embracing an angel, but he was not. At such times it was fear that filled his mind. He dreaded the thought of what he had to do – must do – to stay with her. His mind could not accept the murderous act of plunging a dagger into the flesh of the man called Mistral. He shuddered. It made him physically sick even to contemplate it, yet he knew there was no alternative as he inched away from Adele's back so as not to let his trembling hands waken her.

'Whatever you do,' the officer had warned. 'Don't let him fool you. He comes across as a very friendly, likeable chap. Just remember he is the enemy, a traitor who is going to betray you just as he has betrayed others. Kill him in his house as soon as possible after your meeting and leave him were he drops, with your dagger still in him. Make sure he is dead, and then leave. Turn left out of the house and walk along the street until you come to an empty building on your left with the faded sign *Café Verdun* over the door. Two doors past that is an empty house, number thirty-five. Its front door will be closed but not locked. Inside it is bare, but in a cupboard in the back bedroom you will find bedding, food and water. Remain there until someone comes for you. That may be a day or two, so do not let yourself be seen or heard. The person will have your papers and will help you to return to the Montagne's farm.'

It all sounded so easy, except for the killing, he thought nervously. Would he be able to go through with it?..... *He must!*

It was the morning of the third day after the officer's visit when a tousled-haired youth arrived at the farm and knocked impatiently on the door. The day was pleasant, though chilly, and the lad had enjoyed the cycle ride from the village towing another velo alongside. His orders, from Father Lorrette, were to collect a man from the farm and take him to a yard in another village where he used to live and play as a child. It would be a nice day away from school and home chores, and he looked forward to the long ride there and back, even though he had been told not to speak to the stranger. He wondered, why? With the natural curiosity of all young people he felt intrigued by mystery. Who was he?

Called in from the outhouse by Adele who had answered the door, Eric regarded the old, upright bicycle, propped against the wall, with dismay. Its worn leather saddle resembled a narrow wedge of hard cheese stuck on a stick, like a pointed toffee-apple, and looked painful. Instinct told him the time had come and he didn't want to leave; didn't want to face what he knew he had to face. He felt as though he had a cannon-ball in his stomach.

'Ask him how far I've got to ride that…..thing!' he sighed, looking first at Adele and then at the ancient velo. He could see her lips tremble as she spoke rapidly to the lad.

'A little over twenty kilometres, he says,' she replied pensively, squeezing tears from her weeping eyes and reaching out a hand for his. Did he really mean he would be away for only a couple of days, and be back after assisting in the escape of a group of allied aviators? 'Please be careful, my love.'

He drew her to him, unaware of the boy's interested stare or the haunted look on Jules' face, as he held her in a tight embrace. 'I'll be back before you've even missed me' he said, kissing her on the forehead and then on each wet eye, feeling her body tremble against his and wondering how long it would be before he would hold her again, like this. 'I won't be away for one minute longer than I have to.' he whispered hoarsely into her hair and then kissed her passionately on her full, warm lips. 'I love you,' he said, sotto voce for her ears only, easing her gently away at arms length and watching, sadly, the tears run down her crestfallen face; his own eyes moist.

Reluctantly he released her, and after running upstairs to strap the dagger - his murder weapon - to the inside of his lower leg, he went over to where Jules was sat, and took his hand. 'Au revoir mon ami. A bientot.'

'Bon chance, Rosbif,' answered the Frenchman throatily, forcing a smile to suppress his own tears. He feared for the man who had become a close and very dear friend. His presence on the farm, and in the house, would be sorely missed; not just by himself but also – he knew – by his wife standing heart-broken by the open door. Had he caused her this grief by encouraging her closeness to Eric? Would it have been easier for them had they not started their relationship? One look at her gave him the answer as he recalled a saying he had seen somewhere. *Better to have loved and lost, than never to have loved at all.* **Anyhow**, he would be returning…wouldn't he?

The journey, peddling hard behind the energetic youth through the quiet country lanes, helped Pearman take his mind off his sorrow. He tried to think, and plan ahead, still desperately seeking an alternative to the planned cold-blooded killing, but his heavy heart kept returning his mind to Adele…his Adele, knowing he must go through with the dreaded task to enable him to return, and hopefully spend the rest of his life with her; and Jules of course.

Yet again, he thought of his mates in the Section. If only he knew their fate. Had they made it back home? Somehow he couldn't accept they were dead. Maybe, like him, they had found a safe sanctuary and in a nice warm bed somewhere…well, perhaps not in a bed, not at this time of the day! Maybe they were trudging across the top of a snowy mountain on an escape route to Spain, every step taking them nearer home. At worst - knowing them as he did - they would be living rough, evading the enemy, biding their time and never thinking of surrendering. If they were prisoners - and he thought that highly unlikely - they'd probably talk their way out of jail!

The one and only stop on the long cycle ride, was forced on them by a flock of sheep whose fleeces covered the lane like a slow moving stream of dirty white froth as they bleated passed, seemingly determined to push the two cyclists into the hedgerow. Even the aged, bent shepherd, leaning heavily on his cleft stick, with eyes downcast and looking as sad as a refugee, failed to acknowledge the cheerful greeting of the young guide.

After what seemed an eternity, but was probably only a couple of hours, they rode into a large village, over cobbled streets that shook Pearman's bicycle like a road-drill and put the finishing touches to his misery. Had he not known differently, he would have sworn the wheels had solid tyres. His backside, bruised and battered, ached as though being pounded by a thousand steel-shod hooves, and the insides of his thighs were chafed sore. It felt as though he had been through the Commando assault course a dozen times – and failed.

His relief when they turned off the road into a paved courtyard was profound. He stopped alongside the boy and stretched a foot onto the ground for support…..and almost fell over. Cramp seized the calf muscle and the long-suffering knee gave way. Wincing with pain, he grabbed for the near-by sill of a boarded window. Jesus, he thought, and I am supposed to be a fit, tough, rugged marine?

The boy pointed to a paint-peeling wooden door hanging tiredly in its frame in front of them and, without a word, swivelled his velo around to face back towards the yard entrance. Pearman, realising his guide was about to leave, called out. 'Merci.' The lad smiled a farewell, some of his curiosity satisfied. He could tell by the accent that the man was English. If so, what was he doing in France? Perhaps a spy? He felt a thrill of smug contentment and stuck his chest out. He would be able to boast – at some later date of course – that he had worked with the Resistance.

Pearman watched him ride away with admiration. The boy apparently had no concern for the long return journey. Rather him than me, he thought, leaning the bike against the wall and crossing to the indicated door, on wobbly, aching legs. If he never saw a cycle again it would be too soon. And if anyone had ideas for him to continue using one again tomorrow, next week or next month, they could think again; he'd prefer to walk, thank you very much.

His knock on the door was unanswered, so lifting the latch, he pulled nervously and it opened easily. Stepping into the gloomy interior, he found himself in a large, barn-like space lit only by weak rays of daylight striving to penetrate through two skylights in the sloping roof, both covered in a coating of dirt and bird droppings. Long abandoned cobwebs, swaying like threads of silk, dangled from sagging beams that seemed to silently groan under their burden, adding to the air of complete desolation. Apart from a thin layer of stinking hay strewn across the floor, it was empty. There were no other doors. It had the atmosphere of a neglected mausoleum on a Sunday night and sent shivers down his spine. Was this the right place? Was someone coming to meet him here? If so, when?

He squatted on his haunches, uncomfortably against the wall. It certainly was not the Ritz. He had seen more depressing places in his life, but couldn't remember when. He would wait a while and see what happens; he had no alternative really. They – whoever they were – must know what they are doing….mustn't they?

The only problem of waiting, apart from the discomfort, was the recurring thoughts of his murderous task. He fingered the shape of the dagger under his trouser leg and shivered again. Would his intended victim be the next person to walk through the door? Was he going to commit murder tonight? He felt a stirring in his stomach and retched, almost to the point of being sick as the bile rose in his throat. He must strengthen his resolve, he thought, burying his head in his hands, and stop being so weak. He was supposed to be a soldier, for Christ's sake! Paid to fight the enemy without question. And Mistral *was* the enemy, according to the French. In his mind's eye he imagined plunging the dagger into unresisting flesh, and again the bile burned the back of his throat.

He stood up, intending to walk around and think of other things, including the increasing pressure on his gurgling bladder. He crossed over to the far corner and faced the wall to enjoy the pleasurable relief. It was then he heard the clopping of horse's hooves and the rumbling of iron-rimmed wheels in the courtyard. Quickly adjusting himself, he ran to the door and pushed it open. His eyes stared at what could have been a scene from a Count Dracula film. A man, dressed in a long black coat and wearing a top hat, had stepped down from the driving seat of a polished, black-coloured landau that had glass sides and huge lanterns at each corner and was lovingly rubbing the snorting noses of two magnificent black horses standing quietly between the shafts pawing the ground and tossing their plumed heads.

'Bloody hell!' whispered the amazed marine to himself. 'It's a bloody hearse.'

The man, who must have been several inches over six foot tall, walked towards him, a smile lighting the sombre dignity of his appearance as he removed the stove-pipe hat to reveal a thick mop of heavily greased, slicked-back hair that thatched his thin, pallid face.

Bonjour, m'sieur,' he greeted, extending a claw-like hand. 'You Ereeck?'

'Yes,' answered the stunned marine in English, pouting his lower lip, not knowing what else to say at that very moment, and shaking the hand of the tall, funereal figure towering over him.

The man placed a friendly hand on Pearman's shoulder and looked down with unblinking eyes that appeared to be deep brown in the dim light. 'Welcome mon ami. Me Raymonde. 'ave you been well?' he asked in a mixture of French and fractured English.

'Fine, thanks,' said the marine, allowing the Frenchman to turn him by the shoulders towards another door on the far side of the yard.

The room they entered looked clean and smelled cosily warm compared with the barn. It also had an air of domesticity and frequent use about it. In one corner, an old mattress-covered iron bed had a number of blankets and pillows piled at its head. A table, surrounded by three wooden chairs and covered by a non-to-clean cloth, stood uncertainly in the centre. In the far corner, next to what looked like a partitioned-off kitchen area, two army type sleeping-bags lay on top of each other.

'Sit' ordered the Frenchman as if talking to a trained dog. 'I am put ze 'orses to bed, then we eat, eh?'

Slowly, Pearman lowered his painful backside down onto the unyielding chair, gasping as his weight compressed the bruised muscles, and sat listening to the outside noises of slapping leather, rattling harnesses, and the calming voice of the Frenchman leading his impatient steeds into the barn that the marine had so recently vacated.

'Demain…'ow you say - er - next day?' began Raymonde, sitting himself down again after clearing away the crumbs that were all that remained of the bread, cheese and pickled onion he had prepared. 'We go on more to meet Mistral.'

The very mention of the name sent icy shivers up and down the marine's spine and started him thinking all over again; he had almost forgotten. Talking to Raymonde had pushed it to the back of his mind for a short, blessed period. Now it was back. Tomorrow he was to meet his victim! 'How do we travel?' he asked, dreading that the answer would be "by velo."

A puzzled frown of incomprehension creased the Frenchman's brow, and then cleared as he made sense of the question. He pointed towards the door. 'My 'orses and –'ow you say – cart?'

Pearman's eyebrows shot up like rockets. 'In a coffin?'

Raymonde laughed at the Englishman's dismay. 'Non, Ereeck. Not coffin.' He made a diving, scooping motion with his hand. 'Under ze bottom. It will not be comforting.'

Pearman rightly assumed he meant *comfortable*. At least it would give his backside a rest – or so he hoped.

Woken from a deep sleep - that only seemed to have lasted ten seconds - by the clattering of hooves on the stone paving outside in the yard, he wormed his way out of the sleeping bag; the bruising of his backside starting to hurt as he dragged on his trousers in a one-legged dance. Staggered stiffly to the doorway, he offered a prayer of thanks to the patron saint of marines for not having to mount a bike anymore - not this side of death, anyhow.

A blast of cold, early morning January air hit him as he opened the door. It was almost as shocking as the sight of Raymonde and another man, both dressed in their full undertaker's regalia, harnessing the two horses between the shafts of the hearse. Wrinkly his nose in disgust he looked at his faithful *Everrite* and swore. It wasn't even eight o'clock! …..barely daylight!

Raymonde looked up from buckling a leather strap and saw the dishevelled Englishman standing bleary-eyed in the doorway and raised a hand in salute. 'Bonjour, Ereeck. We go *dans une demi-heure* he called, and then corrected himself. 'In 'alf an 'our.'

The Frenchman's jovial attitude so early in the morning irritated the marine who never was a morning person, and on top of that, his mouth felt like the bilge of a cattle-boat! 'Do we eat before we go?' he asked hopefully, in an early morning croak.

'Non, m'sieur,' replied Raymonde, laughing at the Englishman's serious face. 'No eat. No drink.' He pointed to the glass-windowed hearse and shook his head. 'No toilette.'

Blast!, cursed the marine. He was starving and dying for a drink. 'What – nothing at all?'

'Chaq un a son gout,' came the answer.

Pearman shrugged. He didn't understand the comment but guessed by the tone that it wasn't anything complimentary.

Pre-warned of the long, confined journey ahead he made use of the barn as a last minute toilet. They had shown him his hiding place in the hearse. It was nothing more than an oblong space, about two feet wide and less than eighteen inches high that ran the length of a coffin; with a few refinements built-in for the covert transport of people, like Pearman.

Wrapped like a chrysalis in a cushioning sleeping bag, he laid on a board and was slid, head first, into the claustrophobic hole under what he hoped was an empty coffin; just like a shell being rammed into a gun's breach, he thought. An end cover slid into place at his feet and he felt the thump of the rear doors being closed. Only a faint glimmer of light, filtering through the brass ventilation grilles at each side of his cell, relieved the otherwise total darkness. He could neither twist his body nor bend his knees, and philosophically resigned himself to a seriously uncomfortable ride.

His hopes of maybe getting some sleep, to while away the time, were shattered as the hearse moved off, clattering and bumping over the cobblestones on its iron-rimmed wheels, shaking him like a pea in a pod and sending shock waves the length of his body. He could find no way to ease his discomfort. It was like being put in a straight-jacket and rattled, and he knew there would soon be another mass of bruises to add to his previous days trophies. It was worse than the cycle ride, and going to take twice as long. How many other escapees, he wondered, had endured this torturous confinement? At least those who usually travelled on the next floor up in a padded coffin were dead and beyond feeling, he smiled ruefully.

After the first hour of purgatory he became inured. Acceptance? Resignation? Call it what you will. His training had taught him not to worry about things over which he had no control, such as the weather and live rides in bloody hearses. So, concentrating his mind on other matters, he pushed his suffering to the back of his brain. The only problem now being that the *other matters* were mainly thoughts of killing Mistral; not a subject he wished to dwell upon. In fact, it was beginning to drive him round the bend. He tried mentally counting sheep and miraculously dozed off into a torpid sleep.

Sitting on their high bench seats, like judicial magistrates in the rain, the two coachmen, hunched neck-less into their wet cloaks, allowed the horses to walk through the towns and villages and to trot along the country lanes. The intermittent showers of rain that poured from the brims of their tall hats like overflowing gutters, made pools in their laps that, in turn, spilled over and trickled down to find haven in their boots, among frozen toes.

With the window curtains drawn, the few people who saw their passing were unaware that the only occupant was the hidden marine. Many doffed their caps, bowed their heads, or crossed themselves in reverential awe, receiving an acknowledging nod from one or other of the soggy coachmen. The same appreciative response rewarded those in uniform – German or otherwise – who gave a respectful military salute. The few – all German – giving the Nazi-style salute were disdainfully ignored.

Pearman could not lift his arm when he awoke so had no idea of the time, or of how long he had dozed. It could have been an hour, or minutes, although it felt as if he had been in this hell-hole longer than Nelson had been at sea. The hearse still jolted and swayed on the rutted roads and lanes, and he longed for a breath of sweet fresh air as he strained the toes of his left foot upwards to alleviate the onset of cramp. To occupy his mind, he started counting the hoof beats of the trotting horses, endeavouring to blot out the pain and bruises, and the thoughts he didn't want to think about. He hadn't even reached a hundred when the horses slowed to a walk. Another town or village, he presumed, and was proved wrong as the hearse jerked to a halt. He prayed for it to be the end of his horrendous nightmare, and could have cried with joy when the rear doors were opened and the end cover lifted.

''ere we are, Ereeck,' mumbled the cold lips of a wet and tired Raymonde, as he and his mate pulled Pearman out into the darkness of a yard almost identical to the one they had left from that morning.

Despite their own weary exhaustion, the Frenchmen knew from past experience, that the marine would be weak and stiff after such a long cramped journey, so tucked their shoulders under his arms for support as he stood unsteadily up on his feet.

'We will rest and eat 'ere, for little time,' grunted Raymonde as they virtually carried the marine across to a door that led into what was obviously someone's home. 'Then I take you to Mistral's 'ouse. Only a little walk.'

At that very moment, Mistral was way down on Pearman's list of worries. His legs weren't responding and he felt as weak as a kitten, giddy and nauseous, as he pushed the two Frenchmen away and leaned against a worn leather armchair. His knees were like jelly and he was dying for a pee. One thing at a time, he told himself, get your priorities right. Get your legs to work *then* go for a pee.

Feeling almost human again after a huge bowl of hot soup and mountains of bread and cheese, Pearman - who had the impression that the French seemed to live on bread and cheese at that stage of the war - wanted nothing more than to get his business with this man, Mistral, over and done with; the sooner the better. 'I'm ready when you are Raymonde' he said, looking at his watch and seeing both hands covering the nine.

Reluctantly, the Frenchman – only halfway through smoking a foul-smelling cigarette – rose to his feet. He only had to walk a few steps along the street to show the Englishman the house of Mistral, but he would rather not be going out at all. The long day's journey had taken more out of his old bones than he realised, and he longed for his bed.

They had walked less than two hundred yards when the Frenchman placed his hand on the marine's arm. It was a pitch-black night, and only a few house lights - peeping from inadequate blackout curtains - sparkled in the drizzling rain that the blustery breeze blew in their faces. He pointed across the street to the shadow of a mournful looking, two-storied detached house, unlit except for a frame of light around the edges of one heavily curtained window. 'That is eet, Ereeck. Mistral's 'ome.'

The marine let his eyes follow the pointing finger, surprised that he had no feeling of fear or sickness now; his mind clear and calculating as though someone had switched him off.

Inside that house, behind those curtains, lived a man who - it was said - had betrayed others to the enemy, a traitor who did not deserve to live. He felt no compunction about killing him now; it was only the thought of doing it in cold blood, with a knife that had unnerved him.

'Au revoir, mon ami' he said to Alphonse, taking his hand and shaking it warmly, wondering if the Frenchman knew what he was about to do. Much to his astonishment, and slight embarrassment, the Frenchman withdrew his hand and embraced him, planting a stubbly kiss on both cheeks.

'God go with you, mon ami,' he whispered into the marine's ear. *He knew!*

Pearman crossed over the street, avoiding the worst of the puddles that filled the depressions in the neglected tarmac, and rapped on the door with his bare knuckles. Almost immediately it was opened by a middle-aged man whose high-bridged nose hung like a parrot's beak over a wide beaming smile that seemed to split his narrow face in two.

'Welcome Eric,' he greeted in perfect English, stepping back from the door and gesturing for his visitor to enter as he combed long strands of thinning hair from his forehead with his fingers, brushing them sideways to conceal a balding patch. 'So pleased to see you. Please, sit down. You must be frozen.' Crossing to the log fire blazing merrily in the grate, he attacked it with a brass-handled poker, sending showers of sparks rocketing up the chimney. 'Bet you need a drink, old chap.'

Pearman studied the man's slender back, pleased that he had been forewarned of the over-friendly act. Bonhomie seemed to ooze from the traitor's every pore and, as he accepted a warming glass of brandy, the marine decided, *he didn't like him*. The amiable smile never seemed to reach the grey eyes, and Pearman's dad had always said, never trust a man with grey eyes.

'Have a good journey?' asked Mistral, turning around to carrying on speaking without waiting for an answer. 'You must be a very important person to warrant all this special treatment. I've been told to move you on tomorrow, just the two of us. Normally I have to take four, sometimes five bods, all at once. They assemble here and we travel in convoy, so to speak. Good fun,' he grinned, 'especially with the English.' He pouted his lips. 'The Poles tend to be a bit morose though. They take life too seriously.'

So would you if you had lost everything, thought Pearman. But instead he said. 'You speak excellent English.' He didn't want to become too friendly with his victim and still felt unfeelingly cold, emotionally.

Mistral gave a short, barking laugh, almost like a cough. 'Should do, old chap. That's because I *am* English; born in Shropshire. Mother English, Father French. Moved here ten years ago after Mother died. The old fellow didn't last long – broken heart, don't you know.' His explanation sounded callous. 'Feel I'm doing my bit for the old country by trying to get you chaps back into the action.'

Pearman bit his tongue, wanting to scream. Wanting to tell him he knew he was a traitor and to ask why he wasn't *fighting* for his country. Instead he asked, 'May I use your toilet?'

Mistral watched as the marine crossed the room and went out to the external privy. What a rum character, he thought, doesn't seem to want to be friendly. One of those cloak-and-dagger types, probably. He didn't know how close his guess was - except that Pearman didn't have a cloak!

It wasn't a toilet that the marine wanted, it was privacy. Privacy to unstrap the commando dagger from his leg and stick it under the rope he had around his waist as a belt. I feel like a bloody pirate, he said to himself, still stunned by the fact he was feeling no emotion. Must get this over and done with quickly.

Back in the house, discussing the progress of the war, Mistral made a comment that made the marine's blood boil, and hastened his own demise.

'You've got to give this Hitler chappie *some* credit, Eric,' he said. 'He did wonders for his own people in getting Germany back on its feet after the last little lot, don't you know.' It was the last opinion he would ever express.

The marine took a step towards him, putting a hand inside his jacket to grasp the cold handle of the dagger. Mistral's eyebrows rose as if to ask *'What are you doing, old chap.'* Eric quickly drew the dagger, seeing a fleeting look of alarm cross the man's face as, in one quick move, he rammed it into the traitor's stomach as hard as he could, just below the solar plexus, thrusting upwards under the rib cage towards the heart, feeling it grate against bone, twisting it as he had been taught.

Mistral's look of alarm changed to one of intense, excruciating agony as he sank to his knees, hands scrabbling frantically at the dagger handle as though scratching a massive itch. His pain-filled eyes stared at Pearman and the twitching lips mouthed the one word, *'Why?'* as his body slumped lifeless to the floor.

Something snapped inside Pearman. His hands started to shake, like tree leaves in a gale of wind. His eyes blurred, and vomit surged chokingly up his throat to erupt out over the body curled in the foetal position at his feet. His head started to pound and he dug his finger nails into his cheeks, trying to stop the maddening pain that raced around inside his skull. He found he was shaking, his whole body quivering with a clammy chill; the muscles of his face began twitching convulsively making him grind his teeth. He shook his head wildly to clear the terrifying mist trying to engulf his mind, feeling a surge of fear, wanting to scream.

Tripping over the body and sliding on his own vomit, he staggered to the door and fell out into the street. Somewhere in the back of his swirling brain, a voice was telling him to turn left and to look for a sign...*what sign?*

Weaving like a drunk along the deserted street, he hammered his fists against his tormented forehead. He had to stop the unbearable thumping. Then suddenly, as quickly as it had started, the pain stopped and his eyes cleared. Mistral was standing against the brick wall in front of him, laughing and mocking him. He lashed out, seeing his fist go through the face and smash against the wall. He heard bones break but felt nothing. He lashed out again with both hands, hearing more bones break. Yet still the deriding eyes glared back, untouched. He slammed his forehead into the grinning face, again and again and again, until his world went black... and the face disappeared.

Chapter Twenty Seven.

The drab-grey façade of the Hotel de Ville had the boring sameness as the rest of the block that formed one side of the town square, its three-storey blandness shouldered tightly between the post office and the former museum that now aptly housed the ancient equipment of the fire brigade in its ground floor.

Had passers-by bothered to look, which they didn't, they may have seen a Gendarme and a German soldier gazing despondently out through the windowed front door from the relative warmth and dryness of the entrance hall, waiting to be spoken too, or even acknowledged, as they wiled away their boring hours of duty.

Outside, hanging side-by-side from poles over the doorway like two coloured dish-cloths fluttering in the light wind, the bedraggled tricolour of France and the scarlet and black flag of Nazi Germany dripped in unison onto the broken pave. Not only was the building the administrative centre for the area it also doubled as the German Military District Headquarters - otherwise called the "pig-pen" by the local people, under their breath of course.

On the second floor, in the Mayor's former office - now commandeered - twenty-three year old Oberleutnant Albert Claus Handel sat back in his leather swivel-chair with the neck of his high collared tunic unbuttoned, toasting his stockinged feet in front of a blazing fire. The crackling logs gave only an illusion of warmth to the rest of the ornately decorated room in which the lighter patches on the wallpaper showed where the portraits of past Mayors had hung, prior to their removal.

Despite it being only mid-morning, he felt tired and lethargic after a slight over-indulgence alone in his quarters the previous evening. His Command was a solitary one. There were no other officers to share his off-duty hours with, and the local French dignitaries only socialised with him when ordered to do so. Like all good German officers, he thought the idea of mixing with his six soldiers to be against all the rules and regulations of the Wermacht; bad for discipline, and personally repugnant. They were rough, crude and uneducated. Five were elderly veterans, all old enough to be his father, who had fought in the Low Countries at the beginning of the war – as he had himself. The fifth was a snotty-nosed kid of seventeen, straight from training camp, who's only fighting had probably been in the back alleys behind a slum school somewhere.

He fingered the scar on his cheek, self- inflicted as a youth to give the appearance of being a duelling scar to make him look like an elite Prussian. It had hurt like mad at the time, but the unspoken looks of admiration from others made it all worthwhile.

He stood up carefully, feeling the aching throb in his ankle, a reminder of the small splinter from a Belgian grenade that had resulted in him being withdrawn from his unit in the front-line and posted to this backwater.

Although revelling in his title of District Military Commander, he knew he would never get the coveted iron-cross to decorate his uniform until he got back into the war, among the troops fighting for Fuhrer and country. His back stiffened as his eyes fell on the portrait of Hitler hung prominently where it could best be seen, and never ignored. It had been given to him by the Area Commander who had acquired a bigger one; he treasured it.

He walked over to the window that framed the town-square below and looked down on the deserted streets spreading out from the waterless fountain in the middle like the fleshless rib bones of a giant. Tall, ugly grey buildings stretched in every direction as he watched dead leaves and rubbish paper swirl around in the angry breeze like Dervish dancers, and a mangy dog sniffing hungrily in doorways, continually cocking its hind leg to mark its territory. What a God-forsaken hole! Bad enough in the dry, warm days of summer, but now totally cheerless and dismal with the leaden clouds leaking a cold drizzle of rain….ugh! What a country! He made a mental note to once again plea for a move when he next met with his superior officer, preferably to the Front. Anywhere away from here.

Returning to his chair he twisted it around to face the large oak table that had probably witnessed many a civic occasion, and leaned his elbows on its polished surface on which lay the few hand-written pages of his monthly report to the Regional Commander.

Using an ornate silver lighter – bought to give the impression of wealth – he lit a cigarette and inhaled deeply, narrowing his eyes to keep out the smoke while massaging his throbbing forehead with the finger tips of the other hand. He blew a stream of smoke across the table, his thoughts dwelling on more pleasant dreams, and memories of Hamburg where he had spent his last short leave instead of going home to see his parents. Visions of the gorgeous Gerda filled his mind, and he felt himself becoming aroused as he recalled the nights of passion they had spent together after having declaring his undying love, and making a promise of marriage.

She had been his first, and her obvious experience soon taught him what was expected. Because of her enthusiastic reactions to his frantic fumbling, he was unaware she knew of his virginity, or that she thought him to be a useless, unsatisfying bedmate. In *his* mind, he assumed he had been a great lover who had her begging for more. Needless to say, they had spent most of the days and nights in bed. She had wanted to be taken out, and wined and dined on the arm of her young, handsomely scarred officer, but he had persuaded her that his need of her far exceeded any thoughts of food; and he had saved himself a fortune. Why spend his hard earned money on a good-time girl whom he never intended to see again, let alone marry. He was far more ambitious than that, and foresaw his future as being a much-decorated senior officer who could take his pick of the talent always available to those with power, or money.

He dismissed the girl from his mind as easily as swatting a fly and reached out for his report. He would give it a second reading before submitting it to the critical eye of his superior.

> "………..*a kubelwagon,*" he read, "*driven by Gefreiter Gustaf Lammen of the 217th Field Artillery Regiment stationed at the near-by ammunition storage depot, hit and seriously injured fifty-four year old Paul Benedette, a local resident, on the outskirts of the town. Gefreiter Lammen was under the influence of drink at the time. He was detained at my headquarters until the arrival of the Feldgendarmerie who formally arrested him and took him away. Their full report will be forwarded to you in due course*".
>
> . . . .
>
> "*On January 3rd. Oberschutze George Heimelmann of this Section, reported late for duty by ten minutes without excuse. In answer to my charge he pleaded guilty and was awarded ten days stoppage of leave by the undersigned.*"
>
> . . . .
>
> "*In the early hours of January 6th, an unidentified man was found by the local Gendarmerie near the town square. He had severe head and hand injuries and was rolling around in the street, babbling incoherently. It is not known how the injuries were sustained. He was taken to hospital for treatment and then, on the advice of medical staff, removed to the psychiatric unit at Angers. There was no military involvement. The gendarmerie report will be submitted to you in due course*".
>
> . . . .

"On the 10th of January, the body of a local resident, Alain Greant, aged thirty-seven, was discovered in the downstairs front room of his house at 6, Rue de Lemat by the local Gendarmerie. The man had died as a result of a stomach wound inflicted with a British army-style dagger. Because of the nature of the weapon, I informed the Feldgendarmerie. Their preliminary investigation, and the position of the body, indicates the possibility that the wound was self inflicted, and therefore a possible suicide. Their final report will be forwarded to you on completion".

....

"January 14th. A replacement for Gefreiter Lammen reported for duty with this Section today. He is Gefreiter Wolfgang Keeler, posted in from 18th. Base Hospital, after discharge.

His full service report is attached".

....

"In accordance with your orders, the undersigned acknowledges that he is required to report to you at Regional Command Headquarters on February 1st. at 14.00hrs".

....

Signed:- Oberleutnant Albert Claus Handel. o/c District 4.

Dated January 30th. 1943.

Blowing a huge sigh of relief through puffed cheeks, he bent over and took a silver flask from the drawer under the table and lifted it to his lips, gasping as the raw schnapps bit the back of his throat. For some minutes he sat staring blindly at the empty vase on the mantle shelf. Then, as he put his head back to drain the lasts drips into his gaping mouth, his world seemed to be a much better place.

Chapter Twenty-Eight.

September. 1955. Plourilly. France.

Adele Montagne sat quietly on the edge of the bed, looking down at Eric's untroubled face, seeing the gentle rise and fall of his breathing under the blankets and an occasional flicker of his long eyelashes. She wondered what dreams were running around inside his unconscious mind and hoping they were pleasant as she saw an enigmatic smile twitch the corner of his mouth. This, to her, was the best time of their day. Being with him was always a delight but sitting here in the semi-darkness, watching him with her heart so full of love, was her quality time; the last precious moments of each day when they could talk together in the bedroom, sharing their thoughts until he dropped off. A time to count her blessings.

She sighed inwardly, remembering that her life had not always been so happily and contented. She'd had more than her share of bad times and wretched misery, and even now – today – things could be a little better, but not much. Almost everything she had always wanted, dreamed of, lay in the bed asleep. He was her world, her whole reason for living. Life with him was a pure joy and apart from anything else, they were friends; and yet she felt concern. There was a nervous anxiety niggling away in her stomach that she could not cast aside. How would he take what she would be telling him in the morning? Would his naïve mind accept it philosophically – as she hoped – or upset him? It had always been her intention to tell him on this his special birthday, and tomorrow he would be twelve years old; old enough to understand.

Staring out of the window into the darkening night beyond, her eyes followed a shooting star streak across the clear blue-black sky, miraculously missing the myriad of others until fading into nothingness, like a dying firework. She wondered if any of those twinkling stars could be a heavenly presence of Eric's father – *or was he watching the same grinning moon from a home in England!* She shrugged the thought away, annoyed with herself, and let her thoughts drift into the far corners of her memory, recalling matters of joy and sorrow, some of which had lain hidden for years – hidden, or deliberately forgotten? Her life had been like a ride at the fun-fair, all ups and downs, sad and happy, exciting and painful.

A wayward lock of hair fell across her cheek and she brushed it away, irritably tucking it behind her ear with the fingertips of a hand that was far softer now than it had been on the farm when her days of hard work had been unending. She found it difficult; even now, to imaging just how hard that life had been ten years ago under the German occupation, with no money and barely enough food to keep body and soul together, for her and Jules. Poor Jules; so much suffering. Life had dealt him a bad hand that seemed to lose him every game, even to the very end. He had died alone, sitting in front of the fire - quickly and painlessly according to the doctor - from a blood clot in the brain while she had been outside digging potatoes from their vegetable plot. Finding him slumped in his chair, and having to sit with his body overnight waiting for the morning to ride into the village, had been dreadful; something she would never wish to have to do again. He hadn't even been granted his wish to see the birth of his wife's child, an occasion he had looked forward too as eagerly as she had. A truly wonderful man, an exceptional man.

Her fingers fiddled with the two rings on her left hand, twirling them around, remembering when Jules had bought them. They were the only expensive jewellery she had ever owned……if only their lives could have been different. Tears moistened her eyes as her mind wandered back.

He had been the first man in her life and had changed her from being a naïve young girl to a full-blooded woman during the few months of their exciting, tempestuous courtship and marriage. The envy of the other girls in the village had been a wonderful feeling but then, in a very short time the war came and, like a true son of France, he had left her to fight the Boche; only to get his terrible wounds in the very early days. How had she coped with that? *How had he?* It had been a nightmare. And then, out of the blue – or should it be the blackness of the night? – Eric, the English soldier, had entered her life like a bolt of wonderful lightning. Their loving had been equally as frenzied as her courtship with Jules, and his departure – *"to do something special to get my papers so that I can return and stay with you"* – was heartbreaking, but his failure to keep that promise of returning had devastated her. What had happened to him? If only she knew. Would he have come back had he known she was pregnant?

With her eyes closed and mind elsewhere, her chin slowly drooped forward onto her chest. Just as she was about to fall forward and collapse asleep onto the bed – or more likely the floor – she woke with a start. For one split second she thought she had disturbed her son - his son - but the angelic face still looked peacefully quiet. She straightened her back; it was time to go to her own bedroom. Not the cold, damp and bleak room she had slept in at the farm for so many – too many – years. Now it was warm and cosy with electric lighting.

Her one big stroke of good fortune had come shortly after the war's end, with the sale of her farm to a company that wanted the land for some sort of quarrying. Their offer hadn't been generous, but it was the only one, and more than adequate for her to buy the cottage in the village that had lain empty for three months after the death of dear Albert Dongalue, the gendarme who, with Father Lorrette, had been her saviour during the war. There were few regrets in her heart when the farm buildings were bull-dozed to the ground only a few days after she had sold the animals and moved out.

Climbing the carpeted stairs, now well lit by a shaded light, she was suddenly overcome with weariness. It had been a long day that, as usual, started by walking with Eric the short distance to his school along the wakening village streets in the bright summer-morning warmth. Her own part-time job at the same school finished at twelve noon and enabled her to sit and watch her son playing with other children in the playground during the mid-day break, and then allowing her a couple of hours to shop in the village and gossip with her many new-found friends before collecting Eric at three to return home. Thank goodness tomorrow was Saturday.

Walking barefooted over the carpeted floor, another luxury, she crossed the room to the window and looked down into the shadowy street knowing that not far away, to her left on the village green, stood a small memorial granite stone where she frequently laid a simple bunch of flowers from her own tiny garden and stood reading the short inscription:- *In memory of Father Paul Lorrette, God's servant and a patriot. Taken from his home in May 1943 by the German Occupying Forces and never seen again.*

Sadly, she undressed and changed into her fine cotton nightdress that put the old flannelette one to shame, and slipped between the welcoming sheets. Her last vague thoughts being that she had been almost everything a woman could possibly be; a wife, a mistress, a widow and a mother - not bad going for a forty-year old - and, in a few years when Eric grows up and leaves home, she would be a lonely old woman.

Eric woke her by jumping on her bed demanding his breakfast.

She glanced at the alarm clock on the bedside table with its silent brass bell sitting like a top hat above its round face; both its hands were covering the figure eight. Startled, she almost jumped out of bed before remembering it was Saturday; she hadn't set the alarm and there was no school to rush off to.

'Sorry, my darling,' she apologised to Eric, who was now sat on the bed at her feet tugging at the bed clothes, wanting her to get up. 'I overslept.' She folded back the blankets beside her. 'Come and lay in Mummy's bed while I get us some breakfast.'

Like most children, he loved getting into his mother's warm bed, preferring she stay to be cuddled in to, but hunger prevailed and he laughingly edged her out with his feet as he wormed his way in.

The mist of sleep cleared from her head when her feet touched the floor. 'Happy birthday, darling,' she called over her shoulder, falling back on the bed to reach out for him.

Reluctantly he allowed her to kiss him, desperately wanting to shy away but not wanting to hurt her feelings. He loved cuddles but kissing…ugh! He didn't like it. Two of his so-called friends at school once held his arms to allow that silly Marie-Anne, with her pig-tails and wonky teeth, to kiss him. He *hated* it! Mind you, he didn't like girls much anyhow.

As a special birthday treat, Eric was allowed his breakfast in bed watched by his doting Mum who, after all these years, still couldn't believe she had produced him; couldn't believe that this gorgeous young boy had come from her own body. Birth was truly a miracle.

'Cor, thanks Mum,' he said, giving her a big hug as she climbed back in bed beside him after clearing away the empty cups and plates, and the discarded wrapping of the atlas that was his present from her. 'Just what I wanted.'

If she hadn't known *that* after all the hints he'd been dropping over the last three months she would have been blind as well as deaf. 'You're very welcome dear,' she smiled, leaning forward for a thank-you kiss and then changing her intention by taking hold of his hand when she saw him lean away. 'Now you'll be able to see where all the places you've been learning about at school are, won't you.'

He didn't answer, being far too engrossed in leafing through the pages, fascinated to see flat images of what he had always seen as round ones on the school's globe.

For twenty minutes Adele lay back on the pillows, amused to watch the intense interest on his face as he scanned each page with devouring eyes. Even at his early age he knew he wanted to travel the world, as a soldier or a sailor or, as he once told her in deadly seriousness, on his velo.

Eventually, having answered a million questions as best as she could, she asked, 'Can we talk now? It's about your father.'

He turned to her, a frown of puzzled uncertainty on his face, wondering if he had done something wrong. 'What about him, Mum? He's dead isn't he?' The way he said it wasn't as if he was asking a question.

Adele bit her lip wishing she hadn't started this, but it had to be told – sooner or later – and he was the right age now. Any earlier and he wouldn't have understood. Any later and he would quite rightly be asking why he hadn't been told before. Either way it was a dilemma that many war-time parents had to face. Her heart dropped as his frown deepened. He just stared, waiting silently for her to continue. 'I'm not absolutely sure, darling.'

Choosing her words carefully, trying to talk in an adult manner, wanting to be open and honest while not saying it in such a way as to upset him more than necessary, she told him the story, exactly as it was, leaving out nothing except the sexual aspect that was beyond his young comprehension. Fortunately he hadn't known Jules and that made the telling slightly easier for her.

'So you see, darling……' she concluded, taking a deep breath of relief at having told him at last, '…..Your real father is the man you are named after.' She reached out a trembling hand for his, searching his face for a reaction after his long, listening silence.

For several heart-stopping moments nothing was said. He remained cross-legged on the bed, deep in concentrated thought as if weighing-up the pro's and con's like a politician considering an uncommitted reply to a direct question. Adele's worry lines deepened. Was he thinking bad things of her? Would this news – that must have come as quite a shock to him – create a wall between them? She need not have worried; such thoughts never even entered his head. In fact, when he did finally speak it was not what his mother expected.

His voice sounded bright and his eyes twinkled as he raised his head, almost as if with pride. 'So, Mum. You are saying my real Dad was an English commando who you and Dad (until now he had always referred to Jules as Dad) met during the war after he had done a real brave thing in sinking German ships?'

Not trusting herself to speak, she nodded and tightened her lips against her teeth in a smile; happiness welling-up inside her, trying to fight back tears. *He looked excited!*

'That means he's a hero, doesn't it?' he continued, unconsciously using the present tense, the frown disappearing.

She nodded again, emotional tears streaming down her cheeks.

Not understanding the reason for her crying he put his arms around her neck. 'Don't worry, Mum,' he whispered. 'When I grow up I'll find him and bring him home.'

The dam burst. She buried her head in his young shoulder and burst into a flood of weeping sobs, feeling his embracing arms tighten with concern. *How could she explain that women cry when they are deliriously happy?*

Over the next few days, the tight bond of love between mother and son grew even stronger, if that were possible. He began strutting about like a proud peacock, telling everyone who would listen that his dad was a brave hero who had sunk dozens of German ships during the war. Suddenly he *had* grown up, acting protectively towards his mother and, incidentally, making her *feel* protected. He was nearly as tall as her!

One evening, a few weeks later, they were sat together on the settee engaged in their new game of questions and answers that always seemed to revolve around the topic of his new-found dad. His questions were endless, and her answers sometimes evasive. Her only sorrow being that he never mentioned Jules. *Why should he?* Jules wasn't his dad, and in any case he never knew him. Nevertheless…….

'You look really beautiful, Mum,' he had told her when she came downstairs earlier to show him the new summer dress she'd eventually bought after months of saving, and treated him to a twirl as if he were an admiring husband. 'If I ever marry – and I *won't,*' he added emphatically, 'I want her to be just like you.'

She had run back upstairs again for another good cry.

'Soon be winter again, Mum,' he remarked depressingly, as they sat sipping cups of scalding coffee in front of the cold, empty grate. 'Bet you're glad you're not still living on the farm?'

The thought of those awful days of getting up in the middle of a freezing night and working in the bitter, wind blown fields, sent a shiver up and down her spine that made her hug herself as though for warmth. 'Yes,' she answered. 'It wasn't the……….

A knock on the door interrupted her in mid sentence and made them both jump. They looked towards the door, then at each other, their eyes questioning. *Who would be calling at seven o'clock in the evening?* They rarely had visitors… at any time.

Eric answered the door.

The tall stranger, standing in a long black raincoat and carrying a small battered suitcase, whose pale face appeared almost skeletal in the glare of the electric light, looked at him for a brief second before raising his sunken eyes to gaze over the boy's shoulder and stare at Adele who had come to stand behind her son.

'Adele?'

Chapter Twenty Nine.

Eastney sea-front. August 2002.

Eighty-one year old Albert "Bing" Crosby wasn't asleep, not really. Even with his eyes closed, his mind could still see the hundreds of holidaymakers - strangely silent to his deaf ears - crowding the pebble beach between him and the blue/green waters of the Solent. Many were beginning to pack their belongings into the boots of hot cars parked like rows of dead beetles along the esplanade road, or joining the end of long queues of people waiting impatiently for buses that, in many cases, drove straight by, already full. Others, less fortunate, added to the weary throng having to trudge the whole length of the sea-front, all heavily laden like troops and trailing tired, irritable children full of ice-cream and chips, back to Clarence pier and the day-trip coaches waiting to return them to London, Reading, Bristol or wherever. Many still lay on the hot stones of the beach, basking in the cooling air and enjoying the last of the warming rays, as the sun lowered onto the distant hills of the Isle of Wight like a gold ball in slow motion.

Behind closed lids, tears moistened Albert's rheumy eyes as he relived his many years as a Royal Marine. He'd had plenty of good times, and more tough ones than he cared to remember. The Far East, during the war, had nearly been his lot; scrabbling around in swampy creeks, more frightened of the creepy-crawlies than the Japs who'd chop your head off as soon as look at you. He'd lost good mates on raids that seemed pointless at the time, and even more so now in retrospect, but presumably they'd earned more honours and medals for some red-tabbed staff officer who had signed the order in a cosy office, on a gin-laden table a fortnight's flying time from the nearest hostile. Still, he thought sardonically, that's life, and if you can't stand a joke you shouldn't have joined. He couldn't really complain, he'd done well; far better than some who had "bought it" before they'd even had a chance of a decent life.

Operation Gladstone, the raid on Nantes, had always been his less favourite memory and even now, after all these years, he could still see their faces as they shook his hand, leaving him behind on *Tenacity* in forty-two. Lieutenant Thomas

– who'd probably have been a general by now – "Tonker" Pearman and those two daft buggers "Windy" Nook and "Gravy" Browning.

The unpleasant memory caused another to cross his mind. It was at Colombo, back in forty-four. He had just completed the Senior NCO's course and been called into the Commanding Officer's office with another corporal. He could picture it at clear as day.

Both tired and soaked with sweat, they were standing to attention in front of their C.O. under a slow turning ceiling fan that barely stirred the hot clammy air. The officer, resplendent in immaculate uniform, sat behind a huge desk being fanned by a native *punkah wallah*. It was obvious he wanted the meeting over quickly, so that he could get back to the air-conditioned Officers Mess and be waited on by some poor bastard of a rag-head whose wages were probably less than the price of the glass of gin he was serving.

He couldn't remember what the meeting was about - probably something trivial, like a complaint of a sweating marine with his hands full having failed to salute a crispy clean officer - but during the course of whatever it was they were summonsed in for, the C.O. had said, off-handedly 'You were on *Operation Gladstone* in forty-two weren't you, Corporal Crosby?'

Crosby's ears twitched. Was he going to learn what had happened to the lads after all this time? He had left the UK shortly after returning to Portsmouth on *Tenacity* and, despite making a few discrete enquiries, hadn't been able to find out a thing.

'Yes, sir.'

The grey-haired officer looked up at him through long bushy eyebrows that curled upwards and hid the frown on his forehead. 'Hm…Sorry to hear none of them made it back.'

Crosby was stunned. *None of them?.... All dead?* He couldn't believe it. Not that lot. They must be prisoners of war, or something.

'Still….' continued the officer, shuffling through the papers on his desk importantly, '….according to Intelligence, they had limited success with one ship reported as sunk, and that's what counts, eh!'

Crosby bristled. 'One ship possibly sunk and four good marines dead. Yes, sir!'

The C.O. scowled. The tone had bordered on insolence. 'We don't know that, Corporal!'

Crosby had stared po-faced at the map on the wall over the officer's head, not caring if it was of Ceylon or Timbuktu. He felt cold and numb. There were no other details…….not until after the war when German records were discovered that revealed the atrocities of Lt. Thomas' and Marine Browning's executions, and the finding of Marine Nook's drowned body in the Loire River. No trace of Corporal Pearman, or his body, was ever found so he was presumed dead. Everyone in the Corps was shocked, from the newest recruit up to the highest General. Their shock became anger when the War Department announced that not one of them would receive recognition or award. They had been the bravest of the brave, yet expendable. It was war, and Churchill had made his point.

The news had left Crosby sick, dazed and angry. They were all gone now. He was the only one left. The only survivor.

A ball, kicked by a petulant ten-year - resentful at having been told by his parents it was time to go home - came from out of the blue and bounced against his leg. Crosby flinched as it broke his thoughts away from those dreadful memories…. and his thoughts drifted.

Even though his eyes remained closed, he could still see through the cloud of smoke haze that fogged the Granada's crowded public bar, where fresh air fought a losing battle with nicotine and alcohol fumes.

In the far corner, conveniently propped up against the bar, Tonker Pearman stood surveying the curvy blonde barmaid through the bottom of his upturned glass as she served her thirsty customer with a seductive smile that hid the ache of her large feet crammed into small high-heeled shoes. Standing next to him, grinning like a Cheshire cat, Lieutenant Thomas seemed to be sharing a joke with Windy and Gravy who were laughing too loudly; a sure sign they were nearing the point of having one too many. Surprisingly, none of them appeared to be a day older than the last time he had seen them on board *Tenacity*. Suddenly he found he was shaking, his whole body quivering with a clammy chill that seemed to surge right through him. A cold fog swirled around the bar making the four pale faces shimmer, and yet he could clearly see them looking over in his direction waving their hands, beckoning him over to join them.

It wasn't his round, was it?

An article in Portsmouth's local newspaper

"*The body of an elderly man, found by police on a sea-front bench at Eastney last week, has been identified as eighty-one year old Albert Henry Crosby of St. George's Place, Portsmouth, who died from natural causes.*

Mr. Crosby, a former Colour-Sergeant in the Royal Marines, was awarded the Military Medal for service in the Far East during WW2. Police have been unable to trace any living relatives.

Mr. Crosby will be buried with military honours by the Royal Marines at Milton cemetery on......................"

THE END.

ISBN 1-4120-5458-3

Printed in Great Britain
by Amazon.co.uk, Ltd.,
Marston Gate.